THE SPLENDID AND EXTRAORDINARY LIFE of BEAUTIMUS POTAMUS

Peggy A. Wheeler

THE SPLENDID AND EXTRAORDINARY LIFE OF BEAUTIMUS POTAMUS

A HUGE JUICY thank you to the love of my life, my husband, Steven D. Wheeler. He always supported this book, laughed in all the right places as he read it, gave me wise council even when I pushed back, teared up a little at the book's ending, and faithfully served as my first pair of eyes as I worked through each chapter, and each revision.

Thank you to the two Hemet critique groups, especially to Carrie Elizabeth Allen who loved this tale right off the bat when others in the group were less sure if they liked this strange, otherworldly tale with a talking hippo protagonist. Thank you to my one-time agent, and still friend, Melissa Coleman Carrigee, for taking on this quirky book. Although you are no longer an agent, I'm so very glad we remain friends. A bucket load of thanks to Denise Dumars, also my one-time agent, and a dear friend for more than three decades. You loved this book from the start, and that means the world to me. Thanks, Deb Hoag, too. I so appreciate what you did for me on this book.

I'm beyond grateful to my publisher, Gwen Gades at Dragon Moon Press, for taking a chance on this quirky fantasy.

Special appreciation to my beta readers and "proofers" including Selene Macleod, Kathleen Sauebrei, Marylou Knapik, Laurie Kehoe, and a special shout-out to my lovely friend, Sue Bateman, for reading a much earlier and much messier version of this book, and liking it anyway!

And, thank you from my whole heart to my mother, Opal June, to whom I dedicated this book, the last thing I ever read to her before she died. When I read the final chapter, her only word was, "Beautiful."

DEDICATED TO THE MEMORY OF
OPAL JUNE "LUCKY" PEAVY

February 15, 1923 San Antonio, Texas –
July 7, 2013 Hemet, California

Mom, this book was always yours. I love you
and miss you more than I can say.

People say that what we're all seeking is a meaning for life. I don't think that's what we're really seeking. I think what we're seeking is an experience of being alive, so that our life experiences on the purely physical plane will have resonances within our own innermost being and reality, so that we actually feel the rapture of being alive."

JOSEPH CAMPBELL - THE POWER OF MYTH

CHAPTER ONE

"APPLECHEEKS! AGNES! PLEASE fetch my oracle bag, and be quick about it." Beautimus Potamus had overslept again. Between hot flashes producing so much night sweat that twice already her household help had nearly drowned in it, and her hormone-induced insomnia, rarely did she enjoy a good night's sleep. *It's late in the morning for my daily oracle reading, and I've yet to bathe in the river, or eat breakfast.* As she rose from her pillows her bones and joints snapped and popped, and when she stretched her legs, she groaned.

The house squirrels scrambled atop the altar and pulled the gold brocade pouch onto the floor. Together, they tugged the draw-string bag to the hippo still reclining on her sleeping pillows. Agnes scampered to the cooking pot to make the morning tea, leaving Applecheeks to attend to Beautimus.

"Thank you." The hippo closed her eyes and raised her head in prayer. "Oh, Great Goddess Genesis, thank you for blessing us with your presence." She opened her eyes, and gave a quick nod to the squirrel.

Apple pulled a divining cloth from the bag, spread it on the floor of the abode, and straightened the corners. She put her paw into the bag and withdrew the first of three glyphs.

"Moonmagick," Beautimus said. "Goddess energy strong at work today. Please pull the next."

The squirrel withdrew the second of the stones, placing it to the right of the first.

"Dreamlizard. Ah, yes, my recurring visions. The Goddesses say I must pay attention to them." Beautimus studied the glyphs. "It's rare these two stones appear in that order in a reading. Something is up, Apple. We're to be on the lookout for omens, signs, chance encounters, anything out of the ordinary. You and Agnes keep an eye peeled. Will you?"

Applecheeks nodded.

Beautimus took a cleansing breath. "Now. The outcome glyph."

When the squirrel placed the last of the stones on the cloth, Beautimus leaned in to look, and gasped. "No. No. Please. Not again!" Her eyes rolled back into her head, and she sunk into her pillows.

***

Visions. Beautimus experienced them on and off since adolescence. But they were so infrequent, sometimes a decade would pass without one. Recently, they came at her in bunches, like fruit flies in a mating swarm. One right after another they came. For six days in a row, Beautimus' mother, Sangrina, who'd long before passed into the arms of the Goddess, appeared to her. It was the same each time. Without warning or reason, Beautimus' eyes rolled back, her lids closed, and she dropped to the ground aware of her impending unconsciousness, but as if in a state of paralysis, unable to do anything about it. First, a resonate buzzing originated from inside her head. Then the visions appeared and played out for her like the classic films she streamed from Earth. Only these movies were projected on the inside of her eyelids.

In them, Beautimus sat under a blooming yarron tree. She watched roan mares dancing with red dragonflies in a grassy meadow near the edge of an emerald cenote. A fog bank, the color of spun pink sugar, rose from the water and rolled onto the meadow. Sangrina stepped out of the fog. "Beautimus, it's time."

"Time for what, Mom? Tell me."

"You'll know soon enough."

Without so much as a wink or a nod, Sangrina faded into the aether. The fog cleared, the horses and dragonflies vanished, and Beautimus came around to consciousness, confused and groggy as a drunken coati. The visions stuck to her like a coquillet midge to a sorghum blossom, but try as she might, Beautimus couldn't ferret out their meaning, or why they recurred. Then today for the first time in decades—*the* reading, and *the* glyph, the one that never failed to predict a life-changing event.

Beautimus activated her Crystal Interface and connected with her friend, Lizzy, a mastodon she'd known since she was a bubbit.

"Lizzy, during my reading this morning…White Light."

"Did it land in the outcome position after Moonmagick and Dreamlizard?"

"Yes, exactly as it had when the janitor discovered Áine's body."

"No kidding. What do you think is going to happen?"

"I don't have a bloody clue, but I'm nervous as a Phidippus spider. The last time I'd received *that* glyph in *that* order… who knows what may happen? The Anam Glyph, plus the repeated visions of my mother, it's like…."

"…Bea, you know the Goddess is speaking to you."

"And, if only I had paid attention last time …I mean…I may have been able to prevent Áine's murder."

"Maybe you could have. Maybe not. Don't blame yourself. But, do pay attention *this* time."

"I feel certain I'd have been able to save Áine. I live with this every day of my life."

Many years before, Beautimus had experienced a series of similar visions, and one morning as the squirrels pulled her three daily Anam Glyphs, White Light surfaced in the outcome position of her layout as it had this morning. Back then, Beautimus found her recurring visions and the glyph reading a curiosity, but dismissed their messages.

A few days after, a janitor arrived at dawn as usual to Dr. Pimbly's School of Goodly Educated Adults where Beautimus held the position of History Professor of Earthly Things. That morning, when making his rounds, he discovered the dead body of the beloved Wise Woman, the red fox, Lady Áine.

The Wayflower Quacker printed verbatim what the janitor had told the reporters.

Death of a Wise Woman: The Custodian's Story

That mornin' waz derned flat dark. No moons at all up in that sky. I fumbles arounds a bit until I founds me keys to The Commons so's I could groom the grounds likes I always does.

As I waz a rakin' beneath a two-flowered acacia I stumbled on sumpin' that felt like a lumpy fur-covered sack of tubers. Holy Mother Genesis, what's that? I asks meself. Then me paws slipped in sumpin' wet throwing me clean off balance. Holy Mother! There waz her body right there on the ground under that tree. What I'd a-slipped in waz blood.

When the sunlight busted over The Commons wall, I seen her good. I run full speed out of The Commons. 'Oh me Goddess, she's dead, she's dead,' I hollers. The dead gal waz that pretty red fox, Áine, a Wise Woman, that one next in line fer the High Priestess of Wayflower. Her throat were ripped clean out, poor little thang. Horrible, I tells ya, the most horriblist thang I ever did saw.

News of Áine's murder shocked the whole of Wayflower. The Dean, Sr. Henry, a distinguished grey mole, gave his statement to the reporter from *The Quacker:* "None of us can imagine what kind of fen-sucked evil gudgeon would kill dear

Áine. She was a kind soul, one of our finest graduate students. Beyond her promising future, we all knew her as the sweetest natured fox in the entire District. We are stunned by what is by far the worst tragedy in our institution's history. To ensure the safety of our faculty, staff and students, I will post twenty-four hour guards"

He kept his promise, and hired a trio of lionesses to prowl the grounds. The Guardians arrested the janitor, a slow-witted badger, after witnesses reported him running wild-eyed, squealing in hysterics from The Commons, his fur covered in blood. The Guardians paw printed and questioned him, but in the absence of more substantial evidence or a motive, the Lead Inspector freed the badger.

Few in Wayflower doubted the badger's guilt. He remÁined under suspicion for the remainder of his life. Women hissed as he passed. Children threw rocks and taunted him even long after he'd retired, and had grown old and feeble. By the time crippling arthritis had gripped his hips and paws, blindness had also set in. The badger couldn't get on by himself. Once each day Beautimus stopped by his den to look in on him. She sent Agnes and Applecheeks to dispose of his droppings, tidy his abode, and bring him contÁiners of fruit soup and steamed blue corn. When the badger at last died, the controversy over Áine's murder died with him, even though the Guardians never caught the culprit.

So many years ago. Must have been two hundred at least, maybe more, but Beautimus remembered it as though it had only been a mere half century.

Áine and Beautimus had been friends and neighbors since childhood, and the brutal murder of the fox delivered a gut punch to the hippo, and it hurt that the killer had never been found.

***

Beautimus planned to attend the Wasenia Festival with her best friend, Samuel S. Goodwings, a lime green praying mantis. The hippos of the Wayflower district built their abodes on the River Kwa not far from the Mantis Tribe. Although Samuel and Beautimus lived near one another, there was little reason for them to form a personal bond. Rarely did creatures as large as hippos become friends with creatures as small as praying mantises. But, in spite of their differences, Samuel and Beautimus were close. When the two weren't arguing, Samuel had a way of making her laugh.

"I think you two have some weird co-dependency thing going on. Really, you need to look at that, Bea," Lizzy said often.

Beautimus didn't know if she'd talk to Samuel on their half-day walk to the Festival about her visions or the Anam Glyph reading. He didn't believe in things like mysterious nocturnal messages from the dead, deities, or stone oracles. She and Samuel bickered like old married folks over religion and political ideology. He might ridicule her. Already rattled by the memory of sweet Áine's murder fueled by her recent visions, and the recurring White Light Glyph's appearance, she felt grateful to at least have non-judgmental Lizzy to talk to.

"I only wish I could get Mom's words and the meaning of that Glyph out of my head long enough to concentrate on my classes," Beautimus said to Lizzy. "I'll be too distracted to focus on my students unless I can prevent this thing that is going to happen from happening. And, my publisher is expecting edits to my Earthian Culture text this week. I need to be able to think."

"It's good you and Sam are going to the Wasenia Festival. At least for a short while your mind will be occupied with more pleasant matters."

Beautimus strolled to the river for her morning bath. She looked one direction, then the other to search the landscape for anything or anybody who might offer a clue as to what could be coming her way. She passed a pond where a congregation of alligators and a wisdom of wombats engaged in a heated argument over economics. Nothing unusual in that. Beautimus caught a snippet of their argument.

"...yeah, I wouldn't expect anything more from the Wombat Tribe. Do the wombats at least support the new Rendazian Banking Initiative?" One gator asked.

"As a matter of fact, we *don't* support it. And, the proposed Macro-Economic Stabilization Policy is a pile of stinking horse manure. I can't believe you alligators back it," said a wombat. We wombats..."

"...what exactly do you mean by, 'you alligators'?"

"You're really pulling that alligator card? You're clearly losing this argument so *as usual* you resort to your old trick of deflecting the issue by turning it into speciesism. Un-be-lievable."

"If you weren't such a goddessdamn lizardist, a reptilephobe, a..."

"...you're calling *me* a lizardist, a reptilephobe? I ought to..."

"You ought to what?" The alligator opened his mouth to display a row of rapier-sharp teeth.

"C'mon, guys. No need for threats." Beautimus said. "Why can't you agree to disagree and let it go?"

Right then, she first caught sight of the solitary brown chicken. She'd never seen the hen before, but the chicken's curious behavior piqued her interest. The chicken positioned herself close to Beautimus, keeping herself within the hippo's peripheral vision.

Beautimus left the alligators and the wombats to their arguing, and continued on her way to the river, the hen close behind. She addressed the chicken. "Are you following me?"

The hen ruffled her plumage but didn't respond. Every time Beautimus turned to speak to the chicken, or make eye contact, the hen looked the other way or fluttered off in a frenzy of feathers to one of the ubiquitous purple-wood wattles. The brown chicken re-appeared and continued to shadow the now annoyed hippo. "Excuse me, but who *are* you?"

The fowl remÁined silent.

"Do you not hear me, or are you intentionally ignoring me? If you're trying to be stealthy, you're not doing a good job of it. I can actually see you, you know."

The chicken preened.

"What the hellzabob? I've got enough on my mind as it is, classes to teach this afternoon, and the Wasenia Festival to prepare for. I don't have time for your absurd games." Beautimus decided to ignore the hen.

***

Only on rare occurrence did Beautimus consult her Glyphs in the evening, but tonight felt different. The time for the festival neared. In spite of her night-sweats and bothersome insomnia, she intended to get a few good nights' sleep and wake up the day of the journey clear-minded and joyful rather than disturbed by repeating visions. The squirrel pulled the bag to Beautimus and spread the divining cloth on the ground. Before Apple drew the first stone, one tumbled out of the pouch on its own and landed face-up dead-center of the cloth. *White Light.* Beautimus' throat clenched. As if that wasn't bad enough, as she lay her head on her pillows for the evening, instead of dropping off to sleep, her legs trembled, her eyelids fluttered, and the vision returned. Only, this time the pretty red fox, Áine, also emerged from the pinkish fog alongside Beautimus' mother.

The fox whispered, "It's up to you, Bea. It's all up to you."

CHAPTER TWO

ALL WENT AS expected the following day, uneventful, almost monotonous… until dusk. As Beautimus prepared for her evening bath, her eyes rolled back into her head, her legs buckled, and she sat hard on the packed mud at the edge of the river. "No, please! Not again." She fell unconscious.

But in this vision, it wasn't Áine who appeared to Beautimus alongside Sangrina, but the High Priestess' House Chimp, Priscilla. When the chimpanzee emerged from the pink fog she opened her mouth to speak, but although she mouthed words, no sound issued.

"What is it you want to tell me, Priscilla?"

Priscilla pointed to her neck.

"Why can't you just say what you want?"

Sangrina shook her head. "She's *trying* to tell you, if you'd bother to pay attention." She turned to the chimp. "If my stubborn daughter isn't going to get the message, no need for us to stick around here, is there, Priscilla?"

The chimp and Beautimus' mother disappeared into the pink fog. Beautimus came to, her flanks covered in black mud and slippery moss.

She called Lizzy. "I don't get it. If Priscilla has a problem, she doesn't have to sneak into my 'dead mother' visions. She can contact me on the Interface."

"I'm telling you. Listen to the Goddess."

Beautimus sighed. "You're probably right, but I'm going to ask Priscilla when I see her at the Wasenia Festival."

A foul mood like a wet coverlet dropped over Beautimus. She *hoped* she could enjoy the Wasenia Festival, but given her nightmarish visions, she wasn't so sure.

***

Beautimus had a class to teach, but on the way to the school, she detoured to the Glen of the Ancient Ficus Trees to seek the council of Beard, a 2,000-year-old Banyan tree. The people of Wayflower revered Beard for his infinite wisdom. He stood at least thirty feet above the other trees in the grove, his canopy large enough to shield fifty bull elephants. He earned his name from the profusion of old man beard moss hanging from his limbs. He also happened to be one of only a few talking trees on all of Rendaz, and the only "talker," as Rendazians referred to them, in the whole of Wayflower.

"Good day, Master Beard." Beautimus bowed her head and lowered her eyes.

"Good day to you."

"I have been…troubled. Have you any words of wisdom for me today, Master?"

"You did use the oracle, your Anam Glyphs, this morning didn't you?"

"Yes, I did."

"All right then, answer me this. Why do you seek *my* wisdom when you have a wisdom-source of your own making? In asking me to impart my knowledge to you, you are really saying you don't trust your *own*."

Beautimus hoped the old tree didn't notice her flushed cheeks. "It's that you have lived so long…"

Beard shook his leaves to interrupt her "…because I've lived so long your logic is I must be wiser than you? Is that it? Old grapes don't make good wine. Good grapes make good wine. In the end, the only true wisdom is that which we cultivate for ourselves, Bea, no matter if we've lived 3,000 years, or are naught but wee saplings."

The surrounding trees hummed, vibrated, and buzzed their approval in the way trees do.

On Rendaz, with the assistance of an "Old Mother"—a woman versed in the ways of magic—the ancient trees act as guides to young women wishing to become "Wise Women." There were only a select few Wise Women among the Rendazians, Beautimus not among them.

The old trees also instructed young men in the "Sage Arts." If a young man wanted to become a Sage, he approached a tree, and declared aloud his intention. The ficus willing, a boy would sit for years under its branches absorbing its wisdom until the tree pronounced the boy, "Full of Sap." Sages lived their entire lives as celibate hermits among the trees writing poetry and authoring hefty philosophy tomes. The people of Rendaz greatly honored them, but since Rendazians were social as a whole, and all men are animals who enjoy nothing better than copulating, there were few Sages on Rendaz.

Beautimus sought Beard's wisdom because she knew he'd provide the best council for how to deal with her visions, and perhaps he could ease her distress over her Anam Glyph reading.

"You have something to discuss? You wish to talk about the mystery of Áine's murder perhaps?"

"Yes, Master Beard, I know it's been a long while since her death…but…"

"You'll know more about that when the time is right, and your recurring visions and the message from your Glyph will become clear soon enough."

"How did you know about my visions and the White Light glyph, Master Beard?"

"Old trees know many things, Bea, many things. And, do look out for that brown chicken. She will cause you great trouble."

CHAPTER THREE

THE FOLLOWING MORNING, as Beautimus poked her head through the flap of her abode, a magical dawn greeted her. The larger red sun, Racine, appeared over the peaks of the white-capped volcanoes. The smaller blue sun, Purmoso, rose a scant higher in the dawn sky. Together, the suns cast a hazy violet light.

Beautimus relaxed a little, and allowed a gradual sense of giddiness to overtake her. She often streamed Earth music through her Crystal Interface. Symphonic music and opera were her favorites. As she strolled through the forest, she hummed the overture to Mozart's *Marriage of Figaro*. A much higher octave hum joined hers in a bright duet. Samuel S. Goodwings. "Hi, Sam. What a perfect day."

"Yes, indeed. Beautiful morning. Off to the university?"

She noticed the brown chicken, too, attempting to conceal herself behind a fallen tree. The hen's tail feathers poked out from behind a limb. "You're a complete idle-headed scut." Beautimus said to her.

"Who is a scut?" Samuel asked.

"Oh, just that nosey hen following me around."

"I don't see any hen."

***

In the front row of class, as always, sat her most intelligent and eager student, the white tiger, Cicero.

"So glad to see you, Ms. Bea."

"Why thank you, Cicero. We have a lot to cover today. I assume everyone has read through Chapter Three of their text? I believe during our last meeting we discussed the Crystal

Interface and interplanetary travel. Can anyone tell me where we left off?"

The tiger raised his paw.

"Cicero. Please proceed."

"We discussed how the Crystal Interface is useful as a communication device on Rendaz, but has also been used for over 200,000 moon phases to enable space exploration through wormholes. The Crystal Interface enabled us to discover Earth."

"Yes, Cicero, exactly, thank you," Beautimus said. "No doubt many of you studied Crystal Interface Physics at the Rendazian College of Refined Sciences?"

Several heads nodded.

"For the benefit of those who have not completed a course on the Crystal Interface, can someone please provide a short explanation of how it works?"

Cicero raised his paw again.

"No, Cicero. Let's give someone else an opportunity. You, Jackie, please review for us how the Crystal Interface works."

Jackie, a green woodhoopie who tended toward shyness, had a brilliant mind, but had also earned the reputation as a top-notch Crystal Interface mechanic.

"Please, don't be shy, Jackie. You don't have to fly to the front of the room. Remain on your perch and speak from there if you wish."

The bird ruffled her feathers. Her eyes darted about the room, but as she began to speak, she relaxed. "The Crystal Interface hardware is a flat screen manufactured in sizes from less than a millimeter square to thirty feet or larger. It is constructed from quartz crystal imprinted with codes that enable the user to 'think' a communication. Although the internal driver is complex, for the sake of simplicity we'll say the Crystal Interface works through a combination of quantum physics and magic, which some scientists postulate are one in the same." The bird hesitated.

"Yes. Please continue."

"The Interface can be used as a recording device, for projection, communication, data storage, or reception. With advanced mind training, a captain of a starship can use the Interface to locate wormholes, and propel a ship and its crew to universes light years away, sometimes even into alternate universes."

"Thank you, Jackie." She nodded to the bird. "All right. Let's continue. I've asked Hano, whose ancestor commanded the first Ark of Rendaz, to tell us a little bit about the discovery of Earth. Hano?"

Beautimus sat back onto a pillow. A large male chimp swung hand-over-hand on the rafters and dropped in front of the class.

"My great, great, great, great....maybe 10,000 greats.... grandfather was an astronaut. At a young age the Grand General commissioned Grandfather as Supreme Commander of the first Rendazian Ark. The Butterfly Council ordered him and his crew to seek intelligent life on other planets. According to official historical accounts, and from what I have studied in our family diary, after several light years the Ark came upon a small but beautiful blue planet in a single-sun solar system.

After the ship's engineers tested the atmosphere, and scanned the surface of the planet for probable danger, they declared it 'Most Likely Safe.' Commander Hano...my mother named me after him, you know," He pointed with pride to his chest, "issued the order to land. He put the Ark down in what is known on Earth as the Rift Valley on the continent of Africa." He pointed to an Earth map hanging on a wall. "They discovered a verdant planet, a paradise, with bountiful water, miles of greenery, fecund and rich."

"Sounds a lot like Rendaz," a coati said.

"Yes, indeed, but with significant differences. Other than plants and trees, the exploration team found little life on the planet. Most of the plants did not bear fruit as they do on Rendaz, and other than a few minnows, some krill-like creatures, and corpulent grubs, there initially appeared to be no other beings. After traveling over several continents, the only viable food sources the expedition located were small red, tart berries we named 'cranberry,' because they grew on a plant similar to the cranbush on Rendaz, edible seaweed, and, of course, wild blue corn we discovered in what is known as "The Americas." Hano pointed to the map. "Of course you already know we brought back the blue corn and it is now a staple food on Rendaz. Later we'd return to Blue Earth with flowering and fruiting plants and trees of all kinds."

Hano paused to review the notes he'd had clutched in his toes. "After several moons of exploration, and collecting many samples, The Commander declared the mission a bust. Even though the expedition expended considerable time scouring the entire planet's surface, they'd located no intelligent life. They gathered their equipment and made preparations for the flight home. Only a day before they were to board the Ark one of the Commander's men reported a movement in a nearby blue wattle bush.

Grandfather ordered a group of men to investigate. They discovered a cowering male creature. They captured it and brought it back to camp. The creature walked upright on its hind paws. Save facial, head, and pubic hair it had no significant body fur, and no feathers. Its hide, rather thin and soft, proved a pathetic barrier against the elements. He was the oddest being the explorers had ever encountered. Besides his thin, yielding hide, and his absence of body hair, he lacked sharp teeth and defensive claws. He could neither run fast nor climb well.

Nonetheless, this creature walked with extraordinary adeptness on his two long rear appendages, and his front paws were nimble with strong opposable thumbs. Even with an ape-like structure and general appearance, he demonstrated less intelligence than apes, and did not speak. He only grunted. The records refer to him as 'filthy.' I'll read the report from the ancient log. Hano cleared this throat and opened a book.

This odd creature stinks, urinating or defecating at will, grabbing whatever he wants without asking. He stuffs food into his mouth with his front paws, drools and makes slurping noises as he eats. We have named this new species, Hu Man.

Hano looked up from the book. 'Hu Man' means in the old Rendazian language, 'New Man.' Later, others shortened the name to 'Human'."

"I always wondered what 'human' meant," an owl monkey said.

"Me, too" said a chestnut-backed scimitar-babbler.

"The scientists discovered Hu Mans could use tools quite well, and demonstrated complex speech capability, but simply had never *learned* to speak. The explorers taught the Hu Man to use language, which to the scientists' amazement, the creature picked up with astonishing ease. They gave their Hu Man a name, Dama, meaning in old Rendazian, 'First.' They covered him with protective cloth, and undertook the overwhelming task of teaching him rudimentary manners.

The scientists developed an appreciation for Dama's motor skills and eagerness to learn. They formed search parties to locate other Hu Mans. With Dama as a guide, the crew members found Hu Mans well hidden, mostly in caves or in thick brush living in small family bands, all of them in the same shape as Dama had been when they first heard him rustle the bushes moons before.

Before long, Dama worked side-by-side with the Rendazians to educate and civilize this newly discovered, amazing species of animal, who along with nimble opposable thumbs, demonstrated a capacity for compassion. Also, Hu Mans did something other species did not...smile. At first, our explorers interpreted the Hu Man smile as hostile teeth-baring but soon learned that a smile indicates joy, affection, friendliness, or amusement.

Rendazians came to respect and love this fragile species, and wanted to help them. One problem then, and still remains, Hu Mans' short life span. The Hu Mans died, barely having learned the ways of civilized beings."

Cicero raised his hand.

"Yes," said Hano.

"What happened to the first Hu Man?"

"When Dama passed, the Rendazians gave him a proper funeral with a full Ceremony for the Dead.

Beautimus nodded her head in appreciation. "Thank you. Let's all give Hano a round of applause for his excellent presentation."

The class applauded.

"Ok, next week, we'll move on to Life with the Hu Mans, the Meteor Disaster and subsequent Fall of Earthly Civilization. Please read through Chapter Nine in your texts. Remember, your research papers are due on my Crystal Interface by the end of this moon. Thank you, Cicero, for getting your paper in early as usual."

CHAPTER FOUR

RENDAZ—AN IRIDESCENT JADE-GREEN pearl in a star system of the far reaches beyond Arcturus covered in red sands, ancient acacias, active volcanos, and blossoms larger than an elephant's ear, is double the size of Earth, with two suns, two moons, and one vast ocean. Its sea brims with sea dragons, elder leviathans, and singing orcas. Rendazian rivers are populated by the wisest and most loquacious fish and water mammals, and the lands are inhabited by all manner of talking creatures, many now extinct on the blue planet Earth. Beautimus thanked the Goddess she lived on Rendaz, and not Earth.

This exceptionally beautiful morning, and the Wasenia Festival put Beautimus in a bright mood. Beautimus could barely contain her excitement. She wolfed down a bowl of dragon fruit and walnuts, and headed off to the Mantis Compound. She found Samuel clinging to the bark of his home, a silver mulga sapling. He wore a white cape of gossamer fabric spun from spider webs, attached to it a stiff lace collar giving him the appearance of a pompous miniature emperor.

"Well, don't you look dapper," Beautimus said.

Samuel's journey to the Wasenia Festival might seem odd to those who knew him because he'd been a confirmed, lifetime Non-Believer. Like most on Rendaz, Beautimus followed the ways of The Goddess. Those who honored The Goddesses, and worshiped Mother Nature, as Beautimus did, referred to themselves as Believers.

Samuel, a founding member and Treasurer of the Wayflower Society for Rational Thinking, the district branch of a larger planetary atheist organization, disavowed the existence of any deity. A hard-core scientist specializing in Quantum

Peggy A. Wheeler

Agriculture, he focused on protein plant cultivation and blue corn physics, fervent topics for the mantis. "You have heard about recent developments in blue corn silk string theory, haven't you?" He'd ask at parties, then prattle on about alternate dimensions, quarks, spins, and waves in relationship of blue corn to the universe until the person to whom he spoke would make a polite excuse to get as far away from Samuel as possible.

"Give me a minute," Samuel said. "I'm not quite ready."

Samuel primped in front of his broken chip of mirror propped against a leaf. His brother, Michael M. Goodwings, hopped onto the leaf and shook his head. "Mornin' Bea. My vain brother making you late to the festival? What the hellzabob are you doing, Sam? We're scientists. We're atheists. We don't waste our time on dung like this." Michael turned his head to Beautimus. "No offense," then back to Samuel. "What's up with you going to the Wasenia Festival?"

"Mikey, Mikey, Mikey. Haven't you seen the hot women who go to these things? And, you *do* know they serve mead at these festivals, *free* mead, buckets of it. Do I need say more?"

He jumped in an elegant arc onto Beautimus' head. "I'm going to catch myself on fire with that 'ole time religion in the form of some of fine mantis leg and a few dozen thimbles of hooch. See ya' later, Buddy."

Beautimus let out an exasperated sigh. "You're so irreverent, Sam. If the elders heard you they would..."

"....aw c'mon. I'm just having a little fun."

"Yes, indeed. A little fun. Well, let's get a move-on. I want to have time to browse the vendor booths before the ceremony—and do watch for my star."

He took light steps to avoid the gold pentagram Agnes painted that morning between Beautimus' eyes. The squirrel expended considerable effort to get it right, dipping her paw into the gold dust pot then, with meticulous attention, drawing the star to ensure fine and straight lines.

Within a few minutes, the two friends commenced bickering.

"Sam, I'm proud of the turkey buzzards for standing up for their rights, for speaking their truth."

"Only because you're a bloody idealist who doesn't think anything through. I'm taking a 'wait and see' position on this one."

"Meaning what?"

"Meaning I'm going to wait and see if all their protesting really makes a fuggin' difference. Didn't you even bother to *read* the news today?"

"Of course I did, you cynical bug. *The Wayflower Quacker* specifically stated the *Butterfly Counsel Selects Golden Eagle Tribe to Lead Wasenia Festival Flyover,* edging out the Turkey Buzzard Tribe entirely. They are standing up because they feel discriminated against. Wouldn't you? I support the buzzards' protest. It's brave and noble."

"I may be a cynical bug, Bea, but I'm also a smart bug. Sorry. I think their protest is futile and silly."

They passed a murder of crows roosting in a catechu tree. "You two at it again?" One cawed.

"It's not always like that, Sam, sometimes things…"

"…I'm saying unlike you I don't think the universe is made of daisy petals and bunny fluff so all anyone needs to do to change the world is stand on a corner holding a sign. I don't buy a few bare-headed feathered creatures marching in righteous indignation are going to get what they want, or otherwise make a damned bit of difference."

Clarence Jonas, Esq., a komodo dragon with the firm Darrow, Darrow and Jonas, his tail slashing from side-to-side, scuttled toward a group of protesting buzzards carrying signs in their wings: "Buzzards Are Beautiful. Eagles Are Arrogant" and, "Buzzards Deserve The Right To Fly."

"In the end," Samuel said, "the only one who will win anything is that pox-marked pumpion lizard. He can't wait to get his filthy bacteria-laden teeth into what promises to be the biggest speciesism trial in Wayflower."

"Sam, say what you will. I believe a group of committed citizens who stand firm in their truth and act on their convictions *can* make a difference."

"Whatever you want to believe is fine with me. I respect your idealism, but I don't share it. I wish the buzzards well, and I hope one day you'll stop being so naïve."

"I hope one day you'll stop being an ass."

The two friends passed a congregation of plovers wading in a fen. One cried out to them, "Happy Wasenia Day. May you be blessed by the warmth of the stars."

Beautimus bowed her head slightly, knocking Samuel off balance. "And, may you be blessed by the warmth of the stars."

The odd brown chicken appeared again in a nearby patch of clover, and unabashedly stared at the duo.

"Do you know that chicken, Sam?"

"What chicken?"

The fowl had vanished. Beautimus pondered a relationship between the chicken, her visions, and the White Light Glyph.

The brown chicken emerged from behind a peony bush. When Beautimus attempted to address the bird, it scurried a few yards away and ducked behind a boree tree.

Samuel tugged on Beautimus' ear. "Is that the chicken you've been talking about? Wonder who she is?"

"I don't know. She followed me to the river the other day, and she's been tailing me since." Weary of the chicken, Beautimus refocused her attention on the festival instead.

"Sam, you know the Wasenia Festival is huge. All the districts sponsor celebrations to honor our suns, Purmoso and Racine today, as well as all the other stars who 'graciously share their luminosity' as the words to The Star Song say."

"So, the festival is a big deal. Does that mean there'll be more mead?"

"Hahahaa. Is that all you ever think of, Sam?"

"No, not *all.*"

The exasperated hippo took a breath, then attempted to redirect the conversation. "Lady Rhianna is presiding over the ceremony again this year."

"Really? That old bird still kickin' it at the festivals?"

"C'mon, Sam. She's barely 310-years-old. She's not exactly on her deathbed."

"For a blue crane, 310 years is long in the beak."

"What makes you think cranes have a shorter lifespan than anyone else?"

"Everyone knows cranes, *especially* blue cranes, are susceptible to Avian Shadowfever."

"Don't you think I'd know it if Lady Rhianna were ill?"

Years before, a few moons after Beautimus' mother died, Rhianna stepped in and assumed the role of Old Mother. She did her best to instruct Beautimus in the ways of a Wise Woman. Although bright, Beautimus exhibited no traits whatsoever of a stellar student. Rhianna scolded her for inattention.

"Listen to what I'm telling you. This is critical information you must learn well if you are to ever practice magic or be named Wise Woman."

Although the kind and patient Rhianna stuck by her until she'd completed her early spiritual training, Beautimus never believed herself good enough. She thought she didn't have what it took to be a Wise Woman. "I'm a history teacher, an oracle reader, a mediocre writer and nothing more."

Beautimus felt nonetheless pleased about the prospect of catching a glimpse of her old friend and mentor, with whom she'd not interacted with in quite a long while, at least not since Rhianna had been ordÁined High Priestess of Wayflower. Beautimus hoped to talk to Rhianna about her recurring visions, and the Anam Glyph. Then, she realized Samuel still yammered away.

"...and that's precisely why last year we experienced the highest yield of blue corn in Wayflower history," he said.

"Is that so? Why?"

"I just *told* you. Haven't you been listening? I've been talking for ten minutes about the molecular structure of the soil and subatomic particles. I can't believe you haven't heard even one word of...never mind. I'll go over it again. A proton is comprised of two quarks up, one quark down, and is a subatomic particle. But, you know that already, don't you?"

An exhalation of larks flying overhead called festival greetings to a colony of chinchilla. Beautimus and Samuel, engrossed in their conversation, paid them no heed.

"Not exactly, Sam. I don't know much about the science behind..."

"...we've generated an energy transfer of beetle dung wave packets broken down into a quantum scale. We infused beetle excrement protons into the molecular structure of the soil... and... what nutritional term does the word 'proton' remind you of?

"*Uh*, protein?"

"Exactly. Through the process of infusing the soil with dung proton particles we are now able to increase the protein content of blue corn kernels, and a higher yield per acre. Simple, isn't it?"

"Yeah, sure, Sam. Simple. So—what about jasmine wine? Making any this season?"

"Only if I can get the hydrometer or saccharometer scale denoting the density of specific gravity right this time, you know, the brix."

If the talk about subatomic particles hadn't gotten to Beautimus, the brix thing had. "Sam, why is it quantum physicists have such a goddessdamn tough time answering a simple question?"

The second he launched into a response, Beautimus changed the subject yet again in hopes of extricating herself from Samuel's scientific nattering. "I read an interesting article in *Rendazian Nature* about the beautiful color of hummingbird's tongues…"

"…ah, yes. Two recent studies explore hummingbird tongue design and function, specifically how their tongues are engineered for nectar retrieval. Hummingbirds are….whoa!" Samuel's head snapped around.

A group of attractive praying mantis women buzzed by in their festival finery distracting Samuel from his prattle. One, named Cheeky, with the well-earned reputation for spreading her wings for any male who wanted her, wiggled her hindquarters at Samuel. He straightened his shoulders and flexed his muscles. "My, my, are you ever lookin' sweet today, Cheeky. How 'bout given me a little sugar?"

"Sam, is it going to be like this every time you see a mantis woman today? If you persist in behaving like this, you can hop off now and fly to the festival by yourself."

"I told you mead wasn't all I thought about, Bea."

From behind a bluebush wattle tree, the brown chicken clucked. The hen ducked further in an awkward attempt to conceal herself. When Beautimus stepped closer, the chicken busied herself with a buckwheat stalk.

"Who in hellzabob *is* that?" Asked Samuel.

"I don't know, but Beard warned me about her, and she gives me a bad feeling."

***

A filthy brown rat with a missing tooth scuttled between Beautimus' legs and ran in front.

"There goes that clapper-clawed-swag-bellied-son-of-a-guttersnipe-thieving-pack-rodent, Heatherton. I know *exactly* why he's going to the Wasenia Festival. Hold onto your satchel today, Bea."

"So, you don't trust him, then?"

"Very funny. I'm only warning you not to let him get anywhere near anything you value. That pack rat steals everything he can get his filthy ruttish paws on."

Thundering around a bend, Chance Rockefeller, a surly t-rex, ran right into a small kangaroo. He plowed her over, and when she bumped her noggin on a rock she cried out. Beautimus and Samuel rushed to her side. "Are you okay?" Beautimus asked.

"I'll be fine." The kangaroo rubbed her head. "I don't understand why Chance is so…"

"Because he's a skelpie-limmer bully, and a muck-spout cumberwold if I ever knew one," Samuel said. "He didn't even stop to see if he'd hurt you."

Beautimus nudged the kangaroo to her feet. "Are you sure you're all right?"

"I'm fine. Thank you."

A rustle overhead in the branches of a broad-leaved nealie tree caught Samuel and Beautimus' attention. A single brown feather drifted to the ground.

"Bea, your chicken is with us," Samuel said.

When Beautimus looked up, she saw only leaves and nealie branches. "Well, she's gone now. Maybe without her we can enjoy the rest of our journey."

***

The fairgoers, in great spirits, called greetings to one another, made music, danced, and laughed. With the exception of their encounter with Heatherton the rat, and Chance the t-rex, Beautimus had not enjoyed a nicer day in quite some time. She spied a husk of hares dodging the legs and tails of larger festival travelers. One rabbit bounded in a panic to Beautimus and Samuel. "Ms. Bea. Sam. Have you heard?"

"What's going on?" Beautimus said.

"Ms. Priscilla, Lady's Rhianna's House Chimp."

"Something's happened to her?"

"She left the Blue Crane Compound last night for the Sacred Watering Hole to prepare for Lady Rhianna's arrival. She never made it. A few hours ago, a mew of capons happened upon her body under a needlewood tree. They found her all bloodied, dead, her throat bitten clean out."

CHAPTER FIVE

"SAM, I'VE BEEN considering the similarities between Priscilla's murder and Áine's. I have a gut-feeling Chance killed Áine, and maybe Priscilla. He's got a horrible temper. I can't imagine why he'd murder the High Priestess' house chimp, but as for Áine, she and Chance were never on good terms. I think she pissed him off somehow, and he lost it."

"Perhaps, but why would Chance be in The Compound to begin with, and how could he have gotten in? No one but the badger had a key. And, besides, Áine's murder occurred nearly two centuries ago in a completely different area of the Wayflower District. I don't think the two murders are remotely related."

"Both victims were Believers, and young females with their throats ripped out. What makes you think they aren't connected? That t-rex might have used his family's influence and money to buy his way out of trouble. I think he got away with murder, maybe two murders."

A scratching sound attracted Beautimus' attention. She caught sight of brown tail feathers as the hen scuttled down a shallow embankment. "Sam, I suspect our chicken is getting better at sneaking around."

"Yeah? If she gets in Chance's way, I suspect she'll end up plucked and deep fried."

***

Beautimus and Samuel made their way along the remaining length of the path to the Sacred Watering Hole. They strolled by majestic Japanese maples, magnolias and old camphor trees with spring green trunks. Some of the fairgoers played clay whistles or babuwood flutes as they traversed the path, and others sang or hummed. Samuel and Beautimus passed a knot of toads picking daisies for the festival. The toads sang an old Goddess hymn, "How Great Thou Art."

The two friends picked up the distant strains of the festival's tan river reed whistles, the hypnotic rhythms of pink pebble rumblers and striped pan-pan gourd rattles. The music grew louder and brighter as they at last approached the fair gates. At the entrance, they passed under an arbor of buddleia bushes heavy with plum colored blossoms. Atop the arbor, representatives of the Butterfly Counsel sat in a row attended by eager honey bees.

A particularly stunning swallowtail, Odette, called down to the groups of fair attendees, "Welcome one and all to the festival. Happy Wasenia Day. May you be blessed by the warmth of the stars."

CHAPTER SIX

AT THE ENTRANCE to the festival grounds, a polar bear greeter in an ecstatic yellow bowler and matching cape offered Beautimus and Samuel their choice of complimentary drafts of sparkling mead or mint water. Samuel, being the party mantis he fancied himself, right off chose a generous thimble of mead and downed it in one quaff. Beautimus selected a bulbous hollowed melon of mint water.

Acrobats with tiny bells woven into their feathers and fur, and Manx cat fire eaters in saffron colored satin trousers leapt and twirled about. Yellow-billed cuckoos juggled avocado seeds. Hepatic tanagers and yellow-rumped warblers in groups of five sang ancient Earth madrigals, accompanying themselves on tiny lutes made from corn silk strung across hollowed boa-boa seed pods. A red-naped sap sucker flitted here and there reciting rhyming couplets. Dozens of venders hawked their wares from colorful booths. Heatherton, the rat, scuttled between them, and eyed their cash boxes.

"There's that thieving tardy-gated varlet," Samuel said.

A quartet of horseflies serenaded Beautimus and Samuel with Wagner's *Götterdämmerung Libretto* in perfect pitch. A ceit of badgers, a trip of goats and a fall of woodcocks piled their offerings on the Wasenia alter beneath a carved image of the Goddess of the Fair, the Star Maiden, a stunning white coyote with her nose pointed to the sky.

In spite of Priscilla's murder, the festival atmosphere remÁined light. Yet, everywhere on the festival grounds, attendees talked about the killing.

"I don't know how Rhianna is going to hold up today. Who would kill her house chimp, for hellzabob sake?" One fairgoer asked another.

"Who knows, but I hope they catch the bastard soon."

"The way the killer murdered Priscilla—awful. I mean, why? How could anyone be so vicious?"

"I know. Right? It's inconceivable someone could be so cruel."

"The coroner said Priscilla didn't die right off, meaning the poor dear bled to death or suffocated. There is a truly evil creature in the Wayflower District, and I'm not going anywhere alone, that's for sure."

"Me either. I'll be scared to walk alone at night until the Guardians catch the murderer."

***

A border shepherd, a raven, and a sloth hawked their wares at their shared booth. The dog sold precious grey salt from the Oceanic District packaged in handmade hemp pouches and lovely carved boa-boa boxes. The raven offered frangipani scented macadamia oil formulated for beaks and feathers. The sloth sold mahogany colored hammocks made of hemp fibers dyed with black walnut shells and beet juice. The sign on their stall read, "Goods for the Salty Dogs, Oily Birds, and Lazy Sloths in Your Life." The sloth and the shepherd argued over table space.

"Why do you need all this room for salt? I've got hammocks, lots of them, some large enough for an elephant. Move your stuff over, will ya?" Said the sloth to the dog.

"Hellzabob no," said the dog. "I paid 50 Rendazian Glow Seeds extra for adequate space to display my imported salt boxes. You can bloody well display one of your mundane hammocks and stow the rest under the table. They are all the same anyway."

The raven ignored them. He sat on a perch above them preening, pulling tiny drops of macadamia oil through his feathers with his gaudy painted beak. The raven's feathers were perfect, and he knew it. A dissimulation of birds, bobolinks, vermillion flycatchers, crested caracaras queued to buy the raven's oil, while the salt and hammock sellers continued to yap, squeak, and argue between themselves, ignoring potential customers. First in line for the macadamia nut oil, the brown chicken made her purchase and scooted off in the direction opposite Beautimus.

"That damned chicken," Beautimus said to Samuel.

"Forget about her. Let's go watch the dancers. It'll do us both some good to listen to music and watch happy couples waltzing for a while."

In a grassy meadow, pipers piped and dancers danced. Many tribes were represented on the green. Pairs of tabby cats, grey foxes, and tea cup Chihuahuas showed their stuff on one side of the meadow. Larger animals tangoed on the other. A string of ponies line-danced through a patch of clover. Field mice, fire ants, pygmy bats, and ladybugs whirled about on the surfaces of flat boulders well out of the way of the hooves and paws of bovines and dromedaries. A wake of buzzards danced the Charleston on the limbs of a wallangarra wattle tree. On one broad flat rock to the lee side of the meadow a bullfrog couple tripped the light fantastic. They wore flashy gold and white striped robes bejeweled with dozens of tiny crystals, and the couple sported matching pill box hats. They kicked their long green legs high into the air then commenced to turn, stamp and leap. The duo masterfully executed the Fandango and had attracted a small crowd of bobac marmots and miniature pot-bellied pigs who cheered, hooted, stomped and clapped in time.

"Look at that couple dance, Sam. Wow. They're something else."

Beautimus and Samuel moved a little closer to watch the bullfrogs. Samuel clapped his praying mantis hands and bobbed his head, while Beautimus stamped her feet in rhythm to the bullfrogs' steps. With each stomp the ground shook ever so slightly, but no one minded.

Samuel paid close attention to the dance green. He told Beautimus he'd hoped to catch a glimpse of "fine mantis leg." He looked here and there, bouncing and dancing on Beautimus' head to the beat of the music. He abruptly ceased his clapping and bobbing, and nudged Beautimus' ear.

"Bea! Check out that lone figure near the bullfrogs."

Beautimus halted her stomping, and stared down.

"Is that the brown chicken dancing by herself?" Samuel asked.

Beautimus lowered her head further and squinted to get a better look. She said, "Why, yes it is. Hey, you, brown chicken. You!"

The chicken ceased mid-step, one leg frozen high in the air, took one look at Beautimus and Samuel, skittered off the dance floor all aflutter, and hid behind a butter berry bush. Beautimus shook her head. "I think that chicken is mentally ill, and I give up trying to figure out what the hellzabob she's doing."

As Beautimus and Samuel strolled through the festival grounds they snacked on sugared popped blue corn, and enjoyed the entertÁiners. Then out of nowhere a commotion. The t-rex, Chance!

Chance spent most of his time watching films from Earth streamed onto his Crystal Interface. When he developed a fascination for movies about gangs he adopted the name "T-Bone," and started his own gang "The Wayflower Homies." He referred to the Wayflower District as his "hood," his cave as his "crib," his friends as "dawgs," and his gang as his "crew" or "posse."

He wore a red and blue plaid bandana around his head knotted at the back, his gang's "do-rag." He sported dark, expensive sunglasses even at night. Much to everyone's chagrin, he referred to any woman he encountered as "ho" or "bitch." Although Beautimus found him rude and obnoxious, the Canine Tribe took particular umbrage at his use of the word "bitch." Beautimus called him on his lack of respect, but he didn't care.

He said "yo," "dis" and "mofo," although clear to everyone he didn't understand any of the words' meanings. Chance fashioned a crude weapon from an ash tree limb that looked to her like a cross between an oversized turkey baster and a toilet plunger. He carried his "gat" with him always. When someone annoyed him he'd threatened them with it. "I'm gonna' pop a cap in yo az."

Chance, or rather, T-Bone, recruited two members into his gang, an obese brown weasel named Herbert Smith who called himself M.C. Tweezers. Herbert aspired to be a gangsta' rapper and wore an oversized wooden Earth dollar sign around his neck he'd spray painted silver and referred to as his "bling." A scrawny Jackal, Mortimer Rosenthal, with bad breath and a speech impediment, gave himself the crew name of "Rampage," which he could not pronounce so it came out as "Wampage," joined as well. The gang members threw signs, which they contrived. The signs meant nothing but looked cool. They tagged the neighborhood trees with symbols that also meant nothing but looked cool, and played Earth gangsta' rap from T-Bone's crib day and night. Otherwise, since the three lived well off of T-Bone's ample trust fund, they didn't do much of anything gangbanger-like. For the most part, they were harmless idiots no one liked. T-Bone could be mean-spirited, though, and apparently took pleasure in intimidating anyone smaller and weaker. Beautimus found him loathsome.

Chance bellowed at a mild-mannered little ferret known to everyone as Mr. Grandy of "Mr. Grandy's Candies."

"Yo. Mofo. You tried to cheat me, you stinky-assed ferret. I'm gonna tear down your booth and put yo mofo ugly ass self outta business, then I'm gonna pop a cap in yo az, you farking little cheater."

"But, sir," implored the ferret, "I didn't cheat you. Honest to peewee. I specifically said five Glow Seeds for three honeyed melon balls, not three Glow Seeds for five melon balls. I gave you correct change. I did!"

The bully dinosaur let out a roar so loud fair attendees within twenty meters went running as fast as their paws and claws could scuttle to witness the disturbance at Mr. Grandy's Candy Hut. Chance stomped on the ferret's booth ripping a gash in its striped pop-up cover and splintering the display table. More than half of Mr. Grandy's candies spilled to the ground. The little ferret scampered behind a two-flowering wallowa tree, fearing for his life.

Beautimus bulldozed her way to Chance, stopped short of ramming him, looked up into his face and yelled, "Why in hellzabob did you do that?" She ordered a passing stork to fetch the Guardians. Everyone seemed worried Chance might hurt Beautimus, but no one stepped in to help. Nonetheless, Beautimus stood her ground as the stork flew to the security booth.

Chance, unaccustomed to anyone standing up to him, growled at Beautimus and raised his wooden gun at her in an attempt to cower her. She remÁined unfazed.

He waived and twisted his gat around in one of his tiny arms as though slinging a pistol. "Yo, Bitch. Yo, ugly ho, I'm gonna pop a cap in yo az."

Samuel, who had already ducked behind Beautimus' left ear, held tighter. Chance turned away from her, and high-tailed it to the exit of the fairgrounds.

Beautimus called after him. "Really? You're running away like the spur-galled coward. Is that it? Stay here and face the Guardians like a man!"

Much to her relief, Chance proved to be no exception to bullies who back down when confronted, *or maybe, he doesn't want to appear a coward in front of a large audience.*

He swung around and stood stock still, towering over her with a defiant expression. "Yo, bitch. As though I'd be in any way afraid of stupid-assed unchin-snouted monkeys and a bunch of weakling mofo deer. When the Guardians get here, I'll pop a cap in their az's, too."

The Guardians arrived a moment later, five bull elk and a powerful trio of orangutans, two with imposing truncheons in their hands. The largest of the three orangutans, Sergeant José Saturday, Detective of the First Order, Chief of the Festival Security Team, carried only his badge. When he held it aloft, its silver flashed in the sunlight. The bull elks surrounded Chance, put their heads down, and aimed their massive racks at the dinosaur. The orangutans with truncheons at the ready took their places on either side of Chance, and Sgt. Saturday approached Beautimus.

"Sgt. José Saturday, Ma'am. You sent the stork? Can you tell me what happened here?"

She gave an accounting of the events to the stoic detective. Sgt. Saturday turned his attention to the dinosaur, "You will repair this damage. You will make restitution to the ferret. The alternative is we take you downtown. You clear on this, Mr. Rockefeller?"

Chance mumbled, "Yeah. Uh. Yo. Yeah."

"And, you *will* apologize to Mr. Grandy."

The ferret had only moments before emerged from his hiding place, approached Sgt. Detective First Class Saturday and his men, and thanked them.

"Just doing our job, sir."

Mr. Grandy turned to the crowd. "A round of applause for the brave hippo, Ms. Beautimus Potamus, for having courage to stand up to Chance Rockefeller...alone."

The abashed crowd broke into applause, and the defiance on Chance's face morphed into humiliation.

"My, my," a bornean sun bear said. "Look at this. A big ferocious t-rex, leader of the most feared gang in the whole of Rendaz—never mind *The Wayflower Homies* is the *only* gang on the planet—shamed in front of all us mofo little-assed creatures by a middle-aged hippo ho."

A tower of giraffes broke into raucous laughter.

"I'll pop a cap in all your az's," Chance said. The dinosaur opened his satchel and paid for the expert carpentry of a skilled team of pandas on standby for such emergencies, who in no time, rebuilt the table, repaired the pop-up, and restored the booth. Under the watchful eye of the Guardians, Chance apologized to Mr. Grandy, then paid the ferret for his ruined sweets. Chance spent the rest of the day and evening hawking the remainder of the ferret's candies....threatening to pop a cap in anyone's az who didn't purchase something....until the confections were sold out.

CHAPTER SEVEN

AS BEAUTIMUS BROWSED the stall "Mary's Berries and Jerry's Cherries," she noticed a group of praying mantis people on a patch of lawn feasting on grapes and honey. One of them, a pretty female named Petunia, had eyes for Samuel, and even though he did his best to maintain his reputation as a free-spirited party bug, Samuel returned Petunia's attraction. Beautimus liked Petunia, and thought it a splendid idea to help things along between Samuel and the sweet female mantis. She'd hoped if he found a mate, maybe he'd cease being so damned obnoxious about women.

"Would you mind if I dropped you off with the Mantis Tribe so I can do a little shopping on my own, Sam? I'll pick you up in a short while."

Samuel eyed Petunia. "You betcha, Bea. Take your time."

He groomed himself and straightened his cape and collar. He flew to the picnic circle and settled next to Petunia, "Hey, pretty mama, whatzup?"

Beautimus shopped, paid for her purchases, lingered a bit, then made her way back to the mantis picnic.

"Sam, are you ready?" She called out.

Samuel snuggled close to Petunia and whispered something. The female mantis blushed.

"Hey, Sam, if you'd rather stay here for a bit, I'll catch up with you at the ceremony. No problem."

"No, no, it's okay, Bea. I'll be right there."

Samuel leaned over to the pretty Petunia and planted a kiss on her face. She turned a deeper crimson.

"I'll be seein' you later, little darlin'." He winked at Petunia, flew back onto Beautimus' head and settled in. "Bea, I'd like to go back to Mary's Berries and Jerry's Cherries."

Beautimus knew exactly what he wanted, a bag of dried winter beer-berries to make his own hooch at home. Famous for a brew he fermented in a rusted water tub from beer-berries, blue corn husks, and bottlebrush nectar, he continually refined his brew until he developed a potion that knocked the ever-living slats out from beneath anyone who took more than one sip.

"I plan on sharing a little hooch with Petunia at some opportune moment when we are alone, preferably somewhere like a private romantic room with a red velveteen covered heart shaped bed and a mirrored ceiling."

"Goddess help me." Beautimus wasn't quite sure what else she wanted for herself so she perused the stalls and booths one at a time. Occasionally, Beautimus or Samuel caught sight of the brown chicken shopping at the booths they browsed. The two friends did their best to ignore the crazy hen.

A beautiful chinchilla, Angeline, in a gossamer daffodil colored robe sold dazzling blue pendants. She'd hand-crafted her jewelry from rare crystal mined in the distant Shar District, famous for its unique blue stones said to contain powerful magical properties. Angeline eyed Beautimus as she browsed the jewelry. "I have the very thing for you."

From beneath the table she extracted an enormous heart-shaped shar-stone pendant that changed colors when she held it to the sunlight. "I believe you need this," she said.

The brilliant stone hung on a white silk ribbon. Samuel stepped down onto Beautimus' back as she dipped her head as low as possible toward the chinchilla, who still had to stand on her tip toes to place the ribbon over the hippo's neck.

"The color of the crystal nearly matches the beautiful purple of your eyes, and mimics the heart shaped birthmark on your cheek," the chinchilla said.

"It's lovely. I'll take it, please. What is its magical property?"

She pointed her delicate paw at Beautimus' nose. "That's for me to know and for you to discover."

The merchant called to a bay colored spider monkey in a vest dyed to match Angeline's robe. He sported gold dust on the tips of his ears that flaked off as he moved his head. The monkey rested in a diminutive rocking chair painted peacock blue.

"Jake, please help our customer with her satchel," Angeline said. "That will be 90 Rendazian Glow Seeds please, plus ten for the tax man."

The monkey hopped off his chair, opened Beautimus' satchel and withdrew 100 seeds. He counted them in front of Beautimus then placed them in Angeline's open paw. Beautimus noticed Jake slip a few Glow Seeds into his vest pocket, but said nothing. She wondered if Angeline knew the stealthy monkey might be stealing one or two seeds from each of her customers, taking enough to line his pockets over the course of the day, but not so much that anyone noticed. He scrambled to his chair. Beautimus attempted to make eye-contact with him, but he closed his eyes and rocked, gold dust on his ears flaking into powdery specks with each movement to and fro.

Beautimus wanted to say something to Angeline, to let her know Jake may be stealing, but other customers were in line behind her. It'd have to wait. Angeline bowed, "Thank you for your patronage. Happy Wasenia Day! May you be blessed by the warmth of the stars."

"What a lovely day," Beautimus said. And, would have been more so if it were not for the hot flashes. A few times, Beautimus had to stop short. "Sam! Get off now. I feel another coming on."

She'd trot as fast as her legs could carry her to jump into the nearest pond, or creek, often displacing most of the water and some of the fish, guppies and frogs. Someone with opposable thumbs would run with buckets of water to aid the poor gasping critters. "I'm dreadfully sorry," Beautimus would say.

A few frogs were rather put out. "Those are my guppies you tossed onto the bank, you lubborwort!" One mother said. "For Goddessake, be more careful."

CHAPTER EIGHT

"WHAT IF I'M right, Sam? What if Áine and Pricilla were murdered by the same person, and the killer is still in the District, maybe even right here at the Wasenia Festival? I have received messages from my visions and the Glyphs that I'm supposed to know something, or do something. I'm so upset by all this I can't even sleep."

"It'll work out, Bea. Besides, no offense to you, but your Glyphs and your visions probably don't mean anything."

"Oh, yeah, that's right, Sam. If science can't prove it, it can't be real. Is that what you mean?"

The two continued on the path through the fair grounds. Even with the festive atmosphere, between her argument with Samuel and her recurring thoughts of the murders, Beautimus' mood turned progressively glum. *At least the brown chicken isn't anywhere in sight.*

Beautimus and Samuel turned away from a vendor's booth and nearly ran into a pair of pink flamingos sporting metallic hats resembling dunce caps. Both flamingos wore oversized lavender flowing robes that trailed in the dirt when they walked. Their pink tail feathers stuck out from their robes in awkward angles, and their long legs poked out like pale toothpicks. The flamingos were laden with heavy silver chains from which hung clear crystal pendants cut into the shape of pyramids.

"I'm dreadfully sorry. Excuse me," said Beautimus. She'd almost stepped on the both of them.

"There are no accidents in the cosmos," said one flamingo. "You create your own reality. You have unconsciously asked the Divine Fairies for us to appear to you because of something you need in this exact vibrational moment to expand your cosmic consciousness in preparation for your ascension to the 6th fairy dimension of meaningless emptiness."

Samuel looked down at the birds. "What?"

Beautimus stared at the odd metallic things on their heads. One flamingo reached to touch his cone. "You are wondering what this is? We wear these to protect ourselves from the mighty imagined dark forces to prevent them from penetrating our energy fields with their toxic control waves, and bending our minds to their evil will. You really should wear one yourself. I can sell you one at a good price."

Samuel rolled his eyes, and snickered.

One flamingo made a slight bow and said, "I am 'Floating Blue Moon Wizard Bird' and my companion is 'Starlight Crystal Green Fairy Good-Man.' What may we call you, my universal cosmic brother and sister?"

Samuel eyed them and said again, "What?"

The blue moon flamingo told Beautimus, "My fairy guides from the other dimension have given me a message. They say you are in need spiritual development and soul expansion. They say I must help you, and there is something I must give to you, now."

The mantis bent his head into Beautimus' ear, and said "For crap sake, Bea, say 'no thank you' and let's get the demon fire outta here, *please*."

Beautimus nodded. "Certainly. I'd be happy to see what you have for me."

Samuel groaned, fidgeted and hopped from foot-to-foot like a flea on a hot plate.

Beautimus followed the flamingos to the shade of a large boa-boa bush. The two birds withdrew nine-inch long obelisk shaped crystals from their robes. They closed their eyes and performed an elaborate circular dance waiving the crystals above their heads. They hummed an odd discordant tune that sounded like a cross between "Mary Had a Little Lamb" and "Stairway to Heaven." Once done prancing about and humming, they stopped and gazed into one another's eyes. In a conspiratorial tone, the starlight bird said to the blue moon bird, "Now this space is cleared of all negative galactic ray influences and imagined dark forces, and our chakra energy is in perfect alignment with our auras, it is time."

The blue moon flamingo produced from the folds of his robe a tri-page, full-colored, glossy brochure he spread out on the grass before Beautimus.

"Peruse this information," said the blue moon bird. "What is in this brochure is only for the knowing of a special few the golden light fairies have blessed."

Samuel couldn't take it anymore. He began to laugh hysterically. "You have to be kidding me. Do you think these guys really mean this? Oh, this is rich. Hahahahahaaa."

Beautimus scowled. "Shhhhh, Sam. Stop it."

On the front of the brochure a siege of herons, a colony of weasels, and a cackle of hyenas cast their eyes upwards toward a feline fairy creature with glowing amber eyes and long golden fur. She floated mid-air on what appeared to be a cloud of bleached peanut shells. She wore an azure velvet cape edged in gemstones, and a garnet-studded tiara. A pinkish glow cocooned her body, and she held her tail high in such a way it appeared as a scepter. The hyenas, weasels, and herons stared at her in complete adoration, mesmerized.

Samuel laughed with even more gusto. He began to choke. "Hahahaha....snort, snort, ha ha ha cough, cough, hahaha... ha...ha."

"I mean it, Sam. Knock it off."

"That," said Starlight Bird, "is our spiritual teacher, our leader, our exalted guru, Pretencia Narcissa-Rica, Ultra Queen of the Fairies sent here on a divine mission from the star system, Catlandia. She communicates with golden light fairies from many inter-dimensional spirit realms and has written one hundred books on the subject. She also designed more than fifty packs of Catlandia Fairy Oracle Card Decks. Among her titles are at least a few you certainly know such as 'The Inner Voice of the Outlandish Fairy,' 'You, Too, Are a Big Fairy,' and the ever popular 'Fairies Abound in Our Foodstuff' oracle set. This last set of cards not only provides messages from the fairies, but contains recipes for meals when prepared as instructed and consumed daily, make you holier than thou from the inside out. Pretencia's books and cards are specifically designed to lift you to a higher realm of Righteous Self-Importance."

Samuel peered at the brochure from between Beautimus' ears. "What a load of beetle dung."

"Now," said the blue moon flamingo, "Here's the best part, and you need to listen carefully because this is truly unbelievable."

"Yeah, I'd say this shit is 'unbelievable'," Samuel whispered into Beautimus' ear.

"You can become an officially ordÁined Fairy Counselor and make an abundance of glow seeds helping others to contact their fairy guides and discover their higher sense of self-absorption. Does that sound appealing?"

Beautimus responded with her customary graciousness. "Well, now, that *is* interesting."

Blue Moon continued, "Pretencia is offering a weekend seminar at the beautiful, exclusive Sacred Crystal Emerald Light Dolphin-Ray Energy Isle Resort in the Oceanic District this warm season, and if you act fast you can…"

"…let me take the brochure with me and I'll read it over." Beautimus took a step backwards.

"But, wait!" said the blue moon bird. "Space is limited. We

have only one opening remaining. You, my sister, are in luck. You still have an hour to reserve the last seat before tuition increases by 1,000 glow seeds."

Beautimus edged away from the flamingos. "Thank you so much for your time, Moonbeam Bird Guy and Starcatcher Man Person is it?"

As the hippo blended into the crowd, Blue Moon Bird trotted to Beautimus and thrust the brochure and another piece of paper into her satchel.

"At the very least take this with you as my personal gift. It is a guide I personally developed with the help of pure fairy energy called, 'How to Be Spiritual by Sounding Spiritual'."

Beautimus said, "Thank you so much. Gotta run, now. See you at the ceremony."

Once out of earshot, Samuel said, "I've never seen anything so damned funny as those flamingos dancing the lambada waving those glass things around."

"Don't ridicule what you don't understand."

Samuel's disposition switched from amused to surly. "Actually, as hilarious as it might have been, that whole damned thing resulted in a damned nasty waste of time. Now it's too damned late to even get a damned bite of honey dew melon or another damned sip of mead before the ceremony. Dammit, Bea!"

"Personally, Sam, I appreciated the diversion. At least for a couple of minutes I focused on something other than Glyphs, nightmare visions of my dead mother, and the horrible unsolved murders of two Wayflower citizens. I feel better."

***

Twenty-two coyotes in white capes embellished with gold stars marched one behind the other parade style through the throng and announced, "The ceremony begins in a few minutes. Please make your way to the Ceremony Green."

The fair goers moved toward the Sacred Watering Hole and a broad stage decorated with hundreds of yellow and white streamers. The uprights were festooned with golden star banners fluttering in the late afternoon breeze. The coyotes formed a line with their backs against the stage, faced the crowd and sat, eyes forward.

The melody of the Baboon Harp Trio wafted over the crowd, Pachelbel's *Canon in D Minor*. The eagle and hawk tribes made a spectacular fly-over. At that moment, the Turkey Buzzards took up a chant, "Ugly Heads Are Beautiful! Ugly Heads Are Beautiful! Ugly Heads Are Beautiful!" They waved their signs and stamped their feet. A gossip columnist from *The Wayflower Quacker*, a robust female toad, Hattie Hopper, made her way through the crowd to interview the buzzards. She held a recorderphone, and a few of the more curious onlookers crowded in. The Komodo dragon attorney scuttled toward the buzzards, drooling. Then, with the exception of the harp music, the atmosphere grew silent again.

A clucking came from somewhere within the crowd, but as Beautimus and

Samuel turned, the brown chicken disappeared behind the leg of a wooly mammoth.

"There she went, Bea."

"I saw her. She's probably been following us for hours."

A spot-nosed guenon unadorned except for a gold bhindi between his eyes carried overhead an elaborate carved angico thurible of burning sandalwood incense, and placed it on the edge of the stage.

With great solemnity, a beautiful female coyote dressed in white satin robes, a glittery tiara on her head, stepped onto the stage. She placed herself adjacent to the thurible, closed her eyes and bowed once to the crowd.

Beautimus explÁined to Samuel how The High Priestess

chose the coyote, Belinda, to represent the Star Maiden because of her great beauty, dignity, and devotion. "Today, more than a pretty coyote, she embodies an aspect of the great Goddesses."

Belinda, an exemplary student, Rhianna's best, became well-versed in the ways of the Wise Woman. Everyone knew even as a pup, Belinda had set her intention to become the most powerful woman of The Wayflower District. Over years, with great planning, she positioned herself to ascend to the High Priestess role.

"I think the sole reason Belinda refuses to take a mate, although many young males pursue her, has to do with her single-minded goal to become High Priestess, Sam. Other female coyotes her age would be on their second or even third litter, but from the time she entered puberty and began to bleed, Belinda, has spent hours admiring her reflection in looking glasses and ponds all over Wayflower, proclaiming aloud to any passerby, '*I am to be a queen*. I'll never spend my days cleaning shit out of a dirty den, licking the wax-caked ears of a stinking male, whelping multiple litters of pups while growing fatter by the season. I am meant to save my talents and preserve my beauty for my rightful role as High Priestess.'"

"Wow. Do we want a vainglorious High Priestess to command Wayflower?"

"She's chosen for her other qualities such as her skill in magic, dedication to The Goddess, and her years of training and preparation, not for her personality. I'm sure she'll make a fine high priestess."

A powerful silver-back gorilla named Rufus, sporting a floor-length white cape, walked onto the stage. He bore the entire Wasenia altar above his head with its thousand plus pounds of offerings. Rufus, a clown, big on juvenile practical jokes like flushing cherry bombs down toilets and other such pranks, clung to an ambition to become a professional stand-up comedian. Well-known for his crude jokes, mostly about flatulence and bodily fluids, he chose the stage name "Rufus the Buttmonger," which no one in Wayflower but Rufus thought clever or amusing. He *incessantly* attempted to get laughs, and *always* cracked up at his own bad jokes. However, when it came to ceremonies at the Sacred Watering Hole, Rufus adopted a serious and reverent demeanor. With great solemnity, he placed the altar mid-stage and bowed low to the Star Maiden. "With these gifts, we demonstrate to you our love and great respect. Long Live The Star Maiden."

Belinda turned to Rufus, and spoke the only words she'd say throughout the entire ceremony. "Thank you. May the stars bless you with their light."

With a slight nod, Belinda acknowledged the attending coyotes standing guard over the stage and the altar. For a few minutes, silence fell over The Green, broken only by the sweet strains of harp music.

The music ceased, and the arena became so still not even the banners fluttered. From behind heavy white velvet curtains appeared the beautiful blue crane, Lady Rhianna, High Priestess of the Wayflower District. Five guard wolves followed, stood in a row behind her, and eyed the audience. Rhianna wore a long scarf made of spun gold. In her left wing she held the Wand of Fortuna.

The wand, handcrafted thousands of years before from a revered ancient ash skilled artisans carved, plated in hardened quicksilver, and inlaid with pink tourmaline, yellow diamonds and polished sun stones, glimmered. Assessors placed its value in Glow Seeds as "immeasurable," but its true value lay in its magical powers. The wand could shape-shift the holder. It could send light messages to the moons, the suns and to all the stars in the galaxy and beyond. It could transport the bearer anywhere in the flash of an eye, or render the bearer invisible. The wand could only be used by the High Priestess of Wayflower during sacred ceremonies.

"That wand's gotta be worth a fortune, Bea. Hope she keeps it under lock and key," Samuel whispered.

"When the wand is not in use it's stored in a box carved from solid polished lapis lazuli, inlaid with mother of pearl. The box is bound, locked, and hidden in a niche deep within a secret underground cavern. Its exact whereabouts are known only to the High Priestess and her elite special forces wolf guards who watch over it 24/7. Do you see what the wolves wear?"

"Cool red hats."

"Each of the wolf guards wears a red velvet fez with a gold tassel to indicate his rank. No other wolf but a Wand Guard may wear the Red Fez. Their Captain is Steven D. Lobos, the largest, strongest, and most honored of all the Guards in the Special Forces. He's the one right there in the middle. See? He commands the other Wand Guards. Without hesitation, they are willing to give their life in the protection of the High Priestess and the Wand of Fortuna."

"Shhhhh," someone said. "Lady Rhianna is about to speak."

When Rhianna turned to address the crowd, Beautimus broke into goose bumps from her ears through each of her four feet. "Oh, Sam, isn't she magnificent?"

"I have to admit, she really is."

Rhianna held the Wand aloft in both wings. It pulsated, and emitted a numinous glow. The blue crane turned her head to the sky, and her beak moved in silent prayer. She recited an incantation to invoke the Goddesses of the four corners.

Rhianna held the wand overhead and made a stirring motion with it. Something like a lightning bolt shot from the wand's crystal tip into the sky, and appeared to momentarily cleave the suns in two. For the exception of the tiny wails of a new born Koala Bear cub, the crowd fell silent. Rhianna lowered her wings to her side, tucked the wand into her robes, and addressed the throng. "Happy Wasenia Day. May you be blessed by the warmth of the stars."

The assembly responded in unison, "And, may you equally be blessed by the warmth of the stars."

"Before we begin, I request a moment of silence to acknowledge the untimely passage of my house chimp, and good friend, Priscilla. You undoubtedly heard a mew of capons found Priscilla slain this morning. A kind soul, a devoted servant, Priscilla and I shared a true kinship. My heart is heavy this day as I ask you all to join me in asking the Goddesses to bless Priscilla and ease her passage to the other side."

Beautimus bowed her head, but as she returned her focus to the stage, she noticed something not quite right on stage, something off. She shook her head. *I must be giddy from the ceremony, or maybe my hormones are going wacky again, interfering with my perception. Menopause brain. That must be it.*

CHAPTER NINE

ENTHRALLED, BEAUTIMUS LOST herself in the ceremony.

"…and we are gathered here today in kinship, tribes of all species, to honor the stars who give us warmth and beauty. To all the stars, we thank thee."

The crowd responded to the High Priestess' call. "To all the stars, we thank thee."

Rhianna held the wand aloft in her wing. "Racine and Purmoso, the suns of Rendaz, without you our world would be frozen and lifeless."

The crane pointed her wand at the two suns again, now in perfect alignment, one behind the other. A flash of violet light bright and loud shot from the end of the wand and caused everyone in attendance to flinch. A white glow palpitated from the suns in the rhythm of a hundred butterfly heartbeats. Breathless sighs rushed through the awestruck crowd, and from beaks, muzzles, and mouths, wisps of exhalation escaped the lungs of everyone in attendance.

Rhianna kissed her wand, then tucked it into her robe.

The baboons played a few bars of Beethoven's *Concerto for Violin*.

Rhianna spoke again. "We will now conclude our ceremony with the singing of the Star Song." She signaled the harpists and the stadium resonated with the melody line for the Star Song, Beethoven's *Ode to Joy* from the 9th Symphony. Rhianna raised her wings and sang. The audience joined in.

"Thank you all for being here with us today. May you all be blessed by the warmth of the stars."

The Star Maiden exited the stage in graceful steps, her tail swishing side-to-side. Rhianna pulled the wand from her robes, and held it high above her head. In a gentle pop of light the old blue crane vanished. The crowd gasped.

"My Goddesses. She disappeared into thin air. Wherever did she go?" A rufous-sided Towhee said.

A pair of baboons in gold lamé capes bearing a white banner emblazoned with hot pink letters. "Auntie Nancie's School of Fancy Dancing" marched close to the stage. Close behind followed the gazelle dance troupe twirling, dipping, and prancing on their delicate gold painted hooves.

At the end of the procession, the grand dame herself appeared, Auntie Nancie, a large orangutan with a bulging belly and bulbous cheeks. She maintÁined a perpetual aristocratic, imperious bearing. She wore bright annatto lip rouge applied with such a heavy hand it appeared clownish, and she carried a hot pink parasol to shade her "sensitive skin." Auntie Nancie perched like a prim duchess atop an opulent sidesaddle slung over a mastodon's back.

"Happy Wasenia Day," Beautimus called out.

The mastodon, Beautimus' friend, Lizzy, raised her trunk in greeting.

The Baboon Harp Trio broke into a classic can-can, and the gazelle troupe leapt on stage. They locked their front hooves over one another's shoulders and launched into a precision high-kick routine, sending the crowd into a wild frenzy of applause and cheering. The rest of the evening came alive with a party the likes of which hadn't been seen in the Wayflower District in decades.

Beautimus said, "What a splendid festival. What a splendid day."

Sam wasn't listening—his eyes and his attention were fixed on Petunia.

***

By the time the festival ended, the waxing gibbous twin moons, Ladybeth and Ladyluz, hung suspended overhead side-by-side like slender elderly sisters on a settee awaiting tea. In another few cycles, there'd be a Luna Festival to honor the two moons. The Wasenia Fair booths were not yet even broken down, but already the festival organizers were moving *en masse* to the meeting place to make preparations.

Although the moons were bright this evening, a swath of stars blanketed the sky like a black silk scarf sprinkled with tiny holes from which pinpoints of light shown through. A group of drunken crickets sang the *Star Song* off-key.

Beautimus and Samuel were exhausted but contented.

"Tell me about your favorite part of the day, Bea."

"Seeing Rhianna walk out on stage in her gold ceremonial scarf with the Wand of Fortuna in her wing."

The fairgoers were so subdued on the path home it sometimes seemed to Beautimus she and Samuel were the only two creatures on the entire planet of Rendaz. They passed a sloth of bears dozing beside a stream where the dancing bullfrogs made their home. In the distance, they could hear a mother singing a lullaby to her children in an extraordinarily sweet voice for a bullfrog.

The cool night atmosphere effervesced, and the moons and stars cast an abundance of light to illuminate their way. They passed by the Glen of the Ancient Ficus Trees where Beard lived. They heard the trees humming and vibrating to one another as the exhausted and drunken fair attendees passed them on their way to their homes.

Beautimus said, "I think I'll pay my respects to Beard."

"I'll wait here, if you don't mind." Samuel jumped onto a white oak heavily laden with acorns. He asked the tree, "May I take one of these to eat later?"

The tree buzzed its permission.

"Ya know?" Samuel said to the tree, "If it weren't for the news of Lady Rhianna's chimp, all this Goddess claptrap and abracadabra twaddle, I'd say this could have been one of the better days of my life. By the way, I don't know if you stream *The Scientific Rendazian* on your Crystal Interface, but did you happen to catch the article on the latest developments on the control rate of photon emissions from luminescent imperfections in diamonds? Info can be encoded in spins of electrons and carried through a network via light, one photon at a time. We have been using the technology in our Crystal Interfaces for decades, but now planetary scientists are exploring the application to increasing the production of blue corn. The implications are staggering."

The tree vibrated and buzzed again. Beautimus swore she heard it say something like, "Shut the farkus up. Take the damned acorn and get off my branch."

Beautimus moved further into the Glen to spend a moment with Beard. "Did you notice Rhianna's glow when she walked out from behind the curtain holding the Wand of Fortuna, Master Beard? Wasn't she positively radiant?"

"Yes, indeed, Bea. I witnessed the entire ceremony on my Crystal Interface. Glorious."

"I'm amazed she went on with the ceremony after the news of Priscilla's murder. It must have been a terrible shock for her."

"Lady Rhianna is devastated. She is handling the situation with grace, although don't think she isn't hurting, Bea, and she is faced with grave challenges beyond the tragic death of her house chimp, too. There's more going on with her than I can tell you right now."

"Thank you, Master Beard. I thought something might be wrong, and I am worried for Rhianna. You know? Although I wasn't a great student, I always felt it a profound honor to have studied under her."

"The honor was hers as well. Rhianna only teaches those she believes in, those with a gift."

"Me? She felt sorry for me because my mother died when I was so young, and my father abandoned me. I have no gift."

"Don't underestimate yourself."

"I'm a teacher, an oracle reader, and a mediocre writer. Nothing more. "

"Whatever you say, Bea. But remember this: a person's worth is measured on Rendaz by the value they first place on themselves. If you think you are nothing more than a teacher, oracle reader, and mediocre writer then so it is. You'll never be anything more. It's up to you, dear one."

Beautimus recalled the vision in which Áine appeared and said, "It's up to you." A shiver ran from her spine through the tip of her tail.

A barn owl hooted, and Beard spoke again. "I only wish you could see yourself the way I see you. You have unlimited potential, and I'd love nothing more than to see you live up to it. You have always been one of my favorites."

"I love you, Master Beard."

"And, I love you, Beautimus Potamus. By the way, don't ignore the brown chicken."

"How did you know I... oh, never mind. Good evening, Master Beard."

When Beautimus returned, she discovered Samuel sitting in a pin wattle bush instructing a clutter of tipsy male black widows on how to avoid getting trapped in any one woman's web.

"No matter how glossy her underside, if you allow yourself to get caught up in her messy sticky stuff she'll eat you alive. There's plenty of cuties, so no need to get stuck with one. In fact, there's so much fine, sweet spider around it's like you all are living in a candy shop, you lucky arachnids. Taste as many sweets as you can while you still can breathe from your abdomens. Catch my meaning? "

As Samuel leapt back onto Beautimus' head with his acorn, he turned to the young spiders. "Remember what I told ya, and you'll get plenty of shiny booty before you scuttle off this mortal coil."

Beautimus huffed. "You are beyond gross."

A clowder of cats passed, followed by a baron of mules, and a skulk of foxes. No one said a word, and all dragged their paws and hooves. Now and again, a slow yawn wafted through the crowd of sleepy home goers. They passed a parliament of owls roosting in a blue spruce, too tired to fly the remaining distance home. One owl hooted to another, "Nighty-night."

"Sam, I've been thinking. Do you suppose the brown chicken had anything to do with Priscilla and Áine's murders?"

Samuel didn't respond. He'd been rocked into slumber by Beautimus' rhythmic ambling, but every once in a while he'd snort, hiccup or talk in his sleep. Hiccup..."oh, baby, baby, baby, you know I love you, only you, baby, no one else"…. hiccup, snort, hiccup.

At last, Beautimus reached the silver mulga sapling.

"Sam. Sam. Wake up. You're home."

He yawned and flew from her head onto the bark of the tree. "Good night, Bea. Thanks for the ride. I had a blast."

"Me, too, Sam. Glad we enjoyed the day together. See you later."

Between the dense leaves and blossoms of one of her redbud bushes, Beautimus caught a glimpse of light from the front door of her abode.

CHAPTER TEN

"HOME! SO GOOD to be home." Beautimus inhaled the fragrance of ripe fruit and herbs. *Umm. Agnes must have made minted strawberry soup.*

Beautimus' forest abode, located on the edge of her Tribe's compound, stood on land hippos from the Wayflower District had called their territory for centuries. All the houses were tucked among old-growth trees and red bud bushes. The round structures were oriented toward the river and built close together. The houses were roofed by thatch, sided with windowless walls made from strong woven hemp, and doors were large flaps so hippos could enter and exit with ease.

Inside a river-rock lined fireplace provided warmth, light, and served as a pit for cooking. Through the center of the roof a large circular opening permitted smoke to escape and allowed in fresh air. Sometimes rain came through the hole.

"A few drops of sweet rain never hurt anything," Beautimus often said.

The hippo's home furnishings consisted of her altar, various sized colorful pillows for lounging and sleeping, and two small blue woven hammocks for her house squirrels strung between slender willow branches.

The squirrels cooked and kept the abode tidy, and a troop of hyena from the cleaning company, Dirty Deeds Done Dirt Cheap, cleared the straw from the rammed earth floor every Friday.

Beautimus maintÁined an abundant year-round vegetable and herb garden, along with a small fruit and walnut orchard, and an apiary with a dozen bee boxes, everything well-tended by a team of skilled Saki monkeys.

The exhausted hippo pushed through her front door to be greeted by Agnes and Applecheeks, the two Aber Squirrels who served as Beautimus' live-in help, but were also her good friends. They had been watching reruns of "I Love Lucy" on the Interface, but when Beautimus entered they switched off the crystal and stood to welcome her. Applecheeks wore a red and white candy striped apron smeared with honey, some of which stuck in the tuft of fur over her right ear. Agnes, quite a talker, said in one breath, "Welcome-home-Bea-how-was-the-festival-we-thought-of-you-all-day-and-we-sincerely-hope-you-had-a-wonderful-time-because-you-deserve-it."

"I had a lovely time, thank you."

"We-made-your-favorite-minted-strawberry-soup-and-we-are-preparing-a-nice-bucket-of-hot-chamomile-tea-ooh-what-a-lovely-pendant-is-that-a-shar-stone?-my-aunt-had-one-like-it-but-of-course-hers-was-smaller-it's-gorgeous-and-it-matches-your-eyes-and-your-birthmark-I-hear-they-have-magic-in-them-come-sit-down."

Applecheeks would have spoken, too, if she were not mute, and had been since birth. She let her older sister speak for them both. Apple scrambled onto Beautimus' back to untie her satchel, which she placed on its hook near the door. She climbed back with a warm damp cloth in her paw which she used to clean off the remains of the gold dust star between Beautimus' eyes.

"Thank you, Apple," said Beautimus. She sat on a massive blue chenille pillow stuffed with cattail down.

The two squirrels worked together to pull an oversized wooden bowl brimming with strawberry soup to Beautimus. In times like these Beautimus pondered hiring a troodon or giant panda to help Agnes and Applecheeks, but the squirrels objected.

"We-manage-everything-fine-and-would-rather-work-on-our-own-if-you-don't-mind."

"This looks positively delicious. Thank you so much." Fresh mint leaves were crushed into the cold soup giving off a lovely bouquet, which Beautimus inhaled when she stuck her face into the bowl and began lapping. "This smells and tastes heavenly."

Working together, Applecheeks and Agnes ladled hot chamomile tea into a metal bucket from a large pot over the fire. With potholders so large, they practically eclipsed the small rodents, they lifted the pail off the fire, then pushed and pulled it to Beautimus. The three sipped tea and discussed the events of the day including Priscilla's murder. Agnes pressed Beautimus for additional information.

"No. I'm afraid I don't have any other news about who killed Priscilla."

Beautimus wondered if this would remain yet another unsolved murder in Wayflower. Talking about it upset her, and threatened to spoil her mood. She changed the subject. "You can't know how good it is to come in late after a long day, find a light in the doorway, a warm fire in the hearth, and a fine meal. But, best of all, it's so nice to have such wonderful friends to greet me. Thank you both so much."

The squirrels beamed. After Beautimus finished her supper, the squirrels washed the dishes and the three sat together in front of the fire enjoying one another's company. Beautimus said, "Apple, will you fetch my satchel? I have something in it I'd like to read, and I picked up a couple of candied lemon sticks for you two."

"Really-I-love-lemon-sticks-they-are-my-favorite-sweet-and-even-though-she-can't-say-so-I-know-Applecheeks-likes-them-too-because-we-used-to-eat-them-ALL-the-time-when-Ma-and-Pa-were-alive-and-we-lived-in-the-oak-next-door-to-the-badgers-you-remember-the-badgers-right?-it's-been-a-long-while-since-I've-tasted-a-lemon-stick-thank-you-Bea-how-thoughtful-of-you-to-remember-us."

Applecheeks retrieved from the satchel the rice paper-wrapped candied Meyer lemon sticks, one for herself and one for her sister. She extracted the materials the flamingo stuffed into the satchel earlier. Beatrice instructed Apple to throw away the brochure. She asked her to open the guide. At the top it read:

How to BE spiritual by SOUNDING Spiritual
By Floating Blue Moon Wizard Bird

One cannot BE spiritual without the frequent use of spiritual language. Below is a Spiritual-Speak Generator. All you need do to sound spiritual is randomly choose one word from Column A, one from Column B, and one from Column C. Voila! You have created a handy spiritual phrase you can use any time you need to. The more spiritual language you use, the more spiritual you become.

Spiritual-Speak Generator

Golden	Spiral	Awareness
Ascending	Vibrational	Beingness
Dawning	Crystal	Aura
Mystical	Aquarian	Shift
Cosmic	Chakra	Fairy

"Coming soon, my new Guide, 'How to BE Spiritual by looking Spiritual'—the essential instructional manual to wearing flowing garments, pretentious mystic jewelry, tattoos of obscure meaningless symbols, and silver tinkle bells attached to one's fur or feathers to give others the impression there's something really spiritual going on in you. May you soon enter the Transformative Energy Realm to experience Ascending Aquarian Consciousness."

"I can't *wait* to show this to Sam." Beautimus laughed and turned in to her bed pillows. As she dozed off, a solitary chicken clucked outside her abode.

CHAPTER ELEVEN

THE MORNING FOLLOWING the Wasenia Festival, as customary Beautimus read three Glyphs to set the tone for her day. Applecheeks withdrew the stones for Beautimus, one at a time. The first one, Stone Wheel, she placed symbol-side up on the divining cloth. The second, Open Eye, she placed adjacent to Stone Wheel, and the last Glyph—*once again* White Light.

"Look at these, Apple. The first Glyph indicates movement, the second has to do with intuition, and there it is, the ultimate Glyph, the power stone, the explosion. Every time White Light comes up in the outcome position, a significant event is right around the corner. Sometimes good, but more often not."

Some oracle readings were obvious while others took time and effort to decipher. The meaning of this morning's reading couldn't be more startling clear. Yes, something else big would happen. Beautimus wished she knew what it was, and what she was supposed to do about it.

Beautimus didn't know how or why the Glyphs were accurate. She couldn't say if there might be some "ink blot" mechanism at work, meaning the interpretation of the Glyph's symbols took place only in the mind of the beholder, or if the symbols were magic, or if something mysterious might be at work. She only knew they were truthful, and she could count on 90% or better accuracy with any Anam Glyph reading. Her book *The Anam Glyphs* had become a planetary best seller, and would soon be released in its second printing. Many Believers relied on the Glyphs for direction.

She left Applecheeks to store the Glyphs, and went to the river to bathe. She put one foot into the water, and withdrew it so fast she created a wave, inundating a mallard duck. The duck shook his feathers and glared at her before paddling away in a grand huff.

"Sorry," Beautimus called out. She shook her foot. Beautimus shivered as she stepped back into the water, then with a sharp inhale, she submerged herself. She popped back out of the water like a massive cork, her teeth chattering.

In a small pool enclosed by rocks lived a 100-year-old rainbow trout, Calypso, who she met early mornings now and again.

"Water's chilly this morning, isn't it Bea? Just how we trout like it best."

Beautimus told Calypso—afflicted by A.D.H. D.—about her visions and how this morning's reading turned up White Light again. "I'm deeply bothered by Priscilla's murder, but the Glyphs tell me something else is coming. What do you think? From what I can tell, it's going to be huge."

"Who knows? I don't do land stuff. Oh! Look! On the bank of the river, see? There's a brown chicken. I wonder what she's doing here? Should I swim over and check her out?"

The hippo took notice of the hen. "She's been following me for a few days now, and her sneaking around is becoming tedious. Let's not talk about the chicken. What are your thoughts on the White Light Glyph? Focus, Calypso. I need you to focus."

"Sorry. I get you are worried about your Glyphs, but you know we fish are primarily interested in eating, mating and laying eggs, you know, those sorts of things. Oh! Hear that?"

Beautimus cocked her head to listen.

"Behind the rock over there. Right there, Bea. Might be minnows, or maybe a toad, or perhaps some water bugs. Wonder if they'd like to play a game of Marco Polo this morning? Now, what was I saying? Something about your glyphs, wasn't it? Hey, what's that buzzing sound? I think it is a damselfly, yes a damselfly, or a dragonfly."

"*Please*, Calypso. About the White Light Glyph, what do you think it means?"

"Yes, yes, like I said, I'm very sorry but I'm not at all good with land matters, or stuff about Glyphs."

"I *know*. I get it. You're a fish, but I'm asking because you are wise with strong instincts, and trout have exceptionally keen intuition. I want to know if you have any feeling at all about what might be coming. I'm curious if you or any of the other Trout Tribe have seen or heard anything that could lead to an important event of great magnitude. I value your opinion, and right now I need it. I really do." Beautimus had at last accustomed herself to the brisk water. She dipped in, and gave it a shake to clean her muzzle. When she raised her head, a thin stream of moss hung from the corner of her mouth. Calypso leapt from the water, and helped herself. "I dearly love the taste of fresh river moss. Thanks, Bea."

"Please, Calypso. Let's stick to the topic."

"What topic? Never mind. I remember. Well, like I said, as long as you need an opinion about something that has to do with water…"

Beautimus grew so perturbed with the fish, she raised her voice to a strident pitch. "Calypso, I'm very concerned. Can't you see? I'm trying to tell you something huge is going to happen!"

"Why are you yelling? Worrying about what *could* happen is a waste of time. I don't know what to tell you. Oooooh! Something bright and shiny over there. Could be a gold-grass shoot. Breakfast. See ya later, Bea."

At that, the trout made a mad swim toward the bright and shiny thing before some other fish could beat her to it. Beautimus noticed what Calypso had seen was only sunlight reflecting off the water's surface, but she did nothing to halt the trout. Beautimus emerged from the river to find the brown chicken pecking at rye grass on the river's edge.

***

Over two weeks had passed since the Wasenia Festival. Beautimus had become no closer to understanding what White Light meant to tell her, or the significance of the recurring visions of her dead mother. She grew increasingly frustrated.

The Wayflower Society of Rational Thinking (WSRT) met next door. Of course, Beautimus, a Believer, did not belong to the group. But, the other members of the Potamus Tribe, including many of Beautimus' family, and a growing list of others. She respected the group, but she wasn't up to dealing with the atheists this afternoon.

"I have to spend my energy focusing on what the Glyphs are telling me. I don't have time for participating in a non-believer group," she told Lizzy.

During the first meeting, the larger Rendazian Atheist Organization (RAO) tasked the Wayflower Chapter with finding a name in keeping with the new group's unified anti-belief system that would fit neatly into the RAO charter. The new group met for the first time at the home of Beautimus' Aunt Meg and Uncle Phelan Potamus. Happy for her uncle and aunt who had started the Chapter because they believed the group would help Rendazians become more rational, and therefore happier, Beautimus attended their first few meetings to show her support.

A centipede, Rachel, with the ability to type 200 words per minute (using 90 of her 100 feet on a specially engineered itty-bitty bug-sized keyboard) volunteered as secretary. She'd take minutes and project them onto the Crystal Interface so absent members could access a copy.

Beautimus sat in not out of respect for her uncle and aunt, but out of curiosity. She held back on contributing comments. The group elected Uncle Phelan as President—expected since he started the ball rolling with the RAO in the first place. They voted Aunt Meg in as Vice President, and Rachel as Secretary. They elected Samuel as Treasurer.

After Uncle Phelan called the meeting to order, he covered the agenda items: 1) Chapter name, 2) logo, and 3) tag line. The members decided to select a name reflecting the cohesive team of atheists they were, so they tried names with the word "team" in them. The final selection by consensus would be The Wayflower Atheist Team." One of the attendees, Charles, a silver tabby cat and a printer by trade, offered to mock-up a sample t-shirt for the next meeting. Choosing a logo went fast and easy. The group unanimously voted in a large scarlet letter A with the tag line "Atheists United," to assure everyone who saw it understood they were an organized group who didn't believe in anything spiritual.

At the next meeting, Charles held in his paws a white t-shirt. A huge red letter "A," with the tag line beneath graced the back of the t-shirt. The words "The Wayflower Atheist Team" were printed in brilliant primary colors across the front. The attendees broke into murmurs of approval and applause. Everyone seemed satisfied, that is until Samuel piped up. "Can anyone here this evening see what's wrong with this name?"

The attendees looked to one another.

"C'mon, doesn't *anyone* see what's wrong with this? Am I the only one here who sees a serious flaw in our name? Really?"

Silence.

"Meg, we'll be printing ID cards and promotional materials. Yes? Please spell the acronym we'll be using on our letterhead for "The Wayflower Atheist Team."

"Certainly. T…W…A…." The attendees gasped.

"Oh, my," said Aunt Meg.

Beautimus had to bite the inside of her cheeks to keep from breaking into hysterical laughter.

The group put their heads together to come up with a new name, "Forward Atheists for Rational Thinking"—a popular choice until Charles said, "So, instead of being TWATS we'll be FARTS."

"Back to the drawing board," said Uncle Phelan.

After some deliberation, the group chose "Wayflower Atheists for Rational Thinking," then Samuel had to open his yap again.

"So we don't want to be TWATS or FARTS but we *do* want to be WARTS?"

"I have an idea" said Rachel, "Let's choose a name with an acronym without any vowels." That's how the name Wayflower Society of Rational Thinking (WSRT) came into existence. Beautimus attended one or two more meetings before she dropped out.

With this week's meeting well underway, Beautimus relaxed at home. As she munched on her afternoon heads of romÁine lettuce and reviewed a book called *Flesh Eating and Other Revolting Earth Practices* for a possible class text, a noisy commotion startled her. The young white tiger, Cicero, burst through her door flap without even bothering to announce himself.

"Ms….Bea!" Crazy-eyed and breathless, the tiger struggled to find his words.

"What's going on, Cicero?"

"The Wand…the….Ms. Bea. The Wand. Someone has… stolen it…the Wand of Fortuna."

"It's kept in a well-hidden cavern guarded by the Special Forces Wolves. No, *can't* be."

"Yes, yes. Only this morning the wolves discovered it…I mean….they found it missing while on their rounds."

"This is awful. It simply isn't possible."

"I ran here as fast as I could to….tell you, Ms. Bea. Lady Rhianna is a total wreck over this. First Priscilla's murder then this…she's in the hospital now because when she heard the news her blood pressure sky-rocketed. Doctor Bombay is concerned." The tiger stopped to catch his breath. "I know how important she is to you. The Wand is missing, and no one has a clue who might have taken it."

Beautimus' mouth opened in shock. A head of partially eaten lettuce tumbled out of her maw and onto the straw. Cicero took his leave and Beautimus ran as fast as she could to interrupt the WSRT meeting.

On Rendaz the theft or desecration of a sacred object is a vile offense, and with the inevitable finger pointing, there could be additional conflict between Believers and Non-Believers, therefore, Beautimus knew the WSRT members would want to know right away. She'd volunteer to be on the Recovery Search Committee, and hoped the group would help by offering to volunteer their services, too. The magical Wand of Fortuna was without doubt *the* most sacred of sacred objects in all of Wayflower.

"Oh, no," said Aunt Meg. "This theft is bound to create havoc in the Wayflower District. The fundamentalist Goddess worshipers are sure to blame the atheists. They blame us for everything that goes wrong in Wayflower. No offense to you, dear," turning her head to Beautimus.

Whispers broke out among the attendees.

"You know, Meg's right. With those fundamentalists, it's their way or no way, and if there's any trouble at all, it's always our fault," Rachel said.

"Stop." Uncle Phelan said. "That counterproductive thinking only serves to contribute to the widening gap between Believers and Non-Believers. Bea, let us know how the WSRT can help recover the Wand."

"Thank you, Uncle. I appreciate your offer, and I know the Guardians will appreciate the WSRT's support, too," Beautimus said. "I knew I could count on the WSRT for help."

"I *hope* you don't think this show of support means any of us in the WSRT are intending to become *Believers*, though," said Rachel. "We are sorry someone stole the Wand, and will do what we can to help as way to keep peace in the District, but we don't hold stock in sacred objects."

Everyone at the meeting nodded in agreement.

"I *know*. I'm not here to proselytize. I only hoped you'd join forces with The Guardians to recover the Wand. I've no other motive."

The next morning, Larry, the local paper carrier stork, brought Beautimus' newspaper, *The Wayflower Quacker*. The squirrels opened it and spread it out on the ground so the three of them could read it together. The headline read:

Wand of Fortuna Missing

Guard Wolves discovered the missing wand during their rounds early this morning. No suspects identified. Sgt. Detective First Class, José Saturday, is leading the investigation. Sgt. Saturday and his team questioned the Captain of the Wand Guards, Steven D. Lobos, who said, 'We are always vigilant, sir. My men and I sat in front of the secret cavern all night. Not one of us shut our eyes. I am investigating how anyone could haven't gotten passed us, and we will close the gap in our security. I will personally bite whomever did this.' When asked if any of the Wand Guard Wolves were under suspicion, Sgt. Saturday replied, 'Not at this time. We are pursuing leads. We will not speculate. We seek facts, just the facts.'

Sgt. Saturday assures the Butterfly Counsel the Guardians and the Wand Guards will work together to search day and night until they arrest the culprit(s) and return the Wand to its rightful place. Many citizens, and several District organizations, including the WSRT, have volunteered to join the Search Team.

The High Priestess, Lady Rhianna, who collapsed upon hearing the news, is so distraught she's plucking her tail feathers. The Lady is not available for comment. The entire Wayflower District is in shock over the disappearance of its most sacred object.

According to Sgt. Saturday and the Guardians, the theft of the Wand is unrelated to the murder of Priscilla, Lady Rhianna's House Chimp. Priscilla's murder case is still under investigation. However, some minor thefts occurred during the Wasenia Festival possibly related to the Wand's disappearance. Fair goers reported combs and honeyed melon balls gone from their satchels. Several vendors reported missing boa-boa Goddess figurines, Rendazian Glow Seeds, and grey salt. If you have any knowledge leading to the arrest of the culprit or culprits of these thefts, come downtown and make your report in person to Sgt. Saturday."

Although both squirrels had been home when Cicero barged in with the news of the missing wand, the article upset them anew. Agnes gasped. "I-can't-believe-someone-would-be-so-brazen-as-to-steal-the-Wand-of-Fortuna-for-Goddess-sake-I-hope-they-aren't-stupid-enough-to-actually-believe--they'll-get-away-with-this-the-craven-flapmouthed-thieving-buttholes-would-you-like-breakfast-Bea?"

Applecheeks swished her tail with angry force.

"Yes, Agnes, please I'd like some hot peppermint tea with breakfast this morning, too, and Apple, would you please fetch my Anam Glyphs?" Agnes scurried off to heat a pail of water.

Applecheeks composed herself enough to bring the pouch of Glyphs to Beautimus. The squirrel pulled a stone. Beautimus hadn't realized she'd been holding her breath until Apple withdrew the first glyph, Alma, *New Beginnings*. Then, she exhaled forcefully. Apple pulled the second, Wheat Harvest, *Reaping of Rewards*, then the third. Beautimus' least favorite turned up last, Tricky Boy, the archetypal trickster, a sign she might be fooling herself about something or someone, or perhaps mischievous forces were at work. She interpreted the reading to mean new information would come to light, that the investigation into the murders and the wand would result in a reward, a "harvest," but damned Tricky Boy. Nonetheless, when Applecheeks placed the final glyph on the divining cloth, Beautimus felt a million pounds of pressure lifting from her shoulders. For the first time in weeks, the White Light Glyph had not made an appearance.

CHAPTER TWELVE

IN HER DREAM, Rendaz appeared below her as a tiny green glass bead. Beautimus flew through the air as though a marshmallow floating on warm cocoa. *How is this possible without wings?* Dozens of white-breasted wood swallows, purple iridescent beetles, and giant moths flew about her. A trio of falcons in tight formation tucked their wings, and dove straight down skimming Beautimus' head, scattering the wood swallows. "Yeehaaw," they cried as they came out of their dive and rolled to the left.

The air filled with music, Mahler's *Symphony No. 2 in C Minor.* Beautimus hummed along. "It's so nice and warm. I thought it'd be chilly this far up in the sky," she said to no one in particular. A lone figure swam to her through the ocean of blue sky, a hippo.

"Mom, is that you? In my dreams, not my visions? What's up?"

"Apparently, we are."

"What are we doing up here?"

"Flying above the mundane. Isn't it glorious? I'm here to tell you something."

"What is it, Mom?

"You have a problem."

"I do? What?"

"What do you think the problem is, Bea?"

"I assume my problem is…"

"…no, my daughter, your problem is you assume. Bye!"

"Mom, don't go."

"It's you who are going."

Beautimus felt herself tumbling back to Rendaz, and she awoke.

***

Beautimus prepared to teach her first class of the day at "Dr. Pimbly's School of Goodly Educated Adults," one of her most controversial, "Comparison of Earth and Rendazian Cultures." In spite of the news about the Wand, her concern for Rhianna, and the weird flying dream, she kept her mind on today's class. Lately, her course demonstrated more similarities than dissimilarities between the two cultures. Rendaz, a generally peaceful planet, suffered a recent increase in murders and thefts in the Wayflower District, earning a reputation for being "as burdened by crime as Earth," or so said Hattie Hopper in her gossip column.

Everyone along the river talked about the missing wand. A paddling of ducks quacked up a storm. "It's unimaginable." One said. "The wand has been undisturbed for centuries."

A shoal of bass swam by in search of breakfast discussed the missing wand.

"Who on Rendaz could have stolen the Wand of Fortuna, for Goddessake?" Said one.

"Maybe it's an inside job. No one even knows where the High Priestess and Wand Guard keep it," said another. "Maybe a Wand Guard did it."

"Naw, I don't think so."

As Beautimus rounded the corner leading to the school, she heard voices. Chance outside his "crib," talking to his "crew." Beautimus stopped to listen.

Chance growled and stomped one foot. "Yo, Homie. No one knows the real value of the Wand. Keep this to your mofo self or I'll pop a cap in yo az."

MC Tweezers said, "I'm only sayin' what I think that mofo bling is worth. Quit dissin' me, yo. It's gotta be worth a mofo fortune, T-Bone."

"Shut yo mofo mouth, yo. Don't be spreadin' 'round how much money this mofo thing is gonna fetch 'cause you don't know mofo crap."

Rampage interrupted, "C'mon bwos, stop dissin' each other wid dis mofo shit and let's get us some bwu bewies for bweakfast. I'm hungwee."

The three departed for the blueberry patch.

Beautimus froze. *Chance! I should have known. He and his gang stole the Wand, and now they are trying to figure out its value. Damn. As soon as I'm out of class today, I must tell Sgt. Saturday.*

Since what she overheard preoccupied her thoughts, when she walked onto campus she nearly ran directly into the Dean, Sir. Henry.

"Bea, I'm glad you're here a little early. I want to introduce you to Dr. Lucas Potamway, our new Chief Administrator of the Arts."

"*The* Lucas Potamway?" Beautimus asked, "The same Lucas Potamway known throughout the planet as the foremost famous poet-artist on all of Rendaz. *That* one? I've wanted to meet him for over a century. He's going to be a Chief Administrator here?"

Sir Henry laughed so hard his glasses fell off his nose and into the dirt. Blind without them, he had to pat the soil with his paws to locate them. "Yes, the very same. Lucas, come here for a minute. There's someone here who'd very much like to meet you."

From behind the administration building walked the most elegant hippo Beautimus ever laid her violet eyes on. The closer Lucas came to her, the warmer her shar-stone pendant grew. *Goddess please, no. Not another hot flash. Not now.* But no hot flash. The pendant changed colors: purple, pink, emerald green, back to purple.

Lucas appeared to be about Beautimus' age, but with a boyish air about him. She felt her heart pounding so hard she thought it might crack open. Her warm shar-stone now not only changed colors, it began to thrum against her chest in exact rhythm with her heartbeat. *Oh Goddess, please don't let him see my four knees trembling.*

"Dr. Potamway, meet one of our finest professors, Beautimus Potamus."

Lucas made a small bow of his head, then looked directly into her eyes.

Her heart pounded harder and faster, and the pendant responded thrumming harder and faster.

"It's a pleasure to meet you...is it Ms. Potamus?"

"Yes, but please call me Bea."

"Bea it is, then." He gave her a little nod. "What subject do you teach?"

"History of Earthly Things."

"Ah, yes. I've heard of you. You are quite the scholar of Earthian culture. Didn't you also develop the new oracle and write a book about it, *The Anam Glyphs*?"

"Yes, thank you. Have you read it?"

"I certainly have. It's in my library, and I crafted my own set of Anam Glyphs from river rocks. I don't leave my abode in the morning until I've pulled three."

"Really? I, I, can't...believe...you've even have *heard* of my book or my Glyphs, Dr. Potamway. I'm truly honored."

"Please call me Lucas. It's a good book, and your Glyphs are quite accurate. By the way, such a lovely pendant around your neck. It matches the color of your eyes, and mimics that fetching little heart-shaped mark on your cheek."

Beautimus blushed and cast her eyes down. "Thank you. I mean, thank you about the pendant. Well, and, of course, also, well, thank you for the compliments about my book and Glyphs."

Beautimus fell into an enchantment so profound she hadn't noticed Sir. Henry take his leave, or see her first students, a troop of kangaroo and a route of wolves, enter her classroom. She'd forgotten all about the wand, the conversation she'd overheard between Chance and his gang, her concerns about Rhianna, Priscilla's murder, Áine, her dreams and visions, everything. She'd forgotten the entire world.

"Your class is about to begin, and I've got a lot of paperwork to complete, Bea. I look forward to seeing you again, soon."

"So nice to meet you, Lucas."

"Bye for now," he said.

"Bye for now."

Lucas turned and walked toward the Administration Building. Beautimus floated into her classroom and lectured in a semi-dream state.

***

On her way home she imagined being carried aloft by a million lacewings. The air smelled of jasmine, the suns were brighter, pale pink poppies danced to the beating of her heart. She spied two hippos, a muscular male and a smaller young female together under a corkscrew willow. They leaned against one another and nuzzled. *Lovers.* She felt overjoyed for them...until she recognized the male—Dr. Lucas Potamway. The music in her heart ceased. Her mouth went dry as paper, and the poppies shriveled.

"Well, I guess that's it. What in hellzabob made me think Lucas wants anything remotely to do with me, a scrawny, middle-aged ordinary hippo who can't gain a pound no matter how many bushels of blue corn she eats, when he can have someone as young, plump, and beautiful as her?"

Tonight she would drink a few melon husks of mead to forget the famous Lucas Potamway. Beautimus' heart felt like a sharp rock rattling around in her empty cavern of a chest. She didn't notice the scent of rosemary or the magnificent light of the suns setting. She could only think about her saggy, thin hindquarters and her ordinary face.

She didn't notice the siege of bitterns who greeted her, or the dule of doves flying overhead. She knew they'd said something to her, but she couldn't recall what. She spied the brown chicken by a stream. She didn't care. She entered her abode to the bright greetings of Applecheeks, and Agnes who stopped short. "You-look-exhausted-is-something-wrong-what's-going-on-tell-us-we-are-here-for-you-Bea-something's-wrong-we-can-both-tell-did-something-happen-at-school-did-you-get-fired-or-something-are-you-okay-would-you-like-strawberry-soup?"

"I can't talk right now. Is there mead in the house?"

After she drank one too many melon husks full, she ventured outside. She wobbled and swayed her way to a rainbow gum tree by Sweetwater Pond, a small secluded spot away from the tribe. She sat and sobbed tears into the pond so abundant they caused it to overflow. She cried for hours until, exhausted, she fell into a miserable lump on the cold, damp ground. In an attempt to ease Beautimus' sadness, the tree hummed a soothing Brahm's lullaby.

The following morning she awoke with her head pounding. Her mouth tasted like dried library paste. Every muscle in her body felt stiff. Parched and cold, she took a sip of pond water. Overly salty from her tears, she spat it out and walked with heavy steps into her abode. The squirrels didn't pester Beautimus for information. The two of them pushed a pail of hot lilac tea to her.

"Thank you."

As her two friends stood by, Beautimus lapped her tea, splatting drops of it over the floor of the abode, and dribbling some down her chin. Agnes mopped up the splashes and wiped the hippo's chin. "Thank you, Agnes. Now please get to the school right away and tell Sir Henry I'm not feeling well and I'll not be in class for a couple of days."

Without a word, Agnes scampered out the door. Applecheeks scurried to the altar to retrieve the pouch of Anam Glyphs.

"No thank you, Apple. Not this morning."

The hippo fell into her pillows and slept. This pattern continued for several days, Beautimus sleeping almost all day, declining food and refusing her Glyphs, the squirrels, quiet as field mice, tending to her.

Beautimus' Crystal Interface pulsated and hummed, emitting its familiar pinkish light for the 100th time since her return from school a few days before. Beautimus ignored the pulsing. Agnes finally said, "Bea-aren't-you-going-to-get-that?-it's-been-pulsing-for-days-might-be-important-there-has-to-be-200-messages-stay-in-bed-I'll-answer-it-do-you-w-ant-a-headache-poultice?"

"No thank you, Agnes. Please delete all the messages. I don't care to hear them, and turn off the Interface if you don't mind."

Agnes and Applecheeks were dismayed. They'd been looking forward to streaming reruns of *Gilligan's Island*, *Bewitched* and their favorite, *Wild Kingdom*.

After more than a week, Beautimus came around. "I'm sorry, Agnes and Apple for putting you through a couple of bad days, but you'll be relieved to know my pity-party is over."

"Don't-be-concerned-Bea-we-love-you-and-we-know-you-love-us-back-we-were-worried-because-we've-never-seen-you-quite-like-this-but-we-knew-you'd-come-around-to-being-your-old-self-eventually-breakfast?"

That same morning, Larry brought the early edition of *The Wayflower Quacker*. The headline read:

Suspect Identified In Wasenia Festival Thefts

Working off a lead from an unidentified informant, Sgt. Saturday dispatched Guardians to the den of

Heatherton, the pack rat, for questioning in the case of the missing festival goods. There investigators discovered a pile of combs, honeyed melon balls, pouches of grey salt, a trio of boa-boa Goddesses, and stacks of bright shiny objects. Sgt. Saturday arrested the suspect and escorted him downtown for questioning. Pending a preliminary trial date, and return of the stolen goods, the Guardians released the rodent.

At this time, there is no evidence linking Heatherton to the missing Wand of Fortuna. Steven D. Lobos, Commander of the Wand Guards, told reporters 'If it turns out Heatherton had anything to do with the missing Wand, he will get to know my teeth personally.'

The good news for today is High Priestess, Rhianna, hospitalized when she collapsed after receiving report of the missing wand last week, soon will be released to recuperate at home. Dr. Bombay is optimistic, and is happy to report his magic lotion for quick feather regeneration is working. 'Pin feathers are beginning to appear where she plucked out her tail. Lady Rhianna may be able to resume her duties as High Priestess within the next moon, and could fly again within two."

"I'm glad Rhianna is all right," Beautimus said to the squirrels. "I think I'll take an additional day off to visit her."

She asked Applecheeks to load her satchel with pecans and fresh strawberries for Rhianna. When she reached the crane's abode, she called out to her. "Lady Rhianna. It's me, Beautimus Potamus."

Rhianna opened her door and flung her wings around Beautimus' leg. "Bea! It's been decades. I'm so happy to see you. The sight of you makes my old eyes glad. Step back and let me look at you." Beautimus moved a step, and the old bird beamed at her. "You are as beautiful as ever. What brings you here?"

"I'm sorry about Priscilla and the missing Wand. When I heard you were in the hospital I went straight to see you, but the doctor turned everyone away. I felt so relieved to read in the newspaper you were home. I wanted to make sure you were faring well, and also, if you have a minute, I have something I'd like to talk to you about."

"It's such a beautiful day, let's take a walk, shall we?" said the crane.

With assistance from Rhianna's new helper, a sweet little lemur named Queenie on loan from Belinda the coyote, Beautimus unloaded the gifts.

The old bird hopped from foot to foot in delight. "Oooh, fresh strawberries. My favorite."

The two friends walked side-by-side through the forest. Beautimus' old mentor ambled along painfully slow. The patches where Rhianna had plucked out her feathers were raw and pink. "Are you all right, Lady Rhianna? You seem weary. Would you prefer to ride on my back?"

"No, dear. I'm fine. Thank you."

"It's awful about Priscilla and the Wand. I hope the Guardians catch the criminals soon. Everyone is so upset, Lady Rhianna."

"We are together for our first visit in a long while. Let's change the subject, shall we? What is it you'd like to talk to an old crane about?"

"Can we find a place to sit? This is a matter of the heart and I need to talk it over with another woman."

A slight rustle behind them caught Beautimus' attention. When the hippo turned, she noticed the brown chicken tailing her....again.

The pair found an expansive patch of dichondra under the

shade of a broom wattle and settled in. "So, tell me about this 'matter of the heart,' Bea."

"Lady, Rhianna, I met someone. A wonderful, handsome someone."

"Marvelous." The old bird clapped her wings. "I'm delighted for you. Tell me all about him."

Beautimus recounted the story of how she met Lucas, and how at first sight she'd fallen in love. She also told Rhianna about how she'd spied him nuzzling a young, beautiful hippo. Then she told her old spiritual mentor how she felt undeserving of the affections of the incredible Dr. Lucas Potamway.

"My dear, I will never understand how such a lovely, bright, talented and accomplished creature can hate herself the way you do."

Beautimus averted her eyes.

The crane shook her feathers. "How could you think you are undeserving of any male's love? I want you to promise me you'll go back to school and face Lucas whatshisname as though you deserve every ounce of love in his hide, because you do."

"Lady Rhianna, I can't face Lucas. I just *can't*."

"Oh, yes you can!" The old bird flew into a tizzy—or would have flown had her tail feathers been intact. "You must accept yourself, Bea. I cannot stress how important it is right now that you love yourself. You must." She flapped her wings frantically. "Now promise me right now you'll face Lucas."

"I promise, Lady Rhianna."

The crane thrust out her meaty breast and said, "You dishonor yourself and everyone who loves you with your pitiful low self-esteem."

Beautimus blushed with shame.

"I'm so sorry, Lady Rhianna. I'm so very sorry."

"Quit apologizing. There is an important reason I need you

to recognize your own worth now. I care for you deeply, my dear, and one day…," Rhianna shuddered. Her eyes rolled up toward her forehead, and she crumpled to the ground unconscious.

"Help! Help! Help!" shouted Beautimus. A rafter of turkeys and a gang of elk ran to the aide of the High Priestess. They ferried Rhianna to the hospital. As Beautimus turned to follow them, the brown chicken skittered behind a boulder near where she and Lady Rhianna had been seated.

"What in hellzabob are you *doing* here? Were you eavesdropping on my private conversation with Lady Rhianna? Were you? Well, I hope you got an earful, you goddessdamned driggle-draggle lousy piece of rotten poultry."

***

Beautimus stood for what seemed an eternity in the waiting room of Wayflower General. She prayed to the Goddesses. "Please let Rhianna be well. I beseech you."

Dr. Bombay, a chimpanzee well-respected for his skill in surgery, internal medicine and magical unguents emerged, wiping his hand on a white cloth. "Lady Rhianna is in a coma. We do not yet know what caused it, but for now, she's stable. I have concocted a magical potion, and I will be performing a healing ritual. Hopefully, that will bring her around. Check back with us in a few days for an update."

When Beautimus finally arrived home, she found Sgt. José Saturday and his Guardians waiting.

"What's this about? Has something happened, Sgt. Saturday?"

"Ms. Potamus, you are a suspect in the theft of the Wand of Fortuna. Come with us, please. We are taking you downtown for questioning."

CHAPTER THIRTEEN

THE WAYFLOWER CITIZENS gathered to watch Sgt. Saturday escort Beautimus downtown grew large and unruly. The elks were forced to exert control. "Back away, folks. Do not step on the path. Sir, move your tail away from the accused."

Beautimus knew word of her arrest would spread like marmalade on a hot rock. She couldn't have been more right. It seemed as though the entire population of Rendaz turned out. She couldn't cry. She couldn't speak. She could barely even breathe. She caught pieces of conversation from the burgeoning crowd lining the path between her abode and downtown. She recognized many voices of her friends, students and neighbors.

"Oh no," Cicero said. "It *is* Ms. Bea."

"How awful," the chinchilla, Angeline said.

The house squirrels were in such distress when the guardians took Beautimus away Agnes fainted on the spot. Later, Lizzy told Beautimus, "Applecheeks drug her sister down to the river and had to throw water on her fur to revive her."

Aunt Meg, Uncle Phalen and Lizzy walked behind the elks. Samuel, riding on Lizzy's head, hopped around in circles like a nervous dirt beetle.

"We are right here, sweetie. We'll be with you when you get to town." Lizzy had to shout to be heard over the din. She trumpeted her words.

Beneath the ruckus of the crowd, Beautimus perceived a familiar clucking. *That damned brown chicken. Why in hellzabob won't she leave me alone?*

Clarence Jonas, Esq. pushed his way through the crowd and sidled next to Beautimus. "Well, Bea, looks like you need a good lawyer...."

"Move away, sir," said one of the elks.

"…but I need to talk to her about proper legal representation…"

"Now, sir, move!"

A clattering of red-billed choughs flew low overhead, followed by a fling of dunlins and a gulp of cormorants. "Bea," one of the birds shouted. "We are all pulling for you."

A quiver of cobras lined the path, raised their heads, spread their hoods, and hissed at the Guardians as they passed with Beautimus between them. A mob of emus chanted, "Free Bea! Free Bea! Free Bea!"

Beautimus shuffled with her head hung low. *I can't believe Sgt. Saturday is taking me downtown. Right. In. Front. Of. Everyone.*

Although many hundreds of Wayflower citizens turned out to support Beautimus, far from comforted, she felt sick with shame. She'd blocked out words of encouragement and support, until all she heard was the "How awful" comment from Angeline. The rest came to her as a string of blurred syllables Beautimus took to be taunts.

Sgt. Saturday escorted Beautimus into the Guardian Station and ushered her into an austere, windowless room. He showed her a scratchy cushion and motioned for her to sit. In the corner stood a rusty fan, and in the middle of the room, a bird perch. There were a few air holes poked through the ceiling because the only door into the room was air tight and provided no oxygen source. Without speaking, Sgt. Saturday exited the room. The stout metal door closed behind him with a hollow clang. She shivered in cold and bewilderment. "How can *anyone* think I'd steal the Wand of Fortuna?" she said aloud.

Then the tears—she couldn't stop them. Heavy rivulets rolled down her face in such quick succession they created furrows down her cheeks. Within a short time, at least three inches of salty water flooded the floor of the interrogation cell.

The scratchy pillow became sopping wet. Beautimus cried until at least four more inches of water rose in the room. The tears stopped as suddenly as they had begun, and she sat hiccupping in the flooded cell for an indeterminate amount of time.

The door opened and a deluge of tears spilled out into the building. Someone yelled. "Great Mother Genesis. Get a mop. What the hellzabob is this?" The door slammed again, and the muffled sounds of the clean-up outside commenced. Beautimus pushed the soggy pillow away and continued to sit for what seemed an eternity, cold and shivering, on the damp stone floor, saturated in her own tears.

A female raven entered, not flying, but walking. She paced in front of Beautimus, her claws scraping against the stone floor. Beautimus rose to her feet.

The bird shook her head. "No. Please remain seated, Ms. Potamus." She cawed to the Guardian outside. "Bring in a pail of hot peppermint tea and a blanket."

She turned to Beautimus. "Ms. Potamus, I'm Margaret Glossywings, the interrogator in the case of the missing Wand of Fortuna. I'll be questioning you today, then Sgt. Saturday will have a word with you. Do you know why you are here?"

Margaret Glossywings, a consummate professional, made the perfect interrogator because her emotional character was so muted nothing ruffled her feathers.

"No, I don't. I can't image why *anyone* could think I'd have anything to do with the theft of the Wand. No, Officer. I do *not* know why I am here."

"We have a witness, Ms. Potamus."

"A witness? Someone reported he actually *saw* me steal the Wand of Fortuna?"

"I will ask the questions, Ms. Potamus. This particular witness overheard a loud conversation between you and a certain trout, Calypso, and later a heated argument between you and Lady Rhianna, leading us to believe you may have something to do with the theft of the Wand. We need to clear up a few things before we release you, or decide to send you to Limbo until trial."

The raven paused for a long while, and Beautimus averted her eyes.

"Ms. Calypso said you told her something huge would happen," said Officer Glossywings. "She told us you were quite adamant and appeared highly agitated. She didn't recall anything more. That occurred shortly before the theft of the Wand. Of course, Lady Rhianna is still in a coma and cannot speak. Do you understand what I'm saying to you?"

"I swear on Mother Genesis, I did *not* steal the Wand."

"Where were you an hour before dawn exactly two weeks after the Wasenia Festival, Ms. Potamus?" Officer Glossywings shook and puffed her feathers, turned and cocked her head sideways to get a better look at Beautimus.

Beautimus shivered so hard her teeth chattered. "I was fast asleep on my pillows. My house squirrels, Agnes and Applecheeks, were with me the entire evening."

"Were they awake the whole time you were asleep, Ms. Potamus?"

Someone knocked. The door opened to admit a troodon bearing a blanket and a pail of steaming tea. He placed the blanket over Beautimus' back, and placed the pail in front of her.

"Thank you," said Beautimus.

The troodon departed. Beautimus dipped into the tea and took in its warmth. She raised her head and steeled herself for further grilling.

"Please drink more tea, Ms. Potamus. We don't want you to catch the grippe. Now, back to my question. Were either of the squirrels awake while you slept?"

"No, of course not. They were asleep, too."

"Is there anyone at all who can verify you were home sleeping during the theft of the Wand?"

"I'd rather die than steal that Wand."

"Ms. Potamus, you do understand the gravity of this crime, don't you? Stealing a sacred object is a Rendazian taboo. With a guilty verdict, the Butterfly Counsel may banish you permanently, or even shun you. It will go easier on you if you confess now rather than have it come out in Court."

"I did not take the Wand. I did not!"

"Please settle down, Ms. Potamus. These are routine questions."

Officer Glossywings took a few more steps and hopped onto the perch. "We think there may have been more than one person involved in the theft. Do you know of anyone who might have motive to steal the Wand?"

"No. I have no idea who stole the Wand of Fortuna. None."

"Okay, Ms. Potamus. I am going to leave you alone for a few minutes while I confer with Sgt. Saturday."

The raven cawed, the door opened, and she flew out. Beautimus found herself alone again. Her tea had turned cold, and her back and head hurt. She sat numb under the blanket unable to comprehend the passage of time.

Sgt. Saturday entered the cell and squatted in front of Beautimus. "So, you deny taking the Wand of Fortuna and claim no knowledge of who might be involved?"

"Sir, I did not take the Wand, and I have no idea who might have. I do not have the names of any co-conspirators because I don't know of any." Then Beautimus' eyes flashed wide open. "Wait! I do remember something now. I wanted to tell you this earlier, Sgt. Saturday. A few days ago as I was walking on the path to work, I overheard Chance Rockefeller and his gang in a heated discussion over the value of the Wand. I thought it might be important information, and I meant to come right to you."

"This is *indeed* key information, Ms. Potamus. Why didn't you disclose this fact to me sooner, or tell Officer Glossywings what you'd overheard?"

"To tell you the truth, since I've reached...a certain age...I sometimes forget things. And, there was a lot going on at Dr. Pimbly's school, and I was, well, kind of sick for a few days. Then I went to visit Rhianna and she fell into a coma. A lot going on, a lot, and it was all quite upsetting. And here, today...with Officer Glossywings...I have been so rattled, and with my memory the way it is these days, I simply forgot all about it. I'm sorry."

"Simply forgot? Or just made up the story to deflect suspicion onto Mr. Rockefeller?"

"No, honestly, I forgot."

"In my experience, Ms. Potamus, when someone says 'honestly' they are lying."

"By the goddesses, I'm not lying. I'm telling you the truth."

"What our witness overheard between you and Ms. Calypso, and later the argument between you and Lady Rhianna..." The orangutan paused then sighed. "Let's say your argument with the High Priestess is incriminating. It establishes motive. Perhaps you were angry with Lady Rhianna and wanted revenge?"

"*What?* We weren't arguing. I mean, we were, but not about anything. We were discussing a personal matter and, well, we had concluded, and everything was fine when Rhianna collapsed!"

"Lower your voice, Ms. Potamus. You seem awfully upset for someone claiming innocence."

"Sgt. Saturday, I *am* innocent." She looked away then back again "You've known me for a long time. Do you *really* think I'd steal the Wand? Rhianna can tell you what we talked about. Once she awakens, and you talk to her, you'll discover a simple misunderstanding between two close friends. Rhianna and I love one another. Our argument…I don't know what the witness heard or saw…but it's not what you think. I wouldn't hurt Rhianna for the world."

"Since Lady Rhianna is still in a coma, and we don't know if she'll come out of it anytime soon or at all, there is no one to substantiate anything you say, Ms. Potamus. If she dies, you could be in even bigger trouble than you are already."

The orangutan turned his head as though staring out an imagined window. He turned back. "However, you are correct. I *do* know you as an upstanding citizen of strong character. Because of that, pending further investigation, I've decided to release you on your own recognizance. You will not leave the Wayflower District until this issue is resolved to my satisfaction. Do you understand?"

"Yes, sir. Thank you."

When Beautimus stepped out of the Guardian Station, a boisterous cheer greeted her. "Bea is Free. Bea is Free. Free at Last! Free at Last!" Standing in front, a mastodon with a praying mantis on her head, waited.

Hattie Hopper appeared from nowhere and stuck her recorderphone in Beautimus' face, "A statement for the Press, Ms. Potamus?"

Lizzy used her trunk to push Hattie back a few hops. "This has been a difficult day for Ms. Potamus. No questions right now." She turned to Beautimus, "Damn insensitive reporters. Let's get you home, sweetie."

Beautimus, who had felt sick to her stomach since her arrest, turned green, leaned over and wretched, burying the toad in vomit.

CHAPTER FOURTEEN

THE MORNING FOLLOWING her arrest, Beautimus took her customary dip in the river. Calypso swam to Beautimus. "I'm sorry. I didn't mean to get you in trouble. I'd never say anything to hurt you."

"Don't worry, Calypso. You had no choice but to answer Sgt. Saturday's questions. You were only doing…"

"Oooh, look at that, Bea." The trout made a mad dash through the water to check the "that" out.

Beautimus arrived to Dr. Pimbly's School for Goodly Educated Adults to teach her first class in over a week, A Primary Study of Earthly Civilization. She'd hoped not to run into Dr. Lucas Potamway. He was supposed to return to his district for a few weeks to put things in order before moving to Wayflower, and with any luck he'd be gone when she arrived. But…no…the second she stepped on campus there he stood… waiting. Her pendant heated and thrummed.

Beautimus looked for a way to escape having to talk to him, but she'd promised Rhianna she would face Lucas, so she paused for a moment, bucked up and walked straight to him. "Nice to see you again, Lucas."

"Bea, isn't your Crystal Interface working? I tried for days to call you, and I must have left three dozen messages before I finally gave up."

Her pendant grew so hot it burned against her hide.

"What? That was *you* calling? I'm so sorry. I, I, wasn't feeling well…I couldn't talk. I asked my house squirrels to shut off the Interface, then so much happened. I never checked my messages, I guess. I'm sorry, really. I didn't know you were trying to reach me."

"Bea, *it's fine*. I'm glad you are all right. I only wanted to invite you to a picnic. I heard what happened to Lady Rhianna, and your arrest. I was in the crowd as you were escorted to the Guardian Station. Did you see me? I was concerned about you."

"You want to go on a picnic *with me*? I thought you were involved with…someone else."

"I'm not involved with anyone." Lucas cocked his head one way, then the other. "Why would you think that? I'm leaving Wayflower tomorrow and won't be back for a few weeks. I was hoping we could get together before I had to leave. I guess it will have to wait. How about a date the Sunday after I return?"

"I look forward to it." Beautimus struggled to contain her excitement. She wondered about the young hippo she'd seen Lucas with. *If he says he's not involved with anyone, than he's not involved with anyone.*

Her shar-pendant grew so hot, and beat against her chest with such robust insistence, Beautimus feared it might raise a welt.

"Well, Bea, I have to pack. I'll see you in a couple of weeks."

He leaned over and gave her a tiny kiss on the cheek. Beautimus was so overcome with joy she feared she'd melt into a quivering mass of ecstasy-pudding right in front of him.

"Bye for now," Lucas said.

"Bye for now."

The moment he departed beyond earshot Beautimus gave a loud Hippo "whoop" then she danced into her classroom, but not before she noticed a charm of purple finches hiding in a nearby cutch tree. Finches, being notorious gossips, would spread the word faster about the budding romance than almond butter melts in hot lava. "Oh, Great Goddess, *everyone* is going to know Lucas asked me on a date."

***

After class, the students filed out of the room, and in the door walked Sgt. Saturday. "Good Day, Sgt. Saturday, what can I do for you?"

"I attempted to reach you on your Crystal Interface, Ms. Potamus. Your house squirrel, the one who yammers on in one breath, told me you were here."

Beautimus' stomach tensed. "What is going on?"

"Rhianna came out of her coma and she's doing fine. We interviewed her and she corroborated your testimony, so you are exonerated and are free to leave the Wayflower District, if you so desire. By the way, the witness who reported you turns out to be a nosy chicken who clucked misinformation."

"The *brown* chicken? She has been following me for weeks. So that's what she's been up to, the old hen."

"Yes, she's a know-it-all, a chronic eavesdropper, and a bit of a dalcop, who likes to poke her beak where it doesn't belong. Evidentially, she's been tailing you for quite some time."

"You're telling *me*? I thought she might be a mentally-ill stalker."

"She's been working with the local gossip columnist, Hattie Hopper, who pays for dirt on the most upstanding citizens of Wayflower. We arrested the chicken today on charges of being a nuisance. She told us Ms. Hopper hired her to obtain information on you, specifically. The hen's ambition is to become a gossip columnist one day herself. She overheard bits of conversation between you and Calypso, and the argument between you and Lady Rhianna, took what she heard out of context and jumped to her own conclusions."

"*That's* why I got into all this trouble? Hattie Hopper and the chicken?"

"The hen flew in a crazed frenzy to the guardian station. Because of the nature of the information she provided, we had no choice but to bring you in for questioning. We have her number now, though. The Butterfly Council levied a hefty fine against her. She will never work for *The Wayflower Quacker*, and she is permanently banned from the guardian station. She squawked her head off when we escorted her off the premises."

"Thank you, Sgt. Saturday. I'm greatly relieved. Any leads in the case?

"Nothing solid yet, but based on your testimony, we plan to interrogate Mr. Rockefeller and his gang."

"Is Rhianna still in the hospital?"

"For a day or two longer, but I understand she is well enough to receive visitors."

Sgt. Saturday departed. Beautimus walked into the sunshine. Two groups of students, a colony of beavers, and a coalition of cheetahs chatted. Beautimus overheard one of the beavers.

"I heard it from the bullocks, who heard it from a capuchin, who heard it from an albatross who heard it from an otter who heard it directly from the purple finches who witnessed the two together today right here on campus. Ms. Bea and Mr. Lucas are *dating*."

If Beautimus could have smiled like a human, she would have. *Holy Goddesses, what a gossipy district.*

CHAPTER FIFTEEN

BEAUTIMUS THOUGHT SHE'D never experienced a better day in her life. As she strolled down the path, she heard a familiar voice from a celastrus-leaved acacia. "Hey, girlfriend. How 'ya doin'?"

"Hi, Sam. Did you hear the news about Rhianna?"

"Sure did. I also heard some other news. When are were planning to tell me about this Lucas guy?"

"Great Mother Genesis. *You* know about that? Hop on. I'm going to visit Rhianna. Come with me and I'll tell you everything on the way."

Samuel flew onto her head and settled in his place between her ears.

"I can't believe what a wonderful day this has been, Sam." She told him the story of Lucas from their first meeting up until this morning.

"Everyone knows who Dr. Potamway is. You snagged yourself a winner."

"For craps sake, Sam, I haven't 'snagged' anyone. We are going on a picnic in a few weeks. That's all."

"Yeah, right."

"Sam, two days ago I cried a river in a locked interrogation room. Then, just like that everything in my life turned from a stinking pile of guano into a fragrant bed of rose petals. Today was the best. First Lucas, then Sgt. Saturday's visit to let me know I am no longer a suspect, and now Rhianna is fine. I know who the gobermouch chicken is, too. We probably won't see her again. One thing I've learned is if there is anything on the planet of Rendaz everyone can be assured of is *everything* changes. Everything. In our darkest moments all we need do is remember the worst of times can turn into the best of times in an instant."

"You sound like you've been talking to that preachy Beard again, Bea."

"Oh, shut up, you little bug." Beautimus laughed.

On the way to visit Rhianna, Beautimus and Sam passed a mew of giggling capons. Beautimus heard one say to the others "Y'all heard about Ms. Bea and the new guy at Dr. Pimbly's School, right?"

As they approached the hospital, with Samuel's help, Beautimus chose a pale pink peony blossom for Rhianna. A passing raven bit it from the stalk for her, and balanced it on the hippo's head. "Give the lady my best," the raven said.

They entered the hospital, signed in, and found Rhianna sitting upright in her bed.

Beautimus bowed. "Thank Mother Genesis you are okay, Lady Rhianna. We were worried sick about you."

"I'm fine, dear. A peony. How lovely. Nurse! Nurse! Please take this flower and put it into water."

A pyrrhuloxia wearing white nurse's cap flew in. She took the peony blossom in her beak and dropped it into a small cut crystal vase of water on the bed side table.

"Thank you," said Rhianna.

"Good day, Lady Rhianna. How are you doing?" said Samuel.

"Good afternoon, Sam. I didn't see you there behind Bea's ear. Thank you so much for coming to visit. I'm doing very well, thank you."

Beautimus noticed Lady Rhianna didn't look well at all. Her face and beak were wane, her eyes droopy, and when the old bird stood on her bed, even her remaining tail feathers seemed wilted, but neither Samuel nor Beautimus said anything. Beautimus moved as close to the bed as she could and put her head down so Rhianna could nuzzle her.

"Lady Rhianna, out there in the forest when we had the argument...I wanted to tell you that you were right about everything. And, I have some news for you."

"Would your news have anything to do with a certain Dr. Lucas Potamway and a picnic?" Beautimus jerked her head up so fast she nearly knocked off poor Samuel who had to dig in tight to keep from being flung to the floor tiles. "Jeezcrapomighty, Bea. Will you watch it? You could a' *killed* me."

"Even *you* know, Lady Rhianna? Does everyone know? I can't believe this."

"I'm afraid so, dear. The news Lucas Potamway invited you to a picnic will be all over Rendaz by the time Ladyluz and Ladybeth are in the sky this eve. Didn't I say you were worthy of him, or better yet, he's worthy of *you*?"

"You tell her, Lady Rhianna, because Bea won't listen to me when I say she's a gorgeous hippo. Lucas is damned lucky she agreed to his invitation for a date, if you ask me."

***

That evening the WSRT met. On the agenda was the topic of the stolen Wand of Fortuna, and that's why Beautimus attended. Beautimus, Agnes, Applecheeks, Lizzy and Samuel were all present at the home of Aunt Meg and Uncle Phelan. Uncle Phelan called the meeting to order. Rachel read the minutes from last month. The first agenda item: "The Goddess Who Wasn't There," a film the WSRT produced. Someone mentioned Beautimus' romance with Lucas, which Beautimus squelched immediately. "Really, I don't know where this thing is going between Lucas and me. We haven't even had our first date yet, everyone. So, please back off of this conversation for tonight."

"But, Bea, I saw him the other day while he was looking at property for his abode. He's so handsome. If I were a hundred years younger and unmated, I'd give you a run for your glow seeds, missy."

"Aunt Meg, *please.*"

Uncle Phelan brought the meeting to order. "Let's stay focused on the business at hand, people. We'll discuss Beautimus' love life after the meeting."

Under "New Business," Samuel briefed the WSRT on Quantum Agriculture. The group had always been the agricultural department's largest contributor.

"We have a self-reinforcing pattern machine that induces resonant fractals directly into the energy fields of soil, water and energetic atmosphere of blue corn fields. This self-reinforcing technology improves patterns of lime in the soil related to mineral release, digestion and nitrogen attachment to corn stalks, and combines with atmospheric patterns of silica as they relate to corn photosynthesis. With this innovative technology, we can change rainfall patterns and corn-germ capacity to hold and process water. Isn't it marvelous?"

The only sounds were a few crickets outside drawing their wings across one another to produce stridulation. In other words, chirping. Once everyone's eyes glazed over, and Lizzie began to snore, Uncle Phelan quickly changed the subject. "Thank you, Sam. Our next item of business is the Wand of Fortuna theft. Any suspects?"

"I-think-it-was-Chance-and-his-drate-poke-gang-who-did-it-but-because-his-family-owns-half-the-Randazian-Glow-Seeds-On-the-Planet-his-daddy-will-hire-that-gillie-wet-foot-lizard-Clarence-Jonas-and-the-butthead-and-his-low-life-friends-will-walk-away-free-mint-water-anyone?"Agnes said.

"I know he's a fustilarian boblyne, but I'm not completely convinced of Chance's guilt," said Uncle Phelan. "What do you think Lizzy and Bea?"

"I really don't know," said Lizzy. "I hope they find the Wand soon."

"And you, Bea?" Asked Uncle Phelan.

"After what I overheard that day on the path, I'd been absolutely certain Chance and his gang stole the Wand, and I always suspected him of killing Áine and Priscilla both... that is until the incident with the brown chicken and my going through so much traumatic interrogation because of her assumptions. Now I'm uncertain what I heard actually means Chance or his cronies committed the crime." She glanced around the room. "Already, he's been questioned. There is no reason to believe he did it. I feel terrible now I even reported Chance to Sgt. Saturday. I don't care much for Chance Rockefeller, but I'd never intentionally put anyone through that awful experience, not even him."

Samuel spoke up. "If it wasn't Chance, then who stole the Wand?"

"At this point, no one knows." Said Beautimus

"Are you getting all this, Rachel?" Uncle Phelan said.

"Every word."

"I've an idea," said Aunt Meg said to Beautimus. "You know your uncle and I, and the WSRT, put no stock whatsoever in oracles and magic and such things as you do, sweetie. We in the WSRT believe there is a rational scientific explanation for everything. Magic and fortune- telling to us is either a load of bunk, or perhaps something Science has yet to discover and explain. What I'm getting at is your Anam Glyphs."

Beautimus cocked her head. "What about the Anam Glyphs?"

"What I mean, dear, is well, I'm sure there will one day be a rational explanation for how they work, and none of us is convinced even then we'll recognize any validity in them. All I know is people say they are accurate. Is there a way you can ask them 'yes-no' questions?"

Beautimus paused for a moment and eyed the ceiling. "Yes. I can do that. Apple and Agnes, could I trouble you to run next door and fetch my pouch from the altar?"

"Wait" said Uncle Phelan. "Does anyone have any objections? Should we put this to a vote?"

Samuel said, "I think we should proceed."

"No objections, then?" Asked Uncle Phelan who scanned the room to make certain. "What about you, Rachel? No? Okay, Bea. Send the squirrels for the pouch."

A few minutes later Agnes spread the divining cloth on the floor of Aunt Meg and Uncle Phelan's abode and opened the pouch of Anam Glyphs.

"Shall we start by asking if Chance stole the wand?"

Beautimus set her intention and asked Applecheeks to pull a glyph. The first stone she pulled was Greenleaf.

"According to this, no."

"Try again," said Uncle Phelan.

Three more Glyphs, Alma, Sacred Trio, Waterbug.... all said no, no, no. Uncle Phelan was flummoxed. "I'm certain the odds would eventually turn up a yes." He asked her to pull another stone, and yet another. Each time the result came out the same. He said, "Then, let's ask about Chance's loiter-sack smarmy gang members."

Beautimus asked Applecheeks to pull stones for the Jackal, Herbert, and the Weasel, Mortimer. No, no, no every time.

"All right, then let's try this" Uncle Phelan said. "How about we ask the Glyphs about an unlikely suspect?"

"All right. Applecheeks, pull one for us now, please," asked Beautimus. "My question is, "Did Agnes steal the Wand of Fortuna?"

No, the Glyph stated. "How about Samuel S. Goodwings. Did Sam steal the Wand?" No. "All right, who next?"

"Who'd be the least likely suspect, Lady Rhianna?"

"Did Rhianna steal the Wand?" The Glyphs said no, then no a second time, and no a third time.

"Then who is the *second* least likely suspect?" asked Aunt Meg.

"The coyote, Belinda, since she's so devoted, and she's next in line for the seat of High Priestess."

Beautimus asked, "Did Belinda steal the Wand of Fortuna? Applecheeks pull a glyph, please"

Isa came up. Yes.

"Not possible," said Beautimus. "It's gotta be a fluke. Pull another."

Moonmagick. Yes. She pulled another, Angelwing, Yes. She pulled another and another and another....all yes, yes, yes.

"Oh my Goddesses," said Beautimus. The room became so quiet the attendees could have heard a blossom falling from the lemon tree outside. The sound of broken glass shattered the silence. Agnes had fainted again on her back in the middle of the floor, her legs straight in the air. Her cup had smashed against the rammed earth ground and tea splattered the room. Applecheeks bent over Agnes and, frantic, she fanned her sister's face with both paws.

"Let's compose ourselves," said Uncle Phelan. "Someone get water for Agnes, then let's talk about this thing with Belinda."

After Agnes revived, she and Applecheeks left for the evening.

"As good as Bea's Glyphs are, an oracle reading probably won't hold up in Court," said Lizzy.

"I agree" said Aunt Meg, "We have to find another way to obtain solid evidence, and even if we do, what's Belinda's motive?"

"I've got it" said Sam. "Let's invite Belinda over to dinner. I'll give her some of my home brew and when she's good and drunk, we'll ask her. My beer-berry hooch is not only a steaming hot aphrodisiac, it's a potent truth serum."

"No, Sam, we aren't going to get anyone drunk." Beautimus rolled her eyes.

"We need to find an objective way to obtain evidence to take to Sgt. Saturday," said Uncle Phelan. "I suggest we stake out her den, or tail her to find out what she's up to."

"Good idea, Uncle Phelan," said Beautimus. "Also, Belinda is a Wise Woman."

"So?" asked Samuel.

"So, she keeps a diary. All Wise Women keep a diary that is part grimoire to record spells, healing rituals, things like that. But, they also record important events of their lives and secrets. I know she'll keep a Wise Woman Diary for certain."

"Well," said Aunt Meg. "How do we get our hands on Belinda's diary?"

"It'd be on her Crystal Interface," said Beautimus. "We'll have to break into her den, locate her password, and access her diary from the Interface then project it to Sgt. Saturday."

"Shitolaroma, Bea. How in hellzabob are we going to manage it without getting caught?" asked Samuel.

CHAPTER SIXTEEN

THE MINUTE THE Wasenia Day Ceremony had ended weeks earlier, Belinda walked to the Sacred Watering Hole to say her prayers. Accustomed to going to a secluded spot she thought no one else knew about, Belinda was surprised to find Lady Rhianna there with her wings aloft praying aloud to the stars. The old blue crane must have used the Wand to transport herself there, because she'd arrived ahead of The Wand Guards, who had settled around her with their backs to Rhianna to give her the privacy required for her prayers.

The Captain of the Wand Guard, Steven D. Lobos, respectfully chided Rhianna for having left the ceremony without them. "Lady Rhianna, you never know who you might have met down here by yourself. Anyone could have stolen the wand from you, and could have even hurt you to steal it. You must not travel unaccompanied by my Guards when you are holding the Wand."

"Thank you for your concern, Steven, but I knew I'd be all right here in this sacred place."

Belinda ducked behind a dense copse of long flower catclaw trees and crouched low. One day, she'd be in Rhianna's place. She wanted to know what a High Priestess prayed about after an important ceremony, even though she knew Lady Rhianna would teach her these things as part of her training. But, Belinda, more than curious, was ambitious. She thought it a magnificent idea to eavesdrop and get a leg-up on her training. In the unlikely event there were any other contenders for the High Priestess position, knowing one of the holy prayers might cinch her spot, not that she worried, since she'd personally taken care of her one possible rival, Áine, years ago.

"I will blow Lady Rhianna's tail feathers off by knowing the words to this prayer and reciting it to her before she even teaches it to me."

The old bird put her beak into the air. "Great Goddesses hear my prayer. I've been keeping the secret of my illness and impending death, but now I fear my time is near and must soon disclose my condition to the District. I will name my successor at the Luna Festival."

Belinda became so still she could hear her own breathing, and the blood pulsing through her heart.

"I know Belinda is my natural successor. She is well-trÁined, and prepared on many levels."

Belinda rubbed her paws together, and licked her chops. *Oh, my goddesses, I thought I'd have some decades more to wait after I'd put in my time as an Old Mother. I'll be named successor by the Moon Festival. Rhianna is dying? Well, I'm sorry to hear it…what splendid news!*

"But, by the great holy Goddesses, I'm uncertain Belinda would be the best choice to provide for the spiritual needs of the Wayflower District, and to serve its people."

"What?" whispered Belinda. "What does she *mean* I wouldn't be the 'best choice'? Of course I'm the best choice. I'm her *only* choice."

"Belinda understands her duties. Beard and I trÁined her well, and I named her Wise Woman, but my heart tells me I made a grave mistake. Belinda is too eager, too vain, too caught up in her own ambitions to put her people first."

What? How can she think that? Belinda tightened her jaws and stifled a growl.

"There is another, one pure of heart, a learned woman. Although she thinks little of herself, she loves our people and has a wise soul, but because of her lack of confidence I'd made the mistake of not naming her Wise Woman. I failed to help her to become the Old Mother she could have become." The old crane bowed her head and a single tear rolled down her beak. "It was my mistake that pulled her out of line for natural succession to the role of High Priestess. My heart is heavy because I must rectify my error, which means Belinda will be crushed. I'm so ashamed Mother. Forgive me my bird frailties."

Who in hellzabob is she talking about? Belinda cocked her head.

"With your indulgence and your blessings, Holy Mother Genesis, I exercise my right to break custom and name another to be my successor."

The coyote tensed her shoulders. *"Who? Who? Get on with it, you old bitch."*

The crane lifted her head. "With your approval, I name as my successor, Beautimus Potamus."

What? That old boil-brained hippo? That stampcrap tallowcatch? Is Rhianna fucking kidding?

"Beautimus Potamus is the only woman in our District with the heart of a High Priestess, the only women in Wayflower worthy to hold the Wand of Fortuna."

A breeze rippled the waters of the Sacred Watering Hole. Ladyluz and Ladybeth glowed their permission. In that moment all the Goddesses, even The Great Lady herself, had forgiven Lady Rhianna, and blessed her decision to choose Beautimus.

Belinda knew it, too. Her heart shattered, her tail drooped, and she flattened her ears against her head. She halted, raised her head, and her sorrow instantly transmuted to rage. Hate ascended from her bowels into her solar plexus like caustic bile. Her hackles stiffened. Yes, what she felt was *hate*. She hated Rhianna with every fur follicle on her body. Hated her. *That worn out raggabrash clotpole. She has no idea what I could do to her. I should tear her fucking head off and shove her dead body in the watering hole where she can 'commune' with the Goddesses whenever she wants to from the other world. I'll do to her what I did to the weak, prissy Áine, and Lady Rhianna's weakling house chimp, Priscilla. I've my own lemur, Queenie, in place now, who has so far proven herself as useless as teats on a bull."* She looked into the sky and wrinkled her brow. *I may have to get rid of Queenie, too. Whatever else I might have to do, I will make goddessdamn sure Beautimus Potamus never touches that Wand. I swear it on my dead mother's ashes.*

She growled ever so softly, but loud enough to capture the attention of Steven D. Lobos who jerked his head her direction, although she'd crouched so low she pressed flat against the dirt. He stood, took a few tentative steps toward the trees where Belinda hid, and cocked his head to one side causing the tassel on his fez to fall over his shoulder. He strÁined to see what or who might be there, and lifted his muzzle to the air and sniffed. The wind rustled leaves in the trees and bushes bringing to him the gentle scent of lavender. Steven relaxed, turned his attention to the Guards surrounding the High Priestess, and took his place among them.

When the High Priestess concluded her prayers, she gathered her robes around her. "It's time to take the wand back to its resting place, Steven. Let's go, please."

She took a few steps from the water's edge permitting the wolves to close in around her. Steven D. took point. There was a wolf on each side of Rhianna, and two at the rear. They walked in procession toward the secret place to return the wand to its home. They approached an enormous white granite boulder, maybe ten meters high and twenty meters wide with rows of turpentine bushes in front. Belinda had seen the boulder many times before from a distance. Everyone had. It was called White Rock, a known landmark, but in a dense and frightening part of Dante's Forest no one dared venture into.

Steven D. turned stopped and rose his tail to signal a halt. He pulled one of the turpentine bushes out with his teeth, and placed it on the ground, then took his paw and pushed against a rectangular indentation in the boulder. A well-hidden stone door swung open leading to a passage. The procession entered through the door and proceeded through the dark tunnel. The last wolf stuck his head through the door, and replaced the bush with his teeth, pushing dirt around it with his muzzle. As he disappeared into the cave, the door closed behind him.

Belinda hunkered down, keeping her profile low. She followed. Belinda waited a few minutes, then trotted to the turpentine bush, yanked it out with her teeth, flung it aside, pushed hard against the granite until the door swung open. She pushed it closed it, then padded down the dark passageway a safe distance behind Rhianna and the wolves.

After a long walk down the dark corridor, light flooded the corridor as door opened. Belinda plastered herself against the stone wall of the passageway, hoping she'd blend in with the granite if anyone were to turn around. She held her breath. As the last wolf exited, he shut the door behind him. Belinda sat in the dark for a few minutes listening and sniffing the air. Water dripped from somewhere in the passageway, otherwise, the silence overwhelmed her. She trotted to the end of the tunnel, but even with excellent night vision she ran right smack into the ending of the tunnel. Solid granite. "Ouch. Dammit. Ouch." She recovered, and pushed against the wall until it gave way.

A door opened to a narrow path in the middle of the densest and most remote part of the forest. The atmosphere turned ominous. There was not another creature in sight, not even a yellow jacket or ant. For the first time in her life, Belinda had entered Dante's Forest, a place the Council forbade Rendazians to enter or flyover. As all Rendazians, she'd grown up believing fantastical stories of ferocious flesh-eating demons who dwelled in this forest, and poisonous plants and trees with black sap so toxic it would cause excruciating pain, or even kill any hapless victim who per chance brushed against it. Now she understood why those myths existed, to keep everyone away because in this part of the forest existed the Sacred Cavern of the Wand of Fortuna.

She fell in line a distance behind the others, grateful for all the foliage, the trees close together, the large boulders and rocks. She needed good hiding places because Ladyluz and Ladybeth shown bright.

Damn. Why aren't there clouds tonight?

As she slinked behind the procession, the trees vibrated and hummed. *Good thing there are no talkers around because from what I sense, if they could, they'd give me away to the Wand Guards without hesitation.* One of the trees, a chalker's wattle, attempted to snag her with a low hanging branch, but she ducked out of the way and glared back at it.

"I'll cut your beslubbering ass down if you try that again."

They reached a well-hidden cavern. Rhianna slipped into a small opening.

"Yeah, right. An old hippo could fit through *that*." Belinda put a paw to her mouth to muffle a snicker.

Rhianna reappeared a few minutes later, and four of the Wand Guards took up their posts at the cavern's opening. Steven D. escorted Lady Rhianna to her abode in the Blue Crane compound. Belinda remÁined crouched behind a rock for what seemed an eternity, and waited until Steven trotted back to the cavern to take his place among the Guards.

"I thought you replaced the turpentine bush outside the door of the White Rock?" Belinda perked up her ears as Steve scolded one of the Guards.

"I did, Sir."

"Oh? When Lady Rhianna and I went through, we found it uprooted. You cannot be careless about these things, Private. If

I see this sloppiness again I will bite you. Do you understand?"

"Yes Sir."

Belinda assessed the situation. She decided to go back to her den and return the following night when, according to reports on her Crystal Interface, there'd be cloud cover so she could explore options for breaking into the cavern undetected. She ran all the way back home, and when she got back to her den, she recorded in her diary everything. She deactivated her Crystal Interface, fell asleep exhausted, and dreamt of flesh-eating demons.

CHAPTER SEVENTEEN

THE FOLLOWING NIGHT, Belinda made her way back to the secret cavern, careful this time to replant the turpentine bush at the entrance to the tunnel through White Rock. She hid behind the sizeable boulder again, and surveyed the cavern's exterior. She circled and explored a possible way to enter from the rear, but as she made her way around the cavern, she stepped on a twig, and the snap caught the attention of one of the Guards. He raised himself from his post and advanced toward her, muzzle in the air. She ducked behind the trunk of a large broom wattle and stayed low, making herself as flat as possible. She remained still and silent as a rock. He advanced toward her, one step at a time, until his front paws were barely three inches from her head. *Shit. One tiny step more and he'll step right on me.* The wolf panted and sniffed the air. Her heart banged against her ribs. In the distance, a knocking of stones reverberated. Sasquatch. The wolf turned toward the sound and called out a warning to the creature. "So, it's you making that noise. I warn you. Don't come any nearer." The knocking ceased, and the wolf trotted back to the cavern.

Belinda waited a few moments, then climbed uphill behind the cave. She used her paws and muzzle to test for weakness in the soil. After a while of trying the soil she spied a patch of soft dirt. She pawed at the soil until the dirt gave way, but she met resistance again. She dug harder and deeper into the cavern wall. She shook with nervousness. Purmoso and Racine would soon rise, and with the suns' light, she'd vulnerable to the wolves. She focused her mind, and dug faster until all at once, a small portion of the wall collapsed, and there she discovered a small opening into the secret cavern. She sighed with relief, scratched soil over the opening, pushed a few white pebbles over the spot to mark it, and made her way back to her den right as the suns rose over the peaks. She recorded the evening's event in her diary. "I followed Rhianna and the Wand Guards to the cavern where the Wand of Fortuna is hidden, and…".

Later that morning Belinda set out to find an accomplice. There was no way she could fit through the narrow opening behind the cavern. She went downtown and made inquiries of the shopkeepers and customers.

"I'm looking for a criminal. Someone small. Perhaps a spider monkey or lemur. I was told by a Goddess in a dream that I must bless a little thief today."

Of course, no one would admit to knowing a thief. She asked a black headed junco, a field mouse, and a Holstein cow. They shook their heads, but Belinda persisted. She passed a wake of buzzards headed toward the Civic Building to file their discrimination suit over the flyover incident.

"Do any of you know a thief, perhaps a small fellow, who could use a blessing today?"

One of the buzzards turned his head to her. "Yeah, I know someone who could use a blessing, or a good eye pecking."

"Really?" Asked Belinda. "Who? If he's the right one, he will receive a Goddess blessing that could turn him around."

The buzzard loped his way to Belinda, wings half raised, "Jake, that little tottering pottle-deep monkey."

"Do you mean the same monkey who helped Angelina at her booth during the Wasenia Festival?"

"Yup, same one. That farking little butthole steals anything he can get his spur-galled paws on."

"I thank you, and the Great Goddesses thanks you. Would you also like a Blessing this morning?"

"No thanks. I'm not a Believer. I only wanted an excuse to expose that gleeking dung-headed monkey for what he is."

Belinda ran as fast as she could to the Monkey Tribal complex and there she found Jake snoozing in a hammock strung between two brown salwood trees.

"Excuse me, are you Jake?"

Jake opened one eye and regarded the coyote with amusement.

"Well, well, well what would the 'Star Maiden' want with a little brown monkey today, eh?"

"I need to talk to you in private."

"This outta' be good." Jake hopped out of his hammock. "Climb on my back, and the two of us will take a little stroll."

The monkey complied. They ventured into the forest until they found a secluded spot under a Chippendale's wattle.

Jake climbed off the coyote's back. "So, what's this about? Make it quick. I'd like to get back to my nap if you don't mind." He picked a flea off his stomach and examined it. The poor thing screamed for its life before the monkey popped it into his mouth.

Belinda shuddered. *A meat eater. Loathsome.* "Would you be interesting in making some real money, I mean so many Rendazian Glow Seeds you'd never have to work the festival circuit again?"

The nonchalant monkey's head snapped to attention. He straightened his posture. His eyes grew sharp, and attentive.

Belinda cocked a brow. "What if I were to tell you I know where the Wand of Fortuna is hidden?"

"Say what?"

"I said I know where the Wand of Fortuna is."

"Oh bullshit. Even if you do know where it is, what about the Wand Guard? Are you thinking about stealing it? You wanna get bitten to death, you crazy dumb broad?" The monkey returned to picking fleas from his fur. Each one of the little critters pleaded for its life as Jake crushed it in his teeth.

"I'm telling you I know where the Wand is, and I know a way in that the Wand Guards don't even know about."

The monkey squished a tick between his thumb and forefinger. "You're kidding me, right?"

"No. I'm not kidding you."

"So, what's stopping you? Steal the damn thing. With all its powers, it's gotta be worth a fortune. Why do you need me?" The monkey paused. "Although come to think of it, now that I know, you're gonna have to come up with a nice fat bag of Rendazian Glow Seeds so I don't tell Sgt. Saturday when the Wand shows up missing. Crazy dumb broad."

"What I'm *trying to tell you* is I need a partner. I uncovered an entrance at the back of the cavern. No one except me knows where it is. However, the opening is too small for me to fit through."

The monkey's eyes widened.

"Here's the plan," Belinda said "I take you there. You get into the cave, find the wand and bring it out. Then we sell it, and split the Glow Seeds 50-50."

"Why don't you tell me where it is? I'll get it and bring it back tonight."

"No way, Jake. Maybe I'm not the crazy dumb broad you think I am."

"Yeah, well maybe you ain't a dumb broad, but I never imagined the 'Star Maiden,' next in line for the seat of the uppity-uppity High Priestess seat, wantin' to steal what's gonna be hers eventually anyway. So, I guess that makes you a *crazy* broad, then. What in hellzabob would make you want to steal the Wand in the first place?"

"None of your business. Are you in or not?"

"I'm in."

That night, Belinda and Jake made their way back to the cavern. Both were skilled at being sneaky, so getting to the back of the cavern undetected, although not easy with Steven D. and his Guards present, was doable. Belinda uncovered the hole, and nimble Jake scrambled down. After a long, long while, too long a while, Jake popped out of the hole bearing the Lapis Lazuli box under an arm.

"What took you so damned long? The suns are about to rise. We are going to have to run like hellzabob to make it back before the Guards make their morning rounds, discover the wand missing, and start searching for us."

"Damn, Woman, this thing wasn't easy to find. I found it in a deep well-hidden niche. I'd like to see you try gettin' the Wand without me."

Belinda covered the hole, and she and Jake set out for home. After the coyote and the monkey were a long distance from the wolves, to beat the sunrise, Belinda picked up the pace and as fast as her paws would carry her. She found it very difficult to make her way with a monkey on her back.

CHAPTER EIGHTEEN

ON EARTH, THERE is a thing in some religions called "Karma." The simple meaning of the word is what goes around comes around. As Beautimus teaches her students, under the laws of Karma, if you do something awful, like stealing a sacred object, killing a tree, or committing murder, something bad will happen to you. Belinda was about to face Karma head on, and Beautimus knew it. The Glyphs had told her so.

Heatherton the rat, still under investigation for the thefts at the Wasenia Fair, cased the dens of the coyotes late in the evening of the WSRT meeting. He knew some of the Coyote People were rather well-off, and most seemed to like being out at night. He hoped to discover an unlocked door, a window with a loose latch, or a back entrance to an empty den so he could slip inside and bag a few treasures before any of the band returned from a night of howling and prowling. He peeked through knot holes in wood, and the spaces under doors, and through cracks in windows. Then he came upon Belinda's den. She had a cute little front door and an equally cute little window adjacent to the door because as she said when the Bo Bo Baboon Construction Boss designed her abode, "I'm unlike other coyotes in that I rather like natural light so I want a glass window to let the suns shine through."

She had white curtains on her window she'd bought off the rack on sale from Lacy's store downtown, but they weren't an exact fit. They didn't quite cover the bottom, leaving enough of a gap for a rat standing on his tip toes on a rock to peer through, which is what Heatherton did.

He witnessed Belinda brandishing a wand in her teeth in front of a full length mirror. She did her best to work magic with it. She grew frustrated, then exasperated, because none of her spells worked. She whipped her head from one side to the other, angry, chanting inaudible twaddle. Obvious she really didn't know how to operate the wand, Heatherton, stifled a laugh. The wand interested him, though. He'd seen other Wise Women working with magical tools and sticks, but this one seemed different, somehow familiar. After watching her for an hour or so, he began to think it high time to move on to another den when something happened. With a frustrated growl, Belinda flung the wand across the room and it landed on the floor of her den beneath the window.

The rat squinted to get a better look at the wand, then gasped. *The Wand of Fortuna! How in hellzabob did Belinda end up with the Wand of Fortuna?*

Belinda let out an awful noise. She howled, and wailed. "The goddessdamn thing is useless. I'm going to have to bite the gems out and sell them. Maybe I'll get a *quarter* of what I'd expected on the black market, *that is if I'm lucky.* Dammit, dammit, dammit!" She activated her diary and recorded "The fucking Wand of Fortuna doesn't work. Worthless piece of dung."

On the spot, Heatherton hatched a grand and delicious plan. *I don't need to case more dens. I've found my pot of Rendazian Glow Seeds right here, a never empty pot of Rendazian Glow Seeds.* He chortled and pawed the ground. *Yes-siree-bob, a never empty pot of glow seeds all for me.*

He scuttled back to his abode laughing the entire way home. What he didn't know is in the white oak tree next to Belinda's window, a praying mantis dressed in a black hooded robe with charcoal smeared on his face observed the entire episode. When Samuel witnessed Heatherton linger a bit longer at Belinda's window than seemed necessary for a simple look around, he worked his way down the tree trunk so he could peer into the window, too. He witnessed and heard everything Heatherton had.

After Heatherton departed, Samuel flew nonstop to Beautimus' abode. Wide awake on her pillows, Beautimus watched a rerun of *M.A.S.H.* with the squirrels when Samuel called to her from outside. "Bea. Open up. It's important. I saw something at Belinda's."

Beautimus rose. "What did you see, Sam? Come in."

Samuel flew in and told her all about Heatherton, the wand, and Belinda writing in her diary.

"Ah, she did take the wand, and she does use a Diary. I thought so. Did you see anything else, Sam?"

"Yeah, Heatherton laughed his ass off as he ran back to his rat hole. I think he's got something planned."

"You gotta get back there, Sam, now. You have to see if Belinda tries to contact anyone, or leaves, or if Heatherton returns. You must continue the surveillance because you're the only one of us who can do it. The squirrels, Lizzy and I are too big. We'll be noticed."

"Aw, for gawdessake, Bea. I'm exhausted. I haven't slept since I left your Aunt and Uncle's house."

"Take a quick snooze. I'll get the squirrels to brew some strong caffeinated tea for you. Then, after your nap and tea, go and find out everything you can. I'll stay up, too. I'll be right here awake when you return."

Applecheeks brewed the tea while Samuel took a twenty-minute nap. Agnes woke him and in one gulp he consumed his thimbleful of tea. "I'm on my way."

Beautimus nodded. "Good luck, Sam, and be careful."

He flew to Belinda's den.

***

Exhausted and frustrated, Belinda lapped a bowl of mead and fell asleep. Early the next morning a scratching at her door roused her. She pulled herself up in a haze, made her way to the front of her den. She grasped a rope handle in her teeth and pulled the door open. "May I help you?"

"Yes, Wise Woman, I'm in need of a Goddess Blessing this morning." The rat lowered his head in a gesture of respect.

"It's so early; can you come back in a few hours? I've not even had time for breakfast or grooming."

"No, Mistress, this blessing involves you, too." He lifted his head and stared at her with an intensity and boldness that took Belinda by surprise. "Yes, you, Wise Woman…and a certain Wand."

"I have no idea what you are talking about, sir." A lump of fear hardened in her chest. She regarded the dirty rat with disgust. "What is your name by the way?"

"My name is Heatherton." He made an exaggerated bow. "Pleased to make your acquaintance." He straightened and raised his voice. "I think you better let me in Ms. Belinda before I start talking right here in the open about the missing Wand of Fortuna. What do you think?"

"Shhhhh! Keep your voice down." After she looked one way then the other to see if anyone might be listening, Belinda ushered the rat into her den and shut the door.

Samuel crept up the side of the den wall and squinted through the gap in the curtain. "What do you know about the Wand?" Belinda asked Heatherton. She licked a paw in a casual, unconcerned manner.

"Let's just say I stopped by your window last night, and let's just say you should install more substantial curtains if you don't want anyone to see in."

"What are you talking about? What did you see, because whatever you *thought* you saw was probably me practicing with my own wand. She pulled a lovely beachwood twig off an altar with her teeth and held it out to the rat.

"No, no. Not that wand, the other one. The one you couldn't manage to get to work last night. The one you threw on the floor right down in front of where I peeked in. I got a good look, Ms. Belinda. Why do you have the Wand of Fortuna?"

"I told you I have no idea what you are talking about," Belinda choked the words out.

Samuel pressed tighter to the glass to better hear their conversation.

The rat paced with his hands in his pockets. "Well, I suppose then you wouldn't mind if I told Sgt. Saturday what I saw last night? I mean, he may have a question or two for me about why I looked through your window. I'll tell him I was checking to see if you were home before I disturbed you. I'll tell him I have been so distraught about being searched and interrogated about the Wasenia Festival thefts I sought out the nearest Wise Woman for a Goddess blessing. But...ah.... do you think he'll be more interested in why I peeked through your window, or in what I witnessed when I did?"

"What makes you think he'll believe *you*? You are already under investigation for thievery, Mr. Heatherton. Are you not? I am a Wise Woman, next in line for the chair of High Priestess."

"I already have a call into Sgt. Saturday. He doesn't know what it's about. I could tell him I'm feeling remorseful for stealing goods from customers and venders at the fair, and I'm ready to make restitution without a trial, or, I could tell him I know who has the Wand of Fortuna. I asked him to meet me here. When he arrives, do I tell him I'm here for a blessing and wanted to confess to a Wise Woman, or do I tell him the Wand of Fortuna is there..." He pointed to a bulky red chenille pillow in the corner, "...where I watched you stow it last night? And I wouldn't bother moving it. I've other hard evidence, too." He tapped his hip as though he had a pocket carrying something within.

Samuel kept a sharp eye and an attentive ear on the scene, never letting the rat or coyote out of site. *Shit, I bet that rat doesn't have anything else in his pocket, but she's so scared Belinda will believe anything he tells her right now. That thieving-conniving-scoundrel-of-a-rat played his cards right.*

Heatherton licked his paw. "Up to you, girl."

The coyote ground her teeth. "How much do you want?"

"Oh, let's see. How 'bout 1,000 Rendazian Glow Seeds?"

Her eyes flew open. "Are you out of your mind? I don't even make that much money in a month. I certainly don't have near 1,000 in the bank."

"I suppose you have to find a way to get it, then, say by this time tomorrow?"

"I have no idea how I'd get that kind of money."

"You're an attractive young coyote. There are plenty of well-to-do single male coyotes around who'd probably enjoy a little affection from the beautiful 'Star Maiden' for a few seeds in return. You figure it out."

Her hackles rose. "Why, you dirty rat!"

Heatherton scuttled back a few steps "I hear Sgt. Saturday coming up the path now. What should I tell him, Belinda?" He patted his hip again.

"Okay, okay, I'll figure something out. Don't tell anyone what you saw, please."

"Thatta' girl. By the way, did I happen to mention I expect those 1,000 seeds every month?"

"What? You fucking little…"

"Tisk, tisk. Is that any way for the Star Maiden to talk?" The rat peered under the door. "Oh look. He's coming to your door now. Shall I answer?"

"I'll get your damned money. Don't you dare rat me out."

Someone knocked at the door. She nosed the curtain to one side to look out her window, and saw standing Sgt. Saturday waiting. Samuel remÁined still.

Heatherton scuttled out the front and greeted the Guardian. "Sgt. Saturday. What a pleasure to see you. Thank you for coming today. My conscious is getting to me about the things I took at the fair, and I needed a blessing from a Wise Woman. I thought I might confess and save the people of Wayflower the expense of further investigation and a trial and...."

Belinda slunk toward the back of her den and sat on her haunches in front of her Crystal Interface. "I have to think of something quick to get rid of that damn rat for good," she said.

She entered something into her diary, and afterwards, she tucked her head between her front paws and moaned.

CHAPTER NINETEEN

AFTER HEATHERTON AND Sgt. Saturday departed, Belinda rushed to the Monkey Tribal Compound to find Jake. Samuel flew at a discreet distance behind her. She passed a coterie of prairie cogs chattering and chirping. One of them called out. "Ms. Belinda, Good Morning. Will you please bestow a blessing on me today?"

Belinda whipped her head around to look at the little animal. She bared her teeth and growled. "Shut the fuck up!" The entire coterie fell silent.

When Belinda arrived at the compound, she discovered Jake sleeping in his hammock. She nosed him. "Wake up! Wake up! You tickle-brÁined miscreant."

The monkey yawned. "What the hellzabob are you trying to do. You interrupted a great dream about a hot little monkey with a big…"

"Shut your yap and listen to me. Heatherton looked through my window last night and saw the Wand. He knows *everything*. He's blackmailing me."

"What?"

"You heard me. And, there's another piece of bad news, too, little buddy. The wand doesn't work."

"Whaddayamean the wand doesn't 'work'?"

"I'd heard a story a million times it only works for the reining High Priestess. I guess it wasn't a story."

The monkey leapt out of his hammock. "So, if we try to sell the thing it won't work for whoever buys it? Shitolacrapamunga! The Wand is almost useless."

Belinda sneered. "Exactly, Genius. I'll have to bite out the gems, or you can pry them out, and we'll see if we can't get at least something for them on the black market."

"Uh, no way, girly. First of all, Heatherton knows what's going on, making the Wand waaaay too hot, and secondly, those gems without the Wand are maybe worth, what 1/4th or maybe 1/5th the value of the intact Wand of Fortuna? I'm done. You do what you want to with the farking gems. I want out."

"I don't think so, Jake. If I don't hand over 1,000 Glow Seeds to that stinking rat by tomorrow morning, he's going to Sgt. Saturday." She pointed her paw at Jake's face. "If I go down, I'm taking one stupid little thieving fool-born monkey with me. Savvy? There is no way any Guardian or Jury on the planet will believe I could fit through that tiny hole in the back of the cavern by myself. I'll make damn good and sure they clearly understand who helped me."

The monkey snorted. "What do you propose to do then, kill the rat?"

"What do *you* think I'm going to do?" She bared her teeth.

Jake backed up a step. "You really *are* a crazy broad. You know what the penalty for murder is? Besides, I'm a thief, not a murderer. If you want the rat dead, you have to take care of it yourself."

"Fine, you currish jerk. But remember if I get caught, I'll make certain you suffer right along with me. Got it?"

"Get away from me, Belinda. This whole deal is going south. I don't want to be anywhere near you when it does. Go." The monkey extended his arm and pointed his finger down the path.

"Oh? You want me to leave? Very well, but don't be too surprised if you read in tomorrow's *Wayflower Quacker* about a rank fly-bitten rat discovered poisoned in the woods somewhere. Tonight, I'm going out with my friends to howl at the moon like nothing is at all wrong. Tomorrow when Mr. Heatherton comes by for his money, I will offer him a nice piece of cheese first, a very *special* nice piece of cheese. Then I'll carry his rotten dead carcass deep into the woods and bury him there. If I do by some fluke get caught, you will be an accessory to murder, monkey boy. I'll make sure of it, and you'll go right down with me."

"Keep your murdering plans to yourself, you dark-hearted virago. Just go. Get out of my life."

Belinda turned and trotted off to "Wayflower General's Public Apothecary for Herbal Cures and Magical Healing Potions." She'd buy digitalis, that in a large dose, would mean certain death to a certain rat. *I'll stop that knotted-pated bastard's heart in 30 seconds flat. The pharmacist would never dare question a Wise Woman on the purchase of a natural substance commonly used for healing.*

Samuel flew as fast as his wings would carry him back to Beautimus. There, in Beautimus' abode, he found one tired, awake hippo who had kept her promise, two squirrels and a mastodon fast asleep. The squirrels and Lizzy awoke as he flew in. He recounted to them what he'd witnessed and overheard between the coyote and the monkey.

"Then tonight," Beautimus said, "while she's out in the forest, we'll have to find a way to get into her den. I'll break into her Crystal Interface and project her diary to Sgt. Saturday's Interface before she returns home. First thing tomorrow, we'll show up at her doorstep with Sgt. Saturday right when Heatherton is due to arrive. We have to make certain Belinda doesn't feed him that cheese."

Agnes hopped up and down. "Oh-can-I-help-I-wanna-do-something-anything-to-help-let-me-come-along-I'll-sit-in-the-white-acorn-tree-and-be-a-lookout-no-one-thinks-anything-at-all-of-a-squirrel-in-an-oak-tree-looking-for-acorns-I-can-help-anyone-want-food?"

"Actually, that's a good idea, Agnes. Do come along."

Agnes hyperventilated so hard with excitement Beautimus grew concerned the squirrel might faint again.

Lizzy and Applecheeks were to stay behind in case anyone came by Beautimus' abode. Lizzy would provide an alibi for Beautimus' absence, something like, "The only thing she told me is she's meeting a friend—wink, wink, nudge, nudge—down by a secret hidey-hole on the river." Anyone asking might think Lucas had returned early for a little romantic rendezvous with his sweetheart, and let it go without questioning Beautimus' absence.

That night, Beautimus, Samuel and Agnes took off toward the Coyote Tribal Compound on what would appear to anyone they encountered as a casual evening stroll through the forest. Heatherton was right that most of the coyotes were gone at night. The canines almost always took off into the forest beginning the moment the moons rose high in the sky. No one knew why they did so, but most people accepted their night prowling behavior as a coyote *thang*. The intrepid trio would not meet coyotes, who might question their presence at the dens. As they ambled along, they came across Buford, a Blood Hound. "Hey y'all! Goin' fer a walk? Can I tag along, can I? can I? Pant, pant, pant, drool, drool.

"Ordinarily, Buford, that'd be great, but we have some important business to attend to this evening of a rather secret nature, so can we count on you not to tell anyone at all you saw us?" Beautimus asked.

"Yup, yup. Sho 'nuff. Won't say a thang. My muzzle is good 'n closed tight. Secret? Oh yeah. I love me a good secret. I can keep a secret. Yup. Yup".

"Fine, Buford. Have a nice evening."

"Thank ya, Ma'am and you too over thar little Squirrel lady, and Praying Mantis man."

When the three arrived at the coyote den compound, both

moons were high in the sky. From a distance, they watched Belinda trotting off into the forest with her friends.

"Great timing," said Beautimus. "I think the Goddesses are with us tonight. To reiterate, our plan is to install Agnes in the oak tree near Belinda's window as a lookout. If she sees anything while I'm inside, she'll chatter like she's arguing with another squirrel. Your job, Sam, is to buzz around the abode until you find a way for me to get in unnoticed. I'll hang back here in the trees so I'm unlikely to be seen. Once I'm in, I'll break into Belinda's Crystal Interface. You guard the back, Sam, in case Belinda and her gal friends come in through the forest a different way. When this night is over, we'll all have a big cup of hot spiced mead at my abode. We will have earned it. Let's get going, everyone." She stamped her foot twice.

Beautimus backed into the forest behind a clump of wantan trees to conceal herself.

Agnes jumped off Beautimus' back and scurried down the path, looking both ways to make certain she wasn't seen. She ran up the tree to a high branch to secure the best view of the surrounding area. Samuel flew off to check out Belinda's abode for a suitable entrance. A few minutes later he returned. "We are in huge luck. Ms. Belinda, who is forever remodeling her den, is adding on to the back. There's a big opening covered by a piece of flimsy burlap, plenty of room for you to get inside, Bea."

"Perfect."

Beautimus trotted to Belinda's den. She walked around back, careful not to break any tree limbs that might be noticed by someone walking by. Samuel stationed himself on a white hairy wattle so he could keep an eye on the back side of the den. Beautimus moved the burlap to one side with her head and entered Belinda's abode. There, on the middle of the floor, sat the Crystal Interface. She approached it, tapped it two times and the light came on. "Good, I'm in." But, the second she attempted to focus her mind on the screen, the "Password Protected" image appeared. *Okay. That's expected.* She began to think of possible passwords. "B.E.L.I.N.D.A." Nope, not it. Then she tried Belinda backwards. Then she tried Belinda's mother's name, father's name, friends' names. She tried their names backwards. ACCESS DENIED, ACCESS DENIED, ACCESS DENIED.

After nearly an hour, Agnes chattered and squealed.

"No, it's too early. Can't be!" Sweat broke out on Beautimus' neck. "Oh no!"

Samuel poked his head in. "Bea, they're coming. You gotta get out. They'll catch you."

"No, Sam. I need a minute. Can you stall them? Do something, anything."

The approaching coyotes chatted. "I thought you looked pretty good up there on stage in that tiara, Belinda. You'll make a great High Priestess."

"With the wand missing, there may not be a High Priestess at all for a while." Belinda snorted.

"They'll find the Wand. Surely, it's in Wayflower somewhere. You'll be High Priestess."

Bingo! The password, "High-Priestess" worked. The coyote voices grew closer and louder. The coyotes approached Belinda's den, and would be inside within a minute at most. Samuel buzzed around the coyotes. "Hey, Coyote Women, nice night for a howl. Why aren't you all out in the forest on such a fine night?"

The coyotes ignored him. One took a mindless swipe at him with her paw. They continued talking and walking, closer and closer, right to the door.

Frantic, Beautimus searched the Interface for the diary until at last she found it: "Stunningly Beautiful Belinda's Magical Grimoire and Wonderful Diary." She focused her intention to, "Send to Sgt. Saturday," but nothing happened. The file hung suspended on the screen. *By all that is holy, please no.* She heard the door key turn in the latch.

"Damned. Wrong key," said Belinda to her friends. "It's the one way in the bottom of my pouch, of course, not that one. Give me a minute to find it."

Beautimus' jaws tightened, and she stared hard at the screen. "C'mon, c'mon, c'mon." Then with a soft pop of light the file disappeared and the message "File Sent Successfully" appeared. Beautimus backed out of the den as fast as her big form permitted. As the burlap flap closed shut behind her, the coyotes entered through the door.

"Did anyone hear that stomping noise as we came in?" asked Belinda.

"I think it might be those stupid squirrels outside in the oak tree," said one of the other coyotes.

"Curious. It sounded to me like it came from in here. Oh, look, I left in such a hurry I forgot to deactivate my Crystal Interface. Silly me."

Beautimus and Samuel stood outside holding their breath. Once they heard the coyotes lapping tea and chatting comfortably, Beautimus and Samuel tip-toed out onto the path. There, on her back, all four paws straight in the air, Agnes had fainted and fallen out of the tree.

"Great Mother Genesis, not again." Beautimus nudged the squirrel until she revived her. Agnes climbed onto Beautimus' back without saying a word, and the three returned to hippo's abode. After telling Applecheeks and Lizzy what had transpired, they all fell down into the straw and closed their eyes without taking even one sip of mead to celebrate.

The next morning early, Applecheeks nudged the three awake.

Beautimus woke with a start. "My goddesses! What time is it?"

"Don't worry" Lizzy said, "Racine isn't even in the sky yet. It's barely approaching dawn. We wanted to make sure you were up early enough to get a bite to eat and a dip in the river before heading off to Belinda's."

"No time for the river, I'm afraid, but a little fruit would be nice."

"As we thought. That's why we made up a nice fruit platter and a pail of tea."

"Lizzy, you are the best friend anyone could have. Thank you so much, and thank you, too, dear Apple."

After breakfast, Samuel and Beautimus, at a brisk pace, set off on the path toward the coyote compound. Agnes decided to stay home and nurse her head where she'd received a nasty bump, and a deep scrape from fainting and falling out of the oak tree.

Beautimus and Samuel arrived and hid themselves only minutes before Heatherton scratched at Belinda's door. "Sure hope you got those seeds for me, honey!"

"I certainly do have something good for you, Heatherton. How 'bout we share a little repast together before I hand over the seeds? I procured some special cheese *just* for you."

Beautimus and Samuel went around back where they could better hear the conversation between the coyote and the rat, and observed them through a crack in the temporary covering over the rear of Belinda's abode.

Heatherton cleared his throat. "Under the circumstances, it's gracious of you to make a nice breakfast, sweetie-pie. I am a tad bit hungry, come to think of it." He patted his stomach. "Maybe I've misjudged you. I'm looking forward to a looooong and beautifully prosperous relationship with you. Oooh, I think I'll help myself to a piece of this gouda."

As Heatherton reached to pick up a piece of cheese with his paws for a nibble, Beautimus broke through the burlap flap and kicked the cheese away from the rat. "Don't eat that cheese. It's poisoned!"

Sgt. Saturday and the Guardians broke through the front door. "Ms. Belinda and Mr. Heatherton, you are both under arrest. You," he pointed to the rat, "on charges of blackmail related to the theft of the Wand of Fortuna, and you," he pointed to Belinda, "for the theft of a sacred object, for disrespecting a High Priestess…and for attempted murder."

"My, my, what is this about? We are only two friends enjoying a meal together." Belinda's voice could have melted butter.

One of the Guardians, an orangutan, went straight to the red cushion, and lifted it. Beneath he discovered the lapis lazuli box holding the Wand of Fortuna. Another orangutan picked up the cheese and placed it into an evidence bag. "We'll have this analyzed right away, sir." He said to Sgt. Saturday.

Sgt. Saturday turned to Heatherton. "You'd better thank Ms. Potamus, Heatherton. She saved your life."

Heatherton glared at Belinda. "You traitorous whore. You stinking spur-galled bitch. You tried to kill me."

Belinda put her nose in the air and marched out between two Guardians. On the way, Belinda said to Sgt. Saturday, "By the way, Sir, did you happen to question Jake, the monkey? You know he was in on this, too."

"He's already downtown, Ms. Belinda. We know all about Jake."

On their way home, Beautimus and Samuel came across the same charm of finches in the White Oak Tree that had been at the school when Lucas had asked Beautimus out for a picnic. "The *Wayflower Quacker* will have to act damned fast if the paper wants to get the news out to the District before these gossips do," Beautimus said.

CHAPTER TWENTY

UNCLE PHELAN, AUNT Meg, Lizzy, the Squirrels, Samuel and Beautimus all gathered at Beautimus' abode for brunch, while waiting the delivery a special edition of *Wayflower Quacker*. They were in the midst of a fine meal of bananas, strawberries and lavender tea when Larry showed up with the paper. Applecheeks scurried to the flap and opened it to permit the stork entrance.

The stork bowed and pushed the paper forward with his beak. "Ms. Bea, I think you'll enjoy this edition."

"Thank you, Larry."

After the paper carrier flew away, the squirrels spread out the paper so everyone could read the article.

Wand of Fortuna Recovered. Wise Woman, Belinda, in Custody

Thanks to a one brave hippo, Beautimus Potamus, with assistance from her house squirrel, Agnes, and the prominent Blue Corn Physicist, Samuel S. Goodwings, the mystery of the missing Wand of Fortuna was solved early this morning. Belinda, the Wise Woman coyote, noted for her portrayal of the "Star Maiden" at the recent Wasenia Festival, has been taken into custody along her alleged accomplices, Heatherton the Rat and Jake the Monkey.

The Guardians allegedly charged Ms. Belinda with felony theft of a sacred object, willfully disrespecting a High Priestess, and attempted murder. If found guilty, Belinda could face banishment and possible shunning.

According to the official interrogator, Ms. Glossywings, investigators established a motive for the theft. Allegedly, following the Wasenia Festival, Ms. Belinda inadvertently discovered Madam Rhianna will be naming an alternate successor to the position of High Priestess. Reportedly, Ms. Belinda's only comment was, "How could that old worn out bird even consider anyone but beautiful me to take her place! I've dedicated my entire life to the position of High Priestess."

The local Butterfly Council ordered the press not to release the name of the successor at this time out of respect for Lady Rhianna, who will be allegedly making the announcement at the upcoming Luna Festival. Jake, the monkey, will allegedly be using the "demon defense" per his attorney Clarence Jonas. The demon defense claims insanity by demon possession. Jake's comment to the Wayflower Quacker reporter Hattie Hopper was, "I had to be demon possessed and completely insane to ever consider working with that crazy dumb broad. I'm demon possessed all right." According to witnesses present at the time, after making his statement, Mr. Jake "...bared his teeth, growled like a demented lion, and proceeded to heave. From his mouth issued projectile vomit of a foul smelling copious quantity of green pea soup colored regurgitation barely missing Ms. Hopper."

Heatherton, the pack rat, already under investigation for Wasenia Festival thefts, allegedly attempted to blackmail Ms. Belinda after he allegedly witnessed her in her den in possession of the wand as he looked through the window to see if she was home before disturbing her for a Goddess Blessing. He will plead innocent, per Mr.

Heatherton's attorney, Clarence Jonas, also representing Jake the monkey.

Ms. Belinda allegedly attempted to poison Mr. Heatherton with an overdose of digitalis placed into a slice of Gouda Cheese she'd allegedly purchased for that specific purpose. Ms. Bea broke into Ms. Belinda's den, and kicked the cheese out of the way of Mr. Heatherton in time to save his life. Mr. Heatherton made this statement to the Quacker, "I can't imagine why my good friend, the Wise Woman Belinda, could do such a thing. I'm shocked, shocked, I tell you. No one can image how grateful I am to Ms. Bea. I shall always be in her debt for saving my life."

Steven D. Lobos, head of the special forces team, The Wand Guards, said, "Because of this breach of security, and the theft of the wand, I'll be adding a sixth Wand Guard. We will intensify our training to ensure tighter security for both the Wand of Fortuna and the High Priestess. I thought I smelled coyote and monkey nearby, and if there is ever a next time, I can assure the citizens of Wayflower we'll be investigating all odors more thoroughly. I also smelled a rat, most likely the rat odor was on Ms. Belinda. I am hereby putting all three suspects on notice if they attempt to escape Limbo, I will bite all three of them."

Due to the seriousness of the crimes, all suspects are held in Limbo awaiting further investigation and trial.

"Hey, look! *The Wayflower Quacker* says I'm 'a prominent blue corn physicist.' I kinda like that." Samuel puffed out his chest. "But why in hellzabob do they keep saying 'alleged'?"

"It's the seriousness of the crimes," said Uncle Phelan "The

Butterfly Council wants to ensure the media isn't declaring anyone guilty of anything until all the suspects have been fairly tried."

"I wonder who Rhianna is going to name as successor to the seat of High Priestess?" asked Beautimus.

"There's quite a few Wise Women and Old Mothers in Wayflower. It could be one of several," said Lizzy.

"I can't believe that reeky motley-eyed, Heatherton. We know he's guilty as hellzabob," said Sam. "I listened to every word. I don't know what that farking rat thinks he's trying to pull, but I'm telling Sgt. Saturday exactly what I heard."

"Sgt. Saturday and Ms. Glossywings will be collecting statements today or tomorrow from you, Sam, as well as from Bea and Agnes. Plus, I don't think Heatherton knows about Belinda's diary," said Aunt Meg.

Agnes said nothing.

Further down the paper, another headline of interest appeared.

Turkey Buzzards Win Their Discrimination Suit

Turkey Buzzard protestors filed a complaint with the Butterfly Council earlier this week. They claim they were intentionally excluded from the Wasenia Festival flyover because of their ugly heads. After convening to review the Buzzards' complaints, the Butterfly Council determined the Buzzards were indeed discriminated against. In a statement to the press, Odette, the official greater for this year's Wasenia Festival, made a statement. "Discrimination and Profiling are against the Rendazian Constitution. We hold strong to our 'no tolerance' policy against any kind of discrimination toward anyone for any reason. Flying while ugly is not a crime. All birds with necessary wingspans shall be allowed an opportunity to participate in a festival flyover." In the way of restitution, the Festival Committee has offered the Buzzards the lead flyover for the upcoming Luna Festival. The Buzzards accepted.

As the Buzzards celebrated their victory, Mr. Clarence Jonas, Esq. approached Ms. Hopper, there covering the festivities, and made this statement, "Although I'm immensely pleased the Buzzards won their case, had they hired me I could have also secured them an award of thousands, perhaps hundreds of thousands, of Rendazian Glow Seeds to compensate for their pain and suffering. Folks, if you are a victim of unfair discrimination or profiling, hire the best lawyer in Rendaz, me. Don't go to the Butterfly Council because with them, even if you win, you lose."

One of the buzzards present hissed at the komodo dragon attorney, who promptly departed the scene. "What an opportunistic weenie," stated the hissing buzzard. "Next time he interrupts one of our parties, I might do more than hiss. You are not welcome back here, Mr. Jonas!"

Shortly after, Sgt. Saturday appeared at the door with his Guardians, along with Margaret Glossywings, representatives of the Butterfly Council, and Ms. Hopper to take statements from Beautimus, Samuel and Agnes.

Sgt. Saturday said, "The cheese analysis came back positive for digitalis. In fact, we found so much foxglove in that gouda it could have killed ten rats. It's obvious Ms. Belinda intended Mr. Heatherton to die. Premeditated murder is a serious criminal offense, carries as much weight as needlessly cutting down an old growth tree, and with that much digitalis,

Ms. Belinda will have a hard time convincing a jury of an 'accidental' overdose. As for her diary, you getting it over to me, Ms. Potamus, is going to clench a guilty verdict. The Guardians are appreciative beyond words. I commended all of you for your bravery."

Agnes remÁined uncharacteristically quiet. Beautimus suspected her friend might be depressed. She approached the squirrel and gentle nudged her. "Are you all right, Agnes?"

The squirrel nodded her head, but said nothing.

"Listen to me, my dear Agnes, what you did for us all was so important. If you had not been in that tree and chattered a warning, I may have been caught. You saved me, and I'm grateful to you."

Agnes waived her paws in the air. "Ms.-Bea-I-fell-out-of-an-oak-tree-do-you-realize-how-embarrassing-it-is-for-a-squirrel-to-fall-out-of-a-tree-especially-an-oak-on-top-of-that-I-hurt-my-head-I'll-be-a-laughing-stock-among-the-entire-squirrel-tribe-I'm-humiliated-can-I-go-outside-now?" She dropped her paws and hung her head.

Beautimus nudged the squirrel again, "Of course, if you need to go outside to be by yourself, that's fine, but you have no idea what a good friend you are to me, Agnes. You fell out of that oak in the line of duty, an important and brave duty. I love you anyway, but the risk you took for me, for Wayflower, makes me love you even more. If Belinda had caught you in that tree she would have taken you in her teeth and shaken you to death. You risked your life for me, for all of us. I love you, Agnes."

Agnes sighed and for the longest time she clung to Beautimus' leg.

Beautimus' Crystal Interface glowed and buzzed, and she answered. "Hello."

"Hi! How's my girl? "

Blessed Mother Genesis. He called me 'my girl'. Oh my Goddesses. "I'm doing wonderfully, Lucas, so good to hear from you. How are your plans coming along for your move to Wayflower?"

"Great. I wanted to let you know word of what you did to help solve the mystery of the Wand of Fortuna, and your role in the Wand's recovery, is all over Rendaz. I'm proud of you, Bea."

Beautimus' pendant glowed hot, and so did her cheeks. "Thank you, Lucas. It was nothing."

"No, what you did was not 'nothing.' It was something, really something. You should feel good about yourself. I'll be back late next week and I'm really looking forward to our date. You pick the place, I'll supply the picnic."

"That would be great, Lucas."

"I'll see you real soon. Can't wait."

"Me either."

"Bye for now."

"Bye for now."

A few minutes later, Beautimus' Crystal Interface Glowed again. This poem appeared on the screen:

For Bea

You are the flower I've been waiting for
the wild pink rose, the white lily, the pale golden tulip
the blossoming spring of Wayflower

From, a lowly artist-poet whose heart is filled with the flowers of you

Beautimus sighed. She communicated on her Interface to Lucas one word, "Beautiful."

Dr. Lucas Potamway wrote a love poem just for me. No one has ever done that, not ever. I will treasure this poem for the rest of my life.

CHAPTER TWENTY-ONE

THE NEXT MORNING, Beautimus taught the second half of her Earth History Class. On her walk to the university, she ran into the lovely Angeline, the chinchilla who'd sold the shar pendant to Beautimus at the fair.

"Good Morning, Ms. Bea. Nice day, isn't it?"

"Yes indeed it is, Angeline."

"I see you are wearing the pendant. Have you discovered its magical property?"

"I think so. Does it detect another's genuine love?"

"Yes and no. It cannot detect another's love unless the wearer was born with a gift."

"But, I have no gift, Angeline. That's one reason Lady Rhianna never named me a Wise Woman. To be a Wise Woman I'd have had to have been born with an innate ability to create magic, been gifted with clairaudience, clairsentience, or clairvoyance, or have some other natural propensity for making magic and predicting future events."

"Ms. Bea, there are many kinds of gifts, not all are the 'fortune telling' kind, or the gifts of magic. You were born with the 'gift of heart.' What this means is your heart is good. You have within you a natural ability for loving others."

"I do?"

"Yes, but what is important for you to understand is you cannot receive love from anyone unless love is within you first. Love seeks out Love. When two hearts connect the two 'companion loves' vibrate in exact timbre and pitch. That's the thrumming sensation you feel at times emanating from the pendant. When you come near someone who loves you, your pendant glows, yes?"

"Absolutely."

"What you are experiencing is the physical representation of two hearts responding to one another in accordance with the universal Law of Resonance. Without the gift of heart, when you are in the presence of love, the pendant would not intensify in warmth or vibration. It'd be nothing more than a pretty purple shar-stone that changes color in the sunlight. But, because you have the gift of heart, the pendant works its magic *for you.* You will find the stone serves you in other ways, too, Ms. Bea."

***

Her students had read the *Wayflower Quacker,* or had gotten word from someone, who'd gotten word from someone else, who'd gotten word from the finches about Belinda's arrest, and Beautimus' role in the recovery of the wand. Her students bloated with pride because of their celebrity professor. When she entered the classroom, they broke into applause. "Way to go, Ms. Bea." "We are proud of you." "You're so brave."

"Thank you all, but you must know I didn't accomplish this all on my own. Please do acknowledge the others, too, when you see them. They need to hear their roles were no less important than mine. Without everyone playing their part, and sometimes even risking their lives, the wand would still be gone.

Once again I have an overwhelming amount of information to cover this period. Everyone caught up with their assigned reading, I assume? Today we will cover the rest of the Ark II Mission, Life with the Hu Mans, the Meteor Disaster and subsequent Fall of Earthly Civilization. We'll also touch on Earth Customs and Traditions, a preview of an advanced course I hope you'll all register for next semester. Cicero, can you tell us all where we left off last class?"

"Yes, we were discussing what an honorable mission Ark II was to undertake because its sole objective was to save and preserve Hu Manity."

"Thank you, Cicero. Precisely. The Arc II, like the Arc I, landed in the Rift Valley on Earth on the continent of Africa." She turned to her map and indicated the whereabouts of the Rift Valley with a nod of her head. "Interestingly enough, thousands of years after the landing of the Ark II, human archeologists discovered the remains of one of the early Rendazians who had wandered off and became lost. She evidentially died in the wilderness alone. The crew spent months looking for her to no avail. Finally, they gave up the search. Her fossilized remains were well-preserved. The Hu Man archeologists were way off on their date assessment of on the age of her remains, and they were also wrong about the species they'd located...they mistakenly thought she was an early humanoid and named her 'Lucy.' She was a young ape, the daughter of one of the Ark II shipmen."

"I've heard that legend," said Cicero.

"It's not a legend. Our scientists inspected her remains remotely through a Crystal Interface, and the Earthly remains known as 'Lucy' are definitely the remains of little Zulu Spock, the daughter of the ship's first officer.

To continue, after the Ark II landing, the people of Rendaz began to colonize the Earth. The first settlers set up outposts all over the planet. Some were rather impressive. You can still see remains of their structures in what is known as Egypt, Mexico, Central and South America, and in Europe. Some in Asia, too. A few are nearly intact, such as the Pyramids of Giza humans consider archeological wonders. To this day, people of Earth cannot figure out how those pyramids could have been built without sophisticated tools and the use of mortar humans need to construct their less enduring buildings. There are similar structures such as those in the Yucatan Peninsula of Mexico, and in Peru. There are many hundreds more humans have yet to discover and excavate. Ancient Rendazians built these structures with the help of trÁined humans we needed because so many of us lack opposable thumbs.

We planted fruiting trees and bushes, and furnished seeds for thousands of vegetable varieties, and grains not known on Earth prior to our arrival. We taught early humans the basics of agriculture. We populated the earth with our own species, each uniquely suited to certain geographical areas…that's how elephants came to be in Asia and Africa, Cougars came to be in the Americas, Koalas in Australia, Pandas in China, and so on. We instructed and protected the humans, provided them with sustenance and knowledge, shared what we could with the goal of ensuring the survival of the species.

We established schools to teach humans how to read and write. We taught them poetry, music and art. We offered classes in science and mathematics. Our human students proved quick learners. We developed a fondness for them, and they in turn, developed a fondness for us. Some of us became quite close to humans, wonderful friends, actually, the dogs in particular. Dogs soon became known as *Man's Best friend.* They still are. After a while, the humans knew what we knew, and were so quick and clever they surpassed us in philosophy, art, and poetry. They were, and remain, an extraordinary species. For thousands of years we co-existed in peace as equals in mutual admiration and respect, partners, often close friends, Rendazians and humans side-by-side. Then the meteor hit. Can anyone tell me about the meteor?"

Several students raised their paws, muzzles, claws, wings, tails or trunks eager to be chosen to tell the story of the meteor. Cicero, of course, waived his paw. Beautimus searched the room for students who had rarely spoken in class. In the back was a pony named "Charming Granite" who, next to Jackie, had the reputation as the shyest in class. She had her tail raised a little, enough to indicate that if chosen—and she hoped *not* to be chosen—but if she were, since she knew the story well, she'd be willing to share it with the class.

"Charming, please come to the front and tell us the story of the meteor. Don't be nervous. It'll be fine."

Beautimus backed away motioning to the pony. "Please tell us how the meteor forever changed the dynamics between humans and Rendazians."

"I'm very nervous about talking in front of people, so please bear with me as I get through this, but one of my ancestors was on Rendaz when the meteor hit. He surreptitiously sent his observations back to Rendaz before the Council presumed him dead. No one knows for sure what happened to him, but what we do know is that for thousands of years, and during his lifetime, Rendazians failed to acknowledge his work. Without thought, everyone just assumed he'd continue to relay his experiences. Then one day his communications ceased. But, given what I read in our family accounts, I can share some things that maybe not everyone knows."

"Charming, was your ancestor Täkenfore?" asked Beautimus.

"Yes, Dr. Täkenfore Granite."

"This is exciting. I studied him in graduate school. Students, it is because of Charming's ancestor, Dr. Granite, we know so much about what happened right after the meteor hit. Please continue, Charming."

"In those ancient times, which we refer to now as 'the good old days' when humans and Rendazians lived as equals, a tragic natural event occurred that forever altered life on the blue planet. A meteor, approximately ten kilometers wide, slammed into Earth off the coast of what is known as the

Yucatan Peninsula. Soon afterwards, every dinosaur on earth perished. What most of you may not know is that even after thousands of years of searching, from what we know now, Rendaz is possibly the only planet in the universe where dinosaurs exist."

A pterodactyl, Leslie Ann, gasped.

Beautimus responded, "Yes, Leslie Ann. It is a sorry fact that we've not yet discovered dinosaurs on any other planet. Apparently, dinosaurs only existed here and on Earth. We have found other animals in the universe....dogs and cats seem to live on many planets, for example. They are almost everywhere there is intelligent life, along with ants, flies, midges, cockroaches and dung beetles. Additionally, equine species live on other planets and survive in some surprising environments. For example, humans do not know this, but there is a species of horse barely over a millimeter long living on Mars. Enough from me. Please continue, Charming."

"This catastrophic event resulted in widespread extinction. The resulting toxic cloud blocked the sun and covered the planet creating a dark and frigid atmosphere, hostile to plants and all other species. Then greenhouse gases accumulated beneath the dust cloud, generating sweltering heat. Freezing temperatures followed by extreme heat created a nearly unbearable condition for the survival of life. Within a few short years nearly 70% of all living things on Earth perished. What Humans do not know is that the meteor also carried a very specific virus that affected only Rendazians. Nearly every Rendazian on Earth fell ill from the virus, and many died. When the survivors recovered, most of them had lost their memory, and every single Rendazian who'd caught the virus from the largest whale to the smallest mite had completely lost capacity for speech.

My ancestor survived, retÁined his memory and his ability to speak, only because he lived as a hermit in a deep cavern, well away from anyone else. As I said, for years he lived alone and communicated his observations to us via his crystal interface. The authority made plans for a Rendazian rescue party, but because of the toxic cloud and the unstable Earth conditions, by the time we could launch the rescue ship, he had vanished. Also, our scientists expressed great concern the virus may still be viable, and might be still be so, because even today since there are no talking species on Earth except for humans and a few parrots. Our scientists did not want to bring the virus back to Rendaz and risk infecting our species here. Too dangerous. Evidentially, my ancestor's Interface ceased functioning before he perished. He took his hooves, dipped them in red clay, and did his best to continue to record his observations via his drawings on the walls of the cavern. He even drew figures of humans actually killing and eating animals."

"Oh, my Goddesses, killing and eating the flesh of animals. That's horrific," said a Gila monster, John Wayne, in the back of the room.

"Shhhhhh," "shhhhh," "shhhhh." Several students shushed John Wayne.

"Thousands of Earth years later, humans discovered his cave drawings and assumed they were made by early humans. Now humans and Rendazians question how other cavern paintings discovered on Earth might have come about."

"Thank you, Charming. You do know some things we didn't know about those early days on Earth. I never knew about the cave drawings, did any of you?" No one raised their claw, paw, tail, wing, whatever.

"Let's all give a hand to Charming for sharing with us today. I'll take it from here."

Charming made her way back to her place as her classmates applauded.

"Since food was scarce and becoming more so, to survive

many species had to find other sources of nutrition…each other." A few students recoiled. "Terrible, I know. First humans developed crude weapons, and later more sophisticated weapons, and began hunting and eating other species. Eventually, because of competition among humans for resources, they developed this thing called 'war' where they kill each other out of fear of inadequate stores, or from greed wanting to own and control the rest of the world's resources. As far as we know, humans are the only species in our universe who wage war.

What is sad is that because of the lack of food, species other than humans began hunting and eating one another, too. Some species evolved long teeth and claws, and developed violent predator instincts. They hunted and killed other animals as food. Others evolved hyper swiftness, hyper awareness, and natural camouflage to protect themselves from the predators. Those animals developed prey instincts.

Animals killed and ate humans, too, and still do occasionally. But the most dangerous of all predators then and now are humans. In fact, humans killed off many species to the point of extinction. Do you know, for example, there are no more Do-Do birds anywhere on the face of Earth? Not even in human zoos where often endangered species are protected will you find a Do-Do. Humans wiped them out."

Some students shook their heads, and clucked or tisked.

"Other species on Earth are gone forever, too, and many are endangered."

Cicero stood. "Eating, enslaving, trophy hunting and killing off entire species. Why do we let these evil humans survive? Why not eradicate them? Or, why not at least build an Ark III and bring the other species back home where they'll be protected, Ms. Bea?"

"Cicero, these questions have been asked many times before, and are still being asked. There are no simple answers, but I'll do my best to explain. First of all, there is still danger of the virus that Charming spoke of. For obvious reasons, we can't risk such a virus on Rendaz. Beyond that, so many of the other species on Earth, especially the big cats, raptors, some snakes, sharks, canines, bears and others have become unpredictable, vicious, violent and dangerous."

"You mean, they became too much like humans?" said Cicero.

"Humans, even with their violent ways, are as I've mentioned before, still a magnificent species. If you enjoy streaming films, books, and music from Earth, as I do, you'll discover they possess great intelligence, creative capacity, and the ability to make beauty. I know there are those on Rendaz who disagree with me, but in my opinion, it'd be a sad thing if the universe were to lose its Hu Manity."

Did I answer your question, Cicero?"

"Yes, Ms. Bea. Thank you."

Class ended, the students filed out, and Beautimus left for home. She had a tension headache and hoped Agnes and Applecheeks made nice cold cucumber soup for supper. As she walked out of class, some of her students, a brace of ducks, a skein of geese, and a clutch of chickens were debating that age-old question: "what came first, the chicken or the egg?"

CHAPTER TWENTY-TWO

AS BEAUTIMUS WALKED the path home, she came across a stunning field of red poppies shimmering under the pale light of the setting suns. She took in their beauty, reveled in it. A mutation of wood thrush in a bowyakka tree sang wordless Earth melodies in perfect harmony. They sang *Bach's Brandenburg Concerto Number 4, the little Fugue in G minor.* A slight breeze rustled the leaves of the yarran trees and carried to her the scent of lilacs, honeysuckle and hyacinth. Beautimus' headache eased and she felt as though everything was right in her world again.

When she neared her home, sitting in the Silver Mulga sapling sat Samuel, but not alone. He and Petunia snuggled side-by-side on a slender branch and cuddled with no visible space between them. Lost in one another, they did not even notice Beautimus as she approached. She passed on as to not disturb them. *Well, I think Mr. Sam has finally met his match in Petunia.*

The next morning, as she lapped her tea, Beautimus' Crystal Interface pulsated and thrummed. She tapped on the screen with her muzzle, and answered.

"Good morning, my girl. I'll be back next week. I look forward to our date on Sunday. We are still on, aren't we?"

"I can't wait." If Beautimus' shar-pendant could have glowed any brighter it would have lit up the whole of Rendaz on a moonless night.

"I'll see you on Sunday, then. Bye for now."

"Bye for now."

***

The following morning the headline for *The Wayflower Quacker* read:

Trial Date Set for Wand Theft Suspects

The Butterfly Council and Trees set the trial date for the three suspects involved in the theft of the Wand of Fortuna. Belinda, Jake and Heatherton will be tried the first day of the new moons in a closed courtroom. Because of the high profile of the trial, there will be no Crystal Interface coverage. All but one member of the press will be barred from the proceedings. The Guardians have taken witness statements remotely. The Captain of the Wand Guard, Steven D. Lobos will stand sentry at the door of the Court House, along with select members of the Wand Guard. Steven assures the press, "These suspects will not escape during trial. Not on my watch." At which point he put up his hackles, bared his teeth and growled. Following the trial, in a special edition, The Wayflower Quacker will provide an official outcome report.

Beautimus, Samuel and Agnes had already provided their official witness statements, so would not be questioned in Court, common in Rendazian court proceedings. Agnes and Samuel were disappointed, but Beautimus felt relieved. She had other things on her mind such as Lucas, Lucas and more Lucas. She prepared for a date, her first real date as an adult. Her last love affair had been nothing more than a few passionate trysts with a striking young cad behind a copse of whirrakee wattle trees. She had been a young lass way back then, a teenager by Earth standards. She had been desperately in love with him, but he only wanted between her haunches. That was it. Her only "love affair."

There had been brief "flirtations" as she referred to them. She had a few dates with an arrogant barrister who talked of nothing but himself. At one point during dinner as he went on and on about all the trials he'd won, what a great sportsman he was, and about all the beautiful women he'd bedded, she casually said, "I can do a handstand, twirl a hula hoop on one leg, and hum Ave Maria through my nose while wearing lacy pink Earth woman panties on my head."

He'd missed what she said because of his fabulous stories about his fabulous self. She could have balanced on her front legs and did what she said could do right there during dinner and he wouldn't have noticed. He kept talking, and talking, and talking using the words, "me, me, me, I, I, I" in every sentence. He never once asked a question about her life.

She had a date or two with a plumber who was sweet enough, but dumb as a stump. Buford the Bloodhound could carry on a better conversation than this plumber could. Although she basically liked the fellow, and found him rather cute, she couldn't see herself in a long-term relationship with him so she cut it off early. Beautimus heard he ended up marrying a Ph.D., a neuroscientist, of all things.

Beautimus had one other date more recently with a nerdy Crystal Interface scientist Samuel had set her up with. The Scientist had the hots for her, and on their first date did his best all night to get in between her haunches, but she wasn't even lukewarm about him. Dull, tedious, too young and too horny for her, Beautimus regretted the date from the get-go. He was a mama's boy, too, who had always lived at home, and never wanted his own place. "Why should I have my own abode, when I can live with Mother who does everything for me?" He told her.

When he wasn't trying to get Beautimus into the straw, he talked about his mommy. His conversation alternated between, "You know, Bea, you've got one sweet looking rump on you. If you and I were to hit the straw for a few hours, I'd give you the ride of your life, pretty lady," and "Mother doesn't like any of the women I bring home, but I think she might like you. Mother makes the best pea-flower soup you ever tasted. In fact, no woman in the world one can cook like my mama."

After their first date, when he moved in for what threatened to be a sloppy, wet, kiss, she backed away. "I don't think this is going to work out." She ducked into her abode, closing the flap behind her. She had no idea what happened to him afterwards. *He might be with his mommy eating pea flower soup right now.* Therefore, this relationship with Lucas was the first authentic adult, grown-up real romance she'd enjoy with an authentic adult, grown-up, real man.

***

In Beautimus' "Comparative Culture" class, she taught the differences between Rendazian and Earthian legal system. Since Rendaz is not the utopia one might think, meaning most of its inhabitants suffer the same frailties as Earthly humans, there is a good but simple legal system in place. There are thirty-five straightforward laws on Rendaz that all children memorize from the time they are able to first speak, including the seven "Taboos." Belinda, Jake and Heatherton would be tried for breaking Rendazian taboos. If convicted, they'd all be banished, and maybe even shunned, the worst possible of all punishments.

Monkey and Ape tribes hotly contest the Law of Fidelity. It reads that legally mated Rendazians cannot be unfaithful to their partners. Unlike geese and some other animals, apes and monkeys are not monogamous by nature. They like lots of sex with lots of partners, lots of the time. Monkeys would copulate in their sleep if they could. Of course, Monkeys, like everyone else, have the choice not to take mating vows, then they can copulate all they like with as many willing unmated monkeys of either sex they choose. As Beautimus said to Samuel, "Obviously, besides being persistent and always randy, monkeys like to have their cake and eat it, too."

All this thinking about sex and Lucas meant Beautimus pushed Belinda's trial to the backburner.

CHAPTER TWENTY-THREE

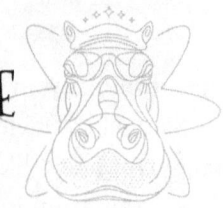

BEAUTIMUS SPENT HER days leading to the trial teaching classes, writing, swimming in the river, and talking with Lucas on the Crystal Interface for hours on end. She visited with Samuel and Lizzy, and regularly checked in on Rhianna. The old crane suffered from some mysterious malady, even though it became apparent that her feathers were growing out, but whenever Beautimus brought up the subject of her health, Rhianna cut her off.

"How are you doing, Lady Rhianna? You look a little tired."

"I'm fine, Bea. Tell me more about Lucas."

That'd be it.

Things progressed between Samuel and Petunia. Samuel still pretended to be a "skirt hound," but since that afternoon when Beautimus saw them getting cozy on the silver mulga tree, Beautimus never noticed Samuel so much as look at another praying mantis woman. One day, as they walked together to check on Rhianna, Beautimus said to Samuel, "So, Sam. Looks like things are getting pretty serious between you and Petunia."

"You know me, Bea. Mate 'em and leave 'em is my motto. I'm having a little fun with Petunia right now, but I'm keeping my options open."

"I noticed you two seem to be spending a lot of time together, Sam."

"That's because you aren't around 24/7. You don't know everything. You only *think* you do."

"Why do you have to act like a pribbline boblyne, Sam? I didn't say I know everything. I'm only making an observation."

Right about that time, the sexy Cheeky, flew by. As she

passed Samuel, she slowed down so Samuel could get a good look at her nicely formed hind legs. She wagged her end a tiny bit, and looked right at him, and winked but Samuel behaved as though Cheeky wasn't there at all. That's when Beautimus knew with certainty that her friend, Samuel S. Goodwings, was in love.

The following week, Beautimus taught her Earth History class, her Long Class. She'd cover the heady topic of Earthly religions.

"Cicero, can you tell me who the first deities were on Earth and why?"

"Yes. Rendazians."

"That is so. Please explain why."

"Because we'd dropped from the sky in starships, and were a species primitive Hu Man had never encountered. They assumed we were all Gods and Goddesses."

"Thank you, Cicero. We never encouraged humans to think of us as deities, and we didn't really want them to, but we have always supported every species' freedom of religion. Humans are known as particularly strong-willed and will do and think as they want regardless of anyone else's wishes.... anyway, thinking we were Gods is why so many of the earliest Earth gods and goddesses look like Rendazians, or are fashioned after half-human and half-Rendazian species. The ancient Sumerians, Celts, Romans, Egyptians, all worshipped Rendazian gods at one time. Are you aware of the Earth deity, Ganesh, who Hindus still worship today? Ganesh has the body of a human and the head of an elephant. Humans worshipped Baal in older times, a golden bull, who some humans revered even some time after 'The Fall,' the period ushered in by the meteor. There were many cultures, from the beginning of our landing on Earth, whose religions honor Rendazian species, tigers, birds, snakes, cows, as well as beetles, buffalo, coyotes, fish, whales, seals, butterflies, crocodiles and even hippos. In fact, all manner of Rendazian species were worshipped as deities in human culture at one time or another, and in some cultures, still are. In the Earth country of Egypt," Beautimus turned to her map and indicated the geographical point of Egypt, "there are many deities in the likeness of Rendazians. Anuket, Hedetet, Apis, Hatmehit, and many others, all of whom are either Rendazian or depicted as human with Rendazian heads. The Egyptians particularly revered felines. There are three or more feline goddesses, including Sekhmet, Bast and Bastet."

At that, a blue-eyed white Persian cat, Maybelle, interrupted. "Of course Egyptians revere cats. Why would they not? Is there any Rendazian more beautiful, more intelligent, more agile, or more graceful than a cat, especially a pure-bred?"

"Maybelle, in my classroom please put up your paw when you wish to speak, but beyond that, what you are saying has little relevance to the discussion at hand. Shall we continue?"

The cat let out a loud hiss.

"Excuse me, Maybelle? Did you hiss at me?"

"Ms. Bea, I think it's important to acknowledge the lofty role of cats in human culture and Earthly religion. You are glossing over the topic of cats. If there are three or more cat deities in Egypt, then what I'm saying is anything *but* irrelevant."

"You are interrupting my lecture, which is rude to the students trying to listen and learn, but beyond that I do not tolerate *any* kind of disrespectful or hostile behavior in my classroom. Growling, baring teeth, raising hackles and hissing are not permitted, not in my class, not ever. Please leave now and I shall decide later if I will permit you to return."

Maybelle plastered her ears to her head, and with her tail down, she trotted out of the classroom.

"To continue with our discussion on Earthly religions, 'The Fall,' as we discussed last week occurred as a result of the meteor strike, which not only altered the relationship between humans and Rendazians, and led to flesh eating, fear and war, but it also effected the way humans worshipped. After the meteor, humans began to perceive Rendazians as 'lesser beings,' as food, slaves, pets, and so forth. In most cultures, Rendazian gods became much maligned, and the female aspect of the divine, The Goddess, disappeared almost completely."

Cicero raised his paw, "Yes, Cicero?"

"Wouldn't the humans feel disrespected by what you're teaching in this class, Ms. Bea? I mean, you are talking about their sacred beliefs. If they heard...you know, how'd they feel about the way we discuss their religions?"

"Cicero, thank you for your thoughtful question. I'm not in any way contemptuous of Earth religions or their deities. Our job as educators, historians, anthropologists, and archeologists is to report, without judgment, what we have observed for millennia. I will not interject my own opinions." Beautimus paused, and stifled a yawn. "I need to clear my head, and it looks like you all need a respite, too. Let's take a break. We'll reconvene in twenty minutes."

The class filed out. Beautimus strolled through campus. She passed the auditorium where another kind of class took place today. A handsome, charismatic, Giant Anole Croaker, Ziggy Robbins, a popular motivational speaker, had rented The Forum, the university's auditorium. When not in use, Dr. Pimbly frequently rented The Forum to citizens of the community for events and seminars, an effective way to bring in revenue for the school. Today, Ziggy Robbins led a seminar for which attendees paid an absurd number of Rendazian Glow Seeds to attend. On an A-Frame board outside the door to The Forum, advertised:

SEMINAR TODAY BY THE FAMOUS ZIGGY ROBBINS

How To Get Whatever You Want

From Whomever You Want,

Whenever You Want It,

As Soon As You Want It.

You, too, can learn to believe and achieve massively better optimal options for 'zestful life-enhanced days'™

Beautimus stuck her head in to listen. Participants from all over the Wayflower District, there for the privilege to learn "how to achieve optimal options for better unfathomably zesty life-enhanced days, and how to get whatever they wanted from whomever they wanted, whenever they wanted it, as soon as they wanted it," packed the forum.

On stage, perched a wobbly table stacked high with the Ziggy Robbins's bestselling book "Achieving Zestful Life-Enhanced Days ©." A Crystal Interface projected an image of Ziggy's face ten feet high onto a white screen. Adjacent to his image were these words:

B-elieve

(and)

A-chieve

M-assively

B-etter

O-ptimal

O-ptions

(for)

Z-estful

L-ife

E-nhanced

D-ays ™

Ziggy stood on a high platform and shouted to the audience through a microphone. "Are you feeling it?"

"Yeah," the crowd shouted back.

"ARE YOU FEELING IT?"

"Yeah."

"I MEAN.... DO....YOU....gesturing to the crowd.... FEEL....IT....TODAY?"

"YEAH!"

The Lizard wrote on a white board:

8-Steps to Achieving Zestful Life-Enhanced Days

1. Embrace your all-encompassing emptiness

2. Accept your vapid spiritual nothingness

3. Acknowledge your inner dissonance

4. Re-align your discordant energy sources

5. Become the essence of nil

6. Rebirth yourself and re-compartmentalize your inner landscape

7. Deconstruct your negative patterning, and...

8. Substitute positive realigned solution-oriented positivity through self-environmentalization.

Ziggy pointed to each of the steps and read them to the crowd. When he came to Number 8 he shouted, "Are you truly ready to substitute positive realigned solution-oriented positivity through self-environmentalization to achieve zestful enhanced days?"

"YEAH," the crowd shouted in unison. The audience members worked themselves into an excited froth, all of them honored to be in the presence of Ziggy Robbins, the best of the best in the motivational industry, each of them convinced their lives would now forever change in a massively better way. They couldn't wait to shell out more Rendazian Glow Seeds for Ziggy's next seminar.

Beautimus sensed a presence beside her, and her shar-stone warmed. Lucas. She turned her head, and there he stood. She bowed in greeting. "I was so hoping you'd be on campus today, Lucas. Welcome back."

Can you believe people actually *pay* to be bamboozled?" Lucas laughed. "I knew you were teaching your Long Class today. But, I couldn't wait until Sunday to see you. I got in way too late to disturb you last night, so I thought I'd come in to complete some paperwork and I stuck around in hopes I might run into you."

The two talked for a few minutes, and a few minutes more, and a few minutes more until Beautimus said, "Great Mother Genesis. I'm late! I've got to get back to class, Lucas. My students are waiting for me."

"Okay, sweetie. I'll see you on Sunday, then."

He called me 'sweetie.' No one has ever called me 'sweetie.'

When Beautimus returned to class, everyone sat at their desks, waiting. She'd wondered how many of them had seen her outside of The Forum talking to Lucas.

After class, Beautimus took the long way home. She needed to clear her head after the intense lecture, but after her unexpected meeting with Lucas, she was in a particularly good mood. Her mind focused on love, sex and children.

As she rounded the corner near a large porknut tree, coming at her in the opposite direction was a sow boar, Lotus Bud Bacon, who had recently given birth to a child, a boy. She pushed his pram with her snout.

"Hello, Lotus. Congratulations on the birth of your son. Kevin, is his name, right? How nice your Soo-ee has a little brother to play with. May I have a look?"

"Certainly. This is his first time out, and he seems to really enjoy the forest, but he's a bit tired. This walk has worn him out."

Beautimus bent over the pram and peered at a sweet boar piglet, chocolate and cream striped, with tiny pink ears and the cutest little nose. The baby nestled in for a nap.

"He's so precious."

"Perhaps one day you'll have a baby of your own."

Beautimus looked away and hung her head.

"Are you okay?" the sow asked.

A tear slipped from Beautimus' eye.

CHAPTER TWENTY-FOUR

IN A FEW days Beautimus would soon be on a picnic with the man of her dreams. She knew where they were going, Sweetwater Pond, where not too long before she'd sobbed all night thinking Lucas wanted nothing to do with her. She spent all morning preparing for her date. She bathed in the river and asked Applecheeks and Agnes to rub rose-scented macadamia nut oil into her hide. She applied cheek rouge, not too much, but a little, and asked the squirrels to tie a lavender colored silk ribbon to her tail. She turned and pronounced, "This is as good as it gets."

Agnes said, "You-look-lovely-Bea-I've-never-seen-you-so-happy-Apple-and-I-know-that-Lucas-will-find-you-completely-irresistable-that-tail-ribbon-is-so-fetching-and-I'm-glad-you-went-easy-on-the-rouge-will-you-and-Lucas-want-tea-before-the-picnic-or-after?"

"I don't know. Maybe afterwards, Agnes. Let's see how the day goes. Thank you for asking."

Lucas appeared outside her abode. He called to her. "Hey, my girl, are you up for our picnic?"

Beautimus composed herself and pushed through the door flap.

Lucas' eyed her from her muzzle to her feet. "You look lovely."

She blushed and cast her eyes down. "Thank you, Lucas. I'm so happy to see you."

"I'm glad to see you, too. *Really* glad to see you. Shall we walk?"

Lucas had hired a proboscis monkey named Jethro, who'd later become Lucas' permanent household help, to come along and set up the picnic. Jethro rode on Lucas' back balancing an enormous willow basket holding abundant delicacies for two good sized hippos. As they strolled beside the silver wattle soap bushes and beneath the corki canji trees they shared stories of one another's past loves and lives.

"I won't lie to you, Bea. There have been others, and a few I've even loved. I was married once when young, but it didn't last. That was well over 100 years ago, though. What about you?"

"I don't date much, Lucas. I've simply not found anyone...that is until now...I've cared to spend much time with. I'm happy on my own. I was in love once, so many years ago it hardly counts. I had a brief affair when no more than a child, really."

"What happened?"

"He left. I haven't seen him since. After nursing my broken heart, I got over him and moved on. There's nothing much else to tell."

They passed a congress of salamanders clinging to the trunk of a southern salwood tree. One called to them. "Perfect day for a picnic, Mr. Lucas and Ms. Bea. You two enjoy yourselves, now."

"Thank you," said Beautimus.

A clamor of rooks flew overhead, and one called down. "Good day, Ms. Bea and Mr. Lucas."

Roberto, a spunky iguana with an attitude, greeted them on the path. "Hey," he said. As he passed by, he looked up at Lucas. He raised his front foot as if he wanted to high five. "Way to go, dude."

Beautimus' had never been able to keep anything about her relationship with Lucas under wraps, even a simple picnic. Everyone knew.

As they rounded the corner they came to Sweetwater Pond. Clear water fell over mossy rocks making a noisy splash. Lazy black and orange Koi lounged just beneath the surface. The Koi paid no attention to the two hippos and the monkey setting up lunch in the meadow beneath the currawong, rainbow gum and moondyne trees. Scarlet hibiscus and deep rust-orange canna lilies bloomed. Freesia and wild iris scented the air—a perfect day for a picnic indeed.

Jethro leapt off Lucas's back, dragging the woven baskets with him. He pulled out a forest green damask picnic cloth. He unfolded it, straightened it, and smoothed the wrinkles with his paws. He pulled out a slender silk bud vase, dipped it into the pond and put in it one perfect white rose barely in bloom and one deep pink rose bud, then placed the vase with the two roses center of the cloth. He pulled out a large covered cut glass pail and removed the lid. It was filled to the brim with sparkling guava blossom honey mead.

"If I didn't know better, Dr. Potamway, I'd think you may have intention of getting me tipsy."

Lucas threw back his head and laughed. "I only want you to relax a little and have a good time, my girl."

Jethro pulled out two clear glass large bowls and two large matching platters. He filled the bowls with crisp cucumbers, sweet sunglow tomatoes, tender purple basil leaves, and fresh crumbled goat cheese. On the platters, he arranged whole honey dew melons and seedless watermelons, peeled bananas and a pile of fresh pineapple slices.

"This is an incredible feast, and these roses are stunning. Thank you for all of this, Lucas."

"Only the best for you."

With the picnic unloaded, and the hippos settled in. Jethro took off swinging through the trees. Beautimus and Lucas sat near one another lapping mead from the glass pail, dribbling some of the icy stuff off their maws and onto their hides. They didn't care. They talked, canoodled, and gazed into one another's eyes like two loved-addled school kids crushing on each other. After a little while, Lucas moved next to Beautimus so his haunch pressed against hers. She thought her shar-pendant would melt from the warmth of him.

Lucas said, "Bea, look at me." When she turned her head toward him, he kissed her. Not a sweet little peck, but a deep, searching passionate kiss. Beautimus kissed back. *The heck with the shar-pendant. I'm the one who is heating up now...and this is no hot flash.*

Then he kissed her a second time with even more passion. Beautimus had never been kissed like that. She believed if she died at that moment, Lucas' kiss would have made her life worthwhile.

When they at last broke apart, Lucas closed his eyes. "You take my breath away, Beautimus Potamus."

After the picnic, as the suns began to set, and the afternoon air turned a little chilly, Jethro returned to pack the goods. Lucas walked Beautimus back home. They ambled side-by-side touching one another the entire time. As they reached the door to her abode, she invited him for tea. He said, "I'd love that, sweetheart, but I've got a big morning tomorrow. I'm meeting with Dr. Pimbly in person and I need to prepare. But....I have to see you again, as soon as possible....say, directly after my meeting? Can we arrange it?"

"Oh, I think so," said Beautimus.

Lucas kissed Beautimus again, a longing kiss. "I'll see you tomorrow after my meeting with Dr. Pimbly, my girl."

"Tomorrow, then, Lucas." She didn't walk through the flap that covered her doorway. She floated through.

Agnes and Apple had peeked through the flap to witness the kiss, and were dancing when Beautimus entered through the door. "We-saw-Lucas-kiss-you-we-didn't-mean-to-be-nosy-but-we-wanted-to-see-him-he's-a-super-handsome-hippo-Bea-and-seems-so-gallant-and-what-a-nice-voice-so-you-are-going-to-see-him-tomorrow-too-then?-we-are-so-happy-for-you-want-tea?"

"No thank you, Agnes. I don't need or want anything right now. I think I'll take a dip in the river." After her return, Beautimus settled into her pillows to grade papers when her Crystal Interface buzzed and pulsated. When she answered, on the screen appeared:

For Bea Again

I am netted by your music.

Your voice more soothing

than the cooing of a morning loon.

Your heart sings to my heart

forever lost in your song.

— Lucas

Beautimus wrote back. "Thank you for everything, Dr. Lucas Potamway, for the beautiful poem, for the picnic, for being a part of my existence. Today was magnificent. "

As she walked back to her pillows, her Crystal Interface buzzed again. She almost tripped herself running back to answer it. "Lucas?" Silence.

"Who is Lucas?" asked a young female voice.

"Sorry, I thought you were someone else. Who is this?"

"This is Cassie, Mom." Silence. "Mom?"

Beautimus' went weak in the knees. "Cassie, is this *really* you?"

CHAPTER TWENTY-FIVE

BEAUTIMUS POTAMUS HAD a secret. Her first love resulted in a teenage pregnancy. Her aunt and uncle were supportive and offered to help Beautimus with her baby. But, Beautimus had concerns her child would be a burden on her Aunt and Uncle, already saddled with enough responsibility having taken Beautimus in after her mother's death and her father's disappearance.

Aunt Meg and Uncle Phelan didn't have much in the way of Glow Seeds back then. They were hard-pressed to feed themselves and Beautimus, and now there'd be *another* mouth to feed? No, she couldn't do that to them. She also knew she was too young to handle being a mother. Beautimus decided to go to the Oceanic District, have her baby there, and hand over her child to a loving couple she'd met through her Crystal Interface. They agreed to foster the baby until Beautimus could return for her. It was the most difficult decision she'd ever made in her life.

Beautimus decided to never speak the name of her baby's father because rampallion buttholes like that don't even deserve a name. He had abandoned Beautimus the second he found out she was carrying his child, scooting off to some far away district never to be seen again. Broken hearted, pregnant, and only a child herself, Beautimus set off alone to the Oceanic district to have her baby.

The day her bubbit calved Beautimus fell in love all over again, this time with her pale grey baby girl. She named her Cassiopeia. "I love you, Cassie. When I'm a little older, and have a real job, I'll come back and get you and we'll have a good life together, I promise."

The day she weaned Cassie and handed her over to the nice couple, Mr. and Mrs. Bopotamus, the baby wailed for her mama. Beautimus left, the cries of her bubbit fading with each step away. Her body wracked with sobs, and more sobs. She sobbed on and off every day for years. She often sent Crystal Interface messages to the Bopotamus' to inquire after Cassie.

"She's doing fine. She said her first word, today." Mrs. Bopotamus said.

"Really, what did she say?"

"Flower."

"How sweet."

"Yes. She's very sweet."

"Do you tell her about me?"

"Not yet. We don't want to confuse her."

"When you do, please let Cassie know that I love her, and I'll come visit as soon as I can, will you?"

"When she's ready, we will do that."

"Thank you for taking care of my little girl. You're angels."

Many seasons went on like this. When Beautimus asked to talk to Cassie, Mrs. or Mr. Bopotamus would say, "Not today, but, when she's ready, we'll tell her you called."

Beautimus wanted what was best for Cassie. She knew the Bopotamus' were well-off, and they were good to Cassie, so she didn't argue with them about talking to her little girl. She would have gone to visit Cassie, but she had no money, no means to get there, and didn't want to take her Uncle and Aunt's Glow Seeds. They'd already paid for her journey, and room and board all those months gestating. Instead she called and called and called.

She finished Mrs. Primjay's Primary School, and entered the Rendazian University Wayflower Campus where she studied Earth History. She secured a part-time job as a teaching assistant. As Beautimus began to earn real money she gave some to her aunt and uncle, and saved the rest so she could visit her little girl. When she'd accumulated enough, she took a hiatus from work and school to see her daughter. After days of walking, she arrived at the doorstep of the Bopotamus' with a little rag doll in her satchel for Cassiopeia.

Mr. Bopotamus answered the door but did not invite Beautimus to enter. He said, "Well, ah, you are, ah, looking quite well, Beautimus."

"Thank you. May I see Cassie?" Her knees trembled with anticipation.

"Oh, I don't know."

"What do you mean 'you don't know'? I've come a long way to visit my daughter. You knew I'd be here. What's going on?"

"To tell you the truth, Beautimus, she doesn't know about you. She thinks Mrs. Bopotamus is her mother."

Beautimus went cold with shock. "You were to tell Cassie about me. Are you saying in all these years you've never spoken of me to her, *never?*"

"We intended to, Beautimus. It never seemed the right time, and, well, we didn't want her to be confused, you know."

"I want to see Cassie right now."

"Of course, Beautimus, but don't be disappointed if she doesn't recognize you. Give her some time. Maybe in a few years when she's old enough to handle it, we can let her know you are her biological mother and arrange regular visits."

"No, not visits, Mr. Bopotamus. We agreed as soon as I could I'd bring Cassie home with me to raise her. Don't tell me you don't remember. I didn't *give* Cassie to you. You agreed to foster her for a few years until I could grow up, finish school, get a job so I could care for her myself. I love Cassie. I never intended for anyone but me to be her mother."

"Let's discuss that later, shall we? Come into the house, and I'll call Mrs. Bopotamus."

He opened the door to permit Beautimus to enter and as he did so, he called out, "Brandie. We have a visitor to see Cassie."

Beautimus had never in her life seen a more lavish, more beautiful abode. It looked large from the outside, but the inside was nothing short of magnificent. Its multiple rooms with fine hewn wooden floors were covered in thick straw blended with white lavender buds, zillions of plush silk pillows, bees wax pillar candles five feet high, and crystal vases filled with roses. The Bopotamuses had many servants, monkeys, troodons, lemurs, and even a giant panda. *Wow, so this is how Cassie has been living. I can never give her anything like this, never.*

The elegant Brandie Bopotamus emerged from one of the rooms, and Cassie followed close behind, the most beautiful little girl on the planet of Rendaz. Beautimus dropped to her knees and cried out, "Oh, Cassie. Cassie. Come here. You've gotten so big. You are beautiful." Tears glazed Beautimus' eyes.

Cassie tucked in further behind, Mrs. Bopotamus. "Mama, who is that lady?"

Beautimus' heart cleaved in two. She didn't know what hurt more, to realize her little girl didn't know who she was, or to hear her call Mrs. Bopotamus 'Mama.' Beautimus had thousands of times imagined Cassie and her taking long walks together on the path through the forest, swimming in the river Kwa, sharing melons for breakfast, picnicking at the pond, going to the festivals, just the two of them, mother and daughter. In all her fantasies Cassie called Beautimus 'Mama." She rose to her feet. "Hello, Cassie. I'm an old friend of your mother's. I've heard so much about you that I wanted to meet you."

Cassie never stepped out from behind Mrs. Bopotamus. A few more awkward minutes passed. Mr. Bopotamus made himself scarce. Brandie asked Beautimus if she'd like a refreshment. "I can have Leslie, my lemur, prepare some hibiscus tea if you'd like. Leslie, come here, please."

"No thank you."

Beautimus said her goodbyes. She spent the night in the darkest part of the forest, alone and cold under a whistling thorn tree. She hurt so much she couldn't even cry. After a long while, fell into a dull sleep and stayed there until the cooing of a piteousness of turtle doves awakened her late the next morning. As she began a slow trek home, she asked a passing crested caracara to take the doll from her satchel and give it to the needy. *Cassie has a hundred dolls, each of them more beautiful than the next. She wouldn't want this one.*

Over the years, she went to see Cassie, each visit more painful than the last. Finally, she stopped going. But, every week, Beautimus called and talked to the Bopotamus' about Cassie, and every time, the same story. "Cassie is doing well. She's happy. She really doesn't want to speak to you right now."

Cassie wanted nothing to do with her.

After some moons had passed, Beautimus called. "I'm coming to see Cassie again, and this time I want her to know that I'm her mother, her true mother. I know you mean well, that you love Cassie, and she loves you. You've given her a good life. I'm grateful, but she needs to know who I am."

"I'm not sure that's a good idea. It will upset her." Mr. Bopotamus said.

"She needs to know her mother."

"I suggest we all tell her together."

"I'll be there next week."

Beautimus didn't know how Cassie would take the news. She'd be about thirteen or fourteen years in human age, and would understand what she could not have when younger. In any event, Beautimus, nervous as hellzabob, prepared to face her daughter for the first time as her "mother."

Brandie Bopotamus opened the door to admit Beautimus. "Cassie, please come here. Ms. Potamus has something she wants to share with you."

"Okay, Mom. Just a minute."

"Now, Cassie. It's important."

Cassie emerged from her room and Mrs. Bopotamus said, "You remember, Ms. Potamus, don't you?"

"Yeah. She used to come here sometimes. She's your old friend."

"Well *sort of.* Ms. Potamus has something she needs to share with you, something important."

Beautimus looked away, then back at Cassie. "I don't know how to say this, Cassie, so it's best I come out with it. I'm your real mother."

"What do you mean, my 'real mother'? Mom, what does she mean?"

"I was a teenager when you were born, Cassie. I loved you very much but I knew I was way too young to care for you, so I arranged with the Bopotamuses to take you for a while until I could grow up and get on my feet, then come get you."

"Bullcrap! Mom, what in hellzabob is this crazy lady talking about?"

"Cassie, don't talk like that. It's disrespectful. I want you to listen to Ms. Potamus."

"Are you telling me this is *true?*"

"Cassie, I know this is a shock, but yes, it's true," Mrs. Bopotamus said.

"So!" Cassie turned angrily toward Beautimus. "You got knocked up by some onion-eyed measle, didn't want your own baby and just gave your baby away. Is that it? And now you want that baby to accept you and love you, and go away, leaving all her friends to live with you happily forever. Is that what you expect? I don't *think* so, Lady."

"Cassie, I thought you should know the truth so you can make your own choice about your life," Beautimus said.

"*The truth*? That's priceless. You are the most self-absorbed, most selfish, most narcissistic person I've ever met. You dumped me because all you thought about was yourself. As for the rest of you?" She motioned with her head to all in the room. "You have been telling me lies my entire whole long life, and *now* you think I should know the truth? I hate you. I hate all of you."

She ran crying from the room with Mrs. Bopotamus running after her. "Cassie, come back, please."

"Go to hellzabob, *Mom*, if that's what I should call you, even."

"Don't you ever talk to me like that, Cassie."

"Oh, don't worry. I don't want to talk to you at all, and I'm not coming out until that lady goes away."

"Cassie!"

Mr. Bopotamus stuck his head into the room, and said to Beautimus, "Don't say I didn't try to warn you."

Beautimus kept tabs on her through the Bopotamuses, of course, but Cassie never wanted to talk to her. One day, Beautimus' Interface buzzed, and when she answered, she recognized Cassie. "Cassie. I'm *so glad* you called, sweetheart."

"I only called to tell you to never, ever, try to contact me again. I want nothing to do with you, not now, not ever. I had to choose between you and them, and I chose them. Leave me alone."

The Interface went dark. That was more than one hundred years ago. Beautimus had not talked to her daughter since that day, so it floored her when Cassie buzzed through on the Crystal Interface, and after all these years, called her "Mom."

"Cassie, I can't believe it's you."

"Yes, it's me. I wouldn't blame you if you didn't want to see me, but I need to talk to you in person."

"Of course I'd love to see you, Cassie. I can be in the Oceanic District in a couple of days. I'll leave right away."

"No need. I'm in Wayflower, downtown. I'm at an interface repair store called 'Can You Hear Me Now?' I borrowed the owner's Interface to contact you. Is there some place we can talk?"

Beautimus left a message for Lucas to let him know something important had come up, to please wait, she'd contact him as soon as she could, but that she'd not be able to see him today. *Mother Genesis, what am I going to tell Lucas?*

Cassie showed up at Beautimus' door an hour later, grown up, gorgeous, taller and lusher built than Beautimus, but she had Beautimus' eyes. Beautimus overflowed with love but resisted the impulse to run to her daughter and nuzzle her. "Come in, please, Cassie." Applecheeks and Agnes fetched a pail of mint tea and put out a bowl of grapes, and left to give the two women privacy.

"I hardly know where to begin," said Cassie.

"It's all right. I'm so glad you're here."

"Thank you, Mom. After ignoring you all these years, and telling you not to contact me, I thought maybe you wouldn't want anything to do with me."

"Cassie, I loved you when you felt like a little butterfly inside of me. When you were born was the happiest day of my life. My saddest day was when I had to leave you with Mr. and Mrs. Bopotamus. I always dreamed one day you'd want to come home. I never gave up on you. I've always loved you, and I always will love you unconditionally."

"Thank you, Mom. I know that. The Bopotamuses cared about me. They gave me so much. But, after I met you and found out you were my real mom, I never felt quite the same. Something changed for them, too. They had other bubbits together soon afterwards and they treated me a little differently. I have a step-brother and a step-sister. I love them, but after they were calved, even though I was technically in the family, I was always the outsider."

"I didn't know any of this, Cassie. I'm so sorry."

"…and they were judgmental, harsh, sometimes, especially

Mom, I mean my *other mom*, of course, not you. I was mad at you, so angry you calved me but didn't want me, and just… gave me away. I didn't want you in my life, and later I felt that I couldn't love you and love them, too. They were the ones who wanted me, cared for me, protected me, not you, so…I hope you understand."

"I'm so sorry. I was so young."

"I know that now, Mom. I don't know how anyone that young could be a mother. I don't know how you went through what you did."

"Thank you for saying that, Cassie. But, I never knew about the other stuff, I mean about how you were made to feel as though you were an outsider. I'm sorry. I always believed you had a wonderful life with them. The one consolation I had in leaving you in their care was knowing you had a better life with them than you'd have had with me, and what you are telling me now…well, this is not easy for me to hear. If I'd known…"

"I did have a good life with them. That wasn't it. It's that I was never really 100% part of the family, which I guess I can understand. I mean, they had their own children together. And, they are also well-off, which sort of throws in a different dynamic altogether."

"Yes, I do know they have an abundance of Glow Seeds. It's one reason why I left you with them. They could give you things I couldn't. And, unlike me, Brandie didn't have to work, so she could be there for you."

Cassie paused to take a sip of tea. "There's more to it, though. Sometimes the 'have' people are not as understanding or accepting of the 'have not' people. When I was in my last year of primary college, I met a wonderful man named Josh, but he didn't have any Glow Seeds. He was a simple man, a common laborer, a forest worker, but he loved me and I loved him. To me, that's all that mattered."

Beautimus nodded. "That is all that matters."

"Mom and Dad didn't agree. They felt I should mate with a man of means. I thought it was because they loved me, but it was more about appearances, fitting in. Josh didn't fit in."

"Would you like me to talk to Mr. and Mrs. Bopotamus for you about Josh?"

"No, don't. Trust me, they don't want to talk to you. They think you are a lowlife gutter snipe, unfit to be a mother, and they are convinced they 'saved me' from you. And, now Josh isn't even around."

"*What?* I'm sorry Josh is not part of your life any more. But...the Bopotamuses? How can they not accept someone you love, and how could they not tell me?"

"Part of that is my fault because after I found out who you were, I never said anything good about you to them." She hung her head. "I was afraid if I did, they'd make me go with you. I wanted them *not* to like you, *not* to tell you, I'm ashamed to say."

"I'm sorry, Cassie." Beautimus shook her head.

Cassie took a mouthful of grapes, chewed and swallowed. "And, of course that means...ah...I suppose they never told you about your grandchildren, either?"

"I have *grandchildren?*"

"Two, a boy and a girl. Both good kids, Mom. I want them to know you, and I want you to know them. That's part of the reason I'm here."

"I have grandchildren. Oh my goddesses, I have grandchildren. Were you and Josh legally mated?"

"I left the Bopotamuses' when I knew they'd never accept Josh, and we were legally mated, yes."

"Tell me about your children. How old are they. What are their names?"

"The oldest is Josh, named after his father, of course. He's a few months under ten Earth years. He's got the biggest brown eyes you have ever seen, Mom. He's got a great personality, real spunky. He loves sports and Earth rock 'n roll. The younger is a girl. She's around six Earth years. Her name is Beautimus and she loves to dance."

"*You named your daughter after me?*"

"No offense, Mom, but not exactly. The reason she ended up with Beautimus as a name had to do with my wanting to name both of my children after family. Josh was easy, but finding a girl's name was more difficult. After they rejected Josh Sr., and never showed interest in knowing my children, I didn't want to name my daughter, Brandie after Mrs. Bopotamus. You were the only female relative I knew of at the time. If I'd remembered another female family member, my daughter's name would have been different, believe me. I'm not saying that to make you feel bad, understand, it's the way it was back then. We call her 'Little Bea' or 'Bea Two'."

"It's okay, sweetheart." Beautimus was pleased and honored anyway.

"And, Mom, as it turns out, Little Bea is a lot like you in some interesting ways. You'll see when you meet her."

"I can't wait to meet Little Bea, and her brother. But, what happened to your mate, Josh?"

Cassie's eyes went sad and dark. "An accident. Some moons ago, when the kids were infants, Josh worked maintaining trees. A big storm came through. A hickory wattle weakened by old age let go of his roots when a big wind came up, and he fell on Josh, killing him instantly."

"Cassie. I'm terribly sorry. I wish I could have been there for you. If I'd only known, I would have..."

"Don't worry about it, Mom. My grief was so intense I could barely get out of bed for weeks. But, because of my children, I came around. I had to for them, and I've done fine since. I'm independent, smart. I landed a job as a teacher and I've managed to take care of the kids on my own."

"A teacher? What subject?"

"Earth History."

"No kidding? I teach Earth History, too. I'm a professor at Dr. Pimbly's School for Goodly Educated Adults."

Cassie's eyes widened. "Really? That's where I want to teach one day, but I can't until I finish my upper-level degree, because with kids to support, you know how it is. Anyway, I don't see Mom and Dad, or my step-siblings, and I've been thinking about moving with the kids to Wayflower since you and Aunt Meg and Uncle Phelan and some of the other Potamus tribe are here. The kids need family, and, so do I."

"Please *do* move here. I'll help. I know my abode is small, but there's room. Come live here with me for a while. We'll hire a troodon and maybe an elephant nanny, and you can go back to school. I'm doing well now. I'll pay for you to build your own abode. Please come, Cassie, please."

"I have other news, too, about Grandpa."

"What 'Grandpa'? Who? You mean Mr. or Mrs. Bopotamus' father?"

"No, Mom, I mean *your* father, Artimus Potamus."

"Daddy? You have been in contact with Daddy? How? Tell me."

"After he left Wayflower, he ended up in Oceanic. He became a meadoholic living on the path under a tough hairy wattle tree begging for Seeds to buy mead. A stoat found Grandpa passed out muzzle down almost drowned in his own bloody vomit, and called for help. Grandpa ended up in a hospital, where he still is. Hospital personnel located me when they were looking for kin in Oceanic. He's far gone with liver heat, and he has Hippodementia, too. I often visit him, but sometimes he doesn't even know who I am. He thinks I'm you. He keeps calling me 'Beautimus.' He asks for you, and he needs someone, Mom. I can't leave him there by himself. Grandpa is the only issue I have about leaving Oceanic and moving to Wayflower."

"We shall bring Daddy here, too, then. I'll take care of him. He is my responsibility anyway, not yours. Cassie, you are staying here tonight, aren't you?"

"I'll take you up on that, Mom."

"Stay as long as you want."

"Only tonight. This has to be a quick visit. I left the kids with a friend, but I need to get back to them, and I have my work. I must leave in the morning."

Beautimus called the squirrels who prepared for Cassie's stay.

"Cassie-your-mother-talks-about-you-all-the-time-or-rather-she-used-to-but-of-course-even-though-she-doesn't-talk-about-you-all-the-time-now-doesn't-mean-she-doesn't-love-you-where-do-you-prefer-we-put-your-sleeping-pillows?"

"Anywhere convenient, Agnes. Thank you."

Beautimus and Cassie took a stroll to the river. On the way, they met a rhumba of rattlesnakes, a host of sparrows, and a hill of ruffs. Each time someone would greet them, Beautimus proudly announced, "This is my daughter, Cassie. She's moving with my grandchildren and my father to Wayflower!"

The standard reply was: "I didn't even know you had a daughter and grandchildren. How nice. Pleased to meet you, Cassie, and welcome to Wayflower."

When they returned to the abode, hot leek, mushroom and pepper soup bubbled on the hearth, and a large watermelon husk of honeysuckle mead waited for the two women. Before settling in to eat, Beautimus tapped on her Crystal Interface. "Lucas, can we meet tomorrow? I have something I need to talk to you about. It has to be in person."

"I've been worried about you, my girl. Is everything all right?"

"Yes, everything is good, Lucas. I didn't mean to worry you. I'm sorry, but what I need to tell you I have to talk to you about in person, not on the Interface."

"I'll come right over."

"No, not tonight. Tomorrow."

"Bea?"

"Yes."

"Are we okay?"

"Lucas, we are more than okay. I care very much for you."

"…and I for you. Then, tomorrow it is. Have a nice evening, my girl. The moons are going to be beautiful tonight. I'm taking a night time walk later, and I'll be thinking of you when I see them."

"I'll be thinking about you, too. Believe me."

"Bye for now, my girl."

"Bye for now."

CHAPTER TWENTY-SIX

THE FOLLOWING MORNING, after tea and breakfast, and an Anam Glyph reading for both of them, Beautimus walked her daughter outside. They nuzzled, the first nuzzle between them since Cassie was a newly weaned bubbit.

"Mom, thanks for everything. I had a very relaxing evening and it's good to reconnect with you. I'll activate my Crystal Interface and contact you as soon as I get home. I'll start making arrangements for the move right away. We'll stay in close touch."

"Have a safe trip, Cassie. I love you."

"I love you, too, Mom."

That was the first time, ever, Cassie told her mother that she loved her. Beautimus' pendant heated up and buzzed like a pillow case filled with bumble bees.

***

Today would be an extension of the semester's Long Class. "Let's discuss the differences between human and Rendazian culture. When comparing the two, on the surface it may not appear that other than our space travel, Earth is the more technologically advanced. Can anyone tell me why?"

Cicero raised his paw.

"Cicero, please come to the front of the class to share your views."

After the tiger made his way to the front of the room and faced the class, he asked, "How many of you are fascinated by Humans' various modes of transportation?"

Some students raised their paws, wings, claws, etc.

"Well, the reason I chose the academic field of Earthian Technologies is because of one thing: automobiles. If you go to the Earthly Things Museum downtown, you'll see a Volkswagen Bug, but there are hundreds of other makes and models of automobiles on Earth. Some of them are magnificent pieces of machinery, and even the common transportation cars used by the average human to commute can travel at speeds over 100 miles an hour. In a car, a human can make it from Wayflower to Oceanic in about three hours traveling at cruising speed, about sixty miles an hour, where it takes us on average three days walking."

Marcel became excited. "Wow. An hour and a half?"

"Yes, and because we don't have cars on Rendaz, we may seem behind in our technology, but there is a reason we don't have cars on this planet. Our culture is different from Earth's. The way we live we simply don't require cars. We exist in an agrarian society where we grow our own food, produce our own goods, and work either at home or within a short walking distance to our work and our educational institutions. Our families live communally in compounds. I can open the flap of my den and see the abodes of my mother, cousins, grandparents, and even those of closest friends."

"I can run 60 miles an hour," said a cheetah named Debbie.

"Yes, Debbie, but most Rendazians can't run that fast, and even a cheetah can't run 60 miles an hour for hundreds of miles. As I was saying, we don't have the same needs. Plus, if we were to build cars in Rendaz, we'd have to design them to accommodate the largest dinosaur and the tiniest flea. Can you imagine the engineering nightmare? And, we'd have to construct highways, put in traffic control devices such as stop signs and lights, and develop an entire legal matrix to regulate driving and traffic laws. Furthermore, cars use costly fuel. Some Rendazians don't know this, but fuel, oil in particular, is one of the reasons why humans wage war. Thousands of humans die every year because one country or another wants to own and control the fuel resources of another. And, don't even get me started on how the excavation and transportation of oil causes huge ecological disasters on Earth. Besides that, cars pollute the atmosphere, cause thousands of deaths annually from accidents, and are one reason why so many humans are sickly." Cicero paused for a moment. "Do you know that even to travel a mile or two, instead of walking in the sunshine and clean air, obtaining the benefit of wholesome exercise, humans get in their cars and drive everywhere? I don't know how any of you feel, but in my opinion, Rendaz is far better off without automobiles, and Earth would be better off without them, too." The tiger turned to Beautimus. "That about covers it, Ms. Bea."

"Thank you, Cicero. What we have instead, of course, is our holiday trains that accommodate any size of species, run on solar energy, are fast, clean, efficient, and travel between all districts on Rendaz. We use these mostly for recreational travel since we are rarely more than a few minutes to a few days walk of anyone we might need to visit in person. If someone so desires, they can also hire a camel, horse, ox, mammoth, dinosaur or mastodon to pull them or their things in wagons, or some smaller animals ride on the backs of larger animals. Cicero, can you please address travel over the water?

"Solar powered transport ships. With our trains, good walking routes, and transport ships, there is no need for cars. Also, no need for airplanes, and since we grow most of our own foods right at home, we don't need to transport food. And, because most our goods are made locally from materials readily available, no need to transport materials or goods, either."

"Cicero, you may take your seat. All right, lack of automobiles, trucks, cars, buses and other such vehicles on Rendaz may make us seem like Earth Luddites. We don't use electricity in our homes. We don't have things like phones or other portable technological gimmicks, or stoves and refrigerators, or air conditioners. We have the ability to develop those things but we don't. Why?"

Cicero raised his paw. "Yes, Cicero?"

"I can answer that question in two words: Crystal Interface."

"That's a huge part of it, yes. Crystal Interfaces replace the need for telephones, computers, word processors, books, television, or devices to enjoy music or film, and our Crystal Interface technology propels our spacecraft. But, there's more. Can anyone address why else we don't require certain Earth conveniences. She pointed to a crested godwit. Ruby?"

"We live in a great climate. Rendaz doesn't suffer from extreme cold or heat like Earth. The only snow or freezing temperatures we have is on our volcano peaks where only Yeti live. And unlike humans, we have dense hides, body hair, feathers and down, or fur pelts to protect us from the elements, so we don't need clothing, let alone heating or air conditioning to keep us comfortable. We don't cook much since more than 90% of our food is consumed raw, so a small flame is all we need to cook a little soup when we prefer it hot, or to heat water for our tea. So, why would we need stoves or microwaves? Since we pick and eat our foods fresh, and unprocessed, why would we need refrigerators or gadgets like toasters or blenders?"

"Precisely, Ruby. Thank you. When the suns are out, we are awake. When the moons are out, we sleep, unless we are nocturnal, of course, than the reverse holds true, but we don't see any reason to put artificial light in our homes. If we wish to stay up after dark and need light, we start a fire in our abode hearths or pits, or we burn natural candles. Our eyes are good and, so unlike humans, most of us see well in the dark. We don't *require* electricity like Earth people do. And, we can travel to any universe, or even parallel universes in a flash using our Crystal Interface technology. What we have is so advanced it responds to *thought waves* and intention. Humans couldn't develop our technology in a million years even if they diverted every dime they spend on war to technology." She hesitated. "Well, maybe if they diverted all their war budget to technology they could develop Crystal Interface technology, but since humans won't ever stop spending trillions on war, it's highly unlikely they'll ever develop Crystal technology that could in any way rival ours." Beautimus stood. "Well, we have exceeded our allotted time, and I have an appointment I must get to. Everyone keep up with your reading, and have a nice week."

After class, Beautimus walked to the Administration Building to Lucas' office, and found him absorbed in paperwork. "Knock, knock," she said.

"Bea, please come in. I've been waiting for you."

Groups of students and faculty members walked by. "Hello, Dr. Potamway and Ms. Bea."

Beautimus tried to speak but the moment she opened her maw, Sir. Henry entered Lucas's office. "Hi, Beautimus. Hope I'm not interrupting anything. Say, Lucas, when you have a minute tomorrow stop my office, will you? I have some art curriculum issues I want to discuss with you."

"Certainly, Sir Henry."

"It's crazy-busy around here," Beautimus said. "Can we go somewhere private to talk?"

"Absolutely, my girl."

The pair lumbered side-by-side to a meadow, apparently deserted apart from an old deaf nag, Oatsie, nibbling on rye grass. "This will do," Beautimus said. "Let's sit."

The two hippos kneeled in the grass.

"So, my girl, what's all this about?"

"I don't know how you are going to feel about me after I

tell you this, Lucas. I was up all night worrying about it, but you have to know."

"Try me."

Beautimus inhaled, "I have a grown daughter and two grandchildren."

Lucas pulled away from Beautimus. "You have a daughter and grandchildren? I see. I thought you told me you were never legally mated."

"I wasn't. Remember my telling you about the tryst with the young beef-witted cad who left me long ago? Well, I ended up pregnant and decided to have the bubbit."

"Why didn't you tell me this, Bea? I was honest with you when we went on our picnic. You weren't honest with me."

Beautimus panicked. *I've lost him. I've lost Lucas.*

"Please, Lucas. I haven't seen my daughter, Cassiopeia, for over 100 years. I haven't even spoken with her. She wanted nothing to do with me. Until yesterday, I didn't even know about my grandchildren. *Please*, Lucas."

She told him the entire story from the call on her Interface the night before through this morning when she nuzzled Cassie goodbye. As she spoke, Lucas didn't look at her. She couldn't feel the space where her heart resided. Her chest felt cold, but her shar-pendant was still warm, though, and the only thing keeping her heart from freezing into a lump of ice. "Lucas?"

"You just dropped a boulder on me, Bea. I need a few minutes to process this."

For an eternity Beautimus and Lucas sat in silence. Oatsie departed, so there were only the two hippos sitting a short distance apart, looking away from one another, not speaking. Beautimus heard the sound of her own breathing, but nothing more.

Finally, Lucas spoke. "If this thing between us is going to work you have to trust me. We can't keep things from one another. This news about a daughter and grandchildren is huge. It's not a trifling tidbit you just happened to forget about. It's unfair that you didn't tell me about this sooner."

"I'm sorry, Lucas, really I am. I thought Cassie was lost to me forever. I never expected to see her again, and honestly, like I told you, I didn't know about my grandchildren. I'm so, so sorry." Tears brimmed in her eyes.

Lucas moved closer. "No more secrets. Promise?"

"Promise." The shar-pendant heated and began to vibrate so hard Beautimus thought Lucas might hear it.

"I will help you with this. Together, we'll bring your family here and I will personally do all I can to ensure they have a good life in Wayflower."

Lucas moved near, licked the tears from her face, and nuzzled her.

The only words Beautimus could think of to describe what she felt in that moment were "Ecstatic Joy." That's what she felt, ecstatic joy, and she wanted to shout her joy to the world.

"Bea, I have something I want to tell you, too. Something important."

Beautimus held her breath afraid of what might come next. "I'm listening."

"I love you."

Beautimus exhaled forcefully. "I didn't expect that. As it so happens, I love you, too, Lucas, and I have since the first time we met."

"That's all I need from you, ever, is for you to trust me and love me."

Lucas leaned in and kissed Beautimus hard and she kissed back equally hard. At last, Beautimus had found a good man. A good man she loved, who loved her in return. At that moment, a movement in the flowering mangium tree above them startled. They looked up to see, sitting a tight knot attempting to conceal themselves on a branch thick with leaves and blossoms, the charm of purple finches.

"Oh no," said Beautimus. "Have you all been there the entire time listening?" Upon being discovered, the finches flew off as fast as their wings could carry them in a frantic rustle of tails and feathers.

CHAPTER TWENTY-SEVEN

THE FOLLOWING DAY, Larry dropped off a Special Edition of *The Wayflower Quacker*.

Wand Theft Trio Guilty!

After two-days of non-stop deliberation a secret jury comprised of rats, monkeys and coyotes, the Council found all three suspects guilty in the Theft of the Wand of Fortuna. They convicted Heatherton, the rat, of one count of knowingly obstructing justice in the theft of a sacred object, and one count of blackmail. In an unrelated charge, the jury found Heatherton guilty in the Wasenia Festival thefts. They convicted Jake, the monkey, on one count each of theft of a sacred object, and conspiring to commit theft. The Council convicted Belinda, the Coyote, of one count of theft of a sacred object, one count of willfully disrespecting the High Priestess, and one count of attempted murder.

The Magistrate, Butterfly Council, and Ancient Trees unanimously agreed to issue an order of banishment for all three suspects. Additionally, Belinda will be stripped of her title of Wise Woman, and all her privileges revoked. Per custom, the head magistrate confiscated and snapped her wand into pieces, and threw it into the River Kwa.

Given the severity of her crimes, and the fact she violated two taboos, protestors are calling for Belinda's shunning as well, but Rhianna has asked for clemency. "If Belinda is shunned, as well as being banished, given she is a pack animal, it would mean pain and suffering beyond what constitutes reasonable punishment. It'd be cruel. For this reason, and because Belinda was devoted for so many years to the Goddesses, I plead for mercy."

As the Wand Guards and members of The Guardians escorted the three convicts across the Wayflower District line into the Wasteland, bystanders allegedly overheard Belinda to say, "I'll be back!" Steven D. Lobos allegedly responded to her with this statement, "Belinda, you got off lucky. You dare show your crook-pated muzzle anywhere in the Wayflower District again and I will tear out your throat," at which time he growled, then lifted his lip and displayed his fangs. The trio's abodes and belongings will go up for auction during the first day of the next moon phase. Sale proceeds will be distributed to the needy.

For weeks, Belinda's banishment was the talk of Wayflower. The Coyote people put up quite a howl. Belinda's friends thought she was treated unfairly and demanded her banishment overturned. Other coyotes were infuriated that one of their own, and a trusted Wise Woman, would dishonor her tribe. They were the most vocal in demanding her shunning.

***

The following days were blissful for Beautimus. She was in love. She reunited with her daughter, who'd be living in Wayflower. She found out she was a grandmother, and she'd see her daddy.

She'd always wondered what happened to her father, and if she'd ever see him again. Now she'd bring him home to care for him during his last moons on Rendaz. Belinda, Jake, and Heatherton were brought to justice. How could life be any better? That evening, she had dinner with her uncle and aunt.

"Cassie was here in Wayflower?" Aunt Meg ceased chewing

mid-bite. "My Goddess why didn't you bring her here to meet us?"

"She was here for a flash, Aunt Meg. We had so much to discuss, and she had to leave early the next morning. I have a surprise, though"

Aunt Meg swallowed. "Yes?"

"She's moving here with the children. You'll see plenty of them, guaranteed."

"How delightful. We are so pleased, aren't we Phalen?"

Phalen nodded.

"And of course we've heard the news going around that Lucas and you are in love. Will we be hearing mating bells soon?"

"Aunt Meg, it's a little too soon to say. Please don't assume anything like that."

"Nonetheless, I think I'll be going downtown to Lacy's to price fabric and ribbons in case we need to put together a mating ritual dress for someone."

"Stop it." Beautimus laughed.

"On a more sobering note, Aunt Meg, I have some news about your older brother."

"What? You've heard from Artimus, too?"

"Not exactly, Aunt Meg. Daddy developed a substance abuse problem and is in a hospital in Oceanic. Addicted to mead, and not doing well. Besides liver failure, the doctors diagnosed him with Hippodementia, and sometimes doesn't know who he is let alone who anyone else is."

"I'm terribly sorry to hear that. When young, Artimus was a bright spot in our family. I love my brother and miss him." Meg shook her head. "Bea, your father's heart broke when your mother passed over. You understand that's why he left?"

"I know, Aunt Meg. I have no rancor or animosity toward my father. He was crushed when mom died."

"We were concerned that he'd take his own life. We were not surprised when he left that he never returned. We thought we might hear from him from time-to-time. When we didn't, and when he didn't respond to any of our communications, we feared the worst," said Uncle Phelan.

Aunt Meg continued, "I guess it was too difficult for him to associate with any place or any person who reminded him of his beloved Sangrina. But, we knew he loved you, and adored you, Beautimus. When he left you with us we thought maybe one day he'd return for you....I think you looked a little too much like your mother. He couldn't take it. You do know he named you?"

"No." Beautimus cocked her head. "Isn't it always the mother who names the children?"

"Yes, but not in this case. The day you were calved, as your father first beheld you, he thought you were the most beautiful baby girl in the world. You were a lovely bubbit, and when you were born, you were almost luminescent. Your hide had an iridescent sheen to it. That, along with your extraordinary violet colored eyes, that little heart shaped birthmark on your cheek, and your perfect head and sweet little tail...well your daddy took one look and said 'She's Beautimus!' Your mother wanted to name you Elizabeth Taylor because of your eyes and the birthmark, but because of your father, Beautimus is the name your mother decided on."

"I never knew that, Aunt Meg. This is the first time I've heard that story."

"We'd hoped one day he'd tell it to you himself."

"I haven't said so, but I'll be bringing him here permanently to care for him. Cassie has been taking care of him until now, visiting him often in the hospital, bless her heart. But, it's my job. It's what I have to do. It's what I *want* to do."

"That's wonderful, Beautimus. We'll do what we can to help, too. It'll be so good to see Artimus again." Aunt Meg looked around, her eyes excited. "Our family is going to expand. I'll plant additional watermelon seeds, and maybe put in hazelnuts. We'll need them."

School was on break. Lucas went out of the District on University business for a few days, so Beautimus had time to herself. She thought she'd take a walk to visit Beard and Rhianna, and catch them up on the latest occurrences of her life, although they she was sure they already knew. She enjoyed a hearty breakfast with the squirrels, during which they discussed the coming changes.

"Don't worry, you two," Beautimus said. "I'll hire additional help. You can help me select a good nursemaid for Daddy, and maybe we'll hire a couple of monkeys, a troodon or panda you can supervise. We'll have a lot of people living with us in the abode for a while. It will be crowded until I can add on. Even with the hyenas' help, there will be more cooking, more cleaning, but you won't have to do all this additional work yourselves."

Agnes and Applecheeks expanded with pride at being promoted to household "management."

Beautimus enjoyed an insightful Anam Glyph reading. She pulled Ram, a sign she had indeed broken through many obstacles, and now wonderful things were ahead. Afterwards, she took a dip in the river that included a quick visit with Calypso.

"Bea! I heard you had a daughter and grandkids coming to live in Wayflower, and who hasn't heard about you and Lucas being in love? I didn't know your dad was moving here, though. That's so…. Oh my! What's that dropping into the water over there?"

"Calypso, it's a leaf."

"Oh, oh yeah, a leaf. Was I saying something? Oh my goddesses! Did you read what Belinda said on her way out of town? Wait…were we talking about something else? I forget."

"Never mind, Calypso. It's nothing."

Beautimus asked the squirrels to load her satchel with jars of milkweed blossom honey for Rhianna, and she set out on the path to the Crane Tribe Compound. The weather turned crisp. The air was cooler than it had been in previous weeks, and the leaves on the mountain aspen, sugar maple, ashburton willows and echidna wattles had already begun turning russet and yellow.

On Rendaz, there are two seasons. The Warm Season is akin to spring and early summer on Earth. The Cool Season is much like Earth's autumn and early winter. In the warmer days, everything is bright and lively. Rendazian citizens are boisterous and active, and sex is absolutely everywhere. Even ancient men and women way beyond their mating years go at each other in amorous, although mostly awkward, attempts to couple. Some of these unfortunate dears get so worked up they end up with pinched nerves and excited bladder conditions. The warm season atmosphere is filled with the scents of spearmint, the damp fur of newborn bunnies, and oils distilled from gardenia petals.

The Cool Season brings muted introspection and silence so deep even atoms and molecular cells are sluggish. During a cool evening if a basset hound woman takes a stroll with her mate on the path along the River Kwa, the couple would surely stop and put their muzzles into the air to take in the lush perfume of raw cocoa, river moss, and roasted pumpkin seeds. They might follow their inclination to bay in harmony at the two moons, but in hushed voices.

Right now, the northern hemisphere of Rendaz in Wayflower entered its Cool Season. Tartarian asters and autumn sunset mums in full bloom provided brilliant splashes of color. The suns spread their golden light across the district reflecting off the ponds, and causing the water of the River Kwa to sparkle in dappled spots here and there. The effect—nothing short of magical.

A shrewdness of apes ambled by, waiving as they passed, and a party of jays flew close for a word. "We are absolutely in a twitter over your daughter, Bea."

A mischief of mice scampered to Beautimus. "Good Day, Ms. Bea. So happy to hear about you and Lucas, and we can't wait to meet your daughter."

"Thank you. You all have a good day, now."

Rufus, the silverback gorilla, approached from the opposite direction. "Hey Bea, did you hear the one about the wallaby who goes to see Doctor Bombay about his farting problem?" Without waiting for Beautimus' response, he launched into the joke. "So, this guy goes to see the doctor and the doctor says: what seems to be the problem?

The wallaby says: Doctor, I've got the farts something bad. I mean, I fart all the time, but my farts are odorless and no one can hear 'em.

The doctor nods and says: Hmmm.

So, the wallaby goes on: I keep farting and farting, but no one can smell 'em or hear 'em at all. Look, I've been here for ten minutes and I've farted at least eight times. You didn't smell 'em or hear 'em, right?

The doctor takes out his pad and writes a prescription.

The wallaby gets excited: So, Doc, will this prescription stop my farting problem?

The gorilla slapped his thigh. "Now listen to this Bea. This is the good part." He leaned in to deliver the punch line. "No, the prescription is to clear up your sinuses, and next week, I want you in for a hearing test. Hahahahahaaa. Get it, Bea? Get it? The guy can't smell or hear his own farts. Hahahahahaaa. Isn't that a riot?"

Rufus extended his index finger to Beautimus. "Hey Bea, pull my finger."

"No thanks, Rufus. I need to get going."

"Aww, c'mon, pull my finger. I won't do anything, I promise."

"Nooooo. Last time you asked me to pull your finger, when I did you gassed the entire forest, Rufus. No thanks."

"Hahahaaaha....Hahaaaaahaha, Bea. You're a stitch. That's what you are."

"I'll be seeing you, Rufus."

"Okey Dokey Artichokey. Don't let the bedbugs bite. Hahahahahaaaa."

As Beautimus departed, Rufus lumbered to a fleet of mud hens. "Hey, you all hear about the Wallaby who went to see Doctor Bombay about his farting problem?"

Beautimus reached the ancient grove to visit Beard. "It's been a while, Master Beard."

"Well, from what I've heard, you've been pretty busy, Beautimus."

"So, you know about my daughter, my grandchildren, my romantic life, my father...anything else you know about, Master Beard?"

"That about covers it."

"It's such a wonderful afternoon, don't you think?"

"Yes indeed it is, Bea. The spirit of the Goddess surrounds us today. And of course, to a woman in love the world is a beautiful place anyway. Through eyes of enchantment, you will behold what no one else sees. When we are in love, we recognize nature as the miracle that it is."

"Can I ask you a personal question, Master Beard?"

"Certainly."

"Have you ever been in love?"

"Many times. I've spread my pollen all over the forest. Many of the trees you see here are my sons and daughters."

"I mean, with someone *special*?"

"To a tree, all people are special. Unlike other creatures, who mate with only one, we tree people spread our love around.

That's one reason why we are so revered...the world needs all the love trees have to share with everything and everybody."

"You are so right, Master Beard. Well...I always enjoy visiting with you, but I need to get going...I'm going to see Rhianna and I don't want to walk home after dark."

"Give Rhianna my healing blessings."

"I certainly will, Master Beard. May I ask....is there a *reason* why Rhianna needs your healing blessings?"

"That's up to her to share with you if she so chooses, Bea. Get on your way. With the Cool Season upon us, Racine and Purmoso set early."

Beautimus arrived to the Crane's abode and called out, "Lady Rhianna, it's me."

Queenie poked her head through the door, "Lady Rhianna is resting right now and is not receiving visitors."

"Is that Bea?" Called Rhianna from her bed chamber. "Let her in. I *do* want to see her."

Beautimus entered and found Rhianna looking thin and tired. "Are you feeling all right, Lady Rhianna?"

"Let's not talk about that now. I have something important I need to discuss with you. Queenie, can you please leave us alone for a few minutes? "

The lemur bowed low and departed.

Beautimus kneeled close to the old bird. "What is it, Lady Rhianna?"

"Are you going to attend the Luna Festival?"

"I'll be there."

"Are you absolutely certain? If there is any chance that you can't make it, you need to tell me now. This is important."

"I'll be there Lady Rhianna."

"Then I must name you a Wise Woman."

Beautimus rose and took a step backwards, nearly tripping over a waddle wood table.

"What? Me? A Wise Woman? Me?"

"You did not hear me correctly?"

"Why, yes, but I never thought of myself as a Wise Woman, Lady Rhianna."

"That's the problem with you, and the one reason I didn't name you Wise Woman sooner. You never thought of yourself as much of anything. High self-esteem and self-confidence are imperative qualities in a Wise Woman."

"But, I…"

"…I don't mean arrogance, narcissism, and vanity like that which controls Belinda, but authentic self-love and self-respect. You must cultivate those qualities within yourself to be a Wise Woman, but if you are willing to do that, I'm ready to name you Wise Woman now and we can work on building your self-esteem afterwards."

Beautimus bowed her head. "I'd be honored."

"Tomorrow when the two suns are high, come to me with a wand. You will go into the forest before you leave for home this evening and ask a sapling ash, a willow, or another suitable tree for a branch of the right length and thickness for a wand. Tomorrow morning, bathe in the river as you always do. Take your wand with you. Bathing is the bonding ritual between a wand and its mistress Wise Woman, and you and your wand must adhere to one another in spirit prior to the ceremony.

Also….I must ask you to say nothing of any of this to anyone, not now, not tomorrow, not after the ceremony, not until I give you permission to speak of it."

"Yes, Lady Rhianna. Is there a reason I cannot talk about this?"

"Because I asked you not to. Do you understand?"

"Yes."

"Good. When you come to me. You will carry me to Beard who will act as our witness for the ceremony in which I will name you Wise Woman. We will begin your wand training after the ceremony. Also, you must name your wand. Your wand will become your good friend, your companion. Our friends and companions have names, don't they? Are you clear on what I need you to do?"

"Yes, Lady."

"It may awhile to find a tree willing to give of itself. You don't have much time. Go now, and use your shar-pendant to help you find what you are looking for."

"How do I do that?"

"You'll know. Hurry. Go."

Beautimus wondered what the rush was all about. It was clear to her Rhianna was ill and didn't want to discuss it, and that worried her. However, without further questioning her High Priestess, she did as she'd been told. She bid Rhianna farewell, and dropped the honey off with Queenie. As she stepped onto the path, she heard Rhianna coughing.

She headed back to the sacred glen. "Master Beard. I have to find a special tree who will give to me of itself."

"Well then do so."

"But, I don't know how to approach a tree about a wand."

"With respect."

"How do I ask?"

"Use your heart, of course. Now, if you have to find this special tree today, I'd get on it if I were you."

Beautimus wandered through the forest. The suns dipped lower in the sky and the air chilled. It would be dark soon. Anxiety niggled at her. "What do I do? What do I do?" She remembered Rhianna had instructed her to use the shar-pendant. Help me, Goddesses. How do I use my shar-pendant to find my wand?"

She heard—what seemed to her to be her own voice inside her head—"All you ever had to do was ask, Bea."

"I'm asking."

"Focus on your pendant as you near a tree."

Beautimus took a breath, then forced all her attention on her shar-pendant, and approached a weeping willow. At first, nothing, then she felt the shar-pendant warm. As she reached the tree, the pendant cooled. *That's interesting.* She tested again. As she moved away from the tree, the pendant warmed. As she moved closer, it cooled. She turned toward another tree, an ash, the shar-pendant warmed, then cooled. She turned to another tree, and another, and the same thing. Frustrated, she looked into the sky. "I'm focusing. It's not working, and it's getting dark, what do I do?"

One word came to her, "Trust."

I get it. I'll keep trying.

She spied a young female corkscrew willow on the shore of the river. As she approached, the shar stone warmed, and grew warmer, warmer, warmer. By the time she reached the tree, the pendant was hot. "I've found the tree. Now, how do I ask?" No response. "All right, I'll try….respect, respect, okay."

She bowed to the tree. "Please. I'm in need of a special wand. Would you honor me by giving of yourself to me, and I will honor you in return by giving my wand your name?" The tree buzzed, hummed, and vibrated, then dropped a slender branch at Beautimus' feet. It was exactly the proper length and thickness.

"Thank you, beautiful tree."

The tree buzzed again, and in her head, Beautimus heard a name. "Ophelia."

"Ophelia? I shall name my wand, Ophelia, then."

Beautimus picked up the wand in her teeth and ran all the way home. She arrived at her abode as Ladyluz and Ladybeth were rising in the sky. She put the wand down by the flap and walked through, and almost directly into….Lucas. "Lucas. What are *you* doing here? I thought you were out of the District on business? I didn't know you were back?" She kissed him.

"I decided to surprise you and come home a day early. I've been waiting here with Applecheeks and Agnes for hours. They told me you'd gone to see Rhianna. Is she faring well?"

"I don't think so. I'm not sure."

"We were all getting a little worried. It's dark now."

"I know, everything took longer than I thought. I didn't mean to worry anyone. Sorry. I'm so very pleased to see you Lucas."

"I was thinking…. since I'm home early, and tomorrow promises to be a gorgeous day, how 'bout I come by in the morning and we spend the day together, my girl, maybe another picnic by Sweetwater Pond?"

I promised Rhianna I'd not speak to anyone. Oh goddesses, have mercy. What can I tell him?

"Lucas, I'd love that more than you know, but…I can't."

"Why not? Dr. Pimbly's not in session tomorrow."

"There's something…something I have to do….and it will take most of the day."

"Bea, let's step outside. We need to talk."

Once outside, Lucas looked Beautimus square in the face. "What's going on?"

"I'm sorry, Lucas, I can't tell you."

"Do you remember the talk we had about not keeping things from one another, you know, the one about trust?"

"Please, this is so important. It's nothing like before. This is something very different, and I promise on my mother's ashes to tell you all about it as soon as I can."

"This isn't sitting well with me, Bea. Why can't you tell me what you are doing tomorrow? What's the secrecy about?"

"Lucas. Trust goes two ways. Right now, I need you to trust me, too."

"All right, but I hope this is the last time that you have an important 'secret' you can't share with me, otherwise, we'll have to rethink this relationship. Contact me on your

Interface when you *do* have time."

He leaned over and gave her an icy peck on the cheek, and retreated in the direction of his own abode. Beautimus drug herself back inside. The squirrels, who had heard everything, said nothing. They pushed a pail of hot chamomile tea toward Beautimus, and tiptoed to their hammocks.

Beautimus said her prayers at her altar then tried to sleep. She tossed and turned all night. She felt heavy, dense with worry. She was stuck in the middle between her promise to Rhianna to tell nothing, and her promise to Lucas to tell everything. The next morning, she arose later than she'd wanted, and without breakfast or tea, she put Ophelia in her teeth and headed to the river. There she said the prayer asking Great Mother Genesis to bind her to her wand as Rhianna had instructed. She put one foot into the water and shuddered. Then she took one deep breath, squeezed her eyes shut, and dove in so she and Ophelia could experience the cleansing water together. Today, she would become a Wise Woman, something she'd longed for. Something she'd wanted for over two hundred years. This should be one of the happiest days of her middle-aged life, but all she could think about was Lucas and how last night he had walked away from her.

She arrived at Rhianna's as the two suns sat directly overhead in the sky. She knelt to ease Rhianna's climb onto her back. Rhianna had become too weak to fly. When they reached the sacred glen, they went before Beard.

Rhianna ruffled her feathers. "Drop your wand at the roots of Beard." Beautimus did so. "Now, kneel before the ancient tree." Beautimus did so.

Rhianna climbed off Beautimus' back and took the wand in her right wing. She pointed it at Beautimus. "You, who kneel before me and the sacred tree, what have you named your wand?"

"Ophelia."

"Repeat after me" Rhianna placed the wand on the dirt before Beautimus.

"I, Beautimus Potamus, pledge myself to Great Mother Genesis, her consorts, and her lesser Goddesses, to honor her and to love her, to give worship to her, and to serve her as her Wise Woman."

Beautimus repeated, "I, Beautimus Potamus, ..."

"Do you, Beautimus Potamus, with your wand Ophelia, swear the oath before the witness, Beard, to obey the charge of the Goddess and to respect that which is taught you, and to be in the service of our Noble Lady until you are ashes, lest you be stripped of your title, rights and powers?"

"I do."

The old bird spat on the wand, and in one wing, and held it to the sky. "I consecrate the wand, Ophelia, and name Beautimus Potamus as Wise Woman."

Rhianna placed Ophelia in Beautimus' maw. She pulled her own wand from her wing and touched Ophelia then Beautimus. "I hereby activate the powers of the wand, Ophelia. May she be used by no one but Wise Woman Beautimus Potamus, and only in the service of healing and good magic. So it is."

Rhianna tucked her wand back into her wing. "Rise Beautimus Potamus."

Beautimus rose to her feet with Ophelia in her mouth.

"You are now a Wise Woman."

Beautimus' heart nearly burst with joy.

"Congratulations, Bea" Beard said "I'm proud of you."

"I had intended to begin your training today, but I'm a bit weary," Rhianna said. "Do you mind taking me back to my abode? You will come again tomorrow afternoon, and we shall begin training you in Wise Woman ways."

"Lady Rhianna, when may I share with others I'm a Wise Woman?"

"After the Luna Festival ceremony, my dear. Not before."

"My, that's several moons from now. A long time to keep this secret."

"But keep it you must. Promise me."

"I promise."

"I thought you'd be happier about this, Bea. What's troubling you?"

"I am happy, really, but there is something bothering me." She told Rhianna and Beard about what had transpired the night before with Lucas.

"I'm pleased you kept the secret, even at the risk of damaging your relationship with Lucas. That confirms I am right to have chosen you," said Rhianna.

"To choose me for Wise Woman?"

"Yes, my dear."

"Don't worry about Lucas" said Beard. "He loves you. His feelings are hurt and he's disappointed because he had his heart set on spending today with you. No matter what happens, you must trust in Lucas' love for you. Now take Rhianna home, then return to your abode and get some rest."

On the way back, Beautimus thought about her new role, what it meant to her, what an honor to be named Wise Woman, and how she'd acquire knowledge to heal and otherwise help the people she loved, her family and the tribes of her community. The air felt cool and gentle against her hide, so nice. She thought about what Beard had told her, that Lucas loved her and she should trust in that love. A kindle of kittens came her way, cute, fluffy little things. She said to them, "Where's your mama, little ones?"

"She's at home takin' a nap….she says now we is all weaned we getta' go out an' play all by ourselves. We is gonna' go roll in dirt, chase blowie-around leaves, and play hide 'n seek 'til we is hungry. Wanna come?"

"No thank you, sweeties. Have fun."

The kittens lightened Beautimus' mood. *As soon as I get home, I'm going to activate my Crystal Interface and tell Lucas I love him.*

She walked maybe a few more meters when she saw a hippo couple by the river snuggled up against one another. *Oh, how sweet.* But, as she drew nearer she recognized one of the hippos...Lucas. He sat with that same beautiful young hippo woman she'd seen him with before. They were so engrossed in intimate conversation neither of them noticed Beautimus who stood frozen in place, too stunned to move. Lucas nuzzled the young woman. When Beautimus finally allowed herself to register what she was seeing, she composed herself enough to pass them unnoticed, then once she had snuck by, she took off at a run to her abode. Out of breath, she entered the door, tears streaming down her face. *It seems as though all I do is cry these days. What's wrong with me? What made me think anything between Lucas and me was more than a silly dalliance anyway?* Grateful the squirrels were not at home, for a few minutes, she sat dumbfounded in the middle of the floor. *I'm a Wise Woman now with huge responsibility, and I have family coming to Wayflower. I'll not have time for romantic folly anyway. It's better I remain alone.*

She activated her Crystal Interface. "Hope you have a good life, Lucas, and I wish you all the happiness in the world. Thanks for the good times. Bye." Then she deactivated her Interface so as not to give him an opportunity to reply.

CHAPTER TWENTY-EIGHT

THE FOLLOWING DAY, Beautimus arose so early the squirrels were still asleep in their hammocks. Mindful not to disturb them, she took Ophelia from the altar and headed to the river for a dip, then after her bath, she departed for the Blue Crane Compound. When she passed the silver mulga tree, she stopped to visit Samuel, who she'd not seen in weeks. Samuel had a way of making her feel better when something had gone wrong in her life, and right now, she needed his friendship in the worst way. She circled the tree and called for him. "Sam, I know it's early, but it's me, Beautimus. Thought I'd stop by."

Michael M. Goodwings, stuck his head out from behind a leaf. "Bea, I'm sorry to tell you but Sam's not here. He took Petunia to the Waterfall for a few days. Not sure when he's due back."

"They went to the Waterfall together? Things must be getting serious between them."

"To hear Sam tell it, they aren't, but all of us can see through his bull crap. He's smitten, taken, trapped. That cutie has him wrapped."

"Well, have a good day, Michael. If Sam comes back before I see him, tell him I stopped by, will you?"

"Sure thing, Bea. See you later."

After a bit, she decided to detour to the Mastodon compound to see if Lizzy might be up and about. She found Liz munching on banana leaves outside her abode.

"Hey, Bea. Long time no see. How are you doing, girlfriend?"

"Not so good. Lucas and I broke up." She choked back tears.

"*What?* Get over here. Tell me what happened."

Beautimus told her the story about catching him at the river bank under a bendee tree cuddled up to the younger female.

"Did you actually see him kiss her on the mouth, or licking her face, anything like that?"

"He nuzzled her."

"Yeah, and I nuzzle my grandmother. How do you know Lucas is actually messing around with this other woman? You don't even know who she is, right?"

"It looked seriously romantic, Lizzy. I mean, I could be wrong of course, but it didn't seem innocent to me. I've seen them together before."

"Who broke it off, Lucas or you?"

"Me."

"You? You broke it off *based on what*? Bea, I love you but you are an idiot sometimes, especially when it comes to men. Go back now, and I mean right now, and find out who this other woman is. How could you break up with the love of your life when you aren't sure he's done anything wrong? Go home and fix this before it's too late."

"I can't. I've got to meet with Rhianna....about.... something important."

"What can be more important?"

"I can't say right now. I'll tell you about it later. Maybe I'll send him another message when I get home."

"You better, or I'll personally come over and kick your fleshy hippo butt, and I'm bigger than you."

Beautimus took her leave and continued down the path. *What if she's right? What if I broke up with Lucas for nothing, and I've lost him forever? Crap. What if I really farkused up this time?* Just then, Rufus came toward her. *Not today, please.*

"Bea, how do you say 'fart' in German? Farfrompoopin! Hahahaha...good one, eh? Haaahaaa."

Rufus, I am not in the mood for jokes. Sorry, not a good day, okay, buddy?

"Wow, you are a bit of a tight ass today, aren't you, Bea?"

"What?"

"I mean your ass is so tight that when you fart only dogs can hear it. Hahahahaaahahahahaaaa."

When she arrived to the Crane Tribe compound, she picked up Rhianna and they went into the sacred grove to commence their training. Rhianna and Beautimus appeared before Beard. Rhianna dismounted and asked Beautimus to withdraw her wand, and Beautimus pulled the wand from her collar with her teeth. Rhianna began. "First, I will show you how to…."

Beard rustled his leaves. "Wait one moment, Lady Rhianna, I have something to say to Bea before you begin the training."

"Certainly."

"Bea, with magic comes great responsibility, and trust."

"Yes, Master Beard."

"I have no doubt, and neither does Lady Rhianna, you will use magic responsibly or you'd not be here today. What I'm concerned about is the 'trust' element."

"I am a trustworthy person."

"Are you? Did I not tell you that Lucas loved you and you must trust in that love?"

"Yes, you did…and how did you know…"

"I told you I know many things, Bea. Among the many things I know is that you lack the trust you say you have. You do not trust Lucas, and you do not trust me, or you'd have been unconcerned about what you witnessed between Lucas and this other woman by the river, no?"

"Well…I…"

"The important questions I have are: Do you trust yourself? Do you trust Ophelia? Do you trust Lady Rhianna? As far as

I'm concerned all that remains to be seen." The tree rustled again. "Lady Rhianna, we'll need to work with Beautimus on trust issues as well as self-esteem and self-confidence if she is to be the...one."

"What *one*?" Said Beautimus

"We'll discuss that later, Beautimus. Right now, you need to learn how to use your wand," said Rhianna. "You and Ophelia will first call in the Goddesses and ask for their protection, wisdom, and guidance. Please do this now focusing on Ophelia with the intention to call in the Goddesses."

Beautimus did as asked.

"What do you feel, Beautimus?"

"I'm not certain. I think I'm feeling a calmness, a warmth."

"Good. The goddesses are with us. We may begin our work. Today, we will train you how to project your thought into Ophelia so that she may help you channel your intentions. You may only do good for another with this wand. You cannot use the wand or its power *or your power* for anything other than in service to others. Understood?"

"Yes."

"The wand will assist you in your healing work. Soon enough, we will venture into the forest to identify and harvest healing herbs, which I will teach you to use. Right now, I will instruct you in how to manifest another's heart desire, not your own, mind you. You will help to grant another's wishes with the help of Ophelia, that is if the other's wishes are pure and in line with what is in their highest and best good. Sometimes we want more for another than they want for themselves, and sometimes what we want for them is not in their best interest. Wisdom prevails in the granting of wishes, Beautimus. You have the wisdom within you, but you must learn to access it and trust it. So today, among other things, we will teach you to access your inner wisdom. Are you ready?"

"I am ready. I have one question, though."

"Certainly."

"Will my wand be able to do what The Wand of Fortuna can do?"

"No. A Wise Woman's wand is either for healing or revealing. Revealing wands help the bearer to know the truth. You have your Anam Glyphs and your Shar Pendent for that, so Ophelia is a Healing Wand. Healing wands help to mend physical and spiritual ills. They can help manifest wishes through healing emotional wounds that are obstacles to achieving one's desires. But, that's all they do. Now, think of someone you love deeply. The first person that comes into your mind is the right person. Don't over think this. Speak the name of the person you want most to help."

"Cassie."

"Now, what do you wish for her?"

"She wants to complete her upper-level studies and teach at Dr. Pimbly's School for Goodly Educated Adults."

"Focus that wish and bring that thought into your inner being, your heart-center. Tell me if you feel a yes or a no. Don't think about it….quickly."

"Yes."

"Good. Anything else going on?"

"My shar-pendent began to heat and vibrate."

"You have been blessed with three magical tools, Bea. Most of us have but one. The wand named Ophelia, and your shar-pendant, both contain powerful magic. The Wand's healing power we shall discover together. Your shar-pendant's power is that it gives you *some* information you require, maybe not the information you want, but the information you need. It can tell you if a person's love for you is genuine, for example. The shar-pendant's magic works well because it is linked directly to your heart. Ophelia's magic is different. She will confirm your wish for another is in that other person's highest and best interest, she'll channel your petitions to the goddesses, and she will help you to heal others."

"What's my third magical tool, Lady Rhianna?"

"Your Anam Glyphs, of course! They provide general guidance for you and others. They help you to locate your true north. The Anam Glyphs contain powerful magic indeed." The old bird cleared her throat. "Let's proceed. You have identified Cassie as the person who you want to help. Close your eyes, and in silence, ask Ophelia for her help and we'll go from there."

Beautimus did as instructed.

"Good. Now set your intention. Hold Ophelia and she will send your petition to the Goddesses. Speak aloud in clear and precise words to ask what you desire for Cassie."

"I want for Cassie to have what her heart desires and...."

"No, no, no...let me help you. Try this instead, "Oh Goddesses of the four corners, if it is in her best and highest interest, let it be that Cassie is healed from any internal emotional wounds preventing her from completing her upper level studies, so that she will be accepted as a Professor into Dr. Pimbly's School for Goodly Educated Adults. So it is."

"Then what?"

"Then your work is done. Thank Ophelia and put her away. Thank the Goddesses of the Four Corners for being present with you, and for considering your petition."

"But...is that really it?"

"Magic is not hocus-pocus. Magic is made through clear intention combined with mental focus, and trust in the potency of your own spells, magical tools, and rites. And of course, a little help and guidance from the goddesses never hurts. There is nothing more to be done. What else did you want...an elaborate snake dance around a bubbling cauldron filled with the scales of dragons, phlegm of feral poodles, and essence of wolfbane?" The crane laughed.

"How often do I make my petition for Cassie?"

"Once."

"Once?"

"Don't you think the goddesses heard you the first time?" The bird laughed again, and clicked her beak. "You must trust them to help heal your daughter and manifest your intention, *if* it is right for Cassie. Are you beginning to understand what Beard meant about the importance of *trust* in working magic? And of course, Cassie plays a huge role, too. She's got to actually *do* something to obtain what she desires. She must be absolutely clear about what she wants, and apply right action to manifest her desires. For example, if someone wants to lose weight, they can act by eating candied Meyer lemon sticks, or by a brisk walk every day. Which do you think is right action in line with losing weight? Do you see what I mean? Wishes mean nothing without action behind them in proper alignment with those wishes, no matter who is working magic on our behalf. Combine trust, with clear intention on direct course with authentic desire, and follow-through with consistent correct action. Add in a good amount of love and the blessing of the goddesses, and you can create any kind of magic you can imagine."

"It sounds so simple. Trust, intention, action, love…so if there's nothing 'mystical' in all of this, why doesn't *everyone* create magic? And, what about some things I've witnessed such as piercing the two suns with the light from your wand at the Wasenia Festival ceremony?"

"The principle behind making magic is simple, very simple, but that does not mean it's easy, Beautimus. Not everyone can do this. To create magic takes a great deal of practice, and not *any* practice but *perfect* practice. If I want to learn to play

Bird Ball, but do not practice the right way, I'll never learn to handle the ball the right way. Understand? Also, magic requires a great deal of discipline, a strong will, and one other thing: a Rendazian magician must have a good heart, my dear. Maybe one in a million people have all it takes in the right combination to be a magician. As for piercing the suns? After decades of perfect practice, I could *intention* it, meaning I focused my intention through the Wand of Fortuna, who acted as a conduit by which my desire was made manifest. That is how a wand works, whether it's a Revealing Wand, a Healing Wand, or the magical Wand of Fortuna. Plus, as I said, I've had a few hundred years of perfect practice."

"I don't know if I can do this, Lady Rhianna."

"Of course you can. Otherwise, you wouldn't be here." The crane clapped her wings together. "Enough for today. Take me home. When you get back to your abode, eat a light meal and rest well tonight. Tomorrow, I'd like you to begin practicing on your own. I want you to spend a lot of time with Ophelia over the next few weeks. Get to know one another. Carry her with you everywhere, and try to make something good happen for someone else through Ophelia. Record what happens as a result of your daily practice in your diary…you do have one, don't you? If not, open one on your Crystal Interface tomorrow morning."

Beautimus bade farewell to Master Beard and took the crane home. She'd spent all afternoon with Rhianna and Beard. She had thought of Lucas, of course, but to learn magic, she had to force thoughts of him from her mind. But, now thoughts of Lucas flooded her, unbidden, unwelcomed and unblocked…. she suffered over perhaps having lost him forever because of her lack of trust. She rehearsed what she'd write to him on her Crystal Interface in hopes she could make things right.

As she approached her abode, she noticed people outside

talking, hippos. *Her Aunt and Uncle? No? Who then? Lucas? Naw…couldn't be. Yes it was Lucas…and her, the young woman, her. He actually has the testicles to bring her to my abode? What the hellzabob?*

She continued, but stopped short when Lucas said, "Juniper, wait here please, and I'll be back in a moment. I'll take you home to my place soon, all right, sweetie?" When he came nearer, Beautimus greeted him, "Good evening, Lucas." She kept her tone controlled and formal.

"Bea, can we talk for a minute?"

"Certainly."

They walked a short distance so they could not be overheard.

"What in hellzabob was that Crystal Interface message? Did you really mean 'bye'? I'm confused. I tried to return your call but Agnes told me that you'd turned off your Interface. I decided to come over in person to find out what's going on. What did I do wrong?"

"It appears, Lucas, in spite of what you've told me, you are interested in someone else. I just wanted to make things easier for you so I….".

"What are you talking about? I'm not interested in anyone but you. What is the matter?"

"Lucas, I saw you! I saw you with that woman, the one waiting for you right now back at *my* abode."

"What woman? You aren't talking about my little sister, are you? She came in yesterday morning to surprise me, and I have been really looking forward to introducing you to her."

"You mean to tell me the young woman you brought to my abode, and are taking home with you tonight, is your *sister?*"

"Well, yes. I told you I had a sister. Who did you think… wait, did you see me and Juniper together at the river and assume…oh that's priceless!" Lucas threw back his head and laughed. "Why didn't you simply ask who she was? Good

Goddess, Bea! You about gave me a heart attack thinking you didn't want me anymore."

Beautimus hung her head. "Lucas, I'm a bonehead. I'm sorry. Honest to Goddess when I saw you two together, and for the second time…well, I thought you wanted someone else. I didn't want to embarrass myself or you by asking about her. I understand not asking was the second best choice I could have made. I just, I…I guess I didn't handle it well. Please forgive me for being such a complete bespawling ditz."

"I told you to trust me, Bea. You're all the woman I want, my girl." Lucas kissed Beautimus, and her shar-pendant lit like a firecracker.

They returned to Beautimus' abode together, hides touching, and he introduced the two women. "Beautimus, this is my little sister, Juniper."

"Bea! I've heard so much about you. You are all Lucas talks about. I'm so glad to finally meet you!"

The three entered the abode. Agnes and Applecheeks rushed to attend the hippos, Agnes at the forefront. "You-left-so-early-this-morning-Bea-and-I-didn't-know-if-I-should-cook-dinner-or-when-you'd-be-home-is-a-fruit-platter-okay?-there's-plenty-will-Lucas-and-Juniper-be-staying?"

"Thank you, Agnes. Lucas and Juniper, would you like to join us for a light supper?"

The five sat down to a simple platter of fruit from Beautimus' gardens, then settled in afterwards to watch an episode of *Gilligan's Island*.

CHAPTER TWENTY-NINE

ONLY A FEW more days and Dr. Pimbly's school would be in session. Beautimus planned to use this time to practice with Ophelia, which wouldn't be easy because everyone kept questioning her about the wand.

"What is that stick you take with you everywhere these days, Bea? You even take it in the river. Why?" Calypso asked.

"It's a little thing that I've become attached to."

"Bea, it's a stick. Mind you, a nice stick, but a stick."

"It's part of something I'm working on that I can't...."

"Oh! Did you hear about Rufus being hired to perform at the Poker Club for Dog's Night Out? It's his first professional gig. Don't be surprised if he tries out his fart jokes on you."

"No Calypso, I hadn't heard."

"Well I'm off. Gotta lay some eggs. Hey, were we talking about something?"

"Never mind. It's not important."

"Alrighty then, bye."

Others were curious, too. The Armadillo twins saw her walking down the path with Ophelia in her mouth. They were so close to one another, they always finished one another's sentences, making for interesting communication.

"Hi there."

"Bea"

"Cool weather we're"

"having"

"isn't it?"

"Nice"

"stick."

Agnes couldn't contain her curiosity. "So-Bea-I-saw-a-stick-on-your-altar-anything-special?-I-mean-I-also-couldn't-help-but-notice-that-you-have-it-with-you-all-the-time-these-days-not-that-it-doesn't-look-in-your-teeth-or-that-stretchy-collar-but-well-what-is-it?"

"I know you and Apple are curious about the stick, but I can't discuss it. You'll know what it's about soon. I promise."

Beautimus took Ophelia to the Sacred Glen and practice with it there where she wouldn't be interrupted, and where she could also spend time with her old friend, Beard.

"Master Beard, I am working on my trust issues. I've finally come to believe that I can trust Lucas, but I don't know why I have so much trouble trusting most people, and why I feel so cruddy about myself much of the time. I don't get it."

"Bea, almost everyone you've loved has turned their back on you, or abandoned you. Your mother died when you were a mere bubbit. And while suffering through the worst grief of your life, and needed him the most, your own father left never to return or to even contact you afterwards. A woman must feel like a reprehensible monster if her own child doesn't love her or want her in her life. Your first love abandoned you and his own baby, leaving you to deal with things on your own when you were a child yourself. Can you see how you may have developed a bit of a low self-esteem problem, some insecurities about yourself, and a few trust issues over the past 200 years or so?"

"I guess you're right, Master Beard. I never saw it that way."

"As tall as I am, you could say I have a view from a height." Then he laughed, and shook his leaves so hard he lost a few.

Is Beard attempting humor? Weird. "What do I do about it?"

"I recommend you keep a journal and record those things you most like about yourself until *you* fall in love with *you*. Once you are in love with yourself, it doesn't matter who else is because you'll have all the love in the world you need right inside your heart. And…know with certainty that you are loved by others, Beautimus. It feels good to be cared about, and if we don't get the love we need from others, it can damage us. But we live in a bountiful world filled with love." He rustled his leaves. "Love is all around you, Beautimus Potamus. Even if you do not realize it there are creatures and beings all over Wayflower who love you. I am one of them."

***

Beautimus continued her practice for the day. As her target, she chose a sickly whiteball acacia damaged by a lightning strike. The tree oozed sap from its wounds. Using her sharpendant, she ascertÁined the tree was in pain, afraid, but retÁined a powerful will to live. So, she concentrated healing intention through Ophelia. Within a few weeks, the acacia perked up. It ceased dropping leaves, and its wounds healed. It grew into a stately specimen with a magnificent canopy. For the rest of her life, every time Beautimus passed, the tree buzzed and hummed at her.

The following day, someone outside her abode woke her. She opened her flap to find Samuel and Petunia buzzing about. "Welcome, you two. Come on in. It's so nice to see you. It's been a long while, Sam." She called over her shoulder. "Apple and Agnes, can you please put on water for tea?"

"We've come here to tell you something that I didn't want you to hear from anyone but me," Samuel said. "Petunia has graciously consented to be my legal mate."

"Oh, my Goddess. Congratulations. I couldn't be happier." Beautimus stomped her foot, rousting a sleeping pheasant from its nap under a nearby redbud bush. "You two will have a beautiful life together. When is the Mating Ceremony?"

"In a few weeks. We haven't set an exact date yet, but soon. Bea, I have a huge favor to ask."

"Certainly, Sam. What is it?"

"Will you be my best man, I mean, I know you aren't a man, but you are my best friend. Please?"

"I'm honored, Sam. Petunia, you've got a good guy here, and I know that at last Sam has a good woman, too. I'm thrilled for you both."

"Thank you," Petunia said. "Sam loves you, and we are both pleased you agree to stand up for him."

"Will you be married by an Old Mother or…?"

"Nope" said Sam. "We are both Non-Believers. In fact, Petunia is a WSRT member. That's where I met her, at a meeting at your Aunt and Uncle's. Atheism is one thing we have in common, well, among others." He winked at Petunia. "We will be officially mated in a civil ceremony, but we are going to have one hellzabob of a party afterwards. Everyone is invited. We might even invite the goddesses to tip a chalice of mead with us, who knows?!"

"Now, Sam, don't be disrespectful, you nasty bug. Apple, forget the hot water for tea. Break out the wildflower mead. We have something to celebrate."

***

Besides working with Ophelia, Beautimus spent a considerable amount of time on her Crystal Interface with Cassie.

"Mom, I've given notice at work, and I've hired a chimp to get us packed. I've lined up a dromedary to carry some of our larger things to Wayflower. I'm thinking this time next month we'll be at your abode. Not sure how we are going to get Grandpa to Wayflower yet, but I'll figure it out. He's got a little 'leaking' problem, too, now on top of his Hippodementia and some weakness in his hips. Long walks are difficult for him."

"Don't you worry. Lucas, my boyfriend, an administrator at the university is taking a leave of absence so he can come with me to help. We'll pay for the chimp and the camel. And, we'll get Grandpa here. I still need to arrange time off from work at Dr. Pimbly's school, but I don't see that as a problem."

"Mom, did you say your boyfriend's name is 'Lucas'?"

"Yes, Lucas Potamway."

"Are you serious? He's famous here in the Oceanic District. He's one of the best artist-poets in Rendaz, and I've taken classes from Dr. Potamway. He was one of my favorite professors."

"No kidding? I have been looking forward to you meeting him, but I guess you already have. I'm delighted. Okay, dear. Keep in touch. Let me know when Lucas and I need to be there, and we'll come right away."

"Okay, Mom. I love you."

"I love you, too, Cassie. Give kisses to my grandchildren from me. Let them know they'll be meeting their grandma real soon."

"I will, Mom, and say hello to Dr. Potamway from me."

"All right, sweetheart. Will do."

***

Beautimus had a special treat for Lucas, a romantic evening, just the two of them at her abode. She clued in the squirrels who became partners in her plan. Beautimus bathed in the river that afternoon, and the squirrels rubbed her hide in rose and lilac scented macadamia nut oil. They painted her nails gold. They prepared a magnificent feast with exotic cheeses, a kaleidoscope of vegetables sprinkled with imported grey salt, rare tropical red fruit breads—well known as aphrodisiacs—drizzled with orange blossom honey, and sparkling mead. The squirrels sprinkled the straw with wild rose petals, and brought in a dozen beeswax pillar candles. They laid out the feast on a white lace cloth, lit the candles, and departed for the evening right as Lucas arrived at the flap of Beautimus' abode. In his teeth, he carried two flawless roses, one white and one pink, identical to those he'd brought to their first picnic.

The evening was magical. Beautimus tingled with nerves because it had been over 100 years since she last mated, and being middle-aged now she didn't know her body "worked right," but she was nonetheless ready to give it a try for the man she loved. He was ready, too. He had been for a long while, but being patient and gracious he never pressed the issue of lovemaking.

The dinner was fabulous, and the mead, sweet and intoxicating. Beautimus pushed the dishes and pails to the side of the abode, and the two hippos sat near one another in the rose strewn straw chatting and nuzzling. At last, Lucas made his move. He pushed close into Beautimus and in a husky whisper said, "You smell lovely, Bea. You are so beautiful, and I want you."

The next morning, Beautimus awoke pressed against Lucas. She felt delicious, lovely, heavenly, gorgeous, radiant, beautiful, sexy—if it was a good feeling for a woman to have, she had it. She left Lucas sleeping and stepped outside of the flap to greet the morning. A pandemonium of parrots roosted in one of her pecan trees, but as soon as she spied them they scattered. Parrots, like finches, are notorious gossips, especially eclectus parrots, which these were. Beautimus knew anything they'd seen or overheard would be parroted all over Wayflower by noon. "Oh crap!" she said aloud.

Lucas emerged from the abode. "What's up, my girl?"

"Parrots were right outside probably all night."

"Eclectus?"

"I'm afraid so, Lucas."

"They are the worst."

***

Lucas and Beautimus sauntered together to the river to take a swim. As they walked, they talked. "Beautimus, last night you enchanted me."

"It was the best night of my entire life, Lucas. I love you dearly."

"And, I love you, Beautimus Potamus. I have never loved anyone this way, not ever."

"What we have between us feels right to me on so many levels. I am so blessed."

They spent a glorious day together, when it came time to part, both were reluctant.

"I hate leaving you, Bea. I will see you tomorrow, won't I?"

"Count on it."

Later that evening, her Crystal Interface glowed and buzzed. When she tapped it open, a poem scrolled across the screen:

> Lover
> The taste of your sweet muzzle,
> The sight of your bare haunch,
> The lilac scent of you,
> The feel of your luxurious hide.
> When I mount you,
> I mount the Goddesses,
> My girl,
> My precious Bea.
> I love you. I love you. I love you.
> —Lucas

"The poem is beautiful, Lucas. Thank you, my love."

"Bye for now, Bea."

"Bye for now."

***

Peggy A. Wheeler

The following weeks passed in a swarm of activity. Beautimus and Lucas spent a great deal of time basking in the warmth of one another's love. They didn't spend every night together, but almost, sometimes at Beautimus' abode, other times at Lucas'.

They were right about the parrots. Everyone in Wayflower knew within hours that Lucas had spent that night in Beautimus' abode, so there was no reason not to be openly affectionate. Beautimus introduced Lucas to Samuel and Petunia. They all took an immediate liking to one another.

The four of them oftentimes picnicked together at the pond, and soon became close friends. Lucas, unknown to Beautimus, also had a keen interest in physics and quantum agriculture, so sometimes the two men would lose themselves in lengthy discussions about the latest developments in Energetic Grow Theories, especially Alchemic Capacitance, Radionics, and Biochemical Sequences in Soil Science. The two women used that time to plan Samuel and Petunia's Mating Ceremony.

"Bea, what do you think about us getting mated at the Luna Festival? We aren't Believers, but a lot of our family and friends are. And, almost everyone in Wayflower will be there. We can open the ceremony to everyone in the community."

"What a grand idea, Petunia. You can rent space in Plush Meadow for very few Rendazian Glow Seeds. Have you hired a ritual Officiant yet?"

"Yes, Odette from the Butterfly Council has agreed to officiate. And, my sister, Pansy will stand up for me."

"This is working out nicely, Petunia."

Lizzy took to Lucas right away. It was as though the two had been friends forever. And Aunt Meg was over-the-two-moons charmed by the handsome Dr. Lucas Potamway. Whenever she was around him she'd flutter about like a member of the Butterfly Council, making Uncle Phelan a little jealous.

In the afternoons, Beautimus made polite excuses to go to the Sacred Glen to practice with Ophelia, and once weekly she'd spend an entire day with Rhianna learning the ways of magic. Lucas became accustomed to her absences. Although curious, he never questioned her. He took it as a matter of course she'd be away for a while each day.

Plans progressed for moving Beautimus' family to Wayflower. Beautimus and Cassie spoke daily. Lucas hired a Wooly Mammoth and a wagon with a ramp to carry Artimus from Oceanic to Wayflower. Lizzy, who had some nursing training, offered to caretaker Artimus. "Now, Bea. You are a close and dear friend. I want to help, and I won't take any Glow Seeds for this."

"Oh, yes you will, Lizzy. Daddy has a leaking problem, his hips and liver are bad, and he has Hippodementia. Even with additional help, we are talking a tremendous amount of work. You have other responsibilities with Auntie Nancie's School of Fancy Dancing."

Beautimus paid Lizzy 50% over the usual price for caretaking.

The squirrels and Beautimus interviewed dozens of applicants from Wayne Rumbly's Clever Helpers Training Center. Wayne, a big, boisterous orangutan, had the hots for Auntie Nancie, but Auntie Nancie had the hots for Sgt. Saturday. The triangle made for entertaining dynamics.

When Beautimus first walked into the Training Center and met with Wayne, one of the first things he'd asked her after reviewing her intake form was, "So, Ms. Bea, you know Auntie Nancie, don't you?"

"Yes," Beautimus said, "but I'm unsure what my relationship with Auntie Nancie has to do with hiring household help."

"I kinda wondered if you'd ever heard her say anything about…me."

"Mr. Rumbly, I know Auntie Nancie, of course. Who doesn't? As a little girl, I took ballet classes from her, but I wouldn't say the two of us are friends. She doesn't discuss with me details of her personal life."

"I'd heard around town that she's been keeping company with that Sgt. Saturday, and I wondered if you knew anything."

"I don't, Mr. Rumbly, but even if I did it'd be inappropriate for me to share anything about that with you. Why don't you ask her yourself? In the meantime, I need to hire some good household help, so can you please set up a series of interviews with your best?"

"Of course, Ms. Bea. I will send applicants to you as early as tomorrow afternoon, if that works for you."

"It does. Thank you."

A string of applicants showed up on Beautimus' doorstep, each one worse than the last. One spider monkey, Jimmy, looked a lot like Jake the banished thief. Beautimus and the squirrels didn't think much of it until part way the interview. "Say, how much does this gig pay anyway?" The monkey asked. "Oooh, nice rocks on your altar. Are those shar stones?" He looked over every object in Beautimus' abode as though he were a hungry crocodile.

Beautimus asked, "Jimmy, not that this has *anything* to do with whether we will hire you, but do you happen to know Jake, the monkey, the one banished?"

"My cousin. And, if you ask me, he got a bad rap. Jake has kinda sticky fingers, if you know what I mean. Who doesn't? But, if it weren't for that sneaky bitch coyote, he'd never been caught for nothin' like stealin' a stupid wand." The monkey rubbed his hands together. "So, I'll take the gig. When do you want me to start?" That pretty much ended the interview. Next....

The applicant after Jimmy, a Panda named Cranberry didn't seem much interested in working. "What hours did you say I'd have to work? It seems like an awful lot I'd have to do, cooking, cleaning, all that. I dunno. How many days off do I get?" Next...

A nimble and beautiful lemur named Tammy walked in. She wore an excess of bright lip rouge, strands of gaudy jewelry, and enough colored ribbons braided into her fur one might assume she was headed to a party rather than a job interview. Through the entire hour, she stared at herself in Beautimus' mirror. She turned her head this way and that to get a better look at her profile. Next....

A young troodon named Redbone came in. He was polite, professional, seemed unafraid of challenging work, and had no objection to reporting to the squirrels. At first, he seemed perfect for the job...that is until he very casually began picking his nose, inspecting his finger afterwards, and eating the boogers. He also passed gas, not little silent toots, but serious rank smelling blasts so loud they could shatter glass. Throughout the remainder of the interview, he continued farting and picking his nose as though no one noticed. Next....

A rhesus monkey named Clancy walked in, or rather he staggered in. He belched and said, "'Scuse me I'm jist a liddle—belch—bit shmired, I mean a liddle tired, I was up – belch—late, uh, watchin' over my poor preedy shick nanny, I mean poor pretty shick granny, I mean my poor shitty sick mammy, I mean my old pretty shick mammy. Sorry. Ah... belch. I might have had a wee nip too much. I drink a liddle... medicinally...ya know. Doc's orders to settle m'nerves. *Belch*." He was excused from the remainder of the interview. Next...

This continued applicant after applicant.

"If this is Wayne Rumbly's best, I wonder what his worst is like?" Beautimus said to Agnes. A few showed up that seemed suitable enough. They finally agreed on a young chimpanzee, Sally, and an older, well groomed, troodon, Jeeves, with over

220 years of experience, but no one else would hire him because of his age. Jeeves was stoic, private, and tended to keep to himself. Sally, however, was vivacious, sociable, with a delightful personality.

"I-like-Sally-it'll-be-so-nice-to-have-someone-around-who-I-can-talk-to-who-can-actually-talk-back-no-offense-Apple-you-know-I-love-you-I-mean-you're-my-sister-and-my-best-friend-really-anyone-want-tea?"

At last, moving day arrived. She and Lucas planned to stop by to visit his family in Oceanic, then head right for Cassie's abode, pack, and go to Shady Grove Invalid Hospital to pick up Artimus Potamus. Sam offered to come along to help. Beautimus and Lucas talked him out of it. "There isn't much you can do, Sam. Why not stay here with Petunia and keep an eye on things here for us while we are gone?"

Lizzy offered to accompany them. "If I come with you, I can meet your father, Bea, and care for him on the way here. It will get him used to the idea that I'll be his nursemaid."

"That's a fine idea," said Beautimus.

The mastodon, the mammoth, the two hippos, with Sally along to help with cooking and other things requiring opposable thumbs, set off together to the Oceanic District.

"My home will be filled wall-to-wall with my family. I can hardly wait," said Beautimus.

CHAPTER THIRTY

THE TRIP TO the Oceanic District assumed a festive atmosphere with lots of chatter and laughter. Now and again, the travelers came across a drove of cattle or a coalition of cheetahs and exchanged greetings. A colony of chinchilla approached from the opposite direction and stopped for a bit. "You are wearing a lovely shar-pendant." One named Charlene said to Beautimus. "You wouldn't happen to know, Angeline? She makes and sells pendants similar to those."

"Why, yes, I do know Angeline. As a matter of fact, I bought this pendant from her at the Wasenia Festival."

"Are you Beautimus Potamus?"

"I am."

"Angeline is my cousin. She speaks highly of you. You do know that shar-pendants contain powerful magic?"

"So, I have heard."

"We are travelling to Wayflower and plan on staying through the Luna Festival. Will you be attending?"

"We certainly will."

"We'll see you there, then." The chinchilla started on her way, then paused. "By the way, the shar-pendant you are wearing is not the kind she sells over the counter. Those are reserved for customers who Angeline feels are in some way deserving, special."

"Really? Thank you for telling me that. I didn't know."

After the chinchillas passed, Lucas asked, "Your pendant has magic. What kind?

"The kind that helped me find you, Lucas."

"No, Bea. It was the magic of you I fell in love with."

On the outskirts of Oceanic, in a lakeside compound,

resided a tribe of Hippos. Within that compound lived Lucas's relatives. Beautimus met Lucas's mother, Betty, and his father, Bob, both lovely people, plus an entire crash of hippos made up of assorted aunts and uncles, cousins, all gracious folk who Beautimus took an immediate liking to.

A beautiful little hippo, Juniper, came running up to greet her big brother. "Lucas! I've been waiting for you all day. Bea. It's so good to see you." She nuzzled both Lucas and Beautimus. "You are staying for lunch, aren't you? Momma made your fav, Lucas, minted strawberry soup."

Beautimus said, "Lucas, I didn't know you liked strawberry and mint soup. That's *my* favorite, too."

After lunch, as everyone exchanged goodbyes, Lucas said to Juniper, "I've got an idea. Why don't you come to Wayflower for the Luna Festival?"

"Yes. I'll be there. Wait a minute, let me check. Mom, Dad is it okay if I go to the Luna Festival with Lucas and Bea?"

"Sure, why not?" Bob said.

"I'm going to the Wayflower Luna Festival. Wait 'till I tell my friends!"

It was in that moment that Beautimus realized how very young Juniper was. "Why, she's no older than I when I calved Cassie. She's a child."

Late afternoon, they arrived at Cassie's abode. The packing chimp loaded things on the back of the camel. Cassie ran out and nuzzled her mother. She said to Lucas, "Professor Potamway, you may not remember me, but I took some classes from you at Rendaz University, Oceanic Campus some moons ago."

"Why, Cassie. I do remember you. You were a fine student. As I recall you had a real feel for Art History."

"It was my favorite subject, Dr. Potamway."

"Please do call me Lucas."

Lucas turned to Beautimus. "Bea, why didn't you tell me your daughter had been one of my students?"

"I'd hoped you'd remember her, and I wanted to surprise you."

"How delightful one of my favorite former students is your daughter."

Two children appeared from behind the abode where they had been playing—a boy with huge brown eyes, and mud stuck to his legs followed by a little girl... *with a luminous hide and violet eyes.*

Beautimus sunk to the ground on all four knees. "They are so beautiful."

Cassie knelt beside her children. "Little Josh and Bea Two meet your grandmother."

The two children nuzzled Beautimus, making her so happy she thought she'd melt into the ground.

"We are going to live at your house in Wayflower, aren't we Grandma?" Said Bea Two.

"Why yes you are, at least until we build you an abode of your own."

"Are there any boy hippos in Wayflower, like, you know, around my age?" asked Josh.

"Yes, there are, Josh."

"I'm ready to go but I want to make sure there'd be boys there first. I'm bringing a kick ball."

"You can bring anything you'd like."

After introductions all around, Lucas said, "What more does the chimp have to load? Can I help? We need to get going soon, because we have to get the mammoth to the hospital and load Artimus into the wagon."

Beautimus sidled up next to Lucas. "Actually, I think we are ready, aren't we? Josh and Bea Two, please go down to the river and wash up. It's time to get on the road."

When the children returned, Cassie took one last look inside her abode, sighed, closed the flap, and said, "Okay, let's go."

She never once looked back. In that abode, she'd lived with the man she loved, and she'd scattered his ashes in the back garden. She'd calved both of her bubbits there. The sorrow in Cassie's eyes cut to Beautimus' core. She hoped her daughter was ready to move on now and start a new life with her children in Wayflower.

The group set off on the path to Shady Grove Invalid Hospital. Beautimus led the way, and skipping next to her, a little girl hippo with violet eyes chatting like a parakeet. Lucas and Josh walked side-by-side. Beautimus turned occasionally to watch them. Seeing the two together, she fell in love with Lucas all over again.

Late in the day, they arrived at the hospital. They beat the wagon by only a few minutes.

Cassie moved to her mother's side. "Mom, are you ready to see your father? Don't be hurt if he doesn't remember you."

The last time anyone had said that to Beautimus, soon after, her heart shattered into a million pieces. She felt trepidation at seeing her father after so many years. She paused for a moment to think it over, took a breath and said, "I'm ready."

She turned to everyone. "Please wait here. We'll be right out."

Cassie led the way through the hospital corridors to the room where Artimus Potamus rested. His things were packed, a couple of scarves to keep away the cold, one big wool blanket, and a small old ratty box that held a few treasures. Beautimus wanted to look in the box, but right now, she wanted to see Daddy.

Cassie walked in ahead of Beautimus. "Grandpa?"

"Is that you, Sangrina?"

"No, Grandpa. It's your granddaughter, Cassie."

"Cassie? Sorry, I get you two confused."

"Grandpa, I have a surprise for you."

"You do? What kind of surprise? Melon Balls?"

"No, something better. Mom, come here."

Beautimus stepped into the room and, with trepidation, she approached her father. He rested on a pile of pillows. He looked so worn, so old, but she could tell it was her daddy for certain. She kneeled. "Daddy?"

He looked at her, cocked his head a little one way, then the other, then squinted at her as though he was trying to peer at a midge on the wall. His eyes flew open. "Beautimus? Is that my little girl? Beautimus!" Tears streamed down his face. "I thought I'd never see you again. Where have you been? Thank the Great Goddess it's you."

Beautimus couldn't contain her own tears. They came in a torrent. "Daddy, I missed you so much. I'm here now. I'm going to take you home. You're going to live with me, and I'll take care of you. Is that all right?"

Artimus nodded his head and buried his forehead, into his daughter's fleshy side and sobbed. After a time, Beautimus stood.

"Where are you going? You aren't leaving me, are you?"

"No, Daddy. We are getting you ready for your trip. I'm not going anywhere. You're coming with me, remember?"

"That's right, to your abode. Now, where is that again?"

"Wayflower."

"Will I see my Sangrina there?" His eyes lit.

"No, Daddy. Mom is gone."

"Yes, yes, of course." He looked sad for a minute. "We are going to your abode in Wayflower, is that it?"

"Yes, Daddy."

"Where's my things? My scarves? Both of them. It might get cold."

"They are packed and on the wagon."

"You sure? Is everything there?"

"Yes, Daddy. I promise."

Eight attending Gorillas entered the room, hoisted Artimus

between them. They helped him walk out of the hospital and up the ramp into the wagon. They laid him on a pile of pillows, and tucked his blanket around him. "You have a good trip, Mr. Potamus. We'll miss you around here."

Artimus looked to his daughter. "Now, where is that we are headed. I forget?"

***

They were quite a sight, a camel piled high with household goods, hippos, a chimp, a mastodon, and a mammoth pulling a wagon. They discussed one thing or another on their way from Oceanic to Wayflower. Beautimus mostly spent time to get to know her grandchildren. "So, Josh, you like sports, I hear?"

"Yup, kickball the most, but I also run pretty fast for a hippo. I like all sports, really."

"I like dancing." Bea Two stretched to her toes and twirled about.

"Shush, Bea Two. Grandma's talking to me, not you."

"It's fine Josh. I'm talking to both of you. What about school? What's your favorite subject?"

"Science. I also play tuba. I might join a rock 'n roll tuba band if there's one in Wayflower."

"That's great, Josh. What about you, Bea Two?"

"Well, besides dancing, which is my number one thing I like in the whole wide world, I like to draw pictures, and I like to write stories, and I play with dollies. I like the goddesses, too. Mama taught me all about them. When I grow up, I wanna be a dancer and a High Priestess."

"You can't be a High Priestess and a Dancer. They don't go together," said Josh.

"She probably can do both, Josh, but maybe not at the same time," said Beautimus.

"Well, I'm going to be a scientist and play in a rock-n-roll tuba band," said Josh.

"That's wonderful."

"….and maybe I'll be a professional kickball player, too."

"That's not fair," said Bea Two. "If he can do all that when he grows up, why can't I be a dancer and a High Priestess?"

"You can both do and be anything you want when you grow up," said Beautimus.

Cassie and Lucas laughed watching Beautimus with her grandchildren.

"These three are going to be a riot together," Cassie said to Lucas.

"She'll be a wonderful grandmother, Cassie, but you better watch out, because I can tell she's going to spoil them until they stink, they'll be so rotten."

"*Ya think?*"

"Hey, you, two," Beautimus said. "I can hear every word. And, for your information, I do plan on spoiling these kids. So there."

To Beautimus' relief, Lizzy and Artimus got along well. Lizzy turned out a patient, loving, and attentive nurse who made Artimus as comfortable as possible. She walked beside the wagon the entire way. She cleaned up his "mistakes" when he leaked a little. She made sure he had fresh pails of water when he needed them. She took him for walks. She fed him. She talked to him.

Once in a while, Artimus called out, "Beautimus, are you here?"

"Yes, Daddy. I'm right in front of you."

"Are we going to Wayflower?"

"Yes. We'll be there in two days."

"Promise?"

"Yes, Daddy. I promise."

"Now, you're sure it's Wayflower we are going to?"

"Yes. Wayflower."

"I'm afraid I don't remember. My forgetter works overtime these days."

"It's okay, Daddy. My forgetter works overtime sometimes, too."

"Beautimus?"

"Yes, Daddy?"

"I love you. I love you a whole bunch."

"I love you a whole bunch, too."

The day they were to arrive in Wayflower, Lizzy asked the mastodon to stop the wagon. Artimus needed to relieve himself. Lizzy helped him down the ramp. He asked for privacy. Artimus walked off in the direction of a pin bush, and disappeared behind it. Everyone waited, and waited, and waited.

Lucas went to check on Artimus. "You all right there, buddy? Hey, Artimus. Where are you? He's not here. I can't find him. Everyone, pick a direction and look for him."

Beautimus searched one direction, Cassie in another, Lucas in another. The children remÁined behind with Lizzy, the camel, and the mammoth in case Artimus returned. Sally shimmied up the highest tree she could find to get a panoramic view, and settled onto a branch.

After a frantic search, Sally called out. "I see him on the path to Wayflower. He's just a few yards behind that zeal of zebras. Right there." She pointed.

They found Artimus strolling down the road as contented as could be. Lucas and Beautimus reached him first.

"Where are you headed, Artimus?" Lucas asked.

"Home, naturally. Sangrina has dinner ready, I imagine."

"Daddy, how about you come back here with us?"

"Where are we going?"

"You are coming home with me to my abode in Wayflower."

"Did you pack my scarves? Both of them? Might get cold."

Lucas and Beautimus escorted Artimus back to the wagon. Lizzy led him up the ramp to his pillows where he reclined, and covered him with his blanket. He fell into a deep snore.

They at last reached Beautimus' abode. Applecheeks, Agnes, and Jeeves helped to unload. Beautimus ordered monkeys to build a storage facility to temporarily house her daughter's furnishings. She had contracted the Bo Bo Baboon Construction Company to build a two-room abode for Cassie. Bo Bo would also add a partition for Artimus' sleeping quarters, and one for Jeeves' sleeping area as well so everyone living under Beautimus' roof could enjoy a little privacy. Beautimus needed her own space, too, especially now that she had a lover.

Lucas and Beautimus fed the mammoth and the camel, paid them and sent them on their way. Everyone had eaten, and the children were down for the evening.

Agnes said, "I-can't-believe-that-Bea-Two-is-like-you-Bea-with-purple-eyes-too-she-is-just-gorgeous-and-really-she-looks-just-like-you-it-will-be-so-fun-to-have-the-children-around-we-should-build-a-play-yard-for-them-will-they-be-starting-school-soon?"

"Yes, Agnes, we'll have them in Mrs. Prim Jay's by next week. I like your idea of a play yard. I'll talk to Bo Bo about it."

Exhausted after the long trip, Artimus fell asleep and the abode grew quiet.

"I think I'll be headed home," said Lucas. "Bea, would you mind walking me outside?"

He pushed through the flap with Beautimus following behind into the coolness of the evening. Ladyluz and Ladybeth shown in all their moonlit splendor.

"Bea, I know we just got your family here today and you need to spend time with them, but is there any way I can see you alone at the pond tomorrow for maybe two hours? I have something important to discuss with you."

"Certainly. What time?"

"Let's make it 3 o'clock."

"I'll be there." Lucas leaned into Beautimus and kissed her. "I love you, my girl."

"I love you, too, Lucas. Thank you so much for all of your help."

"Bye for now."

"Bye for now."

CHAPTER THIRTY-ONE

"WHERE AM I? What is this place? Sangrina! Sangrina! Where *are* you?"

Lizzy and Beautimus appeared together at his bedside.

"Now, now, Mr. Potamus. You'll be fine." Said Lizzy.

"Is that you Beautimus?"

"No, I'm your nurse, Lizzy."

"My nurse? Why do I need a nurse?"

"Daddy, I'm with you, too" said Beautimus

"Where am I?"

"You're in my abode, Daddy, in Wayflower."

"Wayflower? What am I doing in Wayflower? Where's my Sangrina?"

"Mom's gone. You are here living with me. Lizzy and I are going to take care of you now."

"I don't *need* anyone to take care of me." He struggled to get to his feet but fell back into his pillows.

Cassie tended to her children nearby. "Is Great Grandpops okay?" asked Josh.

"He's fine," said Cassie. "Let's go outside you two and see if we can't find the river, shall we?"

"Daddy, I'm here with you. Everything is all right." Beautimus nuzzled her father.

"Yes, yes, Wayflower. I'm at your abode, in Wayflower. That's right. Is Cassie here, too?"

"Yes, Daddy. She's outside with the children."

Lizzy asked the squirrels to brew fresh chamomile tea steeped with valerian root and a little honey to settle Artimus. She stroked Artimus' head with her trunk.

"You are with family who love you, Artimus," Lizzy said.

"Beautimus, Cassie, your great grandchildren are with you. And, I'll help, too. You are going to live a good life here."

"Thank you." He yawned. "I'm so tired."

"Tea is coming, then you can take a nice nap."

Artimus fell back into a deep sleep, during which he relieved himself on the floor. Lizzy and Sally cleaned the mess. Lizzy decided she'd to go Lacy's and see if she couldn't get some sort of diaper made up for Artimus, something with removable, washable pads.

A few days later, Lizzy brought the diapers home but Artimus refused to wear them. "Bea, I don't know what to do."

"Let me handle this one."

Beautimus went to her father's bedside. "You know, Daddy, on Earth the most handsome gentlemen wear these garments called 'trousers' – these things are a kind of trousers, and Liz and I thought you'd look rather rakish in them."

The old hippo hung his head in silence for a moment. "I'll give them a try, but if I don't like them I'm not wearing 'em."

"Fair enough, Daddy."

Most of the day Beautimus stayed by her father's side. Jeeves, Sally and the squirrels made breakfast for everyone. Once Artimus had eaten and rested, he was able to adjust to his surroundings somewhat, and orient himself better. He grew lucid and talkative. "Bea, it's so good to see you again. I thought of you nearly every day after I left. Please forgive me for not coming back or contacting you. After your mother died, I couldn't…"

"Daddy, everything is good. We are here together now, and I'm so happy you share my home with me."

Artimus nuzzled her. "I don't know what I'd do if it weren't for you and Cassie. Now, *who* is that mastodon, again?"

"I'm your nurse," Lizzy said.

"Oh, that's right, *Lizzy*. My forgetter is working overtime. Sorry."

"Don't worry. If you forget who I am again, I'll tell you. No problem at all. Deal?"

"Deal."

Dr. Bombay dropped by to check on Artimus. Afterwards, he asked to speak to Beautimus outside. "I'm afraid your father is in a bad way, Bea. I tested his liver with my pulsometer. His liver function is weak. That, along with his advancing Hippodementia, his failing hips, loose bladder and flabby bowels. You may have him around for ten or twelve more moons, but don't expect much. Keep him comfortable. And, if he develops a tendency to wander, he could get lost in the forest. I'd put the troodoon's bed at the front entrance."

"Thank you, Doctor."

Already after two p.m. and Beautimus still had not gone down to the river to bathe, and she worried she'd be late to meet Lucas. When she thought her father had fallen asleep, she decided to make her exit, but as she nosed through the flap, he called out.

"Beautimus! You aren't leaving, are you? Where are you going? Don't go."

"Daddy, I'll be back soon, I promise. Lizzy and Cassie are here with you."

"Where's Sangrina? Sangrina! Sangrina!"

"Daddy, Mom is gone. I'll be back soon. Rest. Do you want some water? Sally, please get my dad a pail of fresh water." She returned to her father's bed, and with her muzzle, she tucked his pillows around him. "I'll be back real soon."

"Promise?"

"Promise."

Tired, Beautimus took a cool dip in the river, and made her way to Sweetwater Pond. To her surprise she encountered the Baboon Harp Trio playing Debussy's *Claire de Lune*. On the green damask table cloth spread over the soft lawn sat the cut crystal pail filled with cold sparkling mead, and beside it, the vase with the perfect pink and white roses.

Lucas appeared from behind a wild paponax. "Beautimus Potamus, please join me for a sip of mead. I've something to ask you."

"This is lovely, Lucas, but what's this all about?"

"Shhhhh. Come sit near me."

The two hippos sat next to one another on the damask cloth, then Lucas turned to Beautimus. "I love you, my girl, and I know you love me. I want to spend the rest of my life with you. Please honor me by consenting to be my legal mate."

"*What* did you say?"

"I'm asking you to be my legal mate, to live with me and share the good, and bad with me, and all that life has to offer us for the rest of our natural lives."

"Oh my Goddess, my Goddess. Yes, yes, yes!"

Beautimus' eyes filled with tears. Lucas kissed her. "You have made me the happiest man on Rendaz, Bea."

They snuggled against one another, lapping sparkling mead, nuzzling, kissing.

"Maybe the humans are right, maybe there is a spectacular place you go to if you are good, because I feel like I've died and gone to that place. I'm in paradise right now, Lucas Potamway."

The Baboon Harp Trio switched to *Afternoon of a Fawn*.

The pair eventually parted, and when Beautimus arrived home, Aunt Meg and Uncle Phelan were there. Aunt Meg visited with her brother, reminiscing, talking like two normal siblings who'd not seen one another in a long while.

Artimus, in a lucid and lively mood, delighted in his little sister's company. "Bea, look who came by for a visit," he said as Beautimus entered.

"Hello, Aunt Meg and Uncle Phelan. Hello Daddy," she said. "How are you feeling?"

"Pretty darn good."

"Grandma!" said Bea Two. "Me and Josh ate a whole barrel of strawberries today."

Cassie corrected her daughter. "*Josh and I*, Bea Two."

"No, it was me and Josh, not *you* and Josh, Mom. You were looking for a place to build our abode, remember? It was me and Josh who picked the berries."

"You're a bonehead, Bea Two," said Josh.

"No, *you* are a bonehead."

"I called you a bonehead first."

"I don't care. *Mom*, Josh called me a name."

"Both of you stop, *now*," Cassie said.

Beautimus laughed. "I can see things are going to be lively around here." She cleared her throat. "Listen, I'm glad everyone is here. I wish Sam and Petunia were here, too, but I can't wait to tell you this."

"Bonehead, bonehead, bonehead," Josh whispered to Bea Two.

"Mom, make him stop."

"I told you both to stop. Grandma has something to share with us, so please be quiet and respectful. I'm sorry about the kids, Mom. Go ahead."

"Sorry, Grandma," said Bea Two.

"Sorry," said Josh.

"I've got something important indeed to share with you." She looked around at the expectant faces in the room. "Well, I might as well come out with it. Lucas has asked me to be his legal mate, and I've accepted."

"You're kidding me, Bea?" said Aunt Meg, "That's the best news ever. I'm so very happy for you, dear."

Everyone in the abode gave their hearty approval to the finest match in all of Rendaz. Bea Two jumped up and down. "Can I be your flower girl, Grandma? Can I? Please, please, please?"

"Of course, you can be my flower girl."

Because of Artimus' little mead problem, they toasted with apple juice. Afterwards, they shared a fine supper of fresh berries, pecans and goat cheese.

"So, when's this little mating ceremony soiree scheduled?"

"We haven't really discussed it, Uncle Phelan, but it won't be until sometime after the Luna Festival. Besides Sam and Petunia's mating ceremony is going to be at the Festival. I think two mating ceremonies in one day at the same venue would be too much, and since I'm 'best man' for Sam, I can't very well be a bride and a best man on the same day," Beautimus laughed.

Later that evening, after the squirrels cleared the dinner plates, and Aunt Meg and Uncle Phelan had gone home, everyone settled in. Beautimus said, "Daddy, can I open your box? You know, the little brown box you brought with you?"

"Sure, why not?"

With Apple's help, Beautimus unlatched the box. Inside were two things only: a faded, stÁined and frayed white silk ribbon worn by her mother on her mating day with her daddy, and, a slightly creased, very old photo of a small newborn girl hippo with a luminescent hide, violet eyes, and a tiny heart-shaped mark on her cheek.

CHAPTER THIRTY-TWO

WHEN BEAUTIMUS AND Lucas invited Lizzy, Sam and Petunia for picnic, and announced their engagement, the news overjoyed everyone. Samuel suggested a "double mating ceremony" but Beautimus said, "No, no. You need your special day and we need ours, besides that, since Lucas and I are Believers we prefer Rhianna, or the High Priestess after her, to officiate over our ceremony."

Lizzy agreed to be co-Lady of Honor with Cassie. Of course, Bea Two would be flower girl. Beautimus would assign roles for Josh, the squirrels, Samuel, Juniper, all of whom wanted to be involved in the mating ceremony in some meaningful way. Beautimus couldn't decide if she should have the ceremony at Sweetwater Pond where Lucas had proposed, or in the Sacred Glen at the roots of Beard. She'd discuss this with Lucas. She knew she'd hire the Baboon Harp Trio to play Debussy, and would serve minted strawberry soup and sparkling mead after the ceremony. She wanted lots and lots of pink and white roses.

More than anything she wanted her father to be there. He may not be able to escort her down the ceremonial path, or dance with her at the afterparty, but she could put him in a top hat, bring him by wagon with a sign on the back that read *Father of the Bride*, and she'd find some other way to include him in a special way. She accompanied Aunt Meg to Lacy's to pick up silk ribbons in white, pink and lavender, then over to Girly Girl's to get silver paint for her toenails, new cheek rouge, and ylang-ylang scented hide oil.

With planning her mating ceremony, helping Petunia plan hers, teaching at Dr. Pimbly's, helping care for her father, learning magic and healing, overseeing the addition to her abode, working with Bo Bo Construction in building Cassie's abode, and only a moon away from the Luna Festival, to accomplish it all, Beautimus ran a hundred miles an hour with her tail on fire. But, even so, there could be no happier hippo in Rendaz.

Beautimus wanted to bring her father to the Luna Festival. She prepared to hire a wagon and a brontosaurus to pull it, but her daddy weakened by the day. Already Artimus could no longer stand, and required pails full of strong brewed white willow bark tea to keep the pain in his hips at bay. His periods of lucidity were shorter and further apart, and his incontinence worsened. He had begun from time-to-time to hallucinate white mice in red military uniforms dancing on the ceiling, and mysterious humanoid creatures in dark robes coming in through Beautimus' vanity mirror to steal things from him.

When Lizzy said, "Artimus, honestly there are no uniformed mice in the abode," or when Beautimus said, "Daddy, I promise you, no one can get through my mirror." He'd become insistent. "I can see them *right there*. Look." He motioned toward the mirror. "I'm not a liar. I *know* what I see. What's the matter with you? Are you all blind?" After a while, everyone humored him.

Beautimus, Lizzy, Lucas and Cassie had a conference at the pond to discuss the matter of Artimus going to the Luna Festival, and all agreed the trip, even though only a half day's walk, would be too much for Artimus. With all the people and noise, the festival might be confusing to him, maybe even frightening. Although unhappy about it, Beautimus consented to leave him home. Jeeves, not a Believer, hated crowds, and had never been big on social events anyway, offered to stay behind with Artimus so everyone else could go. Beautimus planned to feed Artimus, then dose him with white willow bark, chamomile, and valerian root tincture before leaving in the afternoon in hopes he'd sleep most of the evening. Beautimus set up her Crystal Interface so her father and Jeeves could watch the ceremony if they chose to, and she'd bring them large bags of sugar popped blue corn.

The night before the Luna Festival, Samuel L. Goodwings presided over his bachelor party. Beautimus, being Best Man, would be the only female in attendance, and the only hippo. Petunia expressed delight and gratitude for Beautimus' attendance. A few nights before, in lieu of a bachelorette party, the two women decided on a "Girls Night Out" at Sweetwater Pond. All the women got together for an evening picnic. Besides baskets and baskets of food, they brought rose blossom wine. Later in the evening, Petunia, a lightweight anyway, got bombed. She said to Beautimus, "I'm sooo—hiccup—sooo glad you are going to the bashelour, bachelor's party—hiccup—Bea."

She pointed at Bea's nose. "I heard Michael M. hired that shlut, shlutty, sheap, cheap Cheeky—hiccup—to jump outta a, a, a cup of mead and do a butt-wiggle dance for Sam. If you ask me, I think that sheap shlut always had the—hiccup—hots for Sam and has been hankering toooo latch onto his honker."

"Don't worry, Petunia. If Cheeky shows up, I'll keep her away from Sam's honker. I promise. Hon, I think we should get you home."

"I love you—hiccup—Bea. You're the bestest friend ever, and I mean ever—hiccup—a woman could ever—hiccup—ever, ever have."

At his bachelor party, Samuel drank a bit too much and began blathering about atmospheric reorganizers, cosmic pipes, and electromagnetic spectrums that did not attenuate with distance and were conducted over wires into the blue corn fields. He talked to anyone who'd listen, which turned out to be no one. He didn't care. He enjoyed himself.

Other than that, to Beautimus' surprise, the party goers were subdued. Samuel had to endure some good-natured ribbing from the black widows for being "caught in one woman's web" after his *big* talk to them post-Wasenia festival a short while back. And, his brother and friends teased him. "Well, so much for being a *ladies' man*, Sam," or some variation on that theme.

Michael M. had not hired Cheeky, but had hired Rufus to tell one liners. Rufus brought along a tufted capuchin with a trap drum. The jokes were horrible, and no one except Michael M., laughed, but he laughed so hard he made up for everyone else's *not* laughing.

"So, this guy legally mates with the right woman. He didn't know she'd *always* be right." Badabing

Why did the polygamist cross the aisle? To get to the other bride." Badaboom

"So why fart and waste when you can burp and taste?" Badabing

"Does anyone here know the three stages of sex after legal mating? No one? Ready for this? This is a visual, so pay attention. The three stages of sex in legal mating: tri-weekly; try-weekly; try-weakly." He drew the joke in the sand for the party goers to see." Get it? Hahahahaa. Get it?" Badaboom

"Why do farts stink? For the benefit of the deaf." Badabing.

After he completed his routine, Rufus took a deep bow. "You've been a great crowd, Ladies and Germs. Catch me at Dogs Night Out at the Poker Parlor next moon. Mead one-half off. Bitches get in free. Okey Dokey, Artichokey, don't let the bedbugs bite."

Beautimus laughed. *Petunia will be happy to know that Cheeky wasn't here, and no one attempted to latch onto Sam's honker.*

***

The morning of the Luna Festival, the girls painted their toe nails silver, and tied blue and purple ribbons to their tails. Beautimus asked Apple to paint a silver full moon between her eyes, also one between Lizzy's, one between Juniper's, one between Cassie's and one between Bea Two's. Josh didn't want one "That's for *girls*," he said when Beautimus asked if he'd like a moon on his forehead.

The squirrels dipped their tails in silver paint.

"That's a fine look for you two. Fashionable," Beautimus said.

The squirrels blushed.

There'd be quite a party on the way to the Luna Festival. An abundance of tasty treats in everyone's satchels, and great companionship meant good times on the road. Beautimus carried Samuel and Petunia, who wore matching silver capes, their mating ceremony finery. Lizzy carried Applecheeks and Agnes. Cassie bore Sally who had an enormous white bow on her head, and carried an orange day lily and a spray of blue asters, the official flowers of the Luna Festival.

Last season, when she'd gone to the Wasenia Festival, Beautimus had started off on the path to the Sacred Watering Hole with Sam. Today she went to the Luna Festival with eleven of her family members and closest friends, including her new fiancé, daughter and grandchildren. *What a difference a few moons can make in a person's life.*

The cool season brought forth many kinds of flowers. Joe Pye Weed, Helianthus, Golden Rod, Purple Aster, Chrysanthemum and Sedum were in bloom. The river gave off a rise of mist like soft gray breath. The air smelled of green apples and pumpkin. The forest had become more subdued, introspective and reflective, and those on the walk to the Sacred Watering Hole responded in kind. The overall tone of the procession remÁined festive and congenial, toned down, less raucous than the fairgoers to the Wasenia Festival in Warm

Season.

When the troupe of Auntie Nancie's School of Fancy Dancing passed by, the gazelles, rather than dancing an expansive leaping-twirling Balanchine ballet-flourish kind of thing, took small, refined steps in a series of movements, resembling a modified Bourée. Auntie Nancie, miffed at Lizzy, who declined to bear her this year in favor of accompanying Beautimus—forcing her to ride on a smaller less elegant elephant—demonstrated her disdain by turning her head away.

The Turkey Buzzards swooped low over the crowd, their painted silver beaks glinting in the sun light. The eagles flew closely behind, shamed because they had been relegated to a second place position this time in the festival flyover.

A small zebra, Winnie, her mane and tail braided with long blue, white and purple ribbons, trotted by and greeted Beautimus. "Hello, everyone. May the moons bless you."

"And may the moons bless you, Winnie," Beautimus said.

A gaze of raccoons, a mob of emus, and a nide of pheasants passed by decked out in their Luna Festival caps, capes, hats, bows, ribbons. Each one proffered Luna Festival greetings to Beautimus and her group. A Jackalope named Osiris hopped to Beautimus. At least a dozen ribbons hung from his antlers. "Bea, so nice to see you with your family and friends. May the moons bless you."

"Thank you, Osiris. Same to you."

There is a healthy population of Jackalopes on Rendaz, but most tend to stay to themselves. Osiris, a rare social Jackalope, liked to adorn himself and attend all the festivals. Beautimus recalled seeing him in the mead garden at the Wasenia Festival quaffing a liter of honeysuckle mead with a saber-tooth squirrel. Osiris, unaware that his long ribbons hung in the mead, became sticky with the sweet stuff, attracting a swarm of fruit flies. The mead made the flies drunk, and they stumbled over the fur of the Jackalope, some tumbling to the dirt.

Yellow bellied marmots with the Friends of the Library marched by chanting, "Books, Books, Read More Books." Beautimus gave kazoos to both Josh and Bea Two to occupy them on the way to the festival. The children fell in line behind the Marmots for a while humming into their kazoos as though an official part of the procession.

Beautimus et al, passed the Sacred Glen. Since she'd seen Beard every day while training with Rhianna, and because she had eleven others with her, she decided not to stop on the way. The sounds of clay whistles, rattles and the sweet melodies from a chorus of a mutation of thrush met them as they drew close to the festival. Odette, not atop of the buddleia bush this time to greet them, readied herself at Plush Meadow to officiate at Samuel and Petunia's Legal Mating Ceremony. The other members of the Butterfly Council were there, though, as were the attendant honey bees. The Council appointed a Viceroy Butterfly to act as the head greeter. "May the moons bless you!" He called to fairgoers as they passed under the arbor. Everyone partook of either mead or mint water offered them by the Polar Bear, wearing a blue and silver cape this time. The venders hawked their wares. Musicians, dancers, stilt walkers, balloons were all there. A team of Colobus, Gibbons, Tamarins and Debrazzos dressed in plum colored vests and breeches with silver buttons down the leg performed a complicated and dazzling trapeze act thirty feet above the fairgoers.

***

Keeping everyone together, including two active children, proved a difficult feat. At last, everyone decided to break into groups and, when the time arrived for Samuel and Petunia to exchange vows, meet at Plush Meadow. Beautimus and Lucas, at last to themselves, checked out the vendors. They downed a couple of watermelons from the communal eating table, crunching and spitting seeds in a contÁiner meant for that purpose, shared a bucket of hyacinth blossom ale, then ambled side-by-side through the festival grounds.

They strolled by Jerry's Berries and Mary's Cherries and picked up a small bag of Winter Beer Berries, then they heard...Chance.

"Yo. Mofo. Eat this!"

"Oh no, Lucas, we have to get over to Mr. Grandy's Candies right away."

The hippos trotted to Mr. Grandy's Candy Hut and there they encountered Chance, wearing his dark glasses and do rag...*giving away samples of candy and selling bags of Meyer lemon sticks.* He had his gat with him, but he wasn't threatening to pop a cap in anyone's az.

"Chance, don't stand in one place. Circulate. Take the sample tray *to* the fairgoers." Mr. Grandy issued orders to Chance in an officious tone.

"Mr. Grandy, is everything all right?"

"Never been better, Bea. Chance Rockefeller is the best candy salesman I've ever employed, and he's getting to be a pretty good candy maker, too."

"Chance? The *same* T-Rex who destroyed your booth at the Wasenia Festival? Are you sure?"

Chance approached a fox. "Hey, Mofo, try a melon ball,"

Mr. Grandy nodded. "Funny thing, Bea. After the Wasenia Festival when Sgt. Saturday ordered Chance to make restitution to me, and he had to stand outside my booth selling candies, he came to me afterwards and told me that he'd never had more fun in his life. He asked me for a job. I must admit to skepticism, but against my better judgment, I decided to give him a shot. I got him started part-time at my shop downtown."

"No kidding," said Beautimus. She shook her head in

disbelief.

"He did great. Then after a while, he asked if I'd teach him to make the candies. He took to it right away, even inventing his own. He came up with a beautiful white lavender fudge that's selling like crazy. I can't keep it in stock. As soon as he makes a batch and puts it in the window, it flies out the door."

"Really?"

"Yes Ma'am." The ferret called across the crowd. "Chance, come on over and give Ms. Bea and Dr. Lucas a candied Meyer Lemon Stick."

"Hey, Ms. Bea. Yo. How ya' doin?" Chance placed a lemon stick into her maw. "Best mofo lemon stick you ever ate, right? I made it."

"Yes, Chance. It's delicious. Thank you."

"Yo, you want one, too, dawg?" He asked Lucas.

"Sure. Thanks."

An antelope sauntered by and Chance went after him. "Yo, Mofo. Eat this." Chance gave a Meyer lemon stick to the antelope who chomped down on the candy, crunching so hard he splintered the candy in his mouth. "Wow. This is really good."

"Bet yo mofo self it's good. I made it."

The Antelope bought a bag of lemon sticks on the spot.

"See? what did I tell you?" Mr. Grandy said to Beautimus.

Lucas and Beautimus bought a dozen bags of Sugared Popped Blue Corn, and a fifty-pack of Candied Meyer Lemon Sticks. Beautimus struggled to overcome disappointment that Mr. Grandy had sold out of Chance's White Lavender Fudge before she'd tasted it.

# CHAPTER THIRTY-THREE

BEAUTIMUS AND LUCAS arrived early to Plush Meadow for the mating ceremony. Vases of fragrant purple, white, and orange blossoms were everywhere. In front of a magnificent whipstick cinnamon wattle, heavy with bright yellow blooms, stood tall wooden perches. One, a little taller than the other, Samuel hired a monkey to build for Odette, the Swallowtail who'd officiate over the ceremony, and the others were for Samuel and Petunia, and Petunia's sister, Pansy. Samuel would stand to the right, and Beautimus would stand on the grass adjacent to him.

A quartet of horseflies hovered overhead and hummed, *Love Me Tender, Moon River,* and *When I Fall in Love.* More than 200 guests attended, representing a variety of species from the smallest midge to a Mammoth. After the brief but sweet ceremony, the newly mated couple kissed, and faced their guests, who broke into applause and cheers.

Samuel and Petunia flew to a low branch of a dogwood at the entrance to the meadow, and beckoned Beautimus and Pansy to join them in a receiving line. As the guests filed by to congratulate the joyful couple, a trio of pandas circulated with mead. After a good amount of merry making, the guests disbursed to enjoy the remainder of the festival.

"I can't believe you are really officially mated, Sam. I'm so happy for you," said Beautimus. "And, Petunia, you are an absolutely beautiful bride."

"You'll be where I am very soon. My wish for you is that you and Lucas will be as happy on your Mating Day as we are on ours."

"We will be. I'm sure of it. Thank you, Petunia."

As Lucas and Beautimus walked through the festival grounds, Beautimus spied the two pink flamingos in their oversized robes at a bright purple and lime green booth with pink streamers everywhere. They named their booth, "The Cosmic Pink Fairy." The birds constructed and vended aluminum foil cones for people to wear on their heads because, as one flamingo explÁined, "to wear as protection against the mighty imagined dark forces so they cannot penetrate your energy field with their toxic control waves and manipulate you. That'll be forty Rendazian Glow Seeds, Please. Forty-four including tax."

The other said, "I am 'Floating Blue Moon Wizard Bird' and my companion is "Starlight Crystal Green Fairy Good-Man'. What is your name my cosmic sister?"

He spread the glossy brochure in front of his potential customer.

"My fairy guides tell me you really must do this. Pretencia is only offering this great deal one time ever. This special discount is good for one more hour then the price increases by 1,000 Glow Seeds."

Displayed at the Booth were copies of two handouts: "How to Be Spiritual by *Sounding* Spiritual" and "How to Be Spiritual by *Looking* Spiritual," both by Floating Blue Moon Wizard Bird.

"I have to tell Sam to come by here." Beautimus told Lucas the story of the encounter with the pink flamingos at the Wasenia Festival. Lucas laughed so hard he almost choked on the Meyer lemon stick in his mouth.

"Lucas, I want to go by Angeline's booth to say hello." They walked to the chinchilla's booth, and there Angeline chatted with her cousin, Charlene, who they'd all met on their way from Oceanic to Wayflower. "Nice to see you, again," said Charlene. "Angeline and I were talking about you."

"Nice to see you, too. You have met my fiancé, Lucas?"

"Yes, I believe so," Angeline said. "I'm delighted for the two of you."

"Thank you, and....Wait. Who is *that*, Angeline? My Goddess! That isn't the jackal, Mortimer, known as 'Rampage,' and the weasel, Herbert, known as 'MC Tweezers' is it?"

"Yes. They are both hard working employees, and have proven themselves to be trustworthy. After that unfortunate business with Belinda that Jake got caught up in....what I mean is since Jake is banished now, I had to hire his replacement. These two asked me for a job, and even though neither have opposable thumbs I thought I'd give them a try. They are wonderful. Best hiring decision I ever made."

"Hewo, Ms. Bea. May the moons bwess you."

"Thank you, Mortimer. May the moons bless you, too."

"Yo. Ms. Bea, Dr. Lucas."

"Hello, Herbert," Beautimus and Lucas replied.

They walked a bit further until they reached the booth for "Goods for the Salty Dogs, Oily Birds, and Lazy Sloths in Your Life." The dog and sloth were arguing over space again, ignoring potential customers growing more annoyed by the minute. Some became so exasperated they walked away. The vain raven, oblivious to the other two, paid attention to his customers. He sold his oils faster than he could pull the bottles out from behind the table at the booth.

"At least *some* things remain consistent," said Beautimus.

"Something else that remains consistent, my girl, is how I feel about you. You delight me," Lucas kissed Beautimus' cheek.

A bellowing of bullfinches flew toward them. As they came near, one called out an old Rendazian child's rhyme, "Two little lovers sitting in a tree, K.I.S.S.I.N.G."

Lucas and Beautimus almost ran into Auntie Nancie and Sgt. Saturday walking down the fairway in the opposite direction holding hands, looking very much smitten with one another.

"What a pair," said Beautimus. "Who knows? Maybe there'll be another Mating Ceremony soon. I wonder if we'll be invited?" She laughed so hard her haunches shook.

A murmuration of starlings flew in tight, elegant patterns overhead swooping and dipping down a bit toward Aunt Nancie and Sgt. Saturday. Beautimus could swear she could hear them laughing, too.

Coyotes marched by with whistles in their muzzles and rattles tied to their tails. The lead coyote announced, "Time for the Luna Ceremony. Please make your way to The Green, everybody." Beautimus and Lucas found the agreed meeting place. The radiant newly mated couple, Samuel and Petunia, took their place on Beautimus' head, Pansy with them. Cassie appeared with the children, sucking on Meyer Lemon Sticks, purple balloons tied to their tails. Applecheeks and Agnes rode on her back. Lizzy showed up with Sally. Lucas nuzzled Beautimus. "I can't wait to get you home tonight. My haunches are heating up at the thought of you."

"Hey, we can hear you up here," Samuel said.

"Close your ears. You aren't the only ones in love. And, we'll have our own mating ceremony soon. We're getting a head start on some things, if you know what I mean," said Lucas.

Surrounded by those who loved her, Beautimus had never been happier. Her shar-pendant glowed.

The deckhands had decorated the stage in blues, purples and silver, and put up banners of the deepest blue with bright white moons on them. The coyote sentries took their place. The Moon Maiden, a silver fox named Ariadne, took her position on the stage. Rufus, bearing the altar, walked on the platform in a royal purple cape. He made his respectful greeting to the Moon Maiden. Ariadne bowed to him. The Baboon Harp

Trio played Vivaldi's *IL Gardelino and La Stravaganza*. The music hushed, and from behind the white velvet curtain Lady Rhianna made a grand appearance. She wore a silvery blue robe woven from moonbeams. In her wing, she carried The Wand of Fortuna.

Beautimus shook her head. "She looks thin, too thin. I'm worried."

Samuel said, "Me, too, Bea. Something isn't right."

Ordinarily Rhianna would raise the incense and call in the Goddesses of the four corners. Instead, she spoke.

"Thank you for being here. May the Moons bless you."

Rhianna searched The Green. When she made eye-contact with Beautimus, she relaxed her shoulders as though relieved. "Before we begin, I have an important announcement to make. I am afflicted with Avian Shadowfever and I do not have many moons left on Rendaz."

The crowd grew still. The only sound, a slight breeze rustling the gold dust wattles. A few people whispered, and more than a few wept, including Beautimus. "I knew it, Lucas."

He moved closer to comfort her.

The old bird nodded. "It is for this reason I must name my successor tonight. I've spent moons deliberating and praying to the Goddesses for their guidance. After the Wasenia festival, I made my decision. As you may have read in *The Wayflower Quacker*, Belinda overheard my prayers at the Sacred Watering Hole, and knew she'd not be my choice. That is why, in anger and vindictiveness, she stole the Wand of Fortuna."

A murmur moved through the crowd.

The crane held out her wings and motioned for quiet. "However painful to me, and as much as I knew it would hurt Belinda, I had to make this decision. I know there are Wise Women and Old Mothers among us who'd make excellent High Priestesses. In fact, all of you," She gestured with her wing to the crowd, "who are Wise Women and Old Mothers would make fine High Priestesses, and would well serve the spiritual needs of the Wayflower community. But there is one Wise Woman among us who I feel in my heart will always put her people's needs before her own." She hesitated. "I name Beautimus Potamus as High Priestess of Wayflower."

A clamor arose from the crowd. Some were elated, others shocked. "But, she's not even a wise woman!" Said a crocodile named Rosie. Rosie had been an Old Mother for nearly eighty years and, with Belinda out of the way, she expected to succeed Lady Rhianna.

"Yes, Rosie, Beautimus is a Wise Woman. I named her so in secret and have been training her with her wand and in the ways of magic and healing for some moons now. I felt it best to keep my decision under wraps. Beautimus didn't even know. Since I had to accelerate her training, I needed her to focus 100% on acquiring the knowledge to become eligible for High Priestess. Beard and I did not want her influenced or distracted in any way."

"So, *that's* what you've been up to in the forest every day in secret," said Lucas.

But Beautimus had crumpled to her knees. Samuel, Petunia and Pansy had to fly off her head or they'd have fallen off. Agnes *did* fall off. She had fainted yet again and had landed belly-up on the green. Applecheeks blew short puffs of breath into her sister's face attempting to revive her.

 # CHAPTER THIRTY-FOUR

FOR BEAUTIMUS, THE remainder of the ceremony morphed into a fuzzy dream. Time passed in a disjointed, surrealistic blur. Beautimus lost sense of her own body, unaware of what people around her said. Lizzy, Samuel, Cassie, Lucas all talked to her but she heard them as though they spoke through layers of cotton batting. Bea Two hopped up and down, "Grandma is High Priestess! Grandma is High Priestess!" When Beautimus regained her awareness, her brain filled with a hundred disjointed thoughts: *I can't do this. I want to be mated to Lucas. I'm not ready to be High Priestess. I never wanted this. I have too many things to do. I need to help take care of Daddy. This isn't right. This is a mistake. I already have too many responsibilities to tend to. Oh, my goddesses, Rhianna is dying.*

Samuel said, "So, I guess I'll have to start calling you Lady Beautimus now."

"Don't be silly. Do me a favor and never call me anything but Bea. Besides, I don't even know if I want to do this."

"What do you mean? Of course you'll do this."

After the ceremony, throngs of people crowded Beautimus to congratulate her. She responded to each, but in panic rather than in joy.

Rhianna approached her after the ceremony before heading with the Wand Guards for her prayers to the Sacred Watering Hole. "I'm sorry to have sprung this on you this way, Bea. I'd like you to meet with Beard and me tomorrow first thing."

"I'll be there."

When the festival ended, and the time arrived to walk home, Beautimus asked the others to go ahead. "I need to be alone with Lucas, please."

The group gave Lucas and Beautimus their privacy.

"I'm proud of you, my girl."

"Lucas, do you know what this means?"

"It means we cannot be legally mated."

"But, I want to be your mate. I do not want to be High Priestess. I *can* say no to this."

"No you can't. The people of Wayflower need you. According to Rendazian Law, we can still be together. The High Priestess is permitted a consort. I'd be proud to be yours. And, as far as I'm concerned, we are already mated."

"I love you so much, Lucas. I'm grateful you are in my life."

The hippos nuzzled.

"Lucas, I don't think I'm ready for this. High Priestess is a huge responsibility. What about my classes, and Daddy, and Cassie? The grandkids – I'm finally getting to know my family. Besides that, I don't have the experience. Rhianna only named me Wise Woman a few moons ago. I'm not even an Old Mother yet, and…."

"You know full well Rhianna and Beard would not have chosen you if they didn't think you were up to the responsibility. I'll help with your father, and Cassie understands. She wants this for you, Bea. You can't even think about turning this down, please."

A mob of emus and a wisp of snipe called out as they passed. "Congratulations, Lady Beautimus. Rhianna made a wise choice."

"Thank you, thank you." She turned to Lucas. "I'll do it. With you by my side, I can do anything."

"You'll be the best High Priestess on Rendaz, my girl. I love you."

When they reached Beautimus' abode, Cassie called for cider to toast her mother. Artimus, in deep slumber, muttered "Sangrina" under his breath.

"He's doing well, Lady Beautimus. He's been sleeping most of the afternoon and evening. He woke up once and asked for you, and wanted to know where he was, but other than that, he's been fine."

"Thank you, Jeeves."

"By the way, Lady Beautimus, congratulations. It's an honor to be in your employ."

"Jeeves, please call me Bea or Beautimus. No need to call me Lady."

"I'll not do that. You have been named High Priestess, and I'd never dare be so familiar with you as to address you in any other way than 'Lady Beautimus'."

"Whatever makes you comfortable, Jeeves, but, you don't have to be formal with me."

"Yes, Lady Beautimus."

Uncle Phelan and Aunt Meg burst through the flap of Beautimus' abode.

"Congratulations, niece. You are the most powerful woman in the Wayflower District. How does it feel?" Uncle Phelan said.

"It feels scary."

"You'll do fine, dear," said Aunt Meg. "Your mating ceremony is off I suppose?"

"Yes, Aunt Meg."

"We'll need to return a few things to Lacy's." Aunt Meg sighed in disappointment.

"May-I-still-call-you-Bea?-Apple-and-I-are-so-proud-of-you-we-could-burst-now-we-know-what-that-stick-is-it's-your-wand-isn't-it?-you-will-be-a-great-High-Priestess-are-you-hungry?"

"No thank you, Agnes. Nothing to eat for me. Maybe someone else would like a snack, though, and please do call me Bea."

Lucas spent the night with Beautimus, but neither were in a mood for sex. They cuddled and talked until dawn. The next day, Beautimus awoke late, and rushed to the river to take a dip before departing to the Sacred Glen. She braced herself in preparation for crowds approaching her as she headed to the river. One after another greeted her. "So happy you were named High Priestess, Lady Beautimus," or "Congratulations, Lady Beautimus," or "You'll be a splendid High Priestess," or "We are so proud of you."

"Thank you, thank you, thank you, thank you."

When she at last reached the river, Calypso waited for her with a steam of minnows, a shoal of bass, and a hover of trout. Above the river, a deceit of lapwings held a banner aloft in their beaks that read, "Congratulations, Lady Beautimus."

The fish flapped their fins in the water as a means of applause. "Bravo! Congratulations! Huzzah!" they called out.

Taken aback, Beautimus responded. "How nice. Thank you."

Calypso said, "We are terribly sorry to hear about Lady Rhianna, but are proud of you, Lady Beautimus. We were so surprised when we watched the ceremony on our Crystal Interface when Lady Rhianna named you successor. We had no idea. We know you'll be the best....oh, look! A Pomp of Pekingese." She swam off to investigate the little dogs lined up along the shoreline.

"Thank you all. I need to get in and take my dip. I've got to meet with Lady Rhianna and Beard now."

After her bath, she made her way through all the well-wishers, including the Pekingese who had come to the river to congratulate Beautimus. She entered the Sacred Glen where Rhianna waited. "Where's Ophelia?"

"Great Mother Genesis! I awoke so late. I tried to get to the river and back to my abode to get her, but there were so many people...I totally forgot...."

"You must never, ever, leave without Ophelia again, Bea."

"Yes, Lady Rhianna."

"We must begin your High Priestess training now, but before we do, I need to hear you accept the position of High Priestess in front of the witness, Beard. Do you?"

"I do"

"Good…Tomorrow, the Wand Guards will be here. We will take you to meet The Wand of Fortuna."

"Lady, Rhianna, I'm so sorry about your illness. I am devastated about your announcement about the Avian Shadowfever."

"Thank you, my dear. I've lived a good life. Now that you have accepted the position of High Priestess, I'm ready to go back to Mother Genesis when she calls. Goddesses willing, I'll live long enough to present you as High Priestess at the Genesis Festival. You will be a fine High Priestess, Bea." The crane wrapped her wings around Beautimus' leg.

When Beautimus arrived home, she discovered everyone crowded around *The Wayflower Quacker*. The headline read, *Beautimus Potamus Named Successor to the High Priestess*.

"Hey, Mom, you made the front page," said Cassie.

Artimus awoke. "Beautimus! Beautimus! Where are you?"

"I'm here, Daddy."

"I love you. I love you a whole bunch."

"I love you a whole bunch, too, Daddy."

The following weeks morphed into a busy blur. Beautimus had much to learn, and overwhelmed with concern about Rhianna, she worried the stress of having to train a novice by the next festival would be too much on the old bird. She never said so to Rhianna, though. She applied herself to learning what she must, and never again forgot to bring Ophelia with her. She brought small gifts to Rhianna, a pouch of pecans, a jar of poppy flower candy, a spray of asters. She told Rhianna many times over how much she loved her.

Although she didn't have as much time as she'd have liked

with her grandchildren, she nonetheless managed to sneak off with them occasionally to swim in the river, or play with them in the forest. Lucas and Beautimus spent as many hours together as they could manage, and Cassie and she often stayed up after everyone else had gone to bed to share a glass of mead, or a cup of tea, to talk and get to know one another. Even after the completion of Cassie's abode, several times each week they visited.

Classes at Dr. Pimbly's kept Beautimus busy, too. Her students were proud of her, and darn cocky to have as their professor a High Priestess appointee. Every one of her classes were full. No absences whatsoever, with the curious exception of the white tiger, Cicero, her brightest and best student. He had quit attending classes altogether. She managed a couple of hours with her daddy each day. During Artimus' more cogent periods, they talked about Sangrina.

Once, when he experienced a particularly good day, Beautimus told him she'd been named High Priestess. "Your mother, Sangrina, the goddesses rest her soul, would be so proud of you."

Then by the next day, he'd forgotten…Beautimus understood.

Everyone addressed her as "Lady Beautimus" now, which made her uncomfortable at first, but she accustomed herself to it.

Beautimus woke one morning before class and pulled an Anam Glyph. The last of the three Glyphs she pulled —"Spirit Bridge"—a sign of connecting with spirits. Certain it had to do with her training with Rhianna and Beard, she paid little heed to its message.

On her way out the door her father called to her. "Beautimus?"

"Yes Daddy."

"I love you. I love you a whole bunch."

"I love you, too, Daddy"

She arrived on campus early for her Earth Customs class. A gorgeous day, both suns appeared low in the sky, and the planet lit up in lavenders and purples. Beautimus' mood bright, she addressed her class. "Today we will discuss Earth customs with a focus on the Human tradition of war.

After The Fall, the Human concept of war emerged. Humans, being far more intelligent than we imagined initially, were fast learners, but unfortunately, they used their knowledge of science, agriculture and industry taught them by Rendazians for their own gain, and began to carelessly pollute and overpopulate the Earth that had been a paradise when Rendazians first landed.

For reasons yet unclear to us, Humans separated themselves into color groups called 'races.' They developed separate languages so that racial groups could no longer comprehend one another. This, of course, lead to further suspicion and war. Humans became increasingly fearful, and as we know, fear is always at the root of greed. Out of fear and greed, the stronger racial groups committed genocide against less technically advanced, more peaceful groups, and stole their lands and resources. On Rendaz, we have no war. We perceive our world as plentiful. We know there is enough to go around. No need to hurt anyone or steal anyone else's resources. Earth, too, is bountiful. There is plenty for everyone, but Humans do not believe that. One reason for this difference in our world views, our perspectives on abundance, is that we live much longer than do Humans which…"

At that moment, Sir Henry emerged through the flap. He pushed his glasses further up the bridge of his nose and squinted. "I'm sorry to disturb your class, Lady Beautimus. But I have an urgent message for you. May I please speak to you in private?"

"Certainly, Sir Henry. Class, I'll be back in a moment. Feel free to discuss among yourselves why you think Humans find war necessary."

She stepped outside. She saw from the mole's face something had gone very wrong.

"What is it, Sir Henry?"

"I'm terribly sorry to inform you that your father passed into the arms of Mother Genesis."

Beautimus crumpled. "He'd been so lively this morning when I left. What happened? How?"

"Dr. Bombay thinks liver heat overwhelmed him."

"My daddy, oh no. I've got to go!"

"Of course, Lady Beautimus. I'll dismiss your class, and I'm sorry for your loss."

Beautimus ran all the way to her abode. When she arrived, everyone waited for her...Samuel, Petunia, Lizzy, Cassie, her aunt and uncle.

Lucas approached Beautimus and nuzzled her. "I'm so sorry, my girl."

"I want to see Daddy."

Artimus rested on his pillows, peaceful, as though asleep and dreaming of his precious Sangrina. Beautimus dropped to her knees and pushed her muzzle into his already cold face. "I'm so sorry I wasn't here when you passed. I'll miss you so much. I love you, Daddy. I love you a whole bunch." Tears streamed down her face.

As per custom, the recently deceased lie in state for a day before cremation. People came by to pay respects and placed blossoms on the body. So many people showed up by mid-day flowers buried Artimus. Beautimus stayed by her father's side until time for the cremation.

Family, friends, Beautimus' students, Dr. Pimbly, Sir Henry, Sgt. Saturday, and Auntie Nancie, many of the merchants from downtown, Rufus, Buford, all the Wise Women and Old Mothers of Wayflower turned up for the ceremony. Although so weak she could hardly stand let alone fly, and had to be carried in the arms of a chimp, Rhianna presided over the ceremony. Sacred Attendants cremated Artimus Potamus, and the following morning, spread his ashes over the River Kwa at the same place his beloved Sangrina's ashes had been scattered years before.

"Mommy and Daddy, may you rest together in the arms of Mother Genesis." Beautimus said.

At the post-scattering wake, Petunia and Samuel flew to Lucas and Beautimus. "We are terribly sorry for your loss, Beautimus," said Petunia.

Samuel said, "I know this is not the best time to share this with you, Beautimus, but we wanted you and Lucas to be the first to hear our good news. Petunia is pregnant."

CHAPTER THIRTY-FIVE

BEAUTIMUS GRIEVED HER father, but consoled herself through memories of the better times they shared during his last moons. Again and again she expressed gratitude to Cassie for having brought Daddy back into her life so she could be with him, and help care for him during his end days. She hung her mother's old ribbon and her baby photo on her wall adjacent to a plaque she had made: "Artimus and Sangrina Potamus, dear people who made Rendaz a better world by their existence." Spending time with Cassie, and getting to know her grandchildren brought her great peace, and Lucas, her constant source of joy and comfort, remained steadfast by her side.

Petunia, excited by her pregnancy, babbled like a flea. "Bea, I'll be laying my ootheca soon. I'm certain we'll have at least four nymphs. Sam and I are so delighted."

Samuel and Petunia invited Beautimus and Lucas to a picnic. "We haven't seen the two of you much these days, especially since Artimus' passing. We've missed you," said Petunia, "but, more than that we have something important to ask you."

As they settled down to their lunch, Samuel cleared his throat. "Would the two of you consider being our children's official Alternate Parents?"

Beautimus looked to Lucas for the answer. The roles of Alternate Parents meant a weighty responsibility. If parents died or were incapacitated because of an injury or a disease, the Alternate Parents raise the children as their own. Lucas had expressed no desire to have children, and Beautimus had birthed the only child she'd ever have. But, Lucas wasted no time in responding, "Of course." He chuckled and nodded, "we'd be proud to be Alternate Parents to your children."

"We'd be delighted, Sam and Petunia." Beautimus said.

"Wonderful. We'll make it official at the naming ceremony, then," Samuel said.

Petunia had already decided to name her children after old famous Earth movie stars. She didn't know if she'd have boys, girls or what combination of boys and girls if she had both, but she had chosen eight boys names and seven girls names so she'd be ready. For the girls: Elizabeth Taylor, Marilyn Monroe, Jean Harlow, Ginger Rogers, Betty Davis, Natalie Wood, Clara Bow. For the boys: Kurt Douglas, Sal Mineo, Humphrey Bogart, James Dean, Paul Newman, Burt Lancaster, Rudolph Valentino, Errol Flynn. "I have to wait until the eggs hatch, of course," Petunia said, "but I sense more boys than girls. Samuel loves the idea of boys because siring male offspring is considered manly, and boys will boost his machismo persona. Silly guy. He'll love our children no matter their gender."

The days passed well. Cassie and the children moved into their new abode and planted their garden. Sally went along to help with household chores and to be nanny to Josh and Bea Two so Cassie could return to school.

Beautimus loved her new room the Bo Bo Brothers added onto her abode. She put in vases for flowers, and bought new cattail down pillows in bright colors. The squirrels moved their hammocks behind the partition erected for Artimus, so they had their own "room" affording them and Jeeves more privacy, which he greatly appreciated. Beautimus learned the magic arts, and became adept at using Ophelia and The Wand of Fortuna in preparation for her ascension to the High Priestess position. Under Rhianna's tutelage, she planted a healing garden and made potions, charms, tinctures and unguents. Rhianna had her good days and her bad days, but hung in there.

Beard had taken to telling more jokes, some of which made no sense, and none of which were humorous, but he seemed to think they were. Perhaps his jokes were amusing to other trees, such as this one: "Why does the tree dislike Autumn? Because its leaves fall. Hahaha." Beautimus and Rhianna were perplexed by this shift of personality in the dignified, serious, and wise Beard. They speculated that old trees may get dementia like other creatures.

***

In another part of Rendaz, Belinda, grew more vengeful with each moon. She ran with Heatherton and Jake through the forests, three banished and angry criminals, building an army of other outcasts. Belinda promised her recruits "riches beyond imagining" since she knew the hiding place of the Wand of Fortuna. She planned to kill Rhianna, and kidnap the High Priestess, Beautimus, keep her imprisoned for life forcing her to use the Wand to obtain endless gold, emeralds and Glow Seeds. *I think I shall capture them both and kill Rhianna in front of Beautimus. That would be a fitting punishment* given *it is because of these two that instead of being High Priestess of Wayflower, I've been stripped of my powers and banished. Yes, that is what I'll do.*

She plotted how she'd torture Rhianna, so that Beautimus would experience the horror and pain of watching her beloved mentor suffer before her eyes, while she sat helpless in a locked cage. Belinda also intended to exact revenge on all Wayflower. She'd slaughter as many of the Butterfly Council as she could, murder Sgt. Saturday and his Guardians, obliterate all the Wise Women and Old Mothers and their families, dispatch the Wand Guards, and burn the abodes and gardens of as many of the other Wayflower citizens as possible. No wrath could ever be more powerful, more vicious, or more unmerciful than that of Belinda's. She'd destroy Wayflower, cut down its old growth trees, raze Downtown, burn the blue corn fields, and render the entire district a barren, burned-out husk.

She had to build an army first, though. She recruited powerful wolves, dinosaurs, coyotes, lions, elephants, alligators, gorillas, but did not turn down any outcaste criminal, regardless of species, not even the shunned, who volunteered for the Army of Vengeance, as she named her military. Even the smallest flies could act as spies and messengers for her. She made Heatherton and Jake her field generals. "We will wage the first war ever on Rendaz, and before we are through, the death toll will be astronomical. I will be the most wealthy, powerful, ferocious, and feared woman on the planet," she told them.

In preparation for battle, she sharpened her teeth to lethal points on a whetstone and ordered all her recruits do the same. She promised gold to a metal smith who made helmets for all her soldiers adorned with ostrich plumes ripped out from the tails of the poor unsuspecting birds as they fed. Many ostriches ran about without tail feathers, cold and ashamed.

Since she had been a Wise Woman and knew the ways of magic, and because of her ferocity, no one dared question her. Besides that, she had at her disposal loyal henchmen, a pack of wolves, lions and raptors, who would on her order, tear apart anyone among who dared to defy her, or failed to follow her command. She planned to strike after midnight while all of Wayflower's residents slumbered on their pillows. No one would expect her. She bided her time as daily the ranks of her soldiers expanded. She became Wayflower's very own prodigal daughter, and she'd be coming home very soon.

CHAPTER THIRTY-SIX

ON HER DUE date, Petunia laid her ootheca on the twig of a cassip bush. She pulled the twig inside the abode where she could keep an eye on things until her nymphs hatched. She almost never left. Beautimus stopped by some days after class and the two women shared tea and conversation. Although pregnancy and childbirth for a hippo is very different than for a praying mantis, they both shared the common experience of being mothers. Petunia appreciated Beautimus' friendship since Beautimus was the only woman outside her own family she associated with. The other praying mantis women she'd known with were unmated. Petunia could relate to the older female better than her mantis gal pals who were still into the party and dating scene, and were more concerned about their cheek stain colors coordinating with their wings, than what their futures held.

Petunia had family, her mother and an unmated sister, and they shared a close bond, but the grandma-to-be remÁined constantly nervous about the babies. Petunia's mother had lost her entire ootheca with her first pregnancy, which happens now and again. Because of that, she fretted and worried so much that her presence made Petunia anxious. Pansy wanted to help but didn't know about pregnancies and babies, so Petunia turned to Beautimus.

When the nymphs emerged from their eggs, Petunia got on her Crystal Interface and contacted Beautimus before she even told her own mother or sister. The ootheca produced four perfect little nymphs, three boys and one girl. She named the girl Clara Bow, and the boys James Dean, Humphrey Bogart, and, Rudolph Valentino. The moment Samuel laid eyes on his children, Clara Bow became "Daddy's Girl." He loved his boys, and couldn't wait for them to get old enough to take to the blue corn fields, but Clara became the center of his universe, and his second greatest love next to Petunia. The nymphs were lively, healthy and born with voracious appetites. Beautimus, Cassie, Aunt Meg and Lizzy visited Petunias and the babies a couple of days after they'd hatched. The women brought along a pouch of peanuts which the nymphs fell upon and devoured in seconds. "Next time, we'll bring a lot more," said Beautimus. "I had no idea that at this age they'd eat *so much*."

"I swear," said Petunia, "If I didn't know better, I'd think their appetites so mighty they'd eat each other."

Odette officiated over the secular naming ceremony. Samuel arranged for a wonderful afterparty. Only a moon old, the nymphs buzzed about, and played with other children. Lucas enjoyed watching the nymphs with Josh and Bea II. In less than twelve moons, they'd all be in school together at Mrs. Prim Jay's.

The date for the Genesis festival approached. Once Rhianna and Beautimus stepped from behind the white velvet curtain together, Rhianna would pass the Wand of Fortuna to Beautimus, take a seat stage right, and allow Beautimus to officiate over the ceremony on her own. At the end of the ceremony she'd present Beautimus to the congregation as the official reigning High Priestess. Beautimus, a nervous wreck because she wanted to make Rhianna and Beard proud, practiced her lines and rehearsed her magic for hours on end. She never went anywhere, not even to the loo, without Ophelia. Several times each day she consulted her Anam Glyphs, and much to her frustration she kept pulling Tricky Boy, the archetypical symbol for "the fool." She couldn't be sure if Tricky Boy told her she was a fool for not believing she could do a good job, or a fool for believing she could.

***

Without Beautimus' knowledge, in Dante's Forest near the cavern of the Wand of Fortuna, deep doings were afoot. After Belinda had threatened to return to Wayflower, Steven D. Lobos took her threat to heart and, in secret, he amassed a defending army, the Wayflower Guard. Over time, he recruited and trÁined a formidable team of soldiers, sworn to absolute secrecy. Of the canine tribes, he chose wolves and large dogs. He dared not recruit coyotes because he couldn't trust there weren't coyotes still loyal to Belinda. He had already put together an Intel team of trÁined midges, fruit flies and termites to report Belinda's movements to him.

Belinda's troops captured one of the flies, Geronimo. To the horror of Steven's spies concealed in a buchan blue tree, Belinda ordered a monkey to pull off Geronimo's wings, and torture him into confessing that Steven sent him there to spy. The loyal fly held strong. Eventually, Belinda grew bored of the whole thing, and crushed him with her paw to make him an "example" to any other busy bodies who might dare to sneak around her encampments. Thus, the fly, Geronimo, became the first casualty in the first war on Rendaz.

As a responsible commander, Steven D. Lobos did not want to alarm his community, but he did want them prepared, so he decided to inform the incoming High Priestess of his plans. He'd speak to Beautimus after the Genesis Festival as he escorted her to her abode.

Belinda sent a contingency of horseflies to Wayflower for counter intelligence, but Steven D. Lobos kept his troops well hidden. They trÁined only under cover of dark, and only in Dante's Forest. The flies had little to report to Belinda except a few additional guards around Dark Cavern and the hidden Wand of Fortuna. Belinda swished her tail and scoffed. "Those fools in Wayflower have no idea what's going to hit them." The ranks of her Army of Vengeance swelled with bitter criminals of all species banished or shunned, hungering for revenge, their teeth sharpened for battle.

In stealth, Steven D. Lobos continued to recruit. He brought in Cicero, the Tiger, Beautimus' student. Cicero recruited his brothers, cousins, uncles and father. They brought in other tigers, some from far away districts who wanted to help defend Wayflower. Nearly 300 Tigers would become part of an elite team. Cicero proved to be a natural tactician, so Steven D. Lobos made him his General. Gorillas, skilled in Marshal Arts, joined the Guard, including Rufus. Steven and Cicero trÁined them to hide and jump out in surprise attacks in a style of fighting that would come to be known as "Gorilla Warfare." A hundred razor back pigs with long tusks joined, as well as a team of three dozen mammoths and dinosaurs. Chance joined along with "Wampage" and "M.C. Tweezers."

To avoid rousing the suspicion of the Wayflower citizens, one by one new recruits made their way after nightfall to the military encampments hidden by the dense foliage of Dante's Forest. At last, Steven D. Lobos and the Wayflower Guard were ready for Belinda if she were brazen enough to attack Wayflower with her army of reeky guts-griping criminals.

***

The time for the Genesis Festival approached. Lacy, an orb weaver spider, designed for Beautimus and Rhianna exquisite garments in luscious forest green. They crafted the robes' fabric from web spun from Lacy's own abdomen, shot through with thread spun from gold. The evening before the ceremony, Apple polished Beautimus' toes with gold, and painted a gold bhindi on Beautimus' forehead.

She asked the Guards to take her to the ancient trees. "Master Beard," she bowed her head low. "This is to be my first ceremony as High Priestess. I'm scared."

"Do not be nervous. You are well-prepared for this. Remember what Lady Rhianna and I have taught you about trust, self-love, and self-confidence. These traits are priceless and will serve you far better than your skill with the Wand or your ability to make magic. Hold your head high when Rhianna passes the Wand of Fortuna to you, and do your job."

Steven D. Lobos and two Wand Guards escorted Beautimus to a secret, well-guarded spot on the bank of the Sacred Watering Hole. There she'd spend the night alone in prayer to Great Mother Genesis, and fast in preparation for the ceremony. This would be the first festival in her life Beautimus would miss as part of the audience. "Tomorrow, Lucas, Cassie, my grandchildren, and others I love will walk the path without me," she prayed. "Please keep them well, and hold them in your hand, Mother Goddess."

That night brought both terror and joy to Beautimus. She prayed, rehearsed, prayed, rehearsed and prayed some more. Near dawn, she drifted into a deep sleep. She dreamed the planet spoke to her as a mother might to her small, frightened child. "There, there, Beautimus, my daughter. Everything is as it should be. I will nurture you and protect you." In the dream, Beautimus sank into a warm, dark, place deep within the ground. She felt safe and loved, cradled. Mother Genesis had accepted Beautimus into her blessed womb. Today would be Beautimus' new birthday. She'd walk onstage as a Wise Woman, and walk off stage as the High Priestess of Wayflower, born to the Great Mother.

The following day, at the appointed hour, the Wand Guard escorted Beautimus to The Green. Rhianna waited back stage dressed in her ceremonial garb. She appeared healthy, even radiant, and stood on her own. Lacy ordered an attendant monkey to place Beautimus' robe around her and tie it. The crowd spoke in hushed voices. The baboon harp trio played the second movement of *Sibelius, 2nd Symphony.* Then the music ceased.

Rhianna inspected Beautimus from muzzle to toes. "You are going to be the best High Priestess in Rendaz, Beautimus Potamus. Are you ready?"

They stepped together, side-by-side, through the panels of the velvet curtain onto the stage.

After the ceremony, Rhianna addressed the crowd. "I present to you, Lady Beautimus, your new spiritual leader, The High Priestess of Wayflower."

The applause overwhelmed Beautimus. Her friends, her students, Lucas, and her family including her aunt and uncle who *never* in their lives attended any of the goddess festivals, and would not under any other circumstance dream of attending a spiritual ceremony, clustered together. Beautimus' shar-pendant glowed and pulsated in exact time with her heart beat.

Afterwards, the Wand Guard accompanied Rhianna and Beautimus back to the Sacred Watering Hole for prayers.

"You did well, Bea. I'm proud of you." Rhianna said as they walked.

"Thank you, Lady Rhianna. I'm honored. I will serve the Wand and our people as well as I can for as long as I am able."

"That's why I chose you."

"Thank you for believing in me. I love you Lady Rhianna."

"And, I love you, Bea."

After prayers, two of the Wand Guard escorted Rhianna to the crane compound. Steven D. Lobos and three other of the Wand Guard accompanied Beautimus to White Rock and the cavern to return The Wand of Fortuna. After, Steven D.

Lobos said, "Lady Beautimus, I know you are newly anointed as High Priestess, and this is a difficult way to begin your tenure, but before I escort you to your abode I must speak to you privately of an extremely important matter concerning the safety and welfare of our people."

CHAPTER THIRTY-SEVEN

THE ONLY KNOWLEDGE Beautimus had of war is what she taught in her Earth History class. Sickened war might be waged on Rendaz, and the Wayflower District, her home, could very well be the battlefield, Beautimus' stomach tightened into a cold knot.

"Steven, I appreciate you letting me know about this. We must convene the local Butterfly Counsel immediately. I want my consort, Dr. Lucas Potamway, brought up to speed, and Beard will be included. I think it wise we continue to keep this under tight wraps until you gather more intelligence. No need to alarm the people of Wayflower, or to alert Belinda further about our military defense plans, but I see your point that our people must be prepared if there is even the slightest possibility of invasion. From what you tell me, Belinda is amassing a formidable army of criminals who will not think twice about killing innocents."

"As you say, Lady Beautimus." The wolf bowed.

"This would not be a war waged in the name of someone's religion, or a grab for

resources and land, but violence bred of revenge and hate. From what the Earth History books teach us, hate as a motivator for war results in the most vicious and unmerciful slaughter. I am deeply grateful to you for taking Belinda's threat seriously, and following your instincts to recruit and train soldiers to protect Wayflower. Do you have troops encamped here?"

"Yes, Lady Beautimus."

"I'd like to meet them now, please"

Steven led Beautimus into the thickest part of the forest.

Still in her ceremonial robes, she had to take care lest she catch the rare fabric on a branch or thorn and rip it. Because Steven D. Lobos had ordered the encampment hidden well under the branches of the blue spruce, Douglas fir, incense cedar and the burbridge wattles, Beautimus thought it deserted. The few buildings constructed to house supplies were camouflaged covered under mesh material covered in leaves and needles. On initial inspection, Beautimus did not perceive any buildings at all. The area, dense with brush, and with no delineated paths cut from or to anywhere, appeared as nature intended. Not a sound in the forest disturbed the perfect silence, not even the chirp of a solitary cricket.

Steven raised his head and howled four times. Tigers dropped from the trees surrounding Beautimus. Gorillas and elk appeared as if by magic from behind tall bushes and boulders. Mammoths and dinosaurs rose from behind a ridge that had appeared seconds before as nothing more than a series of dirt mounds. Wolves, dogs and tusked boars trotted in from all directions. Midges, flies and winged termites rose from the soil and tree bark as though stirred with a stick and blown into the air by some fantastic unseen force.

Beautimus and Steven stood in front of over 2,000 creatures, not including the tiny winged Intel reconnaissance teams, of which there were countless, in what had appeared to be only another part of the overgrown forest. Steven howled once, and the Wayflower Guardsmen formed into tight ranks. Dinosaurs and Mammoths to the back, Elk to the middle, wolves, boars and dogs to the front. Tigers lined in disciplined formation on the right flank, gorillas to the left. There in the front of the gorillas—Rufus. At the back, a detail of T-Rex's, but one stood out. Beautimus leaned to Steven. "Is that Chance Rockefeller?"

"Yes, Lady Beautimus."

"I'll be damned."

"He's going to make a great soldier. He's a powerful and determined fighter."

"No doubt."

"He's a rather peculiar fellow though. I believe he speaks either old Rendazian or some Earthly language I do not recognize."

"Oh?"

"During basic training, as I issued commands to him, he continually responded with the oddest phrase."

"I didn't know Chance spoke anything other than modern Rendazian. He's filled with surprises. What phrase?"

"Something that sounds a lot like 'Papacap en joaz'. I took it to mean some sort of acknowledgement."

Beautimus had to choke back a laugh. "That must be what the phrase means, yes, an acknowledgement of your order."

"Cicero padded to the front and faced Beautimus. The reconnaissance team hovered in tight formation.

No one said a word until Steven spoke. "Guardsmen, as you know, Lady Rhianna presented Lady Beautimus today as our new High Priestess. I informed her of Belinda's movements and our training here. She requested to meet you because she has a few words for you. Please give Lady Beautimus your full attention."

Beautimus nodded to the troops. "Thank you, Steven. And…Cicero, I *wondered* why you haven't been in class."

"Sorry, Lady Beautimus."

"No need to apologize. Thank you for joining the Guard."

"Rufus, it's good to see you."

"I'm at your service." Rufus bowed low, scraping his knuckles in the dirt.

Beautimus turned her attention to the troops. "I only heard of Belinda's plans to invade Wayflower a few minutes before arriving here. I am appalled war may be waged on Rendaz. I am completely against war of any kind for any reason. As Earth history shows us, violence begets violence, and no true peace can exist anywhere on our planet when even one District is at war. But, if criminal soldiers are intent on invading our district with the goal of destroying our homes and crops, and killing our people, then we have little choice but to defend ourselves.

For obvious reasons, we want as few people involved with these preparations as possible. However, there will be several more people included in our defense plans. I will be convening a meeting with members of the Butterfly Council, Commander Steven D. Lobos, Beard, General Cicero and my consort, Dr. Lucas Potamway, to formulate an evacuation plan to move as many of our civilian population to safety as possible, to finalize strategy for the defense of Wayflower, and to discuss alternatives to war by means of peaceful resolution.

We will swear the Butterfly Council and Dr. Potamway to secrecy, and will not pull in additional personnel unless necessary. Thank you all for your willingness to put your lives on the line for our people. May we find a swift and non-violent resolution to the problem at-hand so that Rendaz remains a planet at peace, and may Mother Genesis and her many goddesses bless you and keep you out of harm's way."

Steven issued one command. "Dismissed."

Within three minutes everything went back as it had been when Beautimus first walked into the encampment, with no sign that a battalion of Guardsmen comprised of several species, some as big as the largest living dinosaur, had ever been there.

By the time Steven D. Lobos escorted Beautimus home, both moons had passed the midnight point. Lucas paced in front of Beautimus' abode. When he saw Beautimus and Steven approach, he ran to Beautimus. "Thank the Goddesses. We've all been worried sick about you."

"I'm sorry you were worried, Lucas. I'm glad you are outside alone, though. Steven and I must speak to you about an important matter of the utmost secrecy."

"Let me stick my head through the flap to let everyone know you are safe and I'll be right back."

Lucas walked back to the abode, pushed his head in through the flap. "She's all right. No, no, Cassie, don't come out to greet her. We must discuss something in private with the Commander of the Wand Guard. We'll be right in. Apple and Jeeves, bring out the mead pails and some food, I'm sure Beautimus and Steven will be hungry and thirsty. No, she's fine, really. We'll be in shortly."

Lucas joined Beautimus and Steven. The wolf apprised Lucas of the situation, and Lucas grew sullen. "I never thought I'd live to see the possibility of war on Rendaz. Let me know how I can be of service. Thank you for bringing Beautimus home to us safely, Steven, and please do come in and enjoy some food and mead with us."

"Thank you, Dr. Potamway, but I must get back to my men. Lady Beautimus, I bid you a good night. We'll talk tomorrow."

Steven D. Lobos trotted at a brisk clip toward the Forbidden Forest.

Beautimus and Lucas nuzzled one another for a long while. "I'm so glad you are home, Bea. By the way, my girl, you did a splendid job officiating over your first ceremony. You were so beautiful on that stage."

"Lucas, thank you for waiting for me, for worrying about me, for being here with me."

When they entered through the flap, all her family, and many of her friends greeted her. "Congratulations, Bea. We are so proud of you."

"Grandma? Do we have to call you Lady Beautimus now?" Bea Two asked.

"You and Josh will call me Grandma, sweetie, because that's what I am to you."

Everyone celebrated, sipping on lemon blossom mead, and cold pressed apple cider, dining on red pears and Marcona almonds. As the suns' first light appeared over the peaks, the guests departed one by one, and Beautimus and Lucas went outside to greet the violet dawn.

A few hours later, they met Cicero and Steven D. Lobos at the roots of Beard with two members of the Butterfly Council, Odette and Euripides. To avoid inciting curiosity, they opted not to meet Downtown in the Butterfly Council Chambers. Steven D. briefed the butterflies and Beard.

"The question is, how do we avoid war? Can't we send a delegation, maybe from the Butterfly Council, to open a dialogue with Belinda, and see if we can't resolve this issue amicably so no one gets hurt?" Asked Odette

"The problem with that is two-fold. Number one, it's far too dangerous. Remember what Belinda did to Geronimo? Do you think she'd hesitate to pull off your wings and crush you under her paw?" Beautimus said.

"We could send a falcon, and extend an invitation to her for talks here in Wayflower, so we…"

Steven D. Lobos broke in, "Lady Beautimus is prepared to say there is a *second* danger. Lady Beautimus?"

"Yes, thank you. The second danger is that we do not want to alert Belinda that we know of her plans."

"Why not? Why would that be dangerous?" Euripides asked. "If we are open with her, maybe we can build a foundation of trust. Perhaps inviting her here as a guest so we can all sit down and figure this out together could deter an attack. Surely, that would be in the highest and best interest of all."

"Belinda and her soldiers are out for revenge. She intends to hurt Wayflower and its citizens, and talking about it is not going to change her mind. She's already proven herself to be brutal, unmerciful, and violent," said Beautimus.

"There is also a tactical reason we do not want Belinda to know that we are aware of her plans," said Cicero. "Right now, she believes we are defenseless and unprepared. She has no idea we have amassed a well-trÁined, disciplined Guard. She is convinced Wayflower will be easy to conquer; therefore, her confidence is bound to be high and she'll be complacent. If she knows we are prepared, and we have strong defenses at our command, she will become far more aggressive, build larger and better trÁined forces, and attack with an escalated level of ferocity. Belinda is smart and dangerous. She intends to wipe out Wayflower, and if she thinks she has to, she'll hit us much harder."

"Then what *do* we do?" asked Odette

"We've been discussing an evacuation plan," said Lucas

"But, won't masses of people evacuating Wayflower rouse Belinda's suspicion?" asked Euripides.

Lucas spoke up. "The plan is to evacuate a few people at a time, discreetly over a period of days. We can put some on Holiday Trains and others can walk in small groups to the Oceanic District."

"If all goes well, when Belinda invades she will encounter a ghost town. Once she and her forces are subdued, the citizens of Wayflower can return to their homes," said Cicero.

"Do not tell anyone why they are being evacuated. Tell them they are going on holiday. Tell them there's a sick relative somewhere who needs them. Tell them that Rendazian scientists say a volcano is going to blow and people must get to safety. Make up a cover story of some kind, but no matter what, do not tell anyone why they are leaving," said Beautimus.

Just then a winged termite flew in. "Excuse me, Commander. I'm sorry to interrupt, but we have new intelligence."

"Speak up, Guardsman."

"Belinda is planning to burn the blue corn fields, and all our stores of corn kernels."

"Sweet Goddess, no," said Odette. "We won't have enough food to get us through the Cool Season. Children will perish."

"We are going to have to bring Samuel S. Goodwings into these discussions. He's the leading blue corn scientist in Wayflower, and he will know how to protect our fields and corn resources," said Beautimus.

Steven issued an order to the termite: "Dispatch a falcon to Samuel Goodwings and tell him he's needed urgently on a highly sensitive matter that he's to speak to no one about." "Yes, Commander."

The termite flew away to relay orders to the raptor.

It took the falcon a couple of hours to locate Samuel who had been working in the corn fields.

"Samuel, thank you for coming," said Beautimus.

"What is this about?"

Steven D. Lobos brought Samuel up to speed.

"What about my family? Petunia and the nymphs?"

"We'll evacuate them until this is over, Sam," said Beautimus.

"This is what we can do. This is not optimal moon time to reap the corn, but I can order an early harvest. The corn is ripe enough, and I'll say that the harmonic resonance of the soil tuned into a weak energetic frequency so we'll have to get the corn harvested immediately or it will mold on the stalk. That will deflect any suspicion and halt any questions as to why we are harvesting early. I recommend that everyone we evacuate takes with them two or three bags of corn kernels stored in their luggage and satchels so anyone seeing them will think travelers are bringing personal items on holiday. If Belinda is successful in burning the fields and the storage facility, there will be no corn remaining, but we'll have enough viable kernels to replant the fields. Burning will not harm the soil, and in some Earth cultures, farmers frequently used the Swidden Method of agriculture in which they slash and burn brush or forestlands to create fields. The result is a nutrient rich ash that behaves as a natural fertilizing agent, which boosts crop production. Belinda may inadvertently do us a favor if she burns our fields."

"Sounds like a good plan, Samuel. And, it would also relieve troops I'd allocated for protection of the fields. We can redeploy them to protect other areas of Wayflower," said Steven.

"You say you also have a plan to protect the old trees?" Beard asked.

"Yes, Master Beard. With your permission, we will post tigers in your branches, and the branches of the other ancient trees. If Brenda's forces come in with axes, or fire, the tigers will jump them," said Cicero.

"You have my permission, of course. Also, have you plans to evacuate the High Priestess? She must be protected at all costs."

"I'm not going anywhere. My place is here in Wayflower."

"You must go, Bea. You can't stay here." Lucas said. "You'd be in danger. Belinda is probably targeting you personally, and she may even kill you." His eyes betrayed his anxiety.

"Lucas, you'll be with me, and Steven will be with me. What have I to fear? Besides, I know quite a bit about healing now. If any of our Guardsmen are wounded, Dr. Bombay and the medics will need my help. I'm staying."

"Bea, as High Priestess it is your prerogative to stay. But, I'd advise you to leave Wayflower," said Beard

"Master Beard, remember that trust issue we've discussed? I finally understand what it means. I trust everything is going to work out the way it's supposed to. I trust I can use my magic and healing skills to be of help here. I trust Lucas and Steven will protect me and keep me from harm. I trust the Goddess will look over me. I trust in many things now."

"As you wish. May Mother Genesis bless you and hold you in the palm of her hand."

"Samuel, how long will it take your teams to harvest the blue corn and package it?" asked Steven.

"Three, four days, tops."

"Can you make it two? We have intel that Brenda is moving in on Wayflower. We may not have much time."

"We'll give it our all, Commander. I'll leave now so we can get started."

Samuel bid his goodbyes and flew to the blue corn field.

Cicero and Steven outlined their defense strategy to the butterflies, Beard, Lucas and Beautimus. The Commander and his General did an exemplary job of planning to the smallest detail. "When Belinda arrives, she'll see no one, not even a mite. She'll believe the town is deserted, but we'll have men stationed here, here and here." He pointed to a map he'd drawn with his paw in the dirt. "They'll be well-hidden. Tigers will be positioned in trees throughout the District, with the largest concentration Downtown and here in the Sacred Glen. We have additional guards on duty to protect the Wand, and I've stationed gorillas and a dinosaur. We have positioned Guards on the backside of Dark Cavern because Belinda managed to get in from that side. The Wand won't be there. We have already removed it and hidden it elsewhere, but the additional guards will create the illusion that the Wand is still in the Cavern. There will be a detail of Guardsmen stationed inside. If Belinda, or any of her forces, enter the cavern, we'll have a surprise waiting for her in the form of silver back gorillas and lions."

"Where is the Wand of Fortuna, Steven?" asked Beautimus

"I'm sorry, Lady Beautimus, but only one person in all of Rendaz knows where it is hidden. After this is over, we will find a new home for the Wand, a safer place since the location of the cavern is now compromised. In the meantime, if for any reason Belinda's forces capture you it's best you have no knowledge of the Wand's whereabouts."

"I understand. Thank you." *Goddess, help us. What if Belinda comes before we are prepared?*

CHAPTER THIRTY-EIGHT

BEAUTIMUS FIRST THOUGHT of her family, then Rhianna. The old crane would have to leave Wayflower with the others, and because Rhianna had grown so frail by now, Beautimus feared she wouldn't be able to travel. After the meeting, Beautimus and Lucas went to the Crane Compound. When they reached Rhianna's abode, Beautimus called out, "Lady Rhianna, it's me, Bea. I've come with Lucas."

Queenie emerged through the flap. "Lady Beautimus, I'm glad it's you. Rhianna is not doing well at all and she's been calling for you. I tried to reach you on your Crystal Interface but Jeeves told me you and Lucas had left early this morning and no one knew where to. Please come in."

Beautimus and Lucas found Rhianna reclining on her pillows, her beak ashen, and her eyes glazed.

"Lady Rhianna, are you not feeling well?"

"Mother Genesis is calling me home. I'm so glad you are here, my dearest. I wanted to say goodbye to you and let you know one more time that I love you." She stretched her wing to Beautimus' face and stroked her cheek.

"Lady Rhianna, I love you, too. You are like a mother to me. I don't know what I'll do without you."

"You will never be without me, Bea. We will see one another in your dreams. You will live well, you will love well, and you will serve your people well."

The Crane took a shallow breath, her wing dropped from Beautimus' face, and she expired. Beautimus touched the old crane with her muzzle, and wept.

"Bea, we have to go," Lucas whispered. "We need to take Queenie with us, and we have to leave now. We'll have time to grieve later."

"I'm ready."

Beautimus composed herself, covered the crane with a blanket, and kissed her. "Bye, Rhianna. May your journey to Mother Genesis be swift and joyful."

When she informed Queenie that Lady Rhianna had passed away, the lemur wailed, "Lady Rhianna. I will miss her so very much. What am I to do?"

"Come with us," said Lucas. "We'll send someone back for Lady Rhianna later. Gather your belongings and let's go."

Although Belinda had murdered Priscilla, and placed Queenie with Rhianna as a spy, the lemur came to love Rhianna, so became her friend and protector instead. Overcome with grief, the lemur sobbed.

Beautimus did her best to console the smaller mammal. "Everything is going to work out, Queenie."

The two hippos and the lemur walked in silence to Beautimus' abode. As soon as they entered, they gathered everyone around them. They also summoned Aunt Meg and Uncle Phelan, Cassie, the children, and Lizzy.

"Not as your friend or family, but as your High Priestess, I ask you to trust me. You all must leave Wayflower. Do not ask me why, please. Lucas and I will remain here, and we will contact you the moment you can return. Consider this a vacation to Oceanic, if you choose. Please take with you anything of value, but leave everything else behind, and I'm also going to ask you to carry with you bags of blue corn kernels in your luggage."

She gestured to Rhianna's house lemur. "This is Queenie. She has been in service to Lady Rhianna, who I'm sorry to say is now in the arms of The Goddess"

"Oh no," said Lizzy.

"We'll have a ceremony for her, but today, right now, I

need all of you to pack and get to Oceanic. Queenie will be with you as well, since she has no place to go."

"But, Grandma, aren't you coming with us?"

"It's okay, Josh. As High Priestess, I have some things I must take care of here. We'll all be together in a few days. Jeeves, please don't worry about cleaning up. Gather your things and all of you go, now, and please stay together. I don't want you separated. Uncle Phelan and Aunt Meg, you are in charge. I'll contact you as soon as I am able, and stop by Sam and Petunia's. They'll have the bags of blue corn kernels you are to take with you. I ask again that you all trust me, please."

Without further discussion, everyone did as their High Priestess commanded. Cassie, Lizzie, Aunt Meg, the grandchildren, and the squirrels nuzzled Beautimus. They took their belongings, left for Samuel's abode to pick up their bags of corn, and they were off to Oceanic. Later, Beautimus and Lucas went to Samuel's and found him there alone. "Have you sent Petunia and the nymphs away already, Sam?"

"Yes, we have relatives in the Shar District. I boarded them on a Holiday Train only an hour ago. I gave your family ten bags of corn. I have a few more here. The rest are hidden in various locations. The Guardsmen have been doing an excellent job of evacuating citizens. By this time tomorrow, the corn will be harvested and the town empty. Someone started the volcano eruption rumor, and we are letting people speculate."

"Sam, why are you still here? You are planning on joining Petunia and the children, aren't you?"

"No, Bea. I'm staying."

"Sam, your family needs you. Your nymphs are only a couple of moons old."

"I'm staying here."

"As your High Priestess I'm asking....no *commanding*.... you leave Wayflower and go to your family."

"You can banish me for disrespecting a High Priestess when this thing is over, but I'm not going. You are my best friend. You stood up for me at my Mating Ceremony. You and Lucas are the Alternate Parents for my children. Wayflower is in danger and I will help defend it. Petunia and the kids are safe, and if anything happens to me, I know you will take care of them. The best thing I can do right now for my family is to protect their home."

"Okay, you stubborn little bug, but nothing had *better* happen to you, dammit!"

A clutch of chickens and an obstinacy of buffalo passed by Samuel's abode.

"Who knows?" said a buffalo to a chicken, "I don't know what you were told. We were just ordered by a member of the Wand Guard to get on the path to Oceanic with our things and carry some blue corn kernels in our baggage. The wolf gave us no explanation other than to tell us we'd be returning soon. Sounded serious."

"I heard a volcano is going to erupt," said the hen to the buffalo. She ruffled her feathers, and let out a squawk. "Oops, gotta go over there" and she darted across the path.

The buffalo asked another buffalo "Why did the chicken cross the road?"

The other said, "I don't know, maybe to get to the other side?"

***

Heatherton and Jake met with Belinda.

"Bad news, Belinda. Seems we've run out of recruits. We could conscript a few more farmers," Heatherton said.

"Don't bother. We've most of the forests' population among our ranks already. We can probably wipe out Wayflower with half of the soldiers we have. Is the cage ready for Beautimus?"

"Yes," said Jake. "I need to place a few pillows inside and a water pail."

"No pillows. We don't want her to be too comfortable. In fact, I'd prefer you to place the cage somewhere out in the open where that menopausal bitch can experience some of the natural elements of this barren hellzabob of a place for the years that she'll be with us. See how she likes that, eh?"

The rat and monkey laughed.

"My astronomers tell me in two more days the sky will be moonless. Let's break out the mead then get some rest. When the sky is dark, we move on Wayflower."

In a popinac bush, a well-hidden company of midge spies listened to the entire exchange. They reported back to Steven D. Lobos what they'd heard.

"So, Belinda will strike in two days, and her primary target is Lady Beautimus, and her secondary imperative is the Wand of Fortuna. I see. Bring Cicero, Lady Beautimus, Lucas and Sam to me immediately."

"Yes, Commander."

Once everyone convened, Steven D. trotted to Cicero. "General, Belinda and her troops are as yet unaware we have knowledge of her plans, which gives us a tremendous advantage, but let's not become too sure of ourselves. Beginning tonight, deploy the eclectus parrots and purple finches. Place 100 men at the south end entrance Wayflower and one detail along the path from Oceanic and Shar." The wolf addressed Samuel. "All the blue corn is harvested, correct?"

"Yes, Commander."

"Then other than a small lookout contingency, there is no need post troops at the corn fields. Let Belinda burn the field and the storage bin. Since the stalks are still standing, unless someone knows what to look for, they'll not see the corn has been harvested. We concentrate our forces here, here, here and here." He pointed on a map to Downtown, the Sacred Glen, White Rock, the secret cavern and the Sacred Watering

Hole. "As soon as Belinda and her troops enter Wayflower, the parrots and finches will sound the alarm."

Cicero spoke up. "Brilliant, Commander. Belinda will know soon enough we are onto her plan, but allowing her to burn our fields unopposed gives us a strategical edge."

"Exactly. My guess is she'll concentrate her efforts on locating Lady Beautimus, but since we'll have evacuated the Hippo Compound, our first line of defense is Downtown. We will post well-concealed troops." He pointed to where he wanted the soldiers positioned. "When Belinda enters the town, we'll surround her, move in and cut off her exit here." He gestured. "Then we'll strike hard in a surprise defensive attack. Is everyone clear?"

"Commander, what can I do to assist?" said Lucas.

"We will put a detail of Guard Wolves around Lady Beautimus to protect her 24/7 in the civilian compound. But, I need you to remain at her side. If there is any chance Belinda's troops are able to get through the Wand Guards here in the forest, two hippos will be more difficult for her to handle than one. During those times when you cannot be with her, inform the Wand Guard and we'll pull in a mastodon to protect her."

"What about me?" asked Samuel.

"I want you posted with the lookouts at the Blue Corn fields. The outlooks report directly to you, and you report directly to me. If anything goes awry in the corn field, you'd be the best man to recognize it. Afterwards, to avoid civilian casualties, I want you, Lucas, the medics, Dr. Bombay, and especially Lady Beautimus, to stay out of harm's way. Lady Beautimus will assist Dr. Bombay with incoming wounded, but other than that, you are to remain close together in the civilian compound. Understood?"

In Dante's Forest, between Command Headquarters and the cavern, a well-camouflaged medic tent and temporary abodes housed Dr. Bombay, his nurses, Samuel, Beautimus and Lucas. Steven D. Lobos intended for Samuel to return to the Civilian and join the others in safety as soon as Belinda's troops burned the fields.

Beautimus stood tall. "Steven, I think it'd be a good idea to deactivate our Crystal Interfaces. We do not know whether Belinda can hack in and intercept messages. Additionally, we do not want Interfaces buzzing or lighting up once Belinda is inside of Wayflower. The Interfaces could give away our positions. Between our lookouts and spies, we can communicate efficiently with one another. I recommend we call our families and friends to let them know they will not hear from us for a few days, and assure them all is well so they do not worry."

"Sound idea, Lady Beautimus. We deactivate all Crystal Interfaces by night fall. Cicero, issue the orders."

The tiger ran to deliver the order. Then, he posted his troops. Samuel flew off and took up his position in a sweet-briar tree to view the fields and the storage building. He tried several branches until he located one that gave him the best vantage point—high enough to see everything, but low enough to perceive the finer details, such as the faces of the soldiers. If anything were to go wrong, for example if one of Belinda's arsonists were to discover the corn had been harvested and went running back to Belinda, or if the fire grew out of hand, anything that could change the direction of the war against Wayflower, he'd fly back to Steven D. and warn the others.

That evening and through the next day, Wayflower took on an air of surrealism in its serenity. People spoke in hushed tones, even the eclectus parrots and finch tribes curbed their chatter. The Wayflower Guards remÁined on alert and in position. With everything in perfect order, no one could do anything other than wait.

As soon as she fell asleep on her pillows that night, Beautimus dreamed Rhianna, as a young and beautiful crane, appeared to her. "Remember, you have three magical tools at your disposal, Bea. Use your Anam Glyphs, your shar-pendant and Ophelia. Oh, and by the way, your mother and father are quite happy together. They wanted me to relay the message. You should see them, Bea. They are like two teenagers in love."

"Lady Rhianna? Is that you? Don't go."

The image of Rhianna faded, and Beautimus woke from her slumber.

***

Late the following evening, stars were ablaze in the moonless sky but their light too distant to cast more than a dim glow on the path to Wayflower. Much to Belinda's delight, a thin but nonetheless beneficial cloud cover, obscured the light. A mist rose from the rivers Kwa and Redrock further concealing her troops as they marched in perfect formation on Wayflower, feathered helmets affixed, teeth sharpened, eager to commit mayhem and mass murder with a confident Belinda *en point.*

Belinda and her criminal troops advanced in tight formation into Wayflower. The Army of Vengeance, with its hollowed-eyed soldiers gave the impression of a helmeted army of terrible wraiths who had emerged from the bowels of hellzabob to tear the beating hearts from any living being they encountered.

As soon as they reached the path leading to the Hippo Compound, Belinda dispatched a platoon to burn the blue corn fields and kernel storage building, with orders to kill anyone they encountered. She'd personally lead the rest of her troops into the Hippo Compound to capture Beautimus, massacre everyone remaining, loot and burn the abodes and gardens. Afterwards, a detail would take the High Priestess to the cage outside of Wayflower. Belinda's forces would join the platoon at the corn fields, and they'd march together as one unified powerful and swift force on Downtown. After the siege and destruction of Downtown, she'd personally rip off the wings of the Butterfly Counsel before biting them in half.

Belinda planned to dispatch a platoon to the Sacred Glen to destroy the old growth trees. "I want that old molt-worm Beard cut down last so he can witness the destruction of all the ancient trees around him." Simultaneously, she'd take two platoons through White Rock passage to the cavern, kill the Wands Guards, and capture the Wand of Fortuna. But first, Belinda planned a detour to the Crane Compound. "I will enter Rhianna's bode, dispatch Queenie, and capture Rhianna. I will delight in tearing her apart in front of that traitorous swag-bellied bitch, Beautimus Potamus."

Time and time again Belinda imagined Beautimus' horror, helpless behind bars in a barren cage watching her beloved Rhianna rendered into small pieces, one bite at a time. "I will keep a few of Rhianna's feathers to wear as a trophy. Beautimus Potamus will live out the remainder of her life in a cage, my slave, with the persistent memory of witnessing Rhianna's horrible death."

Once she had the Wand of Fortuna and Beautimus, and the whole of Wayflower in ruins, Belinda planned a celebration for her troops, in which the High Priestess of Wayflower would play a significant role as witness to the triumph of Belinda's mighty Army of Vengeance. "Who will be the most powerful woman in Wayflower *then*? No, no. That's not right. Who will be the most powerful woman in *all* of Rendaz?"

Belinda reserved a few special kills for herself: Rhianna, the Butterfly Counsel, Sgt. Joe Saturday, and Steven D. Lobos. She'd give the pleasure of the remainder of the slaughter to her troops who drooled in anticipation, ecstatic at the idea of ripping apart every citizen of Wayflower, from the oldest and largest dinosaur right down to the smallest new-born kitten.

CHAPTER THIRTY-NINE

WHEN BELINDA AND her troops entered the Hippo Compound, silence greeted her. She put her paw in the air to halt her troops, and cocked her head. She'd expected at least the song of a nightingale, the caws and knocks of an unkindness of ravens, a chorus of crickets, but nothing. Water fell over the rocks in the nearby river splashing and gurgling, making the only sound besides a soft wind rustling the leaves on the redbud bushes. She put her muzzle in the air and sniffed. She detected nothing, not the smell of chamomile tea or the fruit rinds leftover from dinner. "Curious" she said. A leaf floated from a klampus tree onto her paw. She shook it off. *Everyone must be deep asleep. This is good.*

She motioned for a detail of boars to accompany her. "The rest of you, enter the other abodes, kill the occupants, take everything of value, then burn the compound, its gardens, apiaries, and orchards to ashes."

Belinda gave the signal. She and the boars crashed into Beautimus' abode through the flap and found…no one. They stopped in their tracks, surveyed the abode in bewilderment. Belinda trotted to Beautimus' second room and found…no one. Most of the contents of the abode were gone save a few pillows, cooking pots, and dirty dishes on the hearth. Belinda motioned to the boars and ran outside to witness her other troops running in and out of the abodes finding…no one. The fruit and nuts had been stripped from the orchards, and most of the vegetables were missing from their vines. The apiaries were empty. No bees. No honey.

Heatherton scuttled to her. "Where is everyone? The compound is deserted."

Belinda growled at the rat.

He backed away. "I'm only asking."

She ordered a few chimps to the river to see if the hippos might be there.

"No, Commander Belinda. We didn't even find a tadpole in the river."

Belinda stood still for a moment, the lifted her snout and howled in fury.

"Commander, shall we burn the abodes?" asked a chimp.

"Not now, you fucking idiot!"

She motioned for the troops to follow her, and she loped full speed toward the blue corn fields, where she saw flames in the distance, and smelled smoke. "Well, it looks like something is going right."

When Belinda and her troops reached the fields, the corn stalks were ablaze, and the conflagration engulfed the large outbuilding used for processing and storing dried kernels. "Commander, mission accomplished. There will be nothing of the corn but ashes," One gorilla reported in triumph.

"Did you encounter resistance?"

"Only one praying mantis in the sweet-briar tree. When we discovered the little fobbing giglet, he went crazy biting everyone. He flew into my face and took a chomp out of my eye. I don't know if I'll be able to see again out of it, the farking little bastard. I swatted him away, and I'm pretty sure he's dead or will be. I couldn't find him, but I hit him hard."

"Well done. Gather the men."

She held an ad hoc meeting adjacent to the burning field.

"Troops, seems the good citizens of Wayflower somehow knew we were coming and have evacuated the hippos. Their compound is deserted." She ordered her spies front and center. "You didn't notice any unusual movement?"

"No, Commander," said one.

Peggy A. Wheeler

"No? You *really* didn't notice groups of animals as large as hippos leaving Wayflower? You *really* didn't notice the Hippo compound had been evacuated you hasty-witted vassals?"

"No commander."

"You failed me, you miserable useless pieces of pottle-deep crap." She raised her voice. "I want everyone to witness what happens to anyone who fails me."

She ordered the midges, flies, and winged termites to the ground. She signaled a mammoth, who crushed them underfoot.

"Change of strategy. You, you and you come with me." She pointed at a cougar, a T-Rex and a chimpanzee. "I also want the gorillas. The rest of you stay here until we return. I'm *personally* leading a reconnaissance to the other compounds. I want to see for myself if anyone else has evacuated. We start with the cranes."

Belinda and her men arrived at the Crane Compound and found...no one. She burst into Rhianna's abode and did find someone...Rhianna dead and cold on her pillows beneath a blanket. Belinda howled in fury. Out of rage and frustration, she whipped her head around and bit the chimp to death standing next to her, and with her paws she shoved his body out of the way. She issued an order to the remaining troops. "Let's get out of here, now!"

They proceeded to the monkey compound, the coyote compound, one compound after another...all empty. She got an idea of where everyone would be.

Belinda trotted with her men behind her to the now smoldering ashes of the blue corn field. "The reason our spies didn't see anyone is because no one has left. I bet the citizens got wind somehow of our invasion and have taken refuge Downtown. We find them, and slaughter *everyone*. I want no prisoners, except that dismal-dreaming bitch,

Beautimus Potamus. And, of course, if Sgt. Saturday and the Butterfly Counsel are present, do *not* touch them. They are mine. Double mead rations to the soldier who kills the most Wayflower citizens. Let's go."

She gave the signal, and they marched triple time to the entrance of Downtown. At first, they detected no one, but Belinda smelled something...something akin to fear. *Excitement? Terror?* She knew for certainty the citizens of Wayflower were Downtown somewhere. She signaled, and the troops marched in. Belinda halted them. She sniffed the air. "They'll be in the buildings."

Belinda signaled again, and the troops headed toward the entrance flaps of the retail shops and official buildings, then it happened. Two sharp wolf howls, and dozens of tigers leapt from trees onto some of her soldiers and tore open their throats. A troop of silverbacks appeared from behind buildings and waded into Belinda's troops. Rufus kicked in the chest of a bear who crumpled dead on the ground. A pack of dogs attacked one of Belinda's horses and ripped out its stomach. An elk gored one of her elephants. The elephant stumbled back injured into the side of the Crystal Interface repair store, "Can You Hear Me Now?" collapsing a wall. One of Belinda's mastodons gored one of Steven's mastodons. The fatally wounded animal stumbled sideways, crashed into Auntie Nancie's School of Fancy Dancing, collapsing a wall. Belinda twisted one way and another in vicious fury biting any of Steven's men who came near her. Her troops fought with mounting ferocity, and killed or injured their share of Steven's troops; however, the coyote, smart enough to know she could not win this battle, ordered her troops to set fire to Downtown. She gave the signal for retreat, but Steven's troops had blocked the town's entrance. She'd have to fight her way though. She ordered the T-Rex's to the forefront, and leapt on the back of the largest, fastest one, the leader of the T-Rex platoon. The dinosaurs stormed the exit flank-to-flank in a mad stampede, killing or injuring many Steven's men, and some of Belinda's soldiers as well.

Once the T-Rexes broke through the line, the Army of Vengeance poured onto the path out of Wayflower and beat a hasty retreat, the town in ruins behind them. Those too injured to keep up, she abandoned to the mercy of Steven D. Lobos. Steven howled twice more and his men pursued Belinda and her men to the border of Wayflower. Once across the bridge over Redriver, she ordered the bridge burned to slow the pursuit. Within Wayflower's borders, in a massive mob, Steven's men chanted and stamped their feet at the retreating army. "Never return. Never return. Never return."

Belinda, still atop the T-Rex, made her way to the bank of the river, as close as she could get to the border of Wayflower. She sought Steven and made eye contact with him. "I'll be back."

"You, or *any* of your troops step one paw into Wayflower again, Belinda, and I will find you and tear off your head."

The two opposing commanders bared their teeth and snarled, hackles stiff.

Belinda issued an order to the T-Rex to move to the front of the line. She resumed her place at the head of her army, and they sauntered down the path disappearing one-by-one into No One's Land.

Steven ordered his best spies, midges and flies, to follow Belinda to her encampment, which although well-hidden could not escape detection. Steven D. Lobos knew her location. Faced with the decision to keep his troops in Wayflower and remain on the defensive, or to counter attack in an offensive strike and wipe her out in No One's Land, he paced in deep thought.

After the medics carted wounded from both sides to the medic tent, Steven convened a meeting with Beautimus,

Cicero, Lucas, and Samuel to assess damage, and adjust strategy. Samuel didn't show. "Where is Sam? Why is he not here?" Steven asked. "Has anyone seen him since I ordered him to the Blue Corn fields?"

Beautimus responded. "Frankly, I'm worried. It's highly unlikely he'd not have flown back to report to us after the cornfield burned."

She managed to control her panic, but she suffered deep angst over what might have happened to her good friend. Lucas grappled with similar feelings, but his primary concern centered on Beautimus.

"I will go to the cornfields and find Sam," Lucas said.

"I don't think that's wise, Lucas. What if Belinda still has troops in Wayflower? You could be killed. Don't go. Steven can send his men to look for him. Please."

"Sam is my friend, and I know what he means to you. I need to do this."

"I doubt Belinda has the ovaries to come back to Wayflower the same day we chased her out," said Cicero. "We can send a detail of Guards with Lucas to ensure his safety."

"Belinda is brazen and vicious, and I'd never underestimate her. Please don't go," said Beautimus.

"Bea, I *need* to do this," said Lucas

"I will order a detail of my best guards to accompany him," Steven said. "Be on sharp lookout, though, Lucas, and make it fast. Certainly, Belinda's spies are here in Wayflower now. I recommend you leave for the corn field as soon as we are finished here."

With the matter of strategy on the table, the tactical team decided it best to use the home field advantage, fortify their defenses and keep their troops strong and unified as a protective force within the borders of Wayflower.

When the meeting concluded, Lucas and Beautimus

strolled a short distance from the team. "It'll be all right, my girl. I'll bring Sam back to you."

"Stay safe. If anything ever happened to you, I don't know what I'd do, Lucas."

"I love you, my girl."

The hippos nuzzled one another and kissed.

"I love you, too, Lucas. Bye for now."

"Bye for now."

A detail of rhinoceroses, mammoths, chimpanzees and cougars departed with Lucas.

Beautimus prayed to the goddesses for their safe return as she watched them trot off on the path toward the Blue Corn Field.

Steven put a mastodon on Beautimus to protect her in Lucas' absence. "Please allow me to escort you back to the civilian compound, Lady Beautimus."

"Yes, I have much work to do with Dr. Bombay. Thank you."

While waiting for the return of her beloved Lucas, and her best friend, Samuel, Beautimus busied herself in the medic tent side-by-side with Dr. Bombay and his nurses caring for the many wounded soldiers.

Belinda had executed most of her spies, but she'd deployed Army Ants who were small and clever enough to avoid detection, plus there were thousands of them. If a few were killed, so be it, there'd be plenty more. Lucas and his Guards kept a lookout for the spies and crushed any ants they came across, but there were thousands of them, and some were well hidden in the trees. A few reported back to Belinda what they had seen on the path to the Blue Corn Field.

"You saw a well-guarded bull hippo? Are you sure you saw a bull? All of the other hippos are gone. Hmmm. That must be Beautimus' consort, Lucas, which means she's still in Wayflower. Splendid news," said Belinda. "Once we have captured the wand, I will find Beautimus, bring her and the wand here, then afterwards we'll wipe out the rest of Wayflower. Bring General Heatherton and General Jake to me immediately."

"I'm sorry, Commander. They haven't been seen since the attack on Downtown."

"What do you mean? I order you to bring them to me now!"

The ant scuttled off to search for them, and returned to her within a few minutes. "The moment fighting commenced during the Downtown invasion, several men witnessed General Jake and General Heatherton scaling the roof of Mr. Grandy's Candies. They leapt off the back of the building and ran into the forest."

"Those fucking, cowardly, sheep-biting deserters. When this is over, I will send every man I have in my army to find them. I will order gorillas to first beat the cowards until all of their bones are broken, then bring them before me so I can burn them alive."

She crushed the ant under her paw.

***

Hours later, Lucas and the troops returned. In his right hand, a chimp cradled the wounded praying mantis.

Samuel groaned. "You should have seen me, Bea. When Belinda's soldiers discovered me, I fought like a tiger. I think I blinded one of the bastards. *Really,* you should have seen me."

"Please rest now, Sam. I'm glad you are back with us."

Dr. Bombay examined Samuel, and asked to speak with Beautimus and Lucas outside.

"I don't know if there is anything we can do for Samuel. His abdomen has been badly crushed and both wings so damaged even if we are able to save him, we'll have to amputate. He'll never fly again. There's internal bleeding, and it's hard to know exactly how much blood he's lost. He is resting now, but I don't want to raise any false hopes."

Beautimus crumpled against Lucas. "Goddesses no. Not Sam, please not Sam." She looked to the doctor. "May I see him?"

"Not right now, Lady Beautimus. He's stable for the time being. Let him rest. We have many other wounded to tend to, and we could use your help."

CHAPTER FORTY

"SAM IS WEAKENING," said Doc Bombay. "He can barely sip water and I'm afraid to give him food not knowing how his digestive track might respond."

"Any chance at all he'll make it?" Beautimus asked.

"I'll do my best."

Injured soldiers of both sides covered every inch of the ground in the medic tent. With their helmets removed, unless they were showing their teeth, no one could tell Belinda's soldiers from Steven's. "They're all so young," Beautimus said. "Some are not even as old as Juniper. Children."

Some whimpered in pain. Most were bleeding. Others suffered broken bones, or had lost paws, wings, legs, or tails. Others were blinded, or disfigured. A few cried for their mates or their mothers, and others begged to die. While making her rounds with Dr. Bombay, she discovered Cicero asleep, scratched and bloodied, with an ear torn and one eye patched with a white gauze bandage.

"What happened to Cicero?" Beautimus asked Dr. Bombay.

"Panthers jumped him in front of the Wayflower Civic Building Downtown. He killed two and injured a third, but lost an eye during the fight, I'm sorry to say."

Belinda touched the wounded soldiers with Ophelia to ease their pain and fear. She prayed to the Great Goddess on the soldiers' behalf. She created a magic healing potion, and when she applied it, the more superficial wounds, cuts, abrasions, minor fractions and contusions healed spontaneously. She made catnip tea to help calm the soldiers and boost their healing process. She proved a tireless worker, who Dr. Bombay and his nurses respected. She stood by as

Dr. Bombay performed surgeries, and worked with the nurses to clean the patients, staunch bleeding, and bandage wounds. All the soldiers thanked her. Her shar pendant warmed and buzzed in response to their gratitude.

Some soldiers healed well, and after a short rest, would be good as new. But she could do nothing for Samuel. She knew her closest friend in the world would die, and her guts clenched at the thought of having to tell Petunia and the nymphs.

Samuel called her to his side, "Bea, I'm so glad that you and Lucas are my children's Alternate Parents. I know I can count on you to take care of Petunia and my nymphs."

"We will, Sam. You know it."

"You should have seen me, Bea." Then, Samuel L. Goodwings died.

Beautimus hurried from the medic tent and leaned against an alumaru tree. She sobbed until her sides ached, and walked to the temporary abode to find Lucas. The moment he saw her, Lucas knew Samuel had gone.

"My girl. I'm so very sorry."

She leaned into him and they wept together. Beautimus composed herself, and returned to the medic tent to help the many who were still alive and needed her. One of the nurses had already moved Samuel's body outside the tent.

"There will be more injured coming in, and we need the space, Lady Beautimus. We are so sorry for your loss," said the nurse.

Many of wounded did not make it through the night. Those who did were held in the medic tent until Steven D. Lobos could interview each one individually, and examine their teeth to separate those in his Guard from those in the Army of Vengeance. When Steven and his guard questioned the injured soldiers about their loyalty, Beautimus used her shar pendant and Anam Glyphs to determine those sincere from those lying out of fear of what Steven might do to them. Since Belinda had abandoned her wounded, who were afterwards cared for with love and kindness in the medic tent, many of them asked to fight with Steven against Belinda. Steven, once again, faced with a difficult choice, met with Cicero, Beautimus, and Lucas to discuss the matter.

"These soldiers are criminals who the Butterfly Council and a Rendazian Court banished. Some even wear the S between their eyes, a symbol they have committed crimes so vile they had been shunned. Under the law, I should have left those shunned on the battlefield, and Dr. Bombay and the medics should never have attended to their wounds, and now we are considering posting them alongside our men in battle?" Steven said.

"We can't simply absorb them into our ranks, Commander. It'd be too risky," Cicero said.

"I think enough of them are disillusioned with Belinda, and so angry having been left behind to die that they'd relish an opportunity to fight against her. They'll probably be among our best Guards because they are highly motivated."

"Beautimus can use her shar-pendant and Anam Glyphs to help sort out those who we should swear into the Guard," said Lucas

"What do we do with the others? Execute them?" Cicero asked.

"Why not build a temporary stockade to hold them, and after the fighting, release them deep into No One's Land?" Suggested Beautimus.

"But what about the shunned, Lady Beautimus? We're talking about hardened criminals here, not petty thieves caught stealing candied melon balls from a vendor booth."

"I understand, Cicero, but my shar-pendant has the power to discern truth, and I can use both the Anam Glyphs and the pendant to help us to find those rehabilitated enough to help us fight Belinda."

"Lady Beautimus, with all due respect, if they were rehabilitated they'd have never joined Belinda's Army to begin with."

"We don't know how many volunteered vs. how many were conscripted and had no choice. Why don't we find out? And, even the soldiers who joined voluntarily may have experienced a change of heart. Those who pose the highest risk, those who have committed the worst crimes, or who The Anam Glyphs and shar-pendant warn us away from, we jail in the stockade. Afterwards, we can deport them deep into No One's Land. It's easy enough."

"I'm not comfortable with this idea," said Cicero

"Then perhaps Steven can put you in charge of the new Guards. They can report to you directly. In that way, you may keep an eye on them."

"You mean my only eye?" Cicero laughed

"Sorry. I didn't mean it that way."

"I know Lady Beautimus. I meant it as a joke…sort of." He touched his paw to his bandage.

"General Cicero, would you be agreeable to personally swearing in the new Guards after we've selected them if they are under your command?" asked Steven.

"Yes, Commander. May I also be a part of the selection committee?"

"Then we'll begin the process today. First, we'll interview those with the most superficial wounds who are ready to return to battle. We'll erect a tent and bring Belinda's men in one at a time, and we all must agree on each of the candidates unanimously. I'll order the construction of the stockade."

By that afternoon, the tent and stockade were ready, and the interviews commenced. One by one, Steve's men escorted

Belinda's soldiers into the tent. By asking a series of "yes/no" questions about their loyalty to Belinda, the crimes they had committed, and whether they were sincere in their desire to fight against Belinda, the Anam Glyphs and the shar-pendant helped the committee to select the best candidates for The Guard.

In the case of indecision, or one holdout among the selection committee, the shar-pendant made the decision. The stone grew warm or cold in response to the captives' responses. The Anam Glyphs were excellent at helping with the questions themselves. They provided clear answers. If the Glyphs' responses were in line with a soldiers' responses, the soldier's answers were authentic. Beautimus, skilled at interpreting the meaning of the Glyphs, instilled confidence in Stephen D. Lobos that her Glyphs were spot-on.

Cicero swore in over 60% of Belinda's men. Stephen ordered the others to the stockade. General Cicero addressed his new men in the swearing-in ceremony. "Any of you step out of line, or show even a hint of allegiance to Belinda, and I'll not bother to ask Commander Steven what I should do with you. I will rip out your guts. I'm watching you. Understood?"

"Yes Sir, General," the troops responded.

The addition of new Guards could not have come at a better time. Late that night, Belinda and her Army of Vengeance returned to Wayflower.

CHAPTER FORTY-ONE

"WAYFLOWER IS CLOSELY guarded now," said Belinda. "We'll have to invade from the North." She pointed her paw at a map in the dirt. We'll enter here at the shallowest, and most narrow neck of the river during the darkest part of the night."

"At night? They'll be watching for us, Commander. They'll be expecting us," said a gorilla platoon leader.

"*Of course* they will, you artless moron. What would you do, attack in the daylight so they can better detect us? Why did I build an army of idiots?" She bared her teeth at the soldier.

"How do we cross the river, Commander?" The gorilla asked.

"The larger animals will cross by wading through the river here," She pointed to the map again. "The water is shallow this time of year. A few will swim and some will, naturally, fly. Others will use rafts. The troodons are constructing them as we speak. We cross the river a few at a time to avoid alerting Steven and his men."

Belinda addressed the entire group of platoon leaders. "Listen well so you clearly understand my plan. If you fuck up, you will burn alive. Understood?"

"Yes, Commander," the troops responded.

"Excellent. My first objective is to capture the Wand. I'll bring a detail with me to the Cavern, and once the Wand is in our possession, we find Beautimus, bring her back over the river. We return en mass and kill every son-of-a-whore left in Wayflower, and burn everything, starting with the ancient trees. When we have finished our work, there will be nothing left but rotting corpses, blood, and black ash. I will rename Wayflower to Wasteland."

Belinda raised her head and howled. Her soldiers stamped their paws, flapped their wings, hooted, howled, squawked, croaked and cawed in a war cry heard for miles.

***

In Dante's Forest, Steven D. Lobos conferred with Beautimus, Lucas and Cicero.

"We aren't sure when Belinda will attack again. But, when she does, I'm inclined to think she'll attack from the north as close to the Cavern as she can position her troops. I'll post reinforcements along the shore bordering the forest, as well as here and here." Steven pointed to a dirt map.

"We've taken a heavy loss of life, and others are too wounded to fight. You need every soldier defending Wayflower you can get. Swear me in as a Guard," said Lucas, "and post me at the Cavern."

"Lucas, no. That's where the fighting is bound to be the most ferocious. Belinda thinks the wand is still there and is determined to…"

"Bea. That's where I'm most needed."

"Lady Beautimus, Lucas is right. Our forces were weakened in the last attack. He is strong and smart. We need his help."

"Lucas, if you die, I swear I'll kill you," said Beautimus

"I guess I'd better not die, then."

Cicero and Steven swore Lucas into the Wayflower Guard on the spot.

"Bea, what do your Glyphs tell us?" said Steven.

"This morning, I pulled Openeye, Zephr, and Yorushi. The first Glyphs tell us vigilance and communication are key to our success in winning the war. Yorushi is the Glyph of Forgiveness. Interesting. My interpretation is that we could win the war, but the outcome is not assured. Winning will not be a piece of cake, and our post war responsibility is not only to bury our dead and rebuild Wayflower, but to forgive our enemies. The primary message is the better we keep our eyes open. The better we communicate with one another, the easier the win."

"I'll post additional parrot lookouts, and set up a line of unbroken communication between the finches," said Steven. "Take your positions. Make certain there are no gaps in our defenses."

Beautimus nuzzled Lucas. "I love you Lucas. Please stay safe. Bye for now."

"I love you, too, my girl. I'll come back, I promise. Bye for now."

Exhausted, Beautimus walked to the tent for a short nap. She wanted to be alert and prepared if Belinda returned that evening. Before she could fall asleep, her legs trembled, she collapsed onto her knees, and dropped into her pillows. A vision. Horses and dragonflies danced in the meadow adjacent to the cenote. Out of the pink fog stepped her mother, Sangrina, her father, Artimus, Áine, Priscilla, Samuel and Rhianna. Behind them marched the host of soldiers from both sides she'd attended to in the medic tent who had passed on.

"Bea. We've all come to show our gratitude. Thank you."

"Mom, I don't know what to say. I miss you all so much."

"You need not say anything. Be strong. We are with you."

"I promise, Mom. I'll be strong."

Rhianna touched Beautimus' cheek with her wing. Beautimus came out of her vision, tears soaking her pillows.

***

The moons were but slivers that night, and the clouds muted the light of the stars. Beautimus pulled a Glyph that confirmed her suspicion. Belinda would return this evening. After consulting with Steven, who nodded his head, Beautimus prayed to the Goddess. "Please watch over our soldiers, and bring Lucas back to me."

***

Belinda addressed her troops. "This will be the defining battle of the war. Lose and I will mount your heads on posts throughout No One's Land. If you want to live, win. Helmets!"

A metallic clacking resounded through the forest as all the soldiers of the Army of Vengeance affixed their helmets.

"Let's go."

The army marched in formation behind Belinda riding atop a T-Rex. When they reached the banks of the River Kwa, they crossed a few at a time. A surge of water hit a raft midway, capsizing it. Dozens of small mammals lost their footing and fell into the river. Their heavy metal helmets dragged the animals under the water's surface. Some powerful swimmers, mostly big cats, returned to rescue them.

"No," Belinda said. "Let them drown. We have no time for currish canker-blossoms who can't even keep their balance on a raft."

Steven's lookout parrots flew on silent wings to alert the finches, who launched a communication chain that wound its way back to Steven.

"She's landed," a finch reported.

Belinda and her troops made their way through the dense forest to Secret Cavern. Out of fear of Belinda, with blind ferocity the soldiers tore their way through Steven's defenses. Belinda signaled for her detail. "Dispatch the guards, dig into the cavern, and retrieve the Wand of Fortuna, then return it to me. I'll wait in that copse of curracabah trees." She pointed with her paw. The remainder of the troops hid with Belinda and awaited further orders.

The Army of Vengeance rushed in with their teeth bared and ripped at the guards, leaving so much blood that soldiers slipped and lost their footing. Casualties were heavy on both sides. At last, all Guards at the cavern's entrance were either dead or had fallen wounded. Belinda's remaining men dug into the cavern to grab the wand, but to their surprise, a contingency of powerful soldiers waited for them. Steven's gorillas jumped out, and bit and ripped the flesh from Belinda's soldiers, all of whom were exhausted already. Those soldiers who managed to get passed the gorillas encountered the rhinos and hippos, among them Lucas. As adrenalin coursed through their bodies, and blood dripped from their sharpened fangs and wounds, Belinda's men tore into Steven's Guardsmen. Steven's rhinos gored many of the coyote's men. Some died on the spot, others toppled over, disemboweled screaming in pain. Belinda's gorillas and lions reached the back of the cavern, slashing Steven's men with their teeth and claws. The Wayflower Guardsmen fell one at a time dead or wounded, but not before taking the lives of many of Belinda's troops.

The battle ended in minutes, but many soldiers on both sides perished. Only two of Belinda's men were still on their feet, both bleeding and limping. They rushed to the niche where the guards hid the Wand of Fortuna and discovered the hole empty. The two soldiers, a cougar and a gorilla, made their way out of the cavern. Outside, Steven's men waited. Steven gave an order to his wolves who tore the gorilla to pieces. The cougar, his side now bitten open, escaped. By the time he crawled to Belinda, he was bleeding to death.

"The Wand. Where's the Wand of Fortuna?"

"I'm sorry, Commander. The Wand is not in the cavern."

"What?"

The cougar gasped and winced. "Steven's men were inside the cavern waiting. They ambushed us. I'm the last one alive, Commander."

Belinda leapt off the back of the T-Rex and trotted to the wounded cougar. "You are telling me you do not have the

Wand? You failed? I made one simple request. Bring me the Wand of Fortuna and you *failed*?"

"There is no Wand in the cavern, Commander. We looked everywhere. I'm sorry."

Belinda ordered a mastodon to the front of the line, signaled, and the mastodon crushed the cougar's head. She ordered a squad of orangutans back to the battle site.

"Bring me one of their wounded."

Steven's medics performed triage on the injured from both sides. The orangutans snuck up on a chimp medic bandaging a wounded wolf on the periphery of the battle field closest to the trees. They grabbed the medic and bit him to death before the chimp could cry out. They drug the unconscious wolf back to Belinda. "Take him to the river bank and rouse him."

Once back at the encampment, Belinda interrogated the wolf.

"Where is the Wand of Fortuna?"

"Even if I knew, I wouldn't tell you."

"Do you have a family? Cubs?"

"Yes. I have a mate and cubs."

"Do you love them?"

"Of course."

"Do you want to see them again? You don't want your cubs to grow up without a father, do you?"

"I'm not telling you anything."

"I'll make a deal with you. You tell me where the Wand is, and I'll see to it that your wounds are tended, and I'll release you to your family."

"I don't know where the Wand is. If I knew, I'd die before telling you."

"No problem. I can see to it that you die. But, first, let's try another way, shall we?"

Belinda ordered a chimp to build a fire. She signaled for a bucket filled with water. Once the fire blazed, she commanded a gorilla to, "Set the wolf on fire."

Two gorillas held down the wounded wolf while another pushed a burning stick into the fur of wolf's thigh. He screamed in pain.

"I imagine that hurts. Tell me where the Wand is and I'll order the gorillas to douse the fire," indicating the bucket with her head. "You want your pain to be over, don't you?"

"Go to hellzabob, you scurvy bitch."

The shrieks of the wolf could be heard all the way into the forest, reaching the ears of Steven D. Lobos and his men who listened to the screams of one of their own burning to death.

CHAPTER FORTY-TWO

AFTER BELINDA KICKED the dead wolf's smoldering carcass into the river, she ordered a detail of lions and gorillas to capture Beautimus. "Find her and bring her to me. If there is no Wand, why do I need a High Priestess? I will see to it she dies slowly, the whore. Bring her now."

Steven's medics, and many of his men, cleared the battlefield, searched for survivors, loaded the wounded into wagons to haul them back to the tent. Belinda ordered a detail to track them from a distance. "The fools will take us directly to her."

In front of the medic tent, a nervous Beautimus paced. The last finch communication reported news that the Battle of the Cavern had ended, and many Guardsmen were dead or wounded. The Wayflower Guard reigned victorious but not without heavy casualties.

No news of Lucas. The soldiers had not yet returned to the encampment, and Beautimus' throat constricted with fear. Dr. Bombay said, "Lady Beautimus, why not take a minute to relax? Get yourself a cup of tea. When the wounded arrive, we'll need you fresh and alert. Until we have further news, there is no use getting worked up."

"Why haven't the finches or parrots brought any further news? It's been hours. Surely, everyone should be back to camp by now."

"After a major battle, I'm certain there's much to do. Medics first treat the most severely wounded and separate the dying from the living. There's massive clean-up. The able-bodied sort through and clear rubble to ensure all soldiers are accounted for. Afterwards, the remaining men load wounded and dead onto wagons. Wagons weighted down travel slow, especially through this part of the forest. There are no cleared roads. Once the fighting is over, the soldiers can't simply run back here. It'll take some time. Please, have a cup of tea."

"I'm concerned about Lucas, Dr. Bombay. If he is uninjured, he'd have sent word."

"I'm sure Lucas is busy helping with the clean-up and maybe loading wounded men onto wagons. Right now every one of us here must be ready. We must be sharp, keep our wits about us so we can care for the injured soldiers who need us. Worrying is not helpful."

The hippo sighed. "Of course, you're right, Doctor. I'll go for a cup of tea."

Instead of going for tea, Beautimus walked a distance from the medic tent, looked around to ensure she wasn't followed, and headed as fast as she could to the battle site. *Dr. Bombay is right. Worrying is counterproductive. The wounded on the battle field can use my help now, and I'm going where I'm most needed. Sorry, Dr. Bombay.*

To avoid detection, Beautimus picked her way through the densest part of the forest. Now and again, she'd cross paths with a finch or parrot. "You are not to communicate to anyone that you've seen me. I'm on a covert mission and if anyone knows I'm here, security is compromised and we could lose the war and many will die."

"Yes, Lady Beautimus."

Littered with evidence of battle, the forest suffered with brush slashed, dead bodies, debris, and branches ripped off trees, vibrating in pain. She nearly tripped over a dented helmet. A broken spear stuck in the side of a broom wattle. She dislodged it. The tree buzzed its appreciation. She found a dismembered marmot and a bloodied severed wolf's paw. From the amount of blood on the ground, it became immediately obvious the wolf had bled to death. There could be no way of knowing if these were Belinda's or Steven's soldiers. She took a minute to dig a hole and bury them together. She prayed over their makeshift grave. "May the Goddess bless you and hold you in her arms."

As she neared the site of the cave, frightened voices assailed her.

"The roof is collapsing, and there's men still inside," one soldier shouted. "We have to get the wounded to safety, Commander!"

"No time. Get out now."

"Men are screaming for help. We can't leave them, Commander."

"I can't risk losing more men. Retreat. Out of the cave. That's an order,"

Beautimus worked up her courage and ran into the fray, disregarding any possible danger to herself, and barged into the entrance of the cavern.

"Lady Beautimus!" Steven shouted. "What are you doing here? It's not safe. Don't go in. You'll be killed."

"Screw that, Steven. I'm going in. There's men alive in there."

She shoved through the rubble and searched the cave. Everywhere were soldiers, some dead some alive. She couldn't tell which side any were on. She didn't care. With her maw she pulled the men through the mouth of the cavern one at a time as fast as she could. A deep rumble came at her as part of the ceiling collapsed onto some soldiers who cried out. Without pausing, she pushed aside the debris and pulled those men to safety, then she found another wounded man and pulled him out, then another and another. "Please, Great Mother Genesis, keep me alive. Help me get these soldiers to safety. Give me strength."

She felt a presence. Near her stood several powerful gorillas, including Rufus, and wolves, among them, Steven D. Lobos, helping her dig through debris to locate and pull men from the cavern. Another rumble followed by a bellowing crash. An explosion of dust roiled out of the mouth of the collapsed cavern. The air grew still and silent.

"Lady Beautimus, are you okay? You barely made it," said Steven.

"The men. Did we get them all out?"

"Yes we did, Lady Beautimus. Every single one. There were thirty-two wounded soldiers in that cavern still alive. Because of your bravery, they will all be going home to their families. Do you realize you single-handedly pulled sixteen men to safety?"

"Thanks to you and Rufus, and the others who helped me to…"

"Lady Beautimus, I ordered the retreat. I had no intention of going back into that cave or allowing my men to enter. If you had not disregarded my orders, thirty-two men would have been crushed to death. We bow to you." The wolf and all his men lowered their eyes and bowed.

Only then did Beautimus notice Lucas on his side bleeding from his head and haunch. Although she'd not realized it at the time, he'd been among the soldiers she managed to pull out by herself. Lucas, a large hippo, unconscious when she dragged him from the cavern, required supernatural strength to pull out unaided. She gazed at the sky. "Holy Mother Genesis, thank you for answering my prayer. Thank you for giving me strength to save the lives of these men, and most of all, thank you for sparing my Lucas."

"Thank the Goddess, you're alive," she said to the unconscious hippo. "We'll be back at the encampment soon and Dr. Bombay will fix you up good as new."

A medic bandaged Lucas' head and leg. She pulled Ophelia from her collar, and focused healing attention through the wand. She touched the wand to Lucas's scrapes and bruises, many of which healed spontaneously. The wound on his leg looked bad, though. Blood soaked through the new bandage and pooled beneath him. She knew if he didn't receive expert medical attention soon, he could bleed to death. She called for a soldier monkey to apply pressure to the bandage. When she touched the tip of her wand to Lucas' head wound he opened his eyes. "Bea."

"Yes, Lucas. I'm here with you. You're going to be all right."

"Thank you, my girl."

His eyes closed.

After the soldiers bearing the wounded returned, because of the severity of his bleeding, Dr. Bombay determined that Lucas be the first moved inside the medic tent.

"Lady Beautimus, I thought you were resting. What in hellzabob are you doing with the soldiers?" Dr. Bombay asked.

"Beautimus is why so many of my men are alive right now, Doc," Steven said.

"But, how? What happened?"

"There'll be time to explain later, but right now, you have to get these soldiers fixed up."

The doctor ordered his nurses and aides to pull the men in and they set to work.

Beautimus worked alongside the medics and nurses. She went to the beds of each of the soldiers touching her wand to their wounds.

"Let the nurses attend to that, Bea. I need to talk to you." Beautimus followed Doc Bombay outside.

"He has lost more blood than we'd hoped, Lady Beautimus."

"Is he going to die?" She trembled. "Please tell me he isn't going to die."

"Right now it's touch and go. The good news is that the head wound is not serious, and there is no brain damage. It's his leg we are worried about."

"Can you save it?"

"Yes, I believe so, but a sharp tooth severed a major artery and some tendons. I want to prepare you. If he makes it, he may not walk again. For the time being, we have clamped the bleeder, and we are transfusing plasma. I've also concocted a magical healing poultice that seems to be helping. That, along with the work you did with Ophelia I think will pull him through. We are doing the best we can, but I don't want to get your hopes up too high. We'll know more by tomorrow."

"Thank you, Doctor. Can I see him?"

"For a few minutes, then he needs to get some rest, and so do you. I want you to go home after this and get some sleep. If there is any change, I'll send someone for you."

Lucas rested under a thick blanket, a fresh bandage on his head. Color had returned to his face and he rested. Beautimus leaned over and kissed him. "Lucas, it's me."

"Hi, my girl. Quite a fight there back in the cavern, you know. I feel awful."

"I know, Lucas. After you rest a bit, you'll be better."

"That's not what I mean, Bea. I took a life. I killed a gorilla. I'll never forget the look on his face before he died. Horrible."

"Shhhhh, shhhhh. You did what you had to, Lucas. I know you'd never hurt anyone, but he would have killed you had you not killed him. You are so brave, and I'm proud of you."

"I'll never forget the look on his face, never. He didn't want to die."

"Please, just rest, Lucas. We'll talk about this later. It's going to be all right. I love you. Bye for now."

"Bye for now."

Beautimus had no idea of the measure of her exhaustion until she walked away from the medic tent. Each step she took, laborious, painful. Her shoulders ached. She yawned, and yawned again, and headed for the river to take a dip. She planned after her bath to head to the temporary abode, and fall into her pillows without dinner. She'd return to Lucas' side first thing in the morning.

When about to step into the river, something heavy dropped over her bringing her hard to her knees. She struggled to stand but could not. "What?" She found herself trapped beneath a thick net, surrounded by a dozen gorillas with sharpened teeth, wearing feathered helmets. One of them grasped a small ferret in his paw. "You scream, or make one noise, and I kill this ferret." He shook the ferret to show Beautimus he meant business. The little mammal cried out in pain and fear. Beautimus' temples pounded. The gorillas loaded her into a wagon hooked to a mammoth and pulled her through the forest to Belinda.

***

"Well, if it isn't Lady Beautimus, the High Priestess of Wayflower. What an honor. Everyone, bow to the High Priestess."

The Army of Vengeance made an exaggerated bow to Beautimus.

"Belinda, it would be in your best interest to release me."

"Let me see. You are alone under a net unable to move. I am here with a well-trÁined army of criminals, none of whom would hesitate to tear you into pieces. All I need do is order your death, and it's done. You are in no position to tell me what I should do or not do, don't you agree?"

Beautimus stared into the coyote's eyes, but remÁined silent.

"I lay on my pillows many nights thinking about how I'd like to kill you, Beautimus Potamus. You ruined my life. You stole my position as High Priestess. It's because of you the old trees and Butterfly Council banished me from the only home I've ever known. Everything that happened to me is your fault," The coyote pointed a paw at Beautimus' face, "and now you will pay for it with your life, you ugly puking ratsbane whore."

"Kill me if you want, but you know what happened to you is your own doing."

"Shut the fuck up!" Belinda signaled to an orangutan holding a sharpened branch spear. He stabbed Beautimus in the flank. The hippo stifled a cry of pain. Blood oozed from the wound.

"So, how shall we do this, Lady Beautimus? Shall we burn you alive? Should we tie rocks around your neck and drown you in your beloved river? We could order the wolves to rip out your intestines, and pull them out of your body inch by inch. Or, we could puncture your hide so many time you bleed to death, screaming for mercy? Eh?"

She signaled the orangutan again who plunged the stick deeper into the hippo in the same spot. Beautimus flinched but did not cry out. Blood poured from the wound.

"Well, well. You are stronger than I thought. This is going to take some time. How fun this is going to be!" She turned to the orangutan. "Go for an eye, this time, but not too deep. We don't want to kill her yet. One eye gone would be good, maybe she'll stop staring at me. What do you think, Lady Beautimus? How lovely you'd look one-eyed."

As the orangutan positioned himself near Beautimus' head to deliver a blinding stab to her eye, a loud rustling averted his attention. He turned in time to see a gorilla pounce, Rufus. Then, a wolf howled twice, and cougars, tigers, dogs, troodons, alligators, rushed in and attacked Belinda and her men. After Rufus beheaded the orangutan, he gnawed through the net covering Beautimus and freed her.

The Army of Vengeance, unprepared for an attack, were frantic, disorganized and sloppy. The Guards overcame Belinda's men who either died or fled. Steven shouted, "Seize her. Hold her."

As Belinda attempted to flee, several silverbacks, including Rufus, grabbed her. She yelped, and tried to squirm out of their hold. She twisted her head and bit in wild fury, but with deft skill the gorillas avoided her teeth. One of them managed to clamp her muzzle shut with his hand. They hoisted her to a seated position and held tight. Her eyes registered panic.

Steven D. Lobos walked over to her, and looked her in the eyes. "I told you I'd personally rip off your head if you ever stepped a pay in Wayflower again." He turned to the gorillas. "Expose her neck."

"No, don't, Steven. Please. Show mercy. I order you to cease." Beautimus said.

"I'm sorry, Lady Beautimus." He bit into Belinda's neck, and ripped one way then the other all but severing the coyote's head. Blood sprayed, drenching the gorillas. Steven stepped away, and the soldiers dropped Belinda into the dirt. Her body twitched for a few seconds, and it was over.

The few remaining Army of Vengeance ran for their lives, waded, flew or rafted their way back into No One's Land. Steven bowed low to Beautimus. "Lady Beautimus, please accept my humble apology for disobeying your orders. I will accept any punishment you deem fit."

Blood dripped from his muzzle, chest, and forelegs. His paws were drenched in blood. Nauseating bile made its way up Beautimus' throat. She swallowed hard.

"Shall I send my men after the enemy, Lady Beautimus?"

"No, Steven. Let them go. With Belinda dead, they are no threat to us. They are no longer our enemies."

"It is for that reason I killed Belinda, Lady Beautimus. I apologize for my willful disobedience, but I had to 'cut the head off the snake' to stop her soldiers."

"I understand, Steven. Thank you, but how did you know I had been kidnapped?"

"Lady Beautimus, with all due respect, given that stunt you pulled at the cavern, I will never allow you to go anywhere unescorted again. I've sworn to protect you, and you could have easily been killed in that cave-in. You did not know I stayed near, but when you left the medic tent, I followed you to the river. When I witnessed Belinda's gorillas drop the net over you, I ran back to the encampment and gathered troops. I'm only sorry we were not able to get to you before that damned toad-spotted orangutan stabbed you."

"It hurts some, but I'll be fine. Ophelia is already helping the wound to heal. I don't know how to thank you, Steven. Rufus? Is Rufus here?"

Rufus bowed. "Lady Beautimus."

"Rufus, I do not know how to thank you for saving my eye."

"I'd protect you with my life, My Lady."

When Beautimus, Steven and the Wayflower Guards returned to the encampment, Lady Luz and Lady Beth were overhead. The men broke out the mead barrel. Beautimus drank from a pail, thanked the soldiers again, and rushed to the medic tent.

"Dr. Bombay has retired for the evening, Lady Beautimus," said a young coati, a nurse.

"How is Lucas? I wish to see him."

"Certainly, Lady Beautimus. Come this way." As they walked into the tent the nurse said, "He seems better."

"Please bring some pillows. I will sleep next to Lucas until Dr. Bombay arrives."

"Yes, Lady Beautimus, although…it is highly irregular…", but when the coati saw the determined flash in Beautimus' eyes, she ran for the pillows.

Beautimus snuggled as close to Lucas as she could, closed her eyes, and listened to his rhythmic breathing.

***

On the banks of a deep lake filled with peacock blue water two women, a hippo and a blue crane, sat side-by-side under a cassie-flower bush. A lovely pale green mist that smelled of fresh lemon peels enveloped them. Hummingbirds flitted, sipping from multicolored eight foot snapdragons growing in profusion as far as the eye could see. Beautimus moved silently through the snapdragons closer to the women. The snapdragons bent out of her way to allow her passage. Beautimus heard the women talking, but couldn't quite make out their words. She couldn't see who see who they were. She moved in a little closer until their features came into focus.

"Lady Rhianna? Mom? What are you doing here?"

They did not respond..

"Can you hear me? Mom? Lady Rhianna?"

"I'm so proud of that girl, Rhianna. Did you see how she handled herself through that war?" Said Sangrina.

"Don't you know it. For a middle-aged woman with slow bones, she managed to save all those soldiers without once thinking of her own safety."

"Did you see when Belinda captured her she didn't even show one sign of fear? She didn't even cry out when that pottle-deep horn-beasted orangutan poked that stick into her flank. And after all that, she begged for mercy for Belinda. She has a wonderful heart, Rhianna. I'm so proud of my daughter."

"We both knew she had it in her."

"She turned into an amazing woman, didn't she, Rhianna?"

"Yes indeed, my old friend, yes indeed."

CHAPTER FORTY-THREE

THE WAYFLOWER CITIZENS returned home, and although Beautimus did not want to face Petunia, she knew she had to be the one to deliver the horrible news.

"No, not Sam, no!" Petunia crumpled. She lifted her head and wailed. "Oh, Bea. He's really dead? Please tell me it's not true."

"I loved Sam, too. For hundreds of years, he's been my dearest friend." Unable to contain herself any longer, Beautimus dissolved into tears. "I'm so sorry, Petunia."

"How do I tell the nymphs they will never see their papa again, Bea? What do I tell them?"

"Tell them their father was the bravest soldier who ever lived, and he died fighting to protect their home. That's what you tell them, Petunia."

"But, what are we going to do? How will we live?"

"You need not worry. Lucas and I will care for you and your children for the rest of your lives. We'll always be here for you."

The two women wept together for a long, long while.

***

Those who had been evacuated returned to find Wayflower ruined—the main bridge burned, many abodes destroyed, the corn fields in ashes, and Downtown a wreck.

The Downtown Square boasted a magnificent botanical garden maintÁined by "Friends of the Flowers," a grist of honey bees dedicated to the care, pollination, and general nurturing of blooms. Also, the square held The Cultural Museum of Earth Artifacts that Dr. Pimbly had built and where he served as curator. Behind glass walls in the museum visitors could view cell phones, ironing boards, pens, table lamps, and other items unique to humans. The flowers in the square were ripped out, the display cases and many priceless objects in the Museum destroyed.

On one corner stood the ruined shell of Lacy's Magnificent Threads owned by Lacy Delaroux, a sweet Doily Weaver Spider. Lacy co-managed her shop with her best friends, a Labyrinth Orb Weaver spider named Fanny, and a Dew Drop spider named Myrtle. Lacy, Fanny, and Myrtle could often be found hanging around the corners of the shop in webs near the ceiling, where they'd drop down to greet customers as they'd enter. Nothing remÁined of Lacy's fabrics and notions but a pile of rubble and ash.

Next to Lacy's, The Crafty Fox, a store that sold handmade paper, parchment by the sheet, and general crafting and office supplies. A fox owned this store, of course, a rather foppish and stuffy fellow named Clarence Tipper. When Clarence laid eyes on his demolished business he dropped his usual decorum and cried like a lost baby panda.

Madam Scheherazade's Magic Eye sold magical supplies, altar accoutrements, carved boa-boa boxes, incense and Goddess figurines. Minnie Buffington, a barn owl who affected the name Scheherazade because she thought it magical, owned this business. With every figurine and box shattered, nothing magical remÁined of Minnie's store now.

Next door to Minnie's psychic shop, the Crystal Interface sales and repair store called "Can You Hear Me Now?" owned by a desert tortoise, Clyde Speeder, known as "Clyde the Geek," and his long time domestic partner, a younger soft-spoken desert tortoise named Manuel Rippington who Clyde affectionately called "Ripper." Gone. Upon seeing the devastation, the two men clung to one another and wailed.

The office of *The Wayflower Quacker*, owned by the

McQuacks, a family of ducks who had been in the newspaper biz for generations, Mr. Grandy's Candy Store, the Wayflower Post Office, the Guardian station, the Civic Building where the Butterfly Council held Court, the Wayflower District Rendazian Glow Seed Bank, gutted, every building.

"Girly Girl," a shop that sold all manner of rouges, ribbons, perfumes and other things one might find on a woman's vanity, had been smashed into a jumble of broken shards. Penelope Freestone, a pretty Triceratops with exceptionally long eyelashes, now matted with tears, owned Girly Girl.

On the corner opposite from Lacy's stood The Clever Helpers Training Center, Wayne Rumbly's business. It'd be moons before the Training Center would hold another class.

Next to the Training Center, the Center for Blue Corn Studies where Samuel worked as head Blue Corn Scientist, and next to that, Mrs. Widgets Kitchen Gadgets 'N Goods that sold pots, pans, culinary herbs. In the back of Mrs. Widget's, once stood Ms. Maggie's School of Fine Cookery. Both were owned by Janice Chartreuse, a nervous Lazuli Bunting known for her gourmet cooking skills. Charred and broken goods were all that remÁined.

The art supply store, "The Artzy Fartzy," a co-op owned by the Wayflower Art Coalition, and Mr. Rumbly's Music School were adjacent to Auntie Nancie's School of Fancy Dancing. Wayne Rumbly owned this store, too. So, he lost two businesses. The "love triangle" between Nancie, José and him, often the topic of local gossip, and a source of embarrassment for Wayne, meant nothing now. Wayne Rumbly stood in shock among the ruins of his life's work, romance the furthest thing from his mind.

The only structure unscathed—a plain looking square building with a sign that read, "The Wayflower Poker Club." For decades, the same group of twelve dogs met there on

Saturday nights. The dogs called themselves "Motley Crew" since they were such a crazy mixed-up group, but despite their size and temperament differences, they were very close and none of them could imagine skipping the Saturday night card game. The only evidence that a battle waged outside its doors—a gorilla spear stuck in the plaster on one wall, and beneath it, a burned body of bobcat with its teeth sharpened.

The cries of men, women and children who had lost family members and loved ones issued from every compound, the atmosphere thick with grief.

Wayflower would never be the same.

CHAPTER FORTY-FOUR

BEAUTIMUS CONVENED A District-Wide Meeting to address her citizens. "We've all lost loved ones, and we've suffered from the devastation of this war. But, not all is gone. Some abodes were damaged, others destroyed, but most still stand. Because of my dear late friend, Samuel S. Goodwings' brilliant planning, there is an abundance of corn kernels for replanting. No one will go hungry. The old growth trees were spared. Not one damaged. The Wayflower Guards fought valiantly, many lives were saved, and we now have heroes in Rendaz who have made the Wayflower District, and the planet, a safer place. Having said that, I do not believe in war. Earth culture has taught us there has never been, *nor will there ever be,* a good war. The only way to achieve lasting peace is to commit to lasting non-violence.

The Butterfly Council and the Old Trees are convening to discuss how to proceed. They are voting to either outlaw war forever and disband the Wayflower Guard, or keep the Guard intact, recruit and train more troops in preparation for the possibility of future war. We defeated Belinda and her Army of Vengeance. I ask the Butterfly Counsel, given the almost impossibility of another war, why even *consider* amassing troops in each of the Districts?"

A murmur passed through the crowd.

"There is another initiative on the table to enact capital punishment for unrepentant and vengeful criminals like Belinda who *might* wage war. I understand the Council's position, but this is the first time in Rendazian history that a banished criminal has reacted in such a manner. It's time for the killing to stop, and I implore the Council to take this initiative off the table.

In the meantime, my deepest sympathies to all of you for your many losses. May the Goddess keep you in her hand."

***

Under the supervision of the Butterfly Council, the citizens of Wayflower banded together to begin the process of rebuilding and healing. The agricultural team assessed the damage to the corn fields. As Samuel had predicted, because of the ash, the soil developed into rich and fertile loam. Field restoration and replanting commenced, giving Wayflower residents a reason to celebrate. But, there many men and women would be forever maimed, some blinded, others missing paws, limbs or tails, others brain damaged, or disfigured. All those who'd fought in the War of Wayflower bore emotional scars that would cause them pain for the remainder of their lives.

Counter to Beautimus' wishes, the Butterfly Council and Old Trees voted against disbanding the Wayflower Guards, and promoted Steven D. Lobos to First General Commander. The initiative for capital punishment passed, but would be up for another vote in ten moons. Beautimus decided to dedicate her life to the cause of peace and would work to overturn the death penalty. She could hear Samuel now:

"What would you have the Butterfly Council, do, Bea? Form a glee club for the criminals? Or, better idea, send them to an exotic island in the Oceanic district to sip mead from fancy glasses with little umbrellas in them while they work on their suntans?"

"Sam, that's not at all what I meant, and you know it. What I'm trying to say is capital punishment perpetuates killing, it doesn't prevent it. The death penalty doesn't make sense."

"What you are saying is if you are someone like Belinda making plans to kill a bunch of people, if you knew you'd be put to death for it instead of banished or shunned, you wouldn't be even at least a little bit deterred?"

"One thing I've learned in all my years of teaching History of Earthly Things is that capital punishment never prevents murder. There are many hundreds of murders committed every day on Earth in places where capital punishment is legal."

"Yeah? Well how do you know there wouldn't be a *lot* more murders if some potential murdering wagtails were *not* deterred by the death penalty?"

"How can we promote peace and tell our children it's wrong to kill *if we kill people*? Can't you understand my logic?"

"What you are trying to tell me is that we should simply forgive the person who slaughtered our families and let them live the rest of their life dancing through the clover, is that it?"

"Sam, *where in hellzabob did you get that*? I didn't say anything of the kind. What I said is that killing is wrong. Capital punishment, therefore, is wrong."

"Yeah, sure, Bea. Even though I'm dead, I can see you're still a bloody idealist who believes the world is made of tulip petals and sweet cream."

"Yeah, Sam, even after you're dead, I can still see you're an ass."

"At least I'm a smartass instead of a dumb ass, Bea."

"Sam?"

"What?"

"I miss you."

***

The day arrived for the Ceremony to Honor the Dead and the Presentation of the Pentagrams of Bravery. Angeline crafted shar-stone pentagrams for each of the award recipients. Everyone dressed in their festival finery and gathered at the Sacred Watering Hole. In tears, Beautimus and Petunia eulogized Samuel. The other dead were given a proper mourning ceremony, and the meercats performed the "Dance of the Dead," accompanied by the Baboon Harp Trio playing *Mozart's Requiem*.

Beautimus said a prayer to usher the souls of the departed into to the arms of the Goddess. Afterwards, Beautimus and Steven D. Lobos scattered the soldiers' ashes into the Sacred Watering Hole as the Wayflower Guardsmen stood at attention, saluting their fallen comrades. The Butterfly Council erected a plaque near The Sacred Watering Hole that read, "This water is blessed by the remains of those who valiantly gave their lives for Wayflower. May their souls rest in the arms of the Goddesses."

Odette and Euripides stood with Beautimus to award the "Pentagrams of Bravery." Queenie helped Beautimus place a shar-stone around the neck of the first soldier on stage. "Rufus, thank you for your bravery," and one around Cicero's neck, "General Cicero, thank you for your Bravery," and one around Petunia's neck "In honor of your mate, Samuel G. Goodwings, we thank him for his bravery." The Butterfly Council unveiled a plaque with the names of the war dead. They'd place it in the Downtown Square once rebuilt. The first name on the plaque? Geronimo. "First casualty of war. Killed in the line of duty protecting Wayflower." Beautimus and Queenie presented Geronimo's widow with his star for bravery.

Steven D. Lobos walked on stage. Queenie placed the shar-stone pentagram around his neck.

Beautimus nodded. "First Commander General Steven D. Lobos, thank you for your bravery."

But, instead of bowing and leaving the stage as the others had, Steven asked Queenie to remove the shar stone and place it around Beautimus' neck. "This is yours, Lady Beautimus."

He told the crowd the story of the cave-in, and how Beautimus was responsible for saving the lives of thirty-two men in the face of grave danger. "Lady Beautimus, thank you for your bravery."

EPILOGUE

"I'M WORRIED WE'LL run out of food, there's so many people," Lizzy said. Today marked the 79th anniversary of the end of the Wayflower War and Beautimus' 300th birthday. Lizzy and Cassie arranged a spectacular bash for Beautimus. Lizzy brought in barrels of mead, and hired the Baboon Harp Trio, sparing no expense for her dear friend.

Cassie organized the decorating at Sweetwater Pond, made out the guest list, and sent invitations through her Crystal Interface. Agnes and Applecheeks scampered up trees and affixed balloons and streamers to branches.

"No, not there, Agnes. Tie the balloons to that wattle tree over there." Cassie directed the activities with the grace of a symphonic conductor.

"Cassie-I'm-not-sure-the-streamers-should-go-in-the-rainbow-gum-there's-already-so-much-color-in-the-tree-and-I-hate-for-us-to-go-through-the-trouble-if-no-one-will-even-notice-them-what-do-you-think-white-balloons-instead?"

"White balloons are fine."

Many people showed up to honor Beautimus, leaving sparse room around the pond for guests. Hundreds of Beautimus' former students brought their families. Angeline and her sister came. Juniper and her mate and tiny new bubbit were there. Odette and Euripides and other members of the Butterfly Council attended. Buford showed up with his mate and new litter of puppies. "See, see? Sho 'nuff cutest puppies, yup." Pant, pant, drool. Osiris, decked out in dozens of ribbons, hopped to Beautimus with his birthday greetings. The armadillo twins scuttled through the crowd to Beautimus.

"Happy"

"Birthday"

"Lady"

"Beautimus."

Aunt Meg and Uncle Phelan, getting on in years, managed to make an appearance.

"They are still so in love," Beautimus said. "Look at them cuddling like teenagers."

Petunia sat on Beautimus' head where Samuel used to perch. "They are indeed cute. I often wonder how Sam and I'd be together if he'd lived. Oh Bea, I miss him so much."

"I miss him, too, Petunia."

"I'm feeling old these days. My kids are grown up, mated, with nymphs of their own. That daddy's girl, Clara Bow, is about to lay her second ootheca any day now. And, you, Granny, what do you think of Josh and Bea II all grown up?"

"I'm proud of Josh. Handsome boy, and so intelligent. I know Bea II is expecting to be named High Priestess in a few decades once I'm ready to put down the Wand, but, Liz, I secretly hope she chooses love. I always regretted not mating with Lucas." She turned. "Well, speaking of the Demon. Hi, sweetheart!"

Lucas limped down a hill toward them. His leg never quite healed after the war, and the limp had become more pronounced over the years. "Hi, my girl." He planted a kiss on Beautimus' cheek. "Happy Birthday."

Chance ambled along behind, holding Lucas' birthday gift to Beautimus, three dozen pink and white roses. "Yo, Happy Birthday. These are from Lucas. I've got a mastodon coming hauling a wagon of mead and bags of Mofo Sweets, too."

Some moons before, much to Beautimus' delight, Chance used his trust fund to buy *Mr. Grandy's Candies* and changed the name to *T-Bone's Mofo Sweets*. His slogan was, "Everybody Eats Mofo Sweets." He hired M.C. Tweezers and Rampage to manage the manufacturing and marketing of dozens of candy varieties, many of which Chance, who'd become a master candy maker, invented. He built a candy plant in Wayflower that employed over a thousand workers and boosted Wayflower's economy. Over time, he expanded *T-Bone's Mofo Sweets* into a popular chain of candy shops with stores in all districts on Rendaz.

Chance had become a philanthropist, and donated part of the proceeds from his candy sales to fund the "Save the Eggs Foundation" he'd built to help Rendazian dinosaur youth graduate from college and avoid gang life. His created a motto: "No T-Rex Left Behind."

Days before Beautimus' birthday party, Ziggy Robbins invited him to join him as a secondary motivational speaker on "The B.A.M.B.O.O.Z.L.E. Tour." Chance co-authored with Beautimus a popular autobiographical book, "Out of the Gang and Into the Melon Balls."

A little later, Bea II, Josh and Josh's girlfriend, a lovely young lady with dark eyes who looked a lot like Sangrina did when young, arrived. It became obvious Josh was smitten with this new girl, but there were no plans for an official mating. Josh still did his best to play the part of the "party guy," not ready to commit to a relationship.

"You know Josh has taken a job at the Blue Corn Science Center, Liz."

"Looks like he's following in his adopted Uncle Samuel's footsteps. He's absolutely passionate about Quantum Agriculture."

"He's like Sam in another way, too. Last night, the WSRT voted him in as Treasurer."

"Really, Bea? I'm glad to hear Sam's legacy lives on in others."

Rufus did not attend. Decades prior, Beard pronounced Rufus "Full of Sap," and the gorilla graduated to the status of a full-fledged sage, one of the most revered in Wayflower's history. Sages never attend secular soirees. He showed up at every one of the Goddess Festivals, though. Beautimus said to Lizzy, "Now we know why Beard told those awful tree jokes."

Cicero came with his mate, a beautiful Bengal. They had two yearling cubs, one white like Cicero, one Bengal like their mother. They played "hide and seek" in the meadow with other cubs, and with Samuel and Petunia's grand-nymphs.

"No fair!" said one of Cicero's cubs, "Mantis kids is way littler than we is, and they hides in sneaky places."

Beautimus found it intriguing that Cicero had become close friends with Zeus, the same panther who had taken Cicero's eye during the war. After his capture, Cicero swore him into the Guard, and the panther became an outstanding soldier who fought bravely for Wayflower. He even formed his own elite "Black Panther" regime who, even after the war, fought to right injustice on the planet. The group tended to be militant, and some people were wary of them, but the Panthers did a lot of good on Rendaz. As part of their uniform, they sported smart looking berets.

After the war, Zeus assimilated into the Wayflower community. He mated with a local girl, and their union produced two children who played today with Cicero's cubs and the other wee ones. Zeus returned to college for his doctorate and earned the title, "Dr. Zeus," and became one of Wayflower's leading citizens. He opened a new shop Downtown, "Sharp Tooth" after the nickname given him since he had sharpened his teeth to points on Belinda's order. Dr. Zeus earned the reputation as the best dentist in all Wayflower.

Although recently retired, Steven D. Lobos appeared wearing his red fez. Always a handsome wolf, in uniform he looked down right rakish. Beautimus had always hoped Steven would become a peace activist, but he remÁined a right-wing soldier to the core. They had many philosophical debates over the subject of peace, and co-authored an enormous book, "War and Peace," showcasing both sides. The book became a classic taught in universities throughout Rendaz. A cute silver wolf, quite a bit younger, accompanied Steven D. Lobos. She adored him, and he adored her. Rumor had it he'd soon propose.

An appalled Auntie Nancie sneered. "Look at that. She's no more than a cub. How disgusting."

"Knock it off, Nancie. Why do you care so much about who Steven chooses as a mate? Pay attention to me, will ya, woman?" Said José Saturday, who'd become a different man after he'd retired. Auntie Nancie and José legally mated some years before, and he enjoyed ribbing his stuffy mate. "How 'bout you and I share a big glass of mead, and talk about what we are going to do behind closed doors at our abode after the party?" He winked at Nancie who turned red as a beer berry.

Cassie never re-mated. "I'm too independent," she said, "besides, I had the best man a woman could ever have. Why would I want anyone else?" She finished her studies, and earned her teaching credential in History of Earthly Things. Cassie had become the youngest tenured professor in the history of Wayflower. Only a moon before, Beautimus sat in on her daughter's class at Dr. Pimbly's School for Goodly Educated Adults. "You are a wonderful teacher, Cassie. A natural. Clearly, your students admire and respect you. I'm so proud."

"Thank you, Mom. I hope I can be half the teacher you were. Do you miss the classroom?"

"Sometimes, but I'm busy with the duties of High Priestess, and there's so much to do for the Wayflower Peace Initiative that I don't have time to dedicate to students. Plus, I'm getting a little older. I don't have the same energy I once did. It's a good thing I retired because it's getting more difficult every year to keep ahead of those mega-bright graduate students. It's your turn now."

***

Ten moons after Beautimus' birthday party, Uncle Phelan contracted hippo-grippe and passed away at home with Aunt Meg by his side. Distraught at having lost her mate of over 350 years, two weeks to the day of Uncle Phelan's death, Meg died in her sleep calling his name. The WSRT gave Uncle Phelan and Aunt Meg a magnificent wake. Afterwards, with the Potamus Tribe, and hundreds of Wayflower's citizens in attendance, Beautimus and Queenie, who stayed on as Beautimus' house lemur after, much to Beautimus' great sorrow, Agnes, Applecheeks and Jeeves all passed away, Beautimus blended their ashes and cast them into the River Kwa.

Many more seasons passed before Lizzy suffered a fatal mastodonian brain attack. Dr. Bombay, nearing retirement, said she died before she hit the ground. A heart-broken Beautimus paid for a granite monument etched with Lizzy's likeness, and planted a memorial rose garden for the Mastodon Compound. She ordered a plaque mounted on the monument that read, "Lizzy, a beloved friend."

Calypso developed trout-dementia, so in addition to A.D.H.D. the fish couldn't remember things or people, and grew increasingly confused. Beautimus often went to the river to check on Calypso. Sometimes the trout recognized Beautimus, and they had wonderful long talks. Other days went like this:

"Hi, Calypso. How are you today?"

"*And...*you are? Never mind. I remember, you're the guy with the funny fart jokes. I remember the one about the dude with the farting problem who goes into see the doctor and..."

"…no, Calypso. You're thinking of the gorilla, Rufus, who tells the fart jokes. I'm Bea."

"Bea. All right *you* are Bea. But, aren't you the gorilla?"

"No, Calypso, I'm a *female* hippo. Rufus is a *male* gorilla."

"You aren't Rufus, but you're a female gorilla, right? Wait! What's that over there? It's a ten-legged water bug. I'm sure of it."

"It's a leaf, Calypso."

"*And*…you are?"

"I'm Bea, your friend. Beautimus Potamus, The High Priestess."

"Nope. The High Priestess is a blue crane. You're fooling with me now, aren't you?"

"You're thinking of Lady Rhianna. She passed away a long time ago."

"She did? Oh, that's too bad. Terribly sorry to hear such sad news. Look! There's something wriggling in the water. Right there. See it? Gotta check this out. See you later, Rufus."

Bea Two fell in love with a dashing barrister. A few moons before she was to be named High Priestess, she brought him to meet her grandmother. "I love the Goddess, Grandma. Since early childhood I've wanted to be High Priestess like you, but I'm in love, and he loves me, too."

"Never trade love for title or position, my child. Go, get mated, live a good life. I'm happy for you."

Beautimus presided over their mating ceremony in the same meadow where Samuel and Petunia were joined, a glorious day in Beautimus' life. Later, Bea Two gave birth to twin girls. She named one Cassie Two and the other Bea Three. Both grew to be beautiful and talented women. The two found wonderful mates and Beautimus presided over their mating ceremonies, also.

Lucas and Beautimus spent many lovely years together, then shortly after her 402nd birthday, Beautimus pulled the glyph, Spirit Bridge. She'd pulled it several times that week. She walked to the pond and sat down under the same tree where Lucas proposed to her so long ago. "It's my time?" She asked. The Goddess answered in the wind rippling the pond water.

That evening, she enjoyed a magnificent dinner of her favorite minted strawberry soup and sparkling mead surrounded by the laughter of friends and family, after which she bathed in her precious Kwa River one last time. When settled into her pillows, she called Lucas and Cassie to her side. "My heart will cease beating tonight."

Lucas kissed her cheek. "Please don't say that, my girl. You've plenty of life left in you."

"Mom, are you sick?"

"I'm not sick. The Goddess is calling me. Please don't worry, my dearest." She turned to Lucas. "Do not waste time grieving. I've led a good life, and now I can go in peace to be with the Great Goddess."

She said to her daughter. "Cassie, take care of Lucas. Make sure he eats his kale and doesn't drink too much mead. He needs burdock tea to strengthen his blood, too, at least one pail every day."

"My girl, please don't talk like that. I love you. I don't know... if I can make it... without you." Lucas' voice broke.

"I love you, too, Lucas. We've had wonderful years together, and you've made me very happy. You'll miss me for a bit, but you'll be fine."

He nuzzled her and kissed her face, her forehead, her mouth. "Bye for now, my girl"

"Bye for now."

***

Beautimus soared in the skies above Rendaz, twisting, turning, and skimming the surface of creamy puffed clouds.

She'd never had so much fun. She kicked all four of her feet as though swimming in the River Kwa. "Whoohoo!"

The white-breasted wood swallows, purple beetles, and giant moths were there with her. The falcons dived and swooped calling out in joy. Beautimus' favorite, Mahler's *Symphony No.2, the Resurrection*, reverberated through the clear air. The entire universe filled with Bach, Mahler, Mozart and Debussy. She spun and pirouetted like a lacewing dancing through the sky.

Two figures flew toward her. She watched them as they approached, first they appeared as two little dots, then larger and larger until she could easily make out a hippo and a blue crane floating alongside one another.

"Well, here you are, Bea. Dancing in the sky, I see." Sangrina said.

"Ready to meet the Great Goddess?" said Rhianna. "She's been asking for you."

"I'm ready."

"Perhaps not so fast," said Sangrina.

"What do you mean, Mom?"

"You might still have work to do on Rendaz."

"I don't think so. I've said my goodbyes and I've made my peace."

"Are you certain?"

"Of *course* I'm certain. I'm ready to meet the Great Goddess."

"Oh, you're going to meet the Great Goddess all right. I'm talking about what happens *after* you meet her."

"What? I'm confused."

"Don't worry, sweet daughter. Everything is in perfect, divine order. Come along with Rhianna and me."

"But, what did you mean about *work left to do*? What are you talking about?"

Beautimus, sandwiched between her mother and Rhianna, soared higher and higher until she could no longer perceive the green glass bead of Rendaz, or sense anything of her physical form. She merged with the birds, the sunlight, and the music. When she at last looked into the eyes of the Great Mother, she'd never experienced such complete joy, such absolute serenity, such pure, holy love.

Then…she felt herself falling, falling, falling.

***

"Lucas, I'm sorry," Cassie said. "Mom is gone." Tears poured down her face. "I love you, Mom. I'll miss you so much."

Lucas burrowed his head into Beautimus' still warm side. He nuzzled and cried. "I love you, Beautimus Potamus. I always have and always will, my girl."

At the precise moment Lady Beautimus' heart ceased beating, her great granddaughter, Bea Three, gave birth to a precious little girl with luminous skin, violet eyes, and on her cheek, a perfect tiny heart-shaped mark.

---

www.ingramcontent.com/pod-product-compliance
Lightning Source LLC
Chambersburg PA
CBHW031103030726
47496CB00002BA/355